P9-DFN-625

RABBIT
&
ROBOT

Also by Andrew Smith

Winger

Stand-Off

100 Sideways Miles

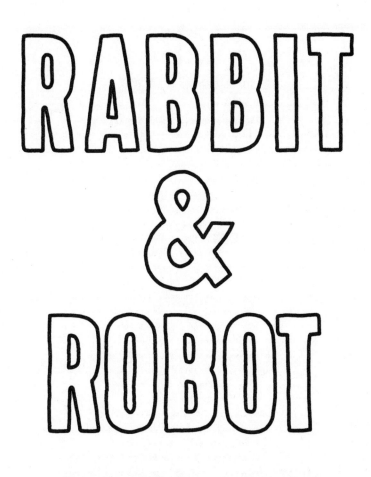

RABBIT & ROBOT

ANDREW SMITH

SIMON & SCHUSTER BFYR

New York   London   Toronto   Sydney   New Delhi

ST. THOMAS PUBLIC LIBRARY

SIMON & SCHUSTER BFYR

An imprint of Simon & Schuster Children's Publishing Division
1230 Avenue of the Americas, New York, New York 10020

This book is a work of fiction. Any references to historical events, real people,
or real places are used fictitiously. Other names, characters, places, and events are
products of the author's imagination, and any resemblance to actual events or
places or persons, living or dead, is entirely coincidental.
Text copyright © 2018 by Andrew Smith
Jacket illustration copyright © 2018 by Mike Perry
All rights reserved, including the right of reproduction in whole or in part in any form.

SIMON & SCHUSTER BFYR is a trademark of Simon & Schuster, Inc.
For information about special discounts for bulk purchases, please contact Simon & Schuster
Special Sales at 1-866-506-1949 or business@simonandschuster.com.
The Simon & Schuster Speakers Bureau can bring authors to your live event.
For more information or to book an event, contact the Simon & Schuster Speakers Bureau
at 1-866-248-3049 or visit our website at www.simonspeakers.com.
Jacket design by Lucy Ruth Cummins
Interior design by Tom Daly
The text for this book was set in Electra LT Std.
Manufactured in the United States of America
First Edition
2 4 6 8 10 9 7 5 3 1
Library of Congress Cataloging-in-Publication Data
Names: Smith, Andrew (Andrew Anselmo), 1959–
Title: Rabbit & Robot / Andrew Smith.
Other titles: Rabbit and Robot
Description: First edition. | New York : Simon & Schuster Books for Young Readers, [2018]. |
Summary: Stranded aboard the lunar-cruise ship, Tennessee, Cager Messer
and his best friend, Billy, both sixteen, are surrounded by insane robots while
watching thirty simultaneous wars turn Earth into a toxic wasteland.
Identifiers: LCCN 2018000353| ISBN 9781534422209 (hardback) | ISBN 9781534422223 (eBook)
Subjects: | CYAC: Science fiction. | Space ships—Fiction. | Best friends—Fiction. | Friendship—
Fiction. | Robots—Fiction. | War—Fiction. | Humorous stories.
Classification: LCC PZ7.S64257 Rab 2014 | DDC [Fic]—dc23
LC record available at https://lccn.loc.gov/2018000353

I've been wading through all this unbelievable junk and wondering if I should have given the world to the monkeys.

—ELVIS COSTELLO

I placed a jar in Tennessee,
And round it was, upon a hill.

—WALLACE STEVENS

Education makes machines which act like men and produces men who act like machines.

—ERICH FROMM

CONTENTS

Tyger Tyger, Burning Bright ◆ Cheese Ball! ◆ I Am the Worm ◆ Cager Messer's List of Things He's Never Done ◆ Hocus Pocus, and Kansas Is Full of Shit ◆ A Visit to the Hotel Kenmore ◆ Getting On Board ◆ Mojave Field ◆ *Rabbit & Robot* ◆ In with the Cogs ◆ Are We There Yet? ◆ Printer Ketchup ◆ Like Nothing Else in Tennessee ◆ Parker, My Valet ◆ The Longest Elevator Ride of My Life ◆ Dr. Geneva, and What Space Does to Teenage Boys ◆ Of Clocks, Cogs, and the Sense of Smell ◆ Captains Outrageous ◆ *Canard à l'Orange* ◆ Good King Wenceslas, and a Serious Obelisk of Friendship ◆ Deck 21 ◆ I Am the Worm ◆ Never Send a Human to Do a Cog's Job ◆ It Really Is Christmas ◆ The Proper Way to Prepare a Curry ◆ I'm Pretty Sure We're Upside Down Now ◆ It Happens Here, I Guess ◆ A Pedestrian Assessment of Alsatian History ◆ A Cruise-Directing Phoenix from the Ashes ◆ Stopped at the Wicket ◆ The Boy from First Class, and a Fire in the Bank ◆ An Infinity of Nevers, and a Mission to Find a Can Opener ◆ Captains Get to Do Whatever They Want to Do ◆ Right Side Up, Upside Down ◆ There's a Bright Side to Just About Everything ◆ Unless You Happen to Be Dying to Die ◆ We Raise Our Hands ◆ A Most Unfortunate Dane ◆ Billy Hinman Goes to Church ◆ Getting Out of the Memphis Hotel ◆ Thanks for Not Killing Me ◆ Out

CONTENTS

of Bed and Into the *Tennessee* ♦ The Lost Girls, and the Boy in the Bucket ♦ Duncan's Horses ♦ Put Your Welcome Faces On! ♦ The Giant Blue Fetus in Space ♦ He Makes a Great Gasket ♦ Tricky Words ♦ The Things We'd Never Seen Before ♦ Happy New Year, Happy No Year ♦ Freedom, and an Unemployed Cog in the Hallway ♦ Billy Hinman, Billy Hinman ♦ This Was the *Tennessee* ♦ We Dance, and Queen Dot Accounts for Mexican Cuisine and Human Evolution ♦ In Which We Find Out Where King Carlos Is and Suffer a Blow to Our Self-Esteem ♦ Herman Melville Would Be Pleased ♦ Eaters and Feeders ♦ First Night of the Neveryear ♦ It's Time to Eat Now, and I Become Aware of My Balls ♦ The Cruise Ship to End All Cruise Ships ♦ The Nicest Giraffe I Ever Met ♦ A Sleep Sandwich ♦ Dumb Pointless Optimism ♦ You Better Watch Out for the Monkeys ♦ Cager Messer's Can Opener and Push-Ups List ♦ Times That Aren't Now ♦ A Normal California Boy ♦ Getting the Wrong Idea ♦ Shakespeare's Crowbar ♦ The Porridge of Officer Dennis ♦ If Thy Right Eye Offend Thee ♦ What Kind of World ♦ Mooney, Mooney! ♦ This Is What We Saw ♦ Are You One of Us? ♦ Moon to Moon ♦ Just Like Home ♦ Helpless, Helpless, Helpless ♦ v.1 Human Beings ♦ Caveman & Spaceman ♦ The Unlock Code ♦ Righting the Ship ♦ The Doctor and the Reverend ♦ Epilogue: It Took Dominion Everywhere smell humans.

I am very happy about that.

Someone else is here on the *Tennessee* with Billy and me. We are not alone after all.

I might begin by explaining that we are either the last or the first of our kind, and I wonder what time it is that this has come to you—how long our story has waited to be told.

We are trapped inside a moon to our moon, in a home—a lifeless jar—called the *Tennessee*, where we spend our time, absurdly enough, with talking animals and machines that grow increasingly human by the hour.

Are you a person, or are you some kind of cog?

Either way, I feel a compelling obligation to tell you what it meant to be a human, at least as far as I can describe it accurately.

None of this is a lie.

Tyger Tyger,
Burning Bright

s that a fucking tiger?" Billy Hinman asked.

"I think it *is* a fucking tiger," I said.

I'll admit that I had never seen a fucking tiger before.

It was certainly a day for checking things off Cager Messer's infinite list of things he's never done.

"An actual fucking tiger," Billy whispered.

Even when you're a half mile away from a tiger and you're standing naked and chest deep in the middle of a lukewarm fake lake, it is an atavistic human instinct to make as little noise as possible.

"I think the Zoo of Tennessee must have broke," I theorized.

"What the fuck are we going to do?" Billy said.

"I have no plan."

"Cager? Do you know what that is?" Parker hollered.

Parker had been hiding up in the branches of a fake pine

tree. It could have been a cedar. I don't know anything about trees. He'd been watching me and Billy swim.

Since I didn't want to draw the tiger's attention to us, I decided to think about things for a while.

So Billy offered, "You should tell Parker it's a tiger, and tigers are friendly, and that he should climb down from the tree and give the tiger a hug because tigers love to be hugged by horny teenagers. That way, while the tiger is distracted by clawing the fucker to pieces, we can make a run for it."

"But what about our clothes?"

Our clothes were scattered on the shore beneath the tree where Parker was hiding.

"Cager. It's a fucking tiger," Billy told me.

For some reason, ever since I'd been forced off Woz, my best friend, Billy Hinman, did make a lot of sense at times.

"I can't tell Parker that," I whispered.

"Why not? He's a fucking machine."

"I know that. I just can't, is all," I said. And, yes, I felt stupid and embarrassed for as much as confessing to Billy Hinman that I had some measured feeling of empathy—or maybe even friendship—for Parker, who was, after all, just a fucking machine.

So I continued, "Besides, the tiger is just a machine too, right? It's a cog. It won't do anything to us."

"What do you mean by *us*?" Billy said.

Damn all this clarity.

"Well, he's *not supposed to* do anything to us."

"You mean *you*."

"Are you daring me to get out of the water and tell the tiger to go away?" I asked.

"Not at all. You should make Parker do it," Billy said. "You said it yourself, Cager: The tiger's just another cog. And cogs don't eat cogs, right?"

That was becoming increasingly debatable on the *Tennessee*.

The *Tennessee* had been going to shit, and neither of us had any idea how to stop it from spiraling completely out of control. Worse yet, Billy and I were alone; we were stuck here.

Parker, who was my personal attendant on the *Tennessee*, called out, "Can you hear me, Cager? What is that thing with stripes and orange hair? Do you know? Will he be kind to me?"

I waded in a little closer to shore, but only about three steps. Then I backed up one. I tried to make my voice as normal sounding and calm as possible. There was no need for me to shout at Parker, because the guy did have pretty good hearing.

"How did you get up in the tree?" I asked him.

But Parker had to yell for me to hear him clearly, which certainly agitated the tiger, who clawed at and chewed on the pants I'd dropped beside the lake. "I floated up here, two days ago when the gravity turned off. The thing with the stripes who is eating your pants right now has been walking around here in Alberta ever since."

When the *Tennessee*'s gravity failed, all the animal cogs must have gotten out of the zoo.

A zoo without gravity can easily become a battlefield for clashing survival instincts.

The tiger chewed and chewed.

"Tell him to stop eating my fucking pants," I said.

I was mad!

And Parker, being the rigidly programmed horny but obedient valet cog that he was, said, "You! Thing! Stop eating Cager Messer's fucking pants!"

And the tiger, being the rigidly programmed large predatory cat cog that he was, snorted and growled, shook my pants wildly in his teeth, and ripped them to shreds.

"Bad idea," Billy whispered.

"Fine. Now I don't have any pants. Stupid fucking tiger."

"Tigers are dicks," Billy said.

"I think I should wait up here in the tree for a few more days, Cager," Parker said.

"It's only a tiger, Parker." But I wondered when—if ever—in the history of humankind, anyone had ever said *It's only a tiger.* "But he's a cog. He won't do anything to us. Watch. I'll show you so you can climb down from the tree."

Then I cupped my hands around my mouth, forming a megaphone with my fingers, and said this: "Attention, tiger! You need to go back to the zoo immediately! My name is Cager Messer, and my father owns this ship! Do you hear me? I am Anton Messer's son, Cager, and I am telling you to return to the zoo!"

And that was when the tiger ate Billy Hinman's pants too.

No animals, not even fake ones, like being in zoos.

Billy Hinman said, "Plan B: Cager and Billy stay naked in the lake for the next five days, waiting for a fucking tiger to die of boredom."

What could I say? I never had a Plan A to begin with.

Fortunately for us, we did not have to wait five days in the lake. Something else, which was enormously tall, judging by the rattling and swaying of the fake cedars or pines — or whatever—that didn't grow or photosynthesize on the recreation deck called Alberta, came crashing toward the lake through the woods.

It was another refugee from the *Tennessee*'s compromised zoo: a giraffe. The thing's head, nearly as high as the branch Parker sat on, came crashing through the canopy of Alberta's fake forest.

And Parker yelled, "Cager?"

What did he want? I refused to be my horny cog's fucking safari guide.

"Giraffes are nice, right?" I whispered to Billy.

Billy nodded. "And they're bisexual."

"*What?*"

"They really are," Billy said. "Totally bisexual. They're, like, the greatest animals ever."

"How do you know that?"

Billy shrugged. "I just do."

The giraffe stopped at the edge of the woods on the opposite side of the trail from where the tiger continued thrashing Billy Hinman's pants. The giraffe looked directly at Billy and me. He cocked his head slightly, as though waiting for one of us to say hello or something.

Also, I may as well admit this: I had never seen a giraffe before. It was very tall. And I was terrified of it too.

"Would you boys like to climb up onto my back, so I can carry you out from the lake?" the giraffe said.

He had a French accent.

"That giraffe is from France," Billy said.

"Why the fuck would your dad make a French giraffe that talks?"

"I think the more important issue is why he would make a fucking tiger that eats pants," Billy said.

The tiger thrashed and thrashed.

"*Bonjour, les jeunes garçons!* My name is Maurice," the giraffe said. And if giraffes could smile, Maurice was smiling at us. "But, please, let me offer you boys a ride on my back. The Alpine Tea House serves magnificent waffles. It's just over there, at the bottom of the hiking trail. Are you hungry? *J'ai très faim.* Heh heh . . . I am, as you say, very hungry."

Cogs were not supposed to get hungry. Ever. Something had been twisting out of whack on the *Tennessee*.

"He seems really nice, and I love waffles," Billy said.

"Billy, I am naked. There's no fucking way I'm riding

naked on a bisexual talking giraffe to go get waffles with you," I argued.

And Billy countered, "Cager, like you said: It's an opportunity for you to do one of those things you may never get a chance to try doing ever again. Who's ever gotten to ride naked on a giraffe to go get some breakfast?"

As it turned out, Billy Hinman and I did not need to carry our argument to any definite conclusion. Maurice, being the hungry French giraffe that he claimed to be, became fascinated by the tiger, who had finished eating Billy's pants and had moved on to his next course, which was my T-shirt.

Maurice looked at Billy and me, then apologetically said, "Excuse me. *Excusez-moi, s'il vous plaît.*"

Maurice spread his front legs wide and stiffly lowered his head toward the oblivious tiger, who was apparently an expert at sorting laundry and was now eating Billy's T-shirt and socks.

Maurice cocked his head back and in one powerful thrust stabbed his pointy giraffe face directly through the tiger's midsection.

Maurice made a sound like *Mmmph mmmph mmmph!* as he wriggled his face deeper inside the tiger's body, gulping and slurping the internal components of the cat's mechanization.

Billy Hinman said, "Okay. I take back the thing about him being the greatest animal ever."

And the tiger, who had no discernible European

accent, said, "Ow! That fucking hurts! This is all there is to life, isn't it? Sadness and pain."

The tiger wept and sobbed as great gushing blobs of viscous, semenlike hydraulic fluid burped from the gaping holes Maurice pierced in his torso.

Maurice ate and ate as the tiger cried and cried.

Maurice burbled, *"Cette viande de tigre est délicieux!"*

Four or five days in the lake was starting to look like a pretty good idea.

Parker shouted, "Cager, what do you suggest I do now?"

"Tell him to ride the giraffe," Billy whispered.

And the tiger wailed, "Sartre was right—I cannot escape anguish, because I *am* anguish!"

Mmmph mmmph mmmph! went Maurice.

Cheese Ball!

There was a time when people theorized the moon was made of cheese.

Up here on the *Tennessee*, though, I can see it is more likely made of ash. Probably all the ashes from all the fires of all our pasts, forever and ever.

And I can turn and, in one direction, see the surface of this enormous cratered ashball as it skims below us like a moving sidewalk; and, in the other, the smoke-shrouded Earth — our lost home — burning itself out, exhaling ash one last time.

Among the enterprises that made my father one of the five wealthiest people in America (and those ventures included a television program called *Rabbit & Robot*, as well as a line of lunar cruise ships like the one Billy and I were trapped on) is transporting deceased loved ones — not their ashes, but their actual bodies — to the surface of the moon, where they are laid out like vigilant sentinels, eternally gazing down, or up, or wherever, at the planet of their origin. They never decay, never change. Billy and I can see the bodies every time the *Tennessee* passes above *Mare Fecunditatis*, which oddly enough means "Sea of Fertility."

There are more than thirteen thousand fertile and dead sentinels floating there atop that sea of ash, staring down at everything that had come before them, and everything that came after.

They just lie there, dressed in their outfit of unquestioned permanence—military uniforms or perfect white smocks, every last dead and fertile one of them.

Billy Hinman and I are trapped inside a moon to our moon called the *Tennessee*.

Because Billy Hinman and I nicked a fucking lunar cruise ship that belongs to my dad.

Well, to be honest, it was kind of an accident. We didn't mean to steal it, but it's ours now, no question about it.

It kind of just fell into our hands, you could say.

And we are at the end of everything.

So, let me back up a bit.

I Am the Worm

Here are some of the things Billy Hinman and I have never done: At sixteen years of age, we have never attended school like other kids. And we also have never seen my father's television program, *Rabbit & Robot*, which, like school, is only for *other kids*—definitely not for Billy and me.

And Billy Hinman, who never lied to me, has also never taken Woz, which is something they only give to *other kids*, to help them learn, so they can become proper bonks or coders, to help them "level down" when watching *Rabbit & Robot*.

Billy never took it, but I am an addict.

It does not embarrass me to admit my addiction to Woz. It's about the same thing as admitting my feet are size fourteen, and that I have a painfully acute sense of smell: all true, all true. The drug became the glue that held me together, even if the source of my cohesion was, according to my caretaker, Rowan, destined to kill me.

This is why Billy and Rowan concocted the scheme to get me up to the *Tennessee*.

Their plan ended up saving—and condemning—all of us.

Cager Messer hears me.

Sometimes when he wakes up in the mornings—no, let's be honest, it's more like the afternoon, and frequently it's evening—he says he feels good and strong, and his head is clear, and he thinks he's not going to smoke or snort or suck down the worm, and I tell him, Cager, who are you fooling? I'll tell you who you're *not* fooling: all of creation minus one, kid.

The kid listens to me, but only because I never tell him what to do. Maybe "listens" is the wrong boy word. He *hears* me. Yeah, that's what he does.

He hears me.

Which is an unbalanced social dynamic, you might say. Right? I've got ears. Look at me. I *hear* him. I know what he wants; what he isn't getting; what he will never get; how he's passively letting that monster-size ball roll down the hill. Gravity, take control, because Christ knows the kid doesn't want to.

I am the Worm.

There was an episode of his father's program, *Rabbit & Robot*, titled "I Am the Worm."

Oddly prophetic, that one.

I need a cigarette, and I don't even smoke. Whenever I ask Cager to bring me some cigarettes, he laughs and tells me I can't smoke. So I say, fine, then bring me a gin and tonic.

In the episode called "I Am the Worm," there are these blue space creatures who can turn themselves into anything they want to be—alligators, Abraham Lincolns (Or is it Abrahams Lincoln? This is why I need a cigarette), Phillips-head screwdrivers, frying pans, whatever—and they send out this little blue worm, wriggling through the solar system, and it ends up crawling up inside Mooney's nose.

The worm, not the solar system.

Mooney is one of the main characters—the robot.

The worm that went up his nose reprogrammed him and made him go insane.

Bad things like that happen to Mooney in practically every episode.

Formula.

The "Rabbit," who doesn't really have a name, is a bonk—a soldier who's come back from one or three, or eighteen, wars. He's insane too.

It's a lot of fun.

And Cager is not allowed to watch it.

Mr. Messer doesn't want the worm to crawl up his son's nose.

Cager Messer's List
of Things He's Never Done

There are things that your friends will do for you that you just don't have the guts to do for yourself.

Because, let's face it: Cager Messer—*me*—I was a messed-up drug addict who had one foot—and probably most of the rest of my body too—in the grave by the time other guys were stressing over getting driver's licenses, and losing or not losing their virginity.

Most people who were allowed to have an opinion on guys like Billy and me would conclude that I was a loser, and that we were both spoiled pieces of shit.

But Billy Hinman was my best friend. I know that now.

He saved me.

Unfortunately, saving me resulted in things no one could ever have foreseen.

Because Billy Hinman and I nicked a fucking cruise ship.

Billy stared out the window as we drifted away on the R & R G G transpod, sad and bleary-eyed. Billy was terrified of flying.

He said, "Good-bye, California. Have a happy Crambox, Mrs. Jordan."

It was two days before Christmas; two days before Billy Hinman and I would find ourselves trapped on the *Tennessee*.

It was also my sixteenth birthday.

Happy birthday to me!

Billy Hinman kept no secrets from me. He and Mrs. Jordan—our friend Paula's mother—had been having sex since Billy was just fifteen years old.

Of course I was jealous, in a sickening kind of way. What sixteen-year-old virgin guy wouldn't be jealous of a best friend who had actual sex as often as Billy Hinman did? He had sex with just about everyone.

But Billy Hinman still called Paula's mother Mrs. Jordan, which was creepier than shit.

One thing I have never done: I do not go to school.

Grosvenor High School's mascot was the Shrieking Weasel. We no longer had competitive sports in high school (a thing I understand was commonplace fifty years before our time), but at assemblies and career fairs the students of Grosvenor High School thrilled themselves by screaming the cry of the Shrieking Weasel, which sounds like this: *Cheepa Yeep! Cheepa Yeep!*

This past summer, Billy Hinman turned sixteen. Also, the United States of America was involved in twenty-seven simultaneous wars.

Twenty-seven!

And up here in heaven, we look down and watch the world burn.

I have this memory from a few months before Billy and Rowan kidnapped me. It was fire season in Los Angeles.

I have never set fire to anything.

Fire season lasted ten months out of the year. The two months that were unofficially not-fire-season were only less flammable because they tended to be a little too chilly for most arsonists—burners—to go outdoors.

Everything that *could* burn in California *had* burned, time and time and time again.

The city was on fire at the time. There was nothing left to burn on the naked, scorched hills, but houses, restaurants, schools, and tax offices still contained combustible components. What would Los Angeles possibly be without its fires and smoke?

"I can smell a school on fire, and a Korean restaurant too," I said.

Billy Hinman and I were standing in an alley at my father's studio, waiting for Charlie Greenwell to show up, so I could get high with him.

"I don't get how you can do that," Billy Hinman said.

I shrugged. "Neither do I. It's just that nothing else

smells like burning smart screens, or a Samgyeopsal-gui restaurant that's been set on fire."

"I guess so," Billy conceded.

Charlie Greenwell wasn't much older than Billy and me when he came back all messed up from War Twenty-Five, or whatever. He liked to hang out around the studio lot where they produced my father's show. And, usually, Charlie Greenwell and I would smoke or snort Woz together in the alley while Billy just watched.

Neither of us liked Charlie Greenwell, so I never really understood why we'd listen to his shit stories about all the people he'd shot, and how great it was to be a bonk. But then again, the way things were, sometimes I'd put up with just about anything to get high, which is why Billy and Rowan, my caretaker, concocted a scheme to get me on board the *Tennessee* and clean me up before I killed myself with the stuff.

Billy was done arguing with me about it a long time ago.

Sometimes we speculated how we might have ended up if we had been born to a regular family—if we'd have ended up bonks or coders. I'm pretty sure Billy Hinman would have gone to war, just like Charlie Greenwell did, and that I would have gone to an industrial lab, but I always told Billy to his face that we would have ended up in the same place together.

Ending up in the same place together is actually exactly the way things turned out for me and Billy Hinman.

* * *

I make lists of things I've never done. I kept them as voice recordings on my thumbphone, until it stopped working on the flight to the *Tennessee*. This book is the list of my life adrift, compiled while we all make a hopeful attempt to get back home.

That's really what all books are, isn't it? I mean, lists of secrets and things you only *wish* you'd done—a sort of deathbed confession where you're trying to get it all out while the lights are still on.

The big difference: It does not matter who my confession is written to, because nobody will ever see this—or, if someone does, it will probably be hundreds or thousands of years from now, and whoever picks this up won't understand a goddamned thing about what it meant to be the last human beings left in the universe.

Anyway, who cares?

Something smells like human.

Cheepa Yeep!

Hocus Pocus, and
Kansas Is Full of Shit

The only time in my life I'd ever seen Rowan look anything close to being embarrassed came when I asked him if he was a virgin.

That was two years ago now. I was fourteen at the time and was just learning so much about all the surprises of life. Also, being fourteen, I was not yet aware that there were certain questions that guys weren't supposed to ask, even if Rowan was closer to me, and certainly knew more about me, than my own parents.

But Rowan wouldn't tell me. He changed the subject to laundry or bathing or driving me somewhere, or some shit like that, which was how Rowan routinely handled me when I asked questions he didn't want to answer.

And even now, at the age of sixteen, I was still constantly monitored by Rowan. At least I was usually permitted to bathe myself, though. But Rowan still did my laundry and got me dressed. And the terrifying thing was that Rowan had told me he was going to teach me how to shave before Christmas, which was something that I really did not think I needed to start doing.

A few days before we ended up marooned on the *Tennessee*, Billy Hinman and I had a play date with kids who were supposed to show us what being normal was all about. Rowan waited for us, as he always did, parked out on the street while Billy and I attended what we called a real-kids party.

It wasn't much of a party.

But Billy Hinman and I were not *real* kids. Until we turned eighteen, or until we were somehow liberated, we considered ourselves to be our parents' fancy pets, tended to by insomniac caretakers like Rowan.

Billy Hinman's caretaker was an actual v.4 cog named Hilda. She was one of the early releases, like most of the cogs who worked on the *Tennessee*, so she had wild and unpredictable mood swings. Most people—humans, that is—didn't like the v.4s. I thought they were hilarious, though. And they also made Albert Hinman—Billy's dad— the richest man in the world.

Not that any of that would amount to shit by the time we got stuck on the *Tennessee*.

Our parents had decided early on that the best way to socialize us, since we were not attending school or watching *Rabbit & Robot* like everyone else in America, would be to create an artificial "friends group" of kids the same age as Billy and me. Our friends group went through several iterations over the years for various reasons. And the kids' families had to apply and go through a screening process.

Not just anyone in the world could be a "play buddy" with a Messer or a Hinman.

Our real-kid friends' parents were paid, naturally.

The only two members of our group who'd been with us since the beginning, when Billy Hinman and I were four years old, were Katie St. Romaine, who was my girlfriend for nearly a year, and a boy named Justin Pickett.

Katie and I had never had sex, although we did come close a few times. It was always me who'd be the one to chicken out. And where did that get me? Stuck on the *Tennessee*, alone, with Billy, Rowan, and a couple thousand v.4 cogs. Ridiculous.

Whatever.

Billy Hinman did have sex with Justin Pickett. Billy told me everything. He was one of those guys who, according to him, didn't like to be pinned down by expectations regarding his sexuality.

Billy Hinman called himself "fluid," which sounded incredibly foreign to me. I just thought he was horny all the time. And, yes, Billy Hinman did ask me more than once if I'd like to fool around sexually with him, to which I answered that if I was too afraid to try anything with Katie St. Romaine, I was definitely too afraid to do anything with him.

And we left it at that, because nothing could really get

in the way of our friendship, especially because of how honest and sometimes sad Billy Hinman was. Also, we needed each other. We were the only real human beings either of us truly knew.

All our fake friends were on Woz. They all went to school, so this was natural. All schoolkids had prescriptions for Woz. It helped you learn things. Billy never had Woz once in his life that I was aware of, but I was pretty much an out-of-control addict ever since I was about twelve. Still, I felt like I'd learned plenty of stuff. Rowan was also my tutor; Billy's, too, when he'd pay attention to stuff.

You couldn't really tell much of a difference between Wozheads at school. The doses they received were perfectly adjusted to help future coders concentrate, or to cull out the obvious future bonks. It was guys like Charlie Greenwell and me who were the unfortunate casualties of the culture of Woz.

I did it for fun, and I had too much fun.

The party was awkward, to say the least. For one thing, it was at Paula Jordan's house, and Mrs. Jordan was there, which meant that I'd probably have to stay around and "wait" for Billy Hinman after all the other kids left.

I had only broken up with Katie St. Romaine two days earlier, and she was there, sitting as far across the room from me as she could possibly get and still qualify her parents for payment for her attending this week's "normal kids" group.

Such fun.

Katie looked unhappy. It kind of made me feel drawn

to her, and simultaneously sad, too, because I worried that I may have hurt Katie St. Romaine's feelings, and nobody likes to do that, right?

I sat on a couch, next to Billy and Justin. There were four other teenagers with us: Paula Jordan; Stuart Michelson; Dani, who was Stuart's twin sister; and another kid who had just joined our play group a few weeks earlier. His name was Craig or Ken or something. Whatever. Craig or Ken tried too hard to talk to me and Billy. He acted like a fucking v.4 cog that was stalled out on friendliness or something. But he was definitely a human. I could smell pee stains in his underwear. Oh well, I'm sure Craig/Ken's parents were beyond thrilled that their boy got to hang out with a couple of kids like Billy Hinman and me.

"Don't mess up the game, Cager," Justin Pickett said.

"I'm not even really playing. I don't care about the game," I said.

I leaned forward and dropped four Woz tabs on the table screen in front of the couch. We were all supposedly playing a game with our thumbphones. The playing field rose up in three dimensions from the table. The game was called Hocus Pocus, and it was one of those trendy party games that was supposed to get people to talk about all kinds of personal stuff, but none of us was really talking that day.

It was Paula's turn. She had to either make a sacrifice to one of the other players, or she had to get up and change something on someone. She decided to change Billy

Hinman's hairstyle. So she walked around the table while I worked at grinding up my drugs, then Paula began combing his hair back from his forehead. It was easy enough for Paula to do; Billy was always loose and relaxed, and his hair was long and hung down in front of his face.

"I like my hair down in my face," Billy protested.

"Nonsense," Paula said. "And you look better this way, besides."

"Nonsense right back at you," Billy told her.

Katie St. Romaine looked sad. I think she'd told everyone else bad things about me. I'd imagined she'd told the other kids things like *Cager Messer doesn't like girls, as it turns out*; or, *Cager tried to force me to have sex with him, and then he got scared when I told him I wanted to*, or dumb shit like that. Whatever. The truth is, I broke up with Katie St. Romaine because how could a guy like me trust anyone who was on my dad's payroll?

But for the record, and now, in light of me being stuck up here on the *Tennessee*, I do sincerely regret having broken up with her, and especially not having sex.

No one wants to die a virgin, unless you really, really believe in God, and, well . . . whatever.

I pulverized my Woz tablets into a small mound of blue powder at the edge of the game field while Paula finished fixing Billy's hair. She was right. Billy Hinman did look good with his hair combed back, but Billy was exceptionally handsome anyway. He would have looked good if she shaved him bald. Some guys get all the breaks. And they're the ones who generally throw most of those breaks away, too.

I snorted the Woz.

I sighed.

"That's too much, Cager," Billy said. "You're going to get sick and puke in the car going home."

Billy put his arm around me and hugged me close. I knew what he was trying to do. Distraction.

I said, "I'm sorry in advance if I puke in Rowan's car, Billy. You know I love you."

And that's about how thrilling our real-kids parties got. Kids got their hair combed, or ended up dressed in new outfits, or had to give away something they liked as a sacrifice to one of the others until our next session of Hocus Pocus.

Also, I passed out, unconscious on the couch beside Billy and Justin Pickett. So I was in a terrible mood, and physically unmanageable, when Billy tried to wake me up and take me to Rowan, who'd been waiting in the car for us for the past five hours.

Mrs. Jordan was disappointed. Nobody got what they wanted that day, I suppose.

"Sometimes you're disgusting," Billy said.

He could say stuff like that to me. I wouldn't put up with it from anyone else, though.

And I said, "And the rest of the time, when I'm not disgusting, what am I?"

"I don't know."

"Fabulous?"

"Whatever."

I leaned all my weight onto Billy's shoulder. He nearly fell over.

"I need to pee before we go," I said. "Come with me and hold me up, Bill, so I don't bust my head open."

"No."

"What do you think I could do to get Cager off this shit, Rowan?" Billy asked from the backseat.

I sat right next to Billy Hinman. He knew I was awake. It wasn't like he was trying to keep any secrets from me.

"You should get hacked up with me sometime, Billy. Rowan too. That would be fun," I said.

"No," Billy answered.

Rowan drove. He said, "Perhaps a birthday vacation is in order. Maybe that would help. You know, take some time away. Take Cager up on the *Tennessee* with you."

My father's ship the *Tennessee* was as big as a midwestern city, staffed by hundreds of v.4 cogs, and affordable only to people like us—or the people who ran the government and military.

"Isn't that the one that got all filled with shit, and the people on board got sick because they had other people's shit all over themselves and in their food and shit?" Billy asked.

One of my father's first lunar cruise ships, the *Kansas*, had a minor "incident," as Mr. Messer liked to call it. It was actually not minor. The toilet systems reversed, spewing tons and tons of shit and other stuff that human beings put in toilets back out into every room and every deck. People got very sick, and a few dozen actually died. Also, nobody wanted to help the ones who were transported back to Earth. Nobody likes to touch someone who's puking and covered in other people's shit.

I said, "No. That was the *Kansas*. The *Kansas* was the one that was full of shit. They fixed it, though. Well, they didn't fix it, really. They just sailed it into the sun."

"Sounds like a reasonable way to clean up a bunch of shit," Billy said.

"Mr. Messer likes simple solutions."

I called my father Mr. Messer. I said, "Nobody would have gone on it after the shit thing. That's why they built the *Tennessee*. No shit problems, so far."

Actually, the *Tennessee* didn't have any glitches yet because it was new and it had never carried any human passengers besides the few coders who'd gotten it online and powered up. I'd visited it one time, before it was fully operational.

Billy Hinman stretched out in the seat, extending his legs over to my side, so our feet touched. Billy Hinman was always horny. I kicked him.

He said, "Well, you'd *never* get me up on one of those shit things. Cruises are what old people do right before they die. Trust me. I learned that."

Billy wasn't entirely wrong about cruises either. When

we were both ten years old, Billy and I went with his parents on an ocean cruise across the Pacific, from Los Angeles to Sydney. It was a very long cruise. Five octogenarians died before we got to Australia.

Cheepa Yeep!

A Visit to the Hotel Kenmore

calculated that at about the same time Billy Hinman and I finished our fourth beer of the afternoon, the twenty-eighth war started.

Twenty-eight!

And it was my sixteenth birthday, too.

Like Charlie Greenwell told us, wars don't just fight themselves.

Bonks were on the move, and this time the boys got to stay close to home. During beer four—or possibly five for Billy—the Canadian Navy sailed across Lake Erie and pounded the shores of Ohio and Pennsylvania with artillery.

Canada was really mad at us. They had their reasons, I'm sure.

Not too many people cared about it, outside of Pennsylvania and Ohio, that is, but the event did provide an opportunity for some undeployed bonks to get to work.

"We should leave this shithole," Billy said.

We drank beer in Mr. Messer's attic office. Well, to be honest, Billy Hinman was doing most of the drinking. I did have some beer, though, just because it was the right thing to do, us being best friends, and it being my birthday and all. Of course Rowan was in on Billy's conspiracy—he got the beer for us—but Billy Hinman was convinced that in drinking beer I'd finally grown some balls, as he put it, and come to my senses about how useless and boring our lives were. Not that I didn't agree with him that our lives were useless and boring. But they were about to get a lot more exciting.

I had no idea.

"You mean we should get out of Los Angeles?" I asked. "It *is* kind of a shithole, isn't it?"

Billy nodded and burped quietly. I was lagging behind him in the number of empty cans I contributed to our pile on the office floor. It tasted awful, but I was already feeling a bit dizzy and energized.

"I'm drunk," I announced.

"Good," Billy said.

"And now I want some Woz," I said.

Billy said, "You practically OD'd in Rowan's backseat last night."

"Oh."

"But if you want, I'll ask Rowan to take us over to Charlie Greenwell's so you can hook some up. Then let's go somewhere and have fun."

"Where?"

"Oh, I don't know," Billy lied. "Somewhere."

This would be fun, right?

Charlie Greenwell's place was a deranged lunatic circus.

Charlie lived in an old hotel in the east end of Hollywood that had been converted to a kind of rehab home for bonks who'd come back from their various wars with holes in their brains. The news about Canada had really cheered up the residents at Charlie Greenwell's complex. The place reeked of Woz smoke. Guns and flags were everywhere.

As we walked into the lobby, Billy Hinman said, "I wonder if Charlie and the other ex-bonks are getting turned on, thinking about killing Canadian rabbits."

He was a little drunk, and he said it a little too loud.

"Rabbits" was what bonks called other bonks.

It was weird, but it was one of those slang words that nobody who wasn't a bonk was ever allowed to use. The unwritten social code: Only bonks can call bonks rabbits. Charlie Greenwell didn't mind if Billy or I used the word around him, but then again, Charlie Greenwell's ability to care about shit had been blasted out of his head four or five wars ago. And "Rabbit" was even in the title of—and the main character in—my father's television program, which was all about getting kids to embrace their inner bonks and coders. Or, at least, that's what I knew about the program, despite never actually having watched it.

Well, to be honest, *never* is an exaggeration. How could *anyone* not catch a glimpse of *Rabbit & Robot* here and there, a few seconds at a time, even if it's just out of the corner of an eye? The show was on almost constantly, in virtually every country of the world, even in most of the twenty-eight we were at war with.

In fact, my father's show was playing on one of the wall screens in the lobby of the Hotel Kenmore when Billy Hinman and I walked in, which was when Billy asked, a little too loudly, a rhetorical question about Canadian rabbits and horny bonks.

The other wall screens in the lobby were playing muted coverage of Canadian rabbits on the rampage in Ohio.

Unfortunately for Billy and me, there were two ex-bonks sitting together in a pair of vinyl reclining chairs watching *Rabbit & Robot* when he said it. One of them—he was shirtless and wore thick eyeglasses with one of the lenses blacked out so you couldn't see the vacated eye socket that was inevitably behind it—stood up right away and puffed out his hairless, tattooed chest. His nipples were pierced with silver barbs that looked like hunting arrows, and he was also holding some type of machine gun.

I have to admit that I felt so nonmasculine for my lack of nipple piercings, as well as my inability to recognize specific models of firearms. It seemed like every boy in America—future coders and bonks alike, thanks to *Rabbit & Robot*—knew the precise make, caliber, and specs of every gun in existence, even if none of our boys could accurately point out more than two or three countries on a map of the world.

Grosvenor was an outstanding school system.

Cheepa Yeep!

"Hey!" The old ex-bonk with a missing eye and a tattoo of the state of Texas on his belly jabbed a finger at us. "What did you just say, little fucking Canadian queer boy?"

All bonks were trained to—or at least *pretended* to—hate homosexuals. It was so fifty-years-ago, but clinging to the past was what armies are good at, right?

And now they hated Canadians, too.

Billy Hinman wasn't exactly queer, though. Billy would have sex with anyone if he liked them well enough. Most people I knew were like that, which made me feel rather odd and isolated. And Billy wasn't Canadian, either. So, kind of wrong on both assumptions.

"Um, your friend doesn't have pants on," Billy Hinman pointed out.

Billy was right. In the tension of our drunken entrance, I hadn't noticed that the other insane ex-bonk who'd been watching *Rabbit & Robot* beside the guy with Texas on his stomach was completely naked except for his old army-issue corporal's shirt and cap. He did have boots on, though.

This was life in the Hotel Kenmore. We'd been there enough times before that seeing such things wasn't ever surprising to Billy and me.

I put my hands up as a conciliatory gesture, and also because everyone knows that putting your hands up when a pair of half-naked insane people are pointing machine guns at you has a generally soothing effect.

"Wait, wait, wait. Billy didn't mean any offense, guys. In fact, he's just on his way down to the recruiter's and stopped by here to say good-bye to our pal Charlie Greenwell before going off to kill Canadians."

"What the fuck are you talking about?" Billy said.

In his defense, Billy Hinman was a bit drunk, so his stupidity was somewhat excusable. He went on, "I thought I told you we were going to do something *fun*."

I persisted in trying to defuse the situation. "Are you guys watching *Rabbit & Robot*? This is my favorite episode!"

I still held my hands in the air. Billy stared at me. The insane ex-bonk with no pants softened a bit and lowered his machine gun so it was pointing at our knees instead of our faces.

"This is my favorite episode too," the naked guy said. "But I wish that fucker Mooney would shut up and die."

Mooney, the "robot" in my father's program, was a v.4 cog who sang ridiculous, overly repetitive songs that helped kids memorize code sequences for school. Mooney was also a cog that was stuck on the emotion of "outrage." For some reason, an awful lot of v.4 cogs were either outraged or elated, both of which are highly unattractive attitudes. Some v.4s were horny, which was extremely awkward. They picked up their emotional tracks from the coders who put them online. I guess some coders, if they weren't outraged or elated, were horny, even on the job.

Whatever.

But it was understandable to me that the naked guy wanted Mooney to die. As far as I could tell, nobody liked Mooney, and he died at one point or another in most episodes.

Billy Hinman hitched a thumb at me. "His dad's Anton Messer."

"Anton Messer?" Texas Dude was so impressed, I'm pretty sure he was getting a boner. It might have been because the screens behind Billy and me were showing the Canadians, though. Who knows for sure?

"You boys should sit down with us and watch the war, and *Rabbit & Robot*," Naked Guy, who may just as well have been an elated v.4 cog, said.

I said, "I'll tell you what. Let us go say bye to our friend Charlie Greenwell, and we'll be right back. Okay with you?"

Texas Dude lowered his gun, grabbed his dick, and then fiddled with one of the silver arrows piercing his nipple. He nodded. "Charlie Greenwell is a hell of a rabbit."

"The best," I agreed.

"Do you realize you almost got us killed down there?" I said.

"Whatever, Cager."

We rode the rickety and urine-fouled elevator up to Charlie's floor.

It was fortunate for everyone, even the insane guys in

the lobby, that we arrived at Charlie Greenwell's apartment when we did.

We didn't knock. Knocking scared Charlie. Walking in on whatever Charlie Greenwell was likely doing scared me, but I was not insane and heavily armed, so we just walked right in, as we always did.

Charlie was attempting to set fire to a Canadian flag that he'd draped over a sofa in his living room. There was a tipped-over can of barbecue starter fluid beside his bare right foot, and Charlie was flicking the flint wheel on a dead plastic cigarette lighter.

Charlie was in his underwear. For whatever reasons, Wozhead insane ex-bonks didn't like to wear clothes very often. Also, like most bonks—insane and otherwise—Charlie Greenwell was covered in tattoos. One of them particularly fascinated me. It was a colorful grizzly bear on the right side of Charlie's chest, walking upright, smiling, and carrying a tattered American flag over his shoulder. The grizzly bear was wearing a flat-brimmed straw campaign hat with a band on it that read VOTE RED OR I'LL TEAR YOUR FUCKING THROAT OUT! It was completely absurd. On the opposite side of Charlie's chest was an octopus wearing a monocle and a derby hat and holding various unidentifiable types of firearms in each of his eight tentacles.

That tattoo made me feel inadequate, because I didn't know what any of the guns were.

Apparently, Charlie Greenwell was a fan of hats and wildlife.

"Hi, Charlie!" I said as cheerfully and calmly as I'd ever spoken to him in my life. "I think those guys downstairs are going to get all bent out of shape if you burn the Kenmore down and kill us all."

"Huh?" Charlie Greenwell's eyes were completely glazed over with Woz. He put the lighter down when he realized who we were, which didn't happen right away. "Oh. Hey, Bill. Cager. Want to get hacked?"

"Got any beer?" Billy asked.

"Sure. Come on in. I was just getting ready to do something, but I don't remember what it was," Charlie said.

"Put on pants?" I guessed.

Charlie looked down at his bare legs and shook his head. "No. That wasn't it."

The Hotel Kenmore burned to the ground that afternoon.

People naturally blamed it on burners—arson gangs—but nobody was too concerned about it. Every one of the insane ex-bonks, in various stages of undress, managed to get out. And they were all rounded up and moved to another abandoned Hollywood hotel that day—a place called the Wilshire Marquis, which had once been made famous for having been the site of a suicide from heroin overdose by one of the original actors who'd played Rabbit in my father's program.

Everyone in Los Angeles—and this is not hyperbolic—always loved stories like that.

But now, despite his plan being in full effect, Billy

Hinman was exceptionally drunk. It was the only way he'd ever get inside anything that flew.

I had no idea.

Billy and I sat in the backseat—Rowan playing the role of chauffeur, as usual—and I watched the blurry, barren landscape of the abandoned and pointless California desert smear past us as we sped out toward Mojave Field.

The Woz was particularly strong.

"So where, exactly, are we going now?" I asked.

"You'll see. It's a birthday surprise," Billy said.

Rowan, who never lied, shifted in the front seat and cleared his throat.

"I need to pee again. Maybe Rowan can just pull over for a minute," I said.

"We're almost there. You can pee when we get there. Trust me," Billy said.

Maybe it was one of my infinite flaws, but I always did trust Billy Hinman.

Getting On Board

'd read something about how people used to complain a long time ago about all the procedures they'd have to go through before being permitted to board an airplane. Whatever. The stuff we had to do to get on a transpod—one that my father owned, no less—for a flight into space was as regimented and absurd as Maoist reeducation.

And although I was out of it on booze and Woz that day, I still suspected something was not right.

"I don't understand why we have to take showers and put on entirely different sets of clothes, just to visit Tennessee," I said.

I have a foggy memory of Rowan and Billy telling me something about taking a train to Tennessee. I had never been to Tennessee. I didn't actually want to go to Tennessee, but I trusted Rowan and I loved Billy, so I would do anything with him, especially because whenever I'd fall into one of my depressed moods, I would generally find myself trying to calculate all the normal human experiences I would never be permitted to have.

"It's a Tennessee thing. A custom. Trust me," Billy told me. "It'll be worth it. I hear they have great food."

On Woz, I wasn't much of an eater, but Woz makes everyone so compliant and malleable.

I countered, "I already took a shower today, and my clothes are nicer than this stupid orange suit."

Ever since the incident with all the shit on the *Kansas*, passengers on Mr. Messer's R & R G G cruises had to go through medical examinations, take disinfecting showers, and put on specially sealed, full-body suits made from recycled paper. Passengers were not allowed to bring anything with them from Earth, not even the clothes they wore into the terminal.

Besides, everything anyone could possibly need was already waiting on the *Tennessee*. Clothes, food, recreation— all managed by my father's company. It only took a quick scan of our eyes—mine, Billy's, and Rowan's—and the v.4 cog at the Mojave Field terminal whisked us through our medical scans and into the changing rooms.

A Messer could write his own ticket anywhere on Rabbit & Robot Grosvenor Galactic.

I still thought we were in a train station, about to go to Nashville.

Embarrassing.

My father's transpods looked ridiculous—all painted in

the clown-suit colors of his television program, with caricatures of Rabbit, the bonk, on one side, and Mooney, the robot, on the other.

The process of preparing to board the transpod was a little personal and awkward for us. Billy felt it was necessary to stay with me so I wouldn't do anything weird, like getting lost or passing out and drowning in the chemical showers. I'd been to space plenty of times—on the *Tennessee* when it was in the final stages of construction, and a couple times on the *Kansas* before the shit thing (I was also lucky that the sewage system on board the *Kansas* worked just fine when I sailed on it)—so I knew the routine.

But I believed Billy Hinman when he told me that nothing out of the ordinary was going on.

Woz.

We completely stripped out of all our clothes and left them in sealed locker vaults. Then we had to endure a medical examination from a depressed male nurse orderly v.4 cog who stared and sighed and put his grabby, poking hands on a little too much of me for my comfort, even if he was a cog—a sad one, at that.

After our exams, the nurse led Billy and me, naked, into a decontamination shower cubicle.

Together.

Yeah. Nothing out of the ordinary.

Billy kept saying, "Isn't this train station great?"

"But we're naked," I pointed out.

"So what?" Billy said.

In all honesty, Billy Hinman had seen me naked plenty of times in our lives. I had seen Billy Hinman, who was thoroughly comfortable without clothes, naked just about every day I'd known him. When we were babies, Rowan, or sometimes Hilda, used to give us baths together.

"We haven't taken a bath together in . . . forever," I said.

"It's almost like we're four years old again," Billy said.

I looked down at my bare legs, like I couldn't believe my pants were missing. I patted my thighs as though trying to convince myself my pockets were actually no longer there. I was a mess. "Where are my clothes? When can I get them back? I left a lot of money in my pants."

Billy didn't answer me.

And I had a feeling I would never see my clothes, or anything I'd left behind, again. I turned out to be right, but for reasons I'd never considered.

The showerheads came on. They sprayed from above and all around us—up from jets on the floor, and out from the sides of our cubicle, which was big enough for more than two people, spraying us with a warm coating of mist and then a downpour of warm water. It was actually very nice.

"Don't worry about it," Billy said. "Trust me. You don't need money or your clothes right now, and we can get some Woz for you in just a little bit."

"You're my best friend. I love you, Billy. And the shower feels really nice."

I felt myself beginning to fall asleep on my feet, standing on wobbly legs in the steaming mist.

* * *

Of course, my caretaker Rowan went through his medical screening and decontamination process ahead of Billy and me, and once we met him on the other side, sterilized and uniformed, the three of us were led down a walkway toward what I still assumed was our train to the Volunteer State, among a group of cogs dressed in identical uniforms.

It was hard for me to tell if anyone among our fellow travelers was human, or if we were isolated in a platoon of cogs. We all smelled exactly the same in our disinfected orange paper flight suits, which was to say we smelled like nothing at all. As soon as someone burped or started sweating, though, Cager Messer's cursed nose would pick it up, and I'd get some clear sense of whether or not we were completely alone.

But I was pretty sure that with the exception of Billy, Rowan, and myself, none of the sixty or so passengers with us were human. But what did I know? Because their coders may have been hungry during final program uploads, some v.4s ate printed food too, which was the only kind of food we'd be getting now. But a cog that can eat may just as well be human, with or without their proclivity for obsessing over a single emotion.

Plenty of v.4s were like that. They were just beginning to exhibit the ability to act with human emotions, although their range was narrowly constrained to just one mood—angry, depressed, horny, happy, and so on. Billy's father,

Albert Hinman, who owned Hinsoft International, the company that manufactured the world's supply of cogs, thought the new, emotional v.4s were funny.

Albert Hinman was also the richest man in the world.

Billy Hinman and I were spoiled pieces of shit, in my opinion.

And Billy detested cogs, especially the ones that were exceedingly happy or mad, or horny, for that matter.

There have always been plenty of human beings like that too—people who only eat, and then obsess on how depressed or outraged or horny they are, and nothing else.

It would end up taking two miserable days for us to get to the *Tennessee*, not that things like days counted up in space the way they counted down on Earth. It was going to be a rough ride, and it was made worse by the flight attendant in our first-class section, a v.4 cog stuck in an endless loop of elation.

The attendant cogs in second class were all outraged, which had to have been even more unbearable.

In fact, before the transpod slid out of the terminal on its gleaming runway rails (I was still convinced we were on a train), we heard a shouting attendant in the cabin behind us. Chances were that she was probably yelling at nobody. Outraged cogs frequently did that.

"Sir! You need to buckle your restraints immediately! This is outrageous! I am so angry right now! I can't take your rubbish! Sir! Hold your rubbish until after takeoff!

This is so unfair to me! I am filled with rage! I can't take your rubbish! This is complete racism! I quit! I fucking quit! Get me out of here!"

Of course, it was already too late for anyone to get out of the transpod, and cogs are not allowed to *quit*, no matter what. The doors had been sealed, and we were about to depart.

They bother most people, but I love v.4s. They were the best things Billy's dad ever made, even if about one-third of them hated human beings. Well, hated everything, really.

I said, "What the fuck is this place, Billy?"

Billy cleared his throat. "Um. We're on our way to Tennessee, Cage. Trust me. Are you hungry or thirsty?"

Billy buckled me into my seat.

"Why are you tying me up?"

"Trust me, Cager. Do you want some more Woz? We can get some in just a little while."

Rowan sat across the aisle from us. We were the only three passengers in first class. Rowan waved at our attendant, and she stepped from her post in the galley as the transpod slid away from the gate.

"Can you bring us three beers before takeoff?" Rowan asked.

"This is so fantastic!" our attendant, whose name tag identified her as Lourdes, said. "I'd be extremely happy to! So happy! I also need to pee! This is so exciting!"

Cogs do not pee. Well, most of them don't. Lourdes was just so happy, she didn't know what to think.

"Would Grosvenor Beer be all right for you gentle-men?" Lourdes's eyes, astonished to the size of apricots, looked at each one of us as she showed a wall of perfect white teeth behind the breach of her smile.

"That would be fine," Rowan said.

"Perfect! Perfect! Perfect!" Lourdes nearly exploded on us.

Then she whirled around to her galley station and sang a Mooney song to herself while she poured our beers.

> *Add Action,*
> *Add Action,*
> *Execute switch void ever never,*
> *Execute switch satisfaction.*

Nobody likes Mooney.

I woke up a bit when the thing we were in started mov-ing. I pivoted my head from side to side, alternately looking out my porthole and the one next to the empty seat beside Rowan.

"Is this a fucking plane?" I asked.

"I promise you it's not a plane," Billy said.

Lourdes returned with a tray of beers. "Drink them fast! We'll be taking off shortly! This is so exciting, I think I just pooped a little!"

Lourdes placed the beers down on each of our service tables and watched us with unblinking and thrilled eyes while we sipped. Well, to be honest, Billy gulped his down in one tip, which made Lourdes even happier.

"If this is a fucking plane, Billy . . . Where are you taking me?" I said.

Billy hated anything that went high or fast. It was impossible for me to consider that he'd ever feel so desperate as to actually get on a plane—and only for me. But it was too late for him to do anything about it now.

As long as I'd known him, Billy Hinman had told me he would rather die than go into space.

"Here, Bill. Maybe you should finish my beer for me," I said.

Billy Hinman emptied my glass, and Lourdes came to collect our service items. Then we reclined our seats flat and waited for all hell to break loose.

Mojave Field

Meg Hatfield knew more about programming than most of the coders who designed the reasoning architecture in the v.4 cogs that Hinsoft International distributed all over the human world.

"It took me a solid week to figure out the code sequence to get in. Writing you into it was easy. The cogs at the gates scan our eyes and they only see code. They think we're a couple of v.4s," Meg said. "Stupid fucking machines."

"I never went to Grosvenor School a day in my life," Jeffrie told her. "I came here with Lloyd when I was ten. I could never figure out something like that."

Jeffrie and her brother Lloyd were burners—arsonists.

"Here" was Antelope Acres—a chain-link-enclosed squatter's camp in the desert north of Los Angeles.

"You set a mean fire, though," Meg said.

"Lloyd does, mostly. I just watch."

Lloyd Cutler had a thing for Meg Hatfield. Meg knew that was why Jeffrie didn't want her brother to come with them. Besides, Meg didn't like Lloyd—she didn't like burners in general, but especially Lloyd, who'd tried to lure her into his camper to have sex ever since she and her father had moved in to Antelope Acres. Meg was afraid Lloyd might get out of control and burn the place down if he came along. So she was relieved that Jeffrie told her not to write him in too, that the girls should go alone.

But Meg liked Jeffrie. Jeffrie Cutler was different from most burners. She didn't just burn things out of anger. Meg Hatfield knew there was something else Jeffrie was trying to get rid of.

A few days before Christmas, the girls hiked down from Missing Boy Mountain on a trail that led to the highway across from Mojave Field's glimmering terminal complex. They sat at the edge of the desert and waited for late afternoon, which Meg explained was the busiest time, and the most opportune for the girls to get inside.

"What happens to Lloyd if we don't come back?" Meg said.

Jeffrie shrugged. "He's grown up. He can take care of himself."

"Won't he worry about you?"

"No." Jeffrie shook her head. "What about your dad?"

"I'll call him. He'll be okay. I'll come back if he needs me to."

"Okay." Jeffrie bit her lower lip and nodded. "What's it like, writing code?"

"It's like talking in dog," Meg said. "It's an ugly language, because there's no space for interpretation, which is the difference between cogs and us."

"I'd rather light stuff up than interpret it," Jeffrie said.

"No burning here once we're in. Okay?"

"I promise." And Jeffrie asked, "Which one of those planes have you been in?"

Across the highway, set a quarter mile behind rows of fencing, sat a rust-smeared and tired old herd of derelict passenger airliners.

"We're not going in one of those. We're going inside the place where the big stuff happens," Meg said.

When it was time, Meg Hatfield drew a rectangle in the air between her thumbs and index fingers. Her thumbphone screen lit up in the space she drew with her hands.

"Are you going to call your dad?" Jeffrie asked.

"No. I'm getting us inside." She entered a sequence of numbers and letters. The screen floating before them in the air scrolled rapidly with line after line of bracketed and meaningless poetry. Then Meg Hatfield hit send, and she said, "Come on, Jeffrie. Let's cross the road now."

Rabbit & Robot

Happy almost-Crambox Eve, Cager," Billy said.

"Fuck, Billy. Why are you guys doing this to me?"

I needed to vomit.

Puking in space is not good; just ask anyone who'd survived the *Kansas* ordeal.

In the absence of gravity, sewage, like hungry tigers and venomous snakes, is incomprehensibly terrifying.

The transpod shuddered and roared as it picked up acceleration down the railway of the takeoff strip. Rowan turned his face toward us and watched what was going on. I could tell he felt bad for me and Billy, so there was a lot of feeling miserable going on in first class.

Except for Lourdes, our flight attendant, who squealed, "Whee! Whee! I am so happy! I am so happy! I could poop myself, I'm so happy! Whee!" From her rear-facing seat, she paddled her high-heeled feet as though she were doing the backstroke.

I couldn't help but catch a glimpse of her panties.

"Well. I thought it would be a nice gift for you, Cager. You know. Just us—well, and Rowan, too—up there on that enormous ship, where we can do whatever we want and basically run the place. Think of it, how much fun that will be."

"Yeah. Whatever, Bill."

"Come on. It will be great. Tell him how fun it will be up there, Rowan," Billy said.

"You may never want to come back," Rowan confirmed.

The transpod got noisier and noisier as it approached liftoff speed.

My hand trembled next to Billy's on our armrest. I watched as my skin drained to the color of skim milk. I felt terrible, so I grabbed Billy's hand.

And I'll admit the truth: When a Grosvenor Galactic cruise transpod lifts off, there are undeniable moments of terror. The noise is so tremendous that you can't hear the other passengers scream, which they always do (and Billy, who had never traveled to space, was doing right now), and the entire craft shakes like it's about to fall to pieces. And then there's that instant when your feet are pointing directly upward and your head fills to capacity with whatever blood was previously circulating in your system. Thankfully, it's all over in a minute or so, and then you're just floating along in silence—and if it's your first time up there, chances are you're wondering if this is what death is actually like.

Billy Hinman's fingernails dug into my hand.

"This may have been the dumbest mistake I've ever made," he said. "Get me down."

"Ow," I said. "Your fingernails are sharp."

Rowan's expression showed a bit of concern—possibly worry—over how I was handling my abduction. And then Rowan said the worst thing imaginable, which was this: "It's all perfectly smooth sailing now, Billy. Look at how high we are."

Rowan extended his hand toward the porthole.

Billy Hinman, who was terrified of flying, groaned. He fired a dirty look at Rowan, and that's when he said good-bye to Earth, and to California.

Billy opened a rectangle between his hands, and his thumphone screen hovered in the air above his lap. I watched without saying anything as Billy Hinman attempted to call his dad, who was somewhere in India.

There was nothing. No message, no fake ringtone. Only static. It was weird, and it made me want to try my phone too, or at least offer to loan mine to Billy, because Hinsoft thumbphones worked everywhere—even in space. But I pretended not to pay attention to what Billy was doing, even though I obviously was doing exactly that.

Billy closed out the screen and said, "Fuck this, stupid no-signal in space."

Behind us, one of the attendants in second class screamed and cried about being unfairly persecuted by a bigoted passenger.

Being on a transpod was almost like being stuck inside *Gulliver's Travels*, I thought. I imagined that if I'd spent a few days in second class, I'd come out acting like the raging flight attendant behind us. As it was, I could only hope that being in the front affected all of our moods in a more positive way.

Lourdes unhooked from her seat and gleefully announced that she would begin in-flight service and entertainment. She activated the transparent screenfield at the front of the cabin and said, "I am thrilled to present our in-flight entertainment selection for first-class passengers on R & R Grosvenor Galactic! Our feature will begin after a brief advertisement! I love this so much!"

Lourdes's face scrunched and she farted. Then she danced. With no music, and for no reason at all that any of us could figure out.

v.4 cogs can fart. There is no Woz in space. Another war was bound to begin on Earth—it was only a matter of time—while the first one between Billy Hinman and Cager Messer was just getting started somewhere between home and the moon.

I did not want to speak to Billy Hinman.

I knew our trip would be tough. There was no turning back, even if I tried using the no-credit-limit impact of my name. And although there was something especially painful in knowing that my best friend was trying to do something nice and positive for me, it was something I didn't want anything to do with. So I found myself pendulum-swinging between regret for being angry at Billy and trying to rationalize the truth that if he'd have let me alone, I would not have lived much longer. I suppose that was selfish of me. And it seemed that every beating I'd ever received at the hands of my mother or father always included some type of it's-for-your-own-good justification, which I knew was bullshit. Just like I knew that what Billy Hinman was doing to me was bullshit too.

Not surprisingly, the brief commercial that played before our in-flight entertainment was produced by Hinsoft International. It was a sure bet that the next advertisement on the flight would be from a Grosvenor brand. After all, there was almost nothing at all in existence that didn't come from the guys whose sperm made me and Billy Hinman.

The Hinsoft ad was all about the New! Revolutionary! v.4 cog, and how seamlessly it blended in to the human world—satisfying the demand for anything people no longer wanted to waste their time doing, which was just about everything you could list, besides being a bonk, a coder, or maybe a department store Father Christmas. The commercial showed happy cogs, which I was already getting sick of after spending about forty-five minutes with Lourdes, shouting cogs, a chorus line of singing cogs, cogs performing surgery on human beings, road-building cogs, and even naked ones. It was perfectly okay to show full nudity in public media displays—as long as the nakedness in question involved unclothed cogs, who were strikingly anatomically

correct—because, after all, cogs were cogs. It was like looking at a Renaissance sculpture of a Greek god or some biblical character's penis or breasts. It was actually like looking
at a naked electric toaster, when you thought about it. As
long as they weren't actually *people*, everyone was pretty
much okay with whatever cogs did.

And the commercial's British-accented and most likely
cog narrator said, "Hinsoft v.4 cogs—so lifelike and func-
tional, so smart and reliable, you might find yourself falling
in love."

Wonderful, I thought.

The more disturbing thing was what followed the v.4
ad. What came next was an episode of *Rabbit & Robot*.

Billy Hinman perked up from the melancholy that
pervaded our cabin. He had an almost conspiratorial look
on his face. Neither of us was ever allowed to watch my
father's program, so this was like sneaking a drink or a
smoke, except those were things that Billy Hinman and I
did whenever we wanted to. Watching *Rabbit & Robot*, on
the other hand, was entirely forbidden in the Messer and
Hinman households.

I glanced over at Rowan. "Hey!"

Rowan said, "Would you like me to have Lourdes turn
it off?"

Billy answered, "No. We're stuck and there's no turning
back at this point. I want to see it."

And on came the opening song. It was meaningless and
absurd, sung as a duet by Rabbit, the bonk, and Mooney,

the cog, but for whatever reasons it brightened my mood. I think it was most likely the case that if there was such a thing, the song was written in the key of Woz, since everyone who was addicted to the program was also, like Cager Messer, addicted to Woz.

> *Oh, Rabbit and Robot, Robot and Rabbit*
> *Behind your eyes, the kingdom we inhabit!*
> *The land of asynchronous transfer mode,*
> *Go fight wars, and write that code!*
> *Oh, Rabbit and Robot, Robot and Rabbit*
> *Oh, Rabbit and Robot, Robot and Rabbit*
> *Oh, Rabbit and Robot, Robot and Rabbit*
> *Oh, Rabbit and Robot, Robot and Rabbit!*

Like I said, it was really dumb, to the point that I felt uncomfortable—embarrassed, even—because I always knew Rowan was exceedingly judgmental about stupid shit. And there was no getting around it here. But I liked it. It made me happy. Just as Billy said, we were stuck on this shit ride.

And while Mooney and Rabbit—and Lourdes—sang to us, a shotgun storm of images blasted all around the screen—scrolling strings of code commands, and short staccato clips of bonks doing what bonks do, the types of things that were big thrilling hits at Charlie Greenwell's "engagement parties."

The last time we'd been to Charlie's apartment on

a Woz buying mission, Charlie Greenwell told us this: "Every week or so, the boys in my unit would get together and drink and get hacked on Woz, and we'd tell our stories about the people we'd killed in engagements. That's what we called 'em—*engagements*. It was an engagement party. Ha ha!"

"Yeah. Funny," Billy had said, completely deadpan.

"I'm not lying," Charlie said.

Neither one of us thought Charlie Greenwell was lying. I could smell the runny eggs Charlie Greenwell had eaten that morning for breakfast, and that he'd drunk some vodka too. It kind of turned my stomach.

"And I'm not embarrassed to say what happened, either," Charlie said. "But, you know, it was weird, but that's what we were there to do. Twenty-seven wars don't just fight themselves, you know?"

"Twenty-eight," Billy corrected.

"What fucking ever, Hinman," Charlie said. "Anyway, it was how we blew off steam—telling about all the rabbits we'd shot, and what it was like. And I ain't lying, neither, but most of us bonks would get pretty worked up after a few hits and all the stories we'd tell about whacking rabbits. Most of us got pretty horned up just thinking about it."

"Wait, wait, wait," I said. "You fucking *got horny* while telling stories about killing people?"

"Well. Yeah. It was no big deal, Hinman. Everyone does," Charlie said.

I could only imagine Charlie Greenwell had no clue

about what *everyone* did, and now there he was, back in the good old United States of America, smoking Woz with me, and walking down the same streets and visiting the same shopping malls as everyone else.

Charlie Greenwell was on state disability. Everyone in America who was old enough to work was either a bonk, a coder, on disability, or maybe on disability *and* doing part-time gigs as human department-store Santas, or completely invisible, except for people like Billy and me, and that was just because of our parents. It had nothing to do with us.

Rabbit & Robot turned out to be meaningless and riveting at the same time. There was something about the song and the images that seemed to connect directly with the Woz receptors in my brain.

I always knew this was why Billy and I had been kept away from the show—and supposedly from Woz—for our entire lives.

When the assault of the song and pictures finally ended, and the quiet opening of the first scene replaced it, I felt my shoulders relax. I slumped comfortably back in my seat.

"I love this show! I love this show so much, I want to rip my clothes off and rub *Rabbit & Robot* all over my naked body!" Lourdes gurgled. Her hair was a mess, and her skirt had twisted around, due to all the wild dancing she'd been doing. If she were a human, she would have been soaked in sweat, and quite possibly ashamed of herself too.

But I love v.4s, even if I was calculating in my mind how unbearably long the two-day journey to the *Tennessee* would actually be with Lourdes running as juiced-up as she was.

Rowan shrugged and shook his head.

If the opening song was stupid, the episode of *Rabbit & Robot* we watched adequately matched or exceeded that quality.

The episode we saw—well, the one I saw, since Billy Hinman was obviously trying to force himself to not watch it—was about a mistake that had been made with Mooney's work classification. He had been drafted into the army, which made Mooney the cog very confused, and Rabbit the bonk extremely angry.

But Mooney, being the patriotic and dutiful cog that he was, reported to boot camp along with his partner, Rabbit (which didn't really make sense, since Rabbit was already an accomplished bonk, but sense making was not something the program was necessarily praised for), and zany high jinks ensued. And even though nearly every episode of *Rabbit & Robot* included Mooney's violent destruction at some point, people regularly told us how hilarious it was, and lavished us with undeserved vicarious praise for our television-program-and-spaceship-producer and cog-and-thumbphone-manufacturing sperm-donor fathers. When the other bonks in Mooney's squad at boot camp found out they were sharing their barracks with a cog, they were understandably outraged. They found out because Rabbit outed Mooney when he was drunk, which was something Rabbit routinely was in the show too.

Oops.

So the other bonks in Mooney's squad waited until after lights-out was declared and, on the third night of boot camp, dragged Mooney the cog outside and set him on fire while he screamed and screamed. Actually, they set him on fire after cutting off his arms and legs so he couldn't run away or attempt to pat out the flames with his cog hands. It was all very funny, especially when the bonk recruits began singing a bonk song called "Making Rabbit Stew."

Everyone knows that it is barbaric and uncivilized to allow cogs to participate in the glories of human warfare. What purpose could that possibly serve? Nothing would ever get solved if people let wars just fight themselves.

Even Charlie Greenwell knew that.

Cheepa Yeep!

In with the Cogs

You two! Go to gate forty-four. Do I have to say it again?" A male cog in a very tight, red Grosvenor Galactic smock flailed his arms as though he were cutting through a swarm of insects flocking between him and Meg. "This is ridiculous! Why are you victimizing me? Why are you doing this to me? What gives you the right to publicly disgrace me like this?"

"What the fuck?" Jeffrie said.

The v.4 in charge of getting the cogs on board was more than mildly huffy.

"I . . . I . . . don't get it," Meg said.

"Why do I have to tell you twice? Why do you feel entitled to demean me?"

Meg Hatfield and Jeffrie Cutler didn't have much experience with cogs at all.

"Are you sure we should do this?" Jeffrie whispered.

"Are you scared?"

"This place needs to burn."

Then Meg asked the cog, "Why are you so mad at us?"

The cog behind the check-in counter gagged and screamed like he was being stabbed. Then he threw himself onto his back and thrashed his arms and legs wildly. "Why? Why are you making me the bad guy in all this? What have I ever done to you? I don't know you! I don't know you! I didn't do anything to you! I owe you no debt of suffering!"

He tugged big handfuls of hair from his scalp and scratched at his cheeks with his perfect fingernails.

This is what v.4 cogs do all the time. Well, at least the irritated ones.

Meg grabbed Jeffrie's arm. "Come on."

The girls joined the assembling crowd of passenger cogs and followed them toward the doorway beneath a sign that read TO ALL GATES.

Although there was no need for medical screenings, since cogs were either alive or dead, running or not running, with no in-between states of disease, all cogs still had to go through the same decontamination showers and suit-up procedures as living human passengers, in order to prevent the transportation of biological pathogens into space. Except cogs, being cogs, were handled a little more roughly than fragile human beings, which was more than a little discomforting to Meg Hatfield and Jeffrie Cutler.

Meg and Jeffrie happened to be in a group that was

mostly made up of very, very happy cogs. A few of the cogs were depressed. One of them wept incessantly, although being a cog, he shed an oily hydraulic fluid, as opposed to actual tears.

The jets in the cog showers were not heated and came on like fire hoses. Eleven cogs, male and female models, were packed with Meg and Jeffrie into a shower stall the same size as those intended for only one or two humans. Jeffrie was lost in the press of naked cogs, all of whom were taller than she was. She squeezed into a corner of the stall away from Meg. It wasn't the best place to be. When the blast of disinfectant came on, Jeffrie was knocked backward and ended up on the floor of the shower, looking up between tangled and nude cog legs.

"Whee! Yippee!" one of the cogs squealed.

"This is the best thing that's ever happened to me!" said another, prancing from foot to foot.

From somewhere in the crush of bodies came, "I never want to leave this place! Except I need to dance! And there's not enough room! I want to dance!"

"I can't stand myself. Can someone please kill me? I don't think I'll ever pull myself out of this hole of darkness," one of the nonweeping depressed cogs added.

The shower lasted exactly ten seconds. When it stopped, most of the cogs were laughing and jumping up and down, which was the only direction they could move.

The sobbing cog continued his sobbing.

Jeffrie got stepped on and kneed in the head. She

couldn't get up from the floor. When the group of naked cogs exited the shower and Jeffrie could finally rise to her feet, she saw that one of the male cogs had broken in half at his midsection. It was hard to tell if he had been one of the happy cogs or one of the depressed ones. But he was broken, naked, and dead, and he was also abandoned and forgotten on the floor of a chemical disinfectant shower.

And things like that happened all the time.

Jeffrie cupped her hands in front of her groin and, dripping, followed all the naked things to the dressing area, where Meg waited for her. Jeffrie was embarrassed and frightened, and felt so terribly small among all the cogs, who despite not being human still had sexually mature human bodies. Jeffrie had been implanted with hormone arrestors, which Lloyd had stolen for her three years earlier, so she wasn't growing and changing the way her body's own code had programmed her to do.

"I thought I lost you," Meg said.

Jeffrie wouldn't look at Meg. She kept her eyes down, watching the parade of feet ahead of her. "I want to go back to Antelope Acres. I want to darf this fucking place with Lloyd."

Meg didn't say anything.

Both girls knew it was too late to leave, much less to light anything on fire now. They were shivering and freezing cold. Of course, none of the cogs had any idea about the temperature of the showers, or that Meg and Jeffrie were not cogs. They were all too overcome by joy, outrage, or deep despair, depending on which cog you paid attention to.

Meg Hatfield and Jeffrie Cutler slid into their orange jumpsuits.

"So. You saw, didn't you?" Jeffrie asked.

"Saw what?" Meg said.

Meg was not good at lying to Jeffrie.

"We're going to the *Tennessee*! We're going to the *Tennessee*! I think I just released my bowels!" one of the cogs burbled.

"Ha ha ha!" laughed a chorus of happy cogs.

"I'm going to clean toilets on the *Tennessee*! I love cleaning human feces and other bodily secretions!" another cog yipped.

"I get to clean bedrooms! Give me a soiled human bed, and I'll be happy for all eternity!"

"I want to release my bowels too!" someone shouted.

"I'm so lonely. I'm so desperately alone. Someone please help me," the sobbing cog cried.

Are We There Yet?

Besides killing off Mooney, and the ridiculous songs containing repetitive sequences of code and the brand names, models, and calibers of the most popular military weaponry, one of the regular components of my father's show, *Rabbit & Robot,* was a weekly feature called "Code from Home," where kids got to send in their own coder programs for Mooney.

Each week, the best submission actually got uploaded into Mooney, so people could witness the ridiculous nonsense some lucky coder enjoyed making the poor cog do.

The episode we watched—well, the one I watched and Billy Hinman tried to ignore—featured a winning code sequence that made Mooney the cog instantly fall asleep whenever he got about one-fourth of the way across a street. It was called "Crosswalk Narcolepsy," and it didn't end well

ANDREW SMITH

for poor Mooney, but I'm sure it was a great hit with the viewers down on Earth.

I thought it was funny.

Rabbit laughed and laughed about it too. So did Lourdes, who floated around the cabin in our gravity-free transpod, not minding at all that her skirt drifted up and down like hypnotic sea fans in an underwater current. I found myself in a desperate dilemma as I tried to figure out what was morally worse: watching an episode of *Rabbit & Robot* or getting turned on by looking at a v.4 cog's panties.

Either way I looked at it, I was completely ashamed of myself.

I was a total mess, and I needed some Woz.

Two days of this was going to be unbearable.

But, apparently no matter what horrible fate Mooney was subjected to, there were always plenty of replica Mooney cogs to stand in and wrap up every "Code from Home" segment. And he'd sing a song that ended with these lines:

> As long as there are young coders like you,
> There's nothing that humans won't eventually
> try to do!

And I thought, yes, as a species, we probably always have had a great need to watch the Mooneys we produce lie down in front of crowded and speeding streetcars.

Pink polka dots. Really small ones. And the cursive

word "Thursday." That was the pattern printed on Lourdes's panties, even though it was a Monday.

I mean, I was pretty sure it was still Monday.

Lourdes pushed herself through the projection of the screen and drifted down the aisle so she could seal off the portal between our first class and the shrieking, laughing, wailing calamity of peasants confined to second class.

Too bad, because I was just starting to smell something, which was probably only Lourdes's food printer as it cranked out some protein-carbohydrate-fiber-mineral replications of shrimp scampi, niçoise salad, or chicken cordon bleu.

After all, there really was nothing we humans wouldn't eventually try to do.

When *Rabbit & Robot* was over, I looked at Billy, who pretended to be asleep.

I said, "I need some Woz. And I need to pee."

And Billy Hinman told me, "Wait. We'll be able to get some Woz when we get there."

I knew he had to have been lying to me. He'd threatened plenty of times that he was going to oversee some forced acquisition of my sobriety.

Fuck you, Billy.

Rowan waved his hand in the air. "Miss? Lourdes? The boy here—my charge—well . . . he needs to use the toilet."

"Oh my! I'm so thrilled to help out! This makes me want to pee too! Have you ever been to space? What a beautiful, heroic, brave, and astonishingly sexy young man! This makes me so happy! This gives me hope for the future and makes me want to deliberately ovulate!" Lourdes burbled. She grabbed the hem of her skirt and, for reasons entirely unknown, flagged it up and down and up and down, as though she were fanning the flames on a blacksmith's forge.

One doesn't simply "pee" in the weightlessness of space, however. That could be a disaster. Fortunately, the *Tennessee* had its own gravity-generation system, which made all kinds of wonderful things possible: swimming pools, urination, and even a full-size zoo, for example. One of my father's first Grosvenor Galactic cruise ships, the *Kentucky*, did not have a gravity generator. Everyone thought people would love to spend some time in zero gravity on a luxury liner, even one with a zoo.

Father quickly learned that floating Siberian tigers and king cobras were very difficult to get along with, however.

It was a real mess, along the same lines as all the shit on the *Kansas*.

But the *Tennessee* was heralded to be the "cruise ship to end all cruise ships."

We certainly found out the truth of that on our own, Billy, Rowan, and I.

In any event, before I could get out of my seat to pee, Lourdes was required to show us a video presentation called "How to Urinate and Defecate On Board Grosvenor Galactic Cruise Ships in Space."

I had been through the identical video lesson on every R & R G G flight I'd been on, and every time I watched, it still made me feel incredibly awkward and embarrassed.

But the vacuum of space leaves no room for personal shyness.

Still, I felt myself turning red and wondering if Billy and Rowan were looking at me as the instructional video ran through its three important sequences: How to Safely Defecate, Female Urination Safety Procedures, and, finally, Male Urination on the Grosvenor Galactic Fleet, during which Billy said, to no one in particular, "That sleeve tube looks like it could be a lot of fun."

It kind of made my stomach turn. But vomiting in weightlessness was potentially worse than peeing, which is why they gave us all anti-nausea injections directly into our stomachs during the ordeal of our physical examinations.

Besides, all the actors in "How to Urinate and Defecate On Board Grosvenor Galactic Cruise Ships in Space" were v.4 cogs, so it wasn't like we were watching actual humans taking dumps and pissing into weird vacuum hoses. But it was still repulsive to look at, even though my brain had been lulled by the subliminal coding effects of *Rabbit & Robot*.

I always tried to hold it to the point of pain whenever I went up into space. Any normal guy would, right?

I unhooked myself from the seat and swam past Lourdes, who opened her eyes as wide as twinned mineshafts and nodded proudly at the prospect of teaching me how to safely urinate as a male in space. Her smile seemed to split her face like an overripe tomato.

I groaned, then turned to Rowan and said, "Are we there yet?"

Printer Ketchup

Meg Hatfield had to figure things out on her own.

There were no instructional videos played for the cogs in second class. It was unnecessary. Cogs knew everything they needed to know and never had to learn anything else.

They also never needed to pee.

It must be very nice.

In fact, after the first few hours of wailing and moaning—and cheering, dancing, and applauding—every one of the second-class cogs, on their way to report for duty aboard the *Tennessee*, the cruise ship to end all cruise ships, went into silent sleep mode while Meg Hatfield and Jeffrie Cutler discussed plans to feed themselves and take care of other corporeal needs.

It didn't matter much, because Meg and Jeffrie could have done anything they wanted to do and they would have

appeared to be invisible as far as the cogs and flight attendants on the Grosvenor Galactic transpod were concerned,
due to the code Meg had uploaded from her thumbphone
earlier that day.

"I could totally darf this thing and nobody would ever
know," Jeffrie said.

"Nobody would know because nobody is actually on
this flight, except for us," Meg pointed out. "We're packed
in with a bunch of machines."

"I saw a boy up there." Jeffrie nodded her chin toward
the barrier that sealed in the privilege of first class. "He
was really cute, but I think he was hacked up on Woz or
something."

Meg said, "*Cute?* I've never heard you call a boy cute
before. How old are you?"

"Fifteen. And shut up," Jeffrie said. "He really is cute."

"He's most likely a cog."

"No. I saw his eyes. I can tell."

"That's what you think," Meg said.

Meg opened up her thumbphone.

"What are you going to do to us now? More code?"
Jeffrie asked. "Why don't you turn this thing around, and
make them take us back home?"

"No. This time I really *am* going to call my dad."

Jeffrie Cutler, like most of the burner kids from
Antelope Acres, did not have a Hinsoft phone implanted
inside her fingertips. "Ask him if he could let Lloyd know
I'm with you."

Nobody liked Lloyd Cutler, and Meg Hatfield's father was no exception.

"Okay."

But when Meg called, nothing happened.

"This sucks," Meg said. "I guess there's no phones up here in space."

"Um, well, in that case, when are we going back?" Jeffrie asked.

"We'll figure out something. Just enjoy the ride, Jeff."

Jeffrie frowned. "I kind of feel weird, like maybe I'm going to puke or something."

"Don't think about it. You're probably just hungry. I am. I'm going to figure out where the toilets are and look for something to eat. Okay?"

"All right."

When Meg came back, she carried pouches of food: hamburgers and fries with bottles of water. It was the kind of food made at places Jeffrie and her brother Lloyd liked to set fire to.

"Food printers," Meg said, waving the girls' meal pouches in front of Jeffrie, "Really cool ones."

"Thanks."

Meg sat down beside Jeffrie and harnessed herself back into the recliner. "But the toilets are weird. It took me ten minutes to figure out how to use their *female urinal*, and by then I thought I was going to piss myself. It's like hooking yourself up to a fucking electronic lamprey eel or something. And the pictures they have on the walls, with the characters from that kids' show demonstrating how to use them, are really disturbing. If I was a guy, I'd be terrified of the male lamprey thing."

Jeffrie tore at the opening of her food pouch. "What's *that* supposed to mean?"

"Nothing."

"Now I kind of have to go too."

"Do you want me to show you how to do it?"

Jeffrie shook her head. "I'm not stupid. And I'm not scared, either."

"Well, do me a favor. When you come back, see if you can print up some ketchup," Meg said.

"No. I can't do the reading and writing thing. Sorry."

Meg said, "Well, then. I guess this pretty much means I can feed you whatever I want."

Jeffrie unhooked her harness and got out of her seat.

"That doesn't mean I'll eat it, though."

Jeffrie pulled herself away from the seat and drifted toward the toilets. She said, "Can you promise me one thing, Meg? Can you promise that you will get us back home before too long?"

"No worries, Jeff," Meg said. "I promise."

Like Nothing Else
in Tennessee

Billy Hinman, who hated to fly, and hated anything that moved fast, had never been to space.

I watched his face, as confused and out of it as I was. Even in my state I knew there was nothing like seeing, for the first time, the massive hulk of the *Tennessee* through the portholes of a tiny Grosvenor Galactic transpod.

The *Tennessee* was so big, it was almost scary.

As a matter of fact, it really was scary to Billy Hinman. The *Tennessee* looked like a gigantic eye, floating in a low orbit over the moon. An eye as big as Boise.

"I don't really want to go on that thing," he said.

Then Billy shook his head and said, "What the fuck did I do, Cager?"

He covered his head with his blanket and turned away from the window.

On the second day of our flight to the *Tennessee*, I began

to sweat and shake. It was just a little at first, but my guts clenched up in protest at the lack of Woz. I could not eat, despite Rowan's pleading with me, and Lourdes's unending manic performances.

Lourdes tried everything to make me feel better. She danced and sang, wrapped me in blankets, swabbed my clammy skin with warm washcloths, and shaved me, which was unnecessary, to be honest.

Billy Hinman, my best friend in life,complained. "You know, he's not the only human passenger in first class," he told her.

So Lourdes put chilled cucumber slices on Billy Hinman's eyelids, and she even asked him if he'd like a hand job, which made me kind of jealous—and horny, too—just thinking about Lourdes and her "Thursday" panties.

Rowan, arching an eyebrow, stared at me silently.

Maybe being in space for two days with a Wozhead in withdrawal was wearing on everyone's sanity, even our nonhuman flight attendant's. And Lourdes's offer to Billy was just typical of my experience around people—and even cogs—who were all so hopelessly attracted to Billy Hinman.

And I wasn't entirely surprised when Billy Hinman told her, "No," and shut his eyes. Some people did like to do sexual things with cogs, but for his entire life Billy Hinman always told me how much he'd hated the things on which his father's empire had been built.

If Lourdes had asked me if she could give me a hand job, I would have probably said yes, but then again, I was in the viselike grips of Woz withdrawal after forty hours' sitting, harnessed in and hopelessly trapped.

"Are you sure? No?" Lourdes asked.

"No," Billy grumbled.

"Oh, well! I'm so thrilled to be part of the Grosvenor Galactic experience! I'm happiest when I can make people happy, and share in their happiness!"

I felt left out, ignored, and unhappy. I also wanted Woz and began plotting some method by which I could access a clinic as soon as we got to the *Tennessee*.

Then Lourdes farted again and did a wild dance that made her look like a terrified, fleeing squid as she floated in the air above our recliners.

"I'm a squid! I'm a squid!" she said. "I am so happy! We are almost at the *Tennessee*! I am a happy flying squid!"

And Lourdes's skirt lifted up again.

Rowan caught me staring at her underwear.

In the weightlessness of space, you might not be able to get Woz, but if you're a sixteen-year-old guy, you can always get erections.

I was embarrassed. Stupid thin paper orange spacesuits.

So I said, "I don't know what's happening to me, Rowan."

"It's been a long trip, Cager. I think we'll all feel better when we get off this transpod," Rowan said.

And I added, "Hand job from a robot or not."

Rowan, as usual, was not flustered by my comment.

And Lourdes gurgled, "Whee! Whee! Strap yourselves in for docking! This is my favorite part! I think I just bubbled out some squid ink in my undies!"

I wondered what color "Friday" was.

And behind us, through the sealed doorway that separated us from second class, as the cogs I'd nearly forgotten about stirred to their active modes, came the muted sounds of imitation humanity: cries of joy, and pained screams of outrage. And inconsolable sobbing, too.

All of human history was with us, hardwired into the circuitry of machines that had never been born and were not predestined to ever die.

The first thing that happens after the docking mechanisms link on the *Tennessee* is the sudden generation of gravity on the transpod. It's a deeply sickening feeling—like suddenly being uncomfortably full after a ridiculously large meal. It hurts in the deepest pits of your stomach—like you've just been kicked in the balls.

It takes a while to catch your breath. Unless you're a cog, that is. The ones in second class were all as noisy, happy, furious, and despondent as they had ever been.

Billy Hinman groaned and cupped his hands under his balls.

I said, "That always happens to me, too."

And before the deck crew on the *Tennessee* opened the portal to allow the first-class passengers out, Lourdes came through the cabin with an eye scanner that would automatically identify us, assign and unlock our cabins, and credit our accounts with money—something that was limitless as far as a Hinman or Messer was concerned.

We also had to sit through one last presentation—a show with Mooney and Rabbit and a bunch of actor cogs in orange flight suits—demonstrating the terrifying procedure for getting into one of the *Tennessee's* lifeboats, which were smaller versions of transpods designed for twenty passengers, if we were ordered to do it. I shuddered to think how horrifying it would be if we ever had to evacuate the *Tennessee*, and what might possibly cause that to happen.

I tried to ignore the show, but it was impossible.

"Don't worry, folks!" Mooney told us. "We've *never* had to use lifeboats on a Grosvenor Galactic cruise ship! Yet! Ha ha ha! Just kidding, folks!"

Then Mooney got sucked out an open bay door on the lifeboat deck and shrieked wildly as he contorted dancelike in the weightless black of space.

It was the stupidest and most frightening thing I ever had to sit through.

The hatch finally came open, and I was immediately assaulted by all the strange smells of the *Tennessee*. It definitely did not smell anything like burning and toxic Los Angeles.

"I hope you feel better! Have a wonderful time on the *Tennessee*! It made me so happy to spend this time with you! I can't wait to see you again!" Lourdes squealed as Billy passed her. Then Lourdes threw her arms around

Billy Hinman and clutched his hair passionately in her coggy fingers and began humping her hips into his.

"Whee!" she gurgled. "Whee! Whee! Whee!"

Things like that just seemed to happen to Billy all the time.

Rowan pried his hands between them like he was shucking apart an enormous part-man, part-machine oyster. "Please. Lourdes. Get a grip on yourself."

Then Lourdes farted and started dancing again.

We left the transpod and stepped out into the vast arrivals hall of the *Tennessee*.

I sighed. The next couple of days were going to be impossible.

Parker, My Valet

nce Billy and I were inside our room, I came unglued, then went back together the wrong way, and fell apart again.

It felt like bugs were crawling all over my skin.

I tore at the paper spacesuit I'd been wearing. Billy tried to calm me down, told me to take a shower. Although there were showers on the transpod, I hadn't taken one in days. Billy pointed out the clean clothes and underwear that had already been prepared for us in advance of our arrival, but nothing he did seemed to make any difference to me.

I panicked. I was covered with bugs.

I tore the spacesuit off and began scratching everywhere, leaving railroad tracks of red welts all over my skin.

"Dude. Get into the shower. You'll feel better."

"I can't make them go away," I said.

Billy Hinman ran to the bathroom and turned on the

water, then wrestled me into the shower, holding me under the stream until I stopped scratching.

It must have been pathetic and frightening for Billy.

I finally calmed down. The water poured through my hair and into my mouth. Billy was soaked. He looked like he was in pain, like he was about to cry.

But crying was something I had never in my life seen Billy Hinman do.

And then I said, "You're so perfect, Billy. Everyone loves you. If I hadn't watched you grow up, I'd swear you were a fucking cog."

Billy turned off the water. He managed to get me to lie down on my bed and tried to cover me with a sheet, but I kept kicking it away.

"Whatever," Billy said. "I'm going to get Rowan. I'll find some help for you, Cager."

"Fuck you, Billy. Get me some Woz. You promised you'd get me some Woz."

I had no idea how long I'd been dead.

That's what it was like, crashing from Woz. There were no dreams, just an empty and sweat-soaked blackness. When I woke up—maybe it was two hours later, maybe it was four days, not that such measurements amounted to much up here where time loses its calibration with suns and shadows—I was twisted up in my sheets, completely naked, and I felt as though I'd been entirely hollowed out, as though the skin that contained what there was that made Cager Messer Cager Messer was nothing more than an eggshell. It was like I was a desiccated husk that if you pressed into it hard enough would dissolve into a faint puff of dusty smoke.

Billy Hinman was gone, and the room was dark.

I had a dim memory of being on the transpod, of tearing off the orange paper suit that had been required flight gear.

"Billy? Are you here?"

Nothing.

I wobbled to my feet, wrapping my sheet into a toga, and made my way to the bathroom so I could put water on my face. I ended up drinking three glasses and got a stomachache.

Rowan's room was next door. Maybe Billy was with Rowan, I thought.

I stepped out through our door and into the hallway.

"Hey! Are you guys in there?" I called out.

I leaned against the wall between our door and Rowan's. I opened my thumbphone. I thought about calling Mr. Messer, or my mom. That would have been stupid. What had they ever done to fix anything in my life? I punched in Katie St. Romaine's number. Nothing. No answer there, either.

Something was wrong. Something was wrong with everything.

"It's quite impossible to lock yourself out of your room."

I hadn't noticed that my personal *Tennessee* attendant had been standing in the hallway, watching me.

There were personal valet cogs assigned to me on every one of my father's ships. Their job was to take care of anything a young, unmonitored teenage Messer could possibly want. And, given the number of cogs on board, and since the three of us—me, Rowan, and Billy—were the only human beings on the ship, it meant that each of us had hundreds of helpful and potentially angry, happy, depressed, horny, or condescending v.4 cogs all to himself.

What fun.

It turned out that my *Tennessee* valet was incredibly needy and simply would not leave me the fuck alone.

My deck valet—a young, soft-voiced male v.4 made to look like some big-eyed and innocent teenage bellhop—continued, "Simply wave your palm in front of your door and it will unlock for you. Here. Do you want me to show you how?"

I closed my phone screen. The cog walked toward me. I said, "No."

The valet stopped on the other side of Rowan's door and tilted his head slightly as he stared at me. I know that cogs are just machines, but I've always been a bit creeped out by people—especially ones who are not exactly *alive*—who stare directly into my eyes.

"My name is Parker," he said. "I'm your personal valet, here to help with whatever you want or need, Cager Messer."

Parker kept staring and staring at me. I looked at the floor.

"Let me show you how to do it," Parker said.

Well, he certainly was not outraged, depressed, or overjoyed. I was trying to decide if Parker was one of those know-it-all, smug v.4s, or if maybe he was a horny one. Either way, I immediately decided I did not like Parker, my personal valet.

"No thanks. Really. I know how, and I'm not locked out."

Then Parker touched my naked arm.

I said, "Um. Parker."

Undeterred, my valet continued, "But, poor thing, haven't you found your clothes? Do you need me to show you where the clothing we've prepared for you is located? I could help you get out of this bedsheet and dressed into something nicer. Wouldn't that feel better? You'll need a tie and jacket for dinner, besides. Please allow me to serve as your valet and help you dress and groom. It's my job, after all."

Parker was still staring into my eyes. And he was uncomfortably close. He brushed his fingers over my hand, and that was it.

"Look. Parker. I'll tell you what: You go back to your post over there, and I *promise* I will come get you when I need help getting dressed for dinner. Okay?"

Parker stared and stared. His mouth hung open slightly. If cogs could drool, Parker would be doing it right now, which was completely disgusting.

Then Rowan's door opened and my caretaker stepped out into the hall.

If Rowan had ever looked surprised and shocked in his life, he was both of those things in that instant when he stumbled into the moment I'd been sharing with a v.4 cog personal deck valet named Parker who wanted to put his hands on me and undress me. I can only assume that Rowan must have thought Lourdes and her polka-dotted "Thursday" panties had gotten me a little too excited over the course of our two-day flight to the *Tennessee*.

But Rowan would have been wrong about that.

Whatever.

Rowan raised one eyebrow and looked at me, then at Parker, then at me again without saying anything.

"I. Um," I said.

"Good morning, Cager." Rowan glanced at his wrist. "Well, nearly evening, to be precise. I'll just get a dinner outfit ready for you."

And Rowan, being the dutiful caretaker that he had always been throughout my life, went into my room and selected an entire outfit for me.

"No necktie," I said, standing in the doorway, wrapped in my sheet. "I'll put it on before we go to dinner."

And Parker—if he could feel such things besides horniness—would have been so jealous that I had my own valet, who most likely was not a cog, to help me get dressed. But Rowan was so *Rowan* all the time.

"Does he help you get dressed?" Parker asked.

I looked down at my sheet, at my pale bare legs sticking out from the bottom. Then I shook my head and went inside, leaving my personal valet alone in the dark of the hallway.

And as I slipped on the clothes Rowan had picked out, I thought, I am a spoiled piece of shit rich brat who lets some other dude draw my bath and choose my outfits down to my socks and underwear, and whose best friend most likely thinks I hate him.

Once I'd gotten dressed, I went in the bathroom and puked until nothing would come out of me.

Then I left without telling Rowan where I was going.

That's what addicts do, right?

Maybe the ship's doctor could give me some Woz—just like he would any regular teenage kid, not that regular teenage kids would ever be allowed up here on the *Tennessee*.

The Longest Elevator Ride of My Life

No! Gah—what the holy fuck are you doing?"

My valet, Parker, stuck his finger in my mouth as soon as I asked him to take me to see the ship's doctor.

"What the fuck, Parker?"

Disgusting. I spit on the floor. Everything suddenly smelled and tasted like cog fingers, which smell and taste like nothing, to tell the truth, but I was still completely repulsed by the insertion of Parker's hand into my mouth.

"I can advise Dr. Geneva if you have a fever or not," Parker explained, still trying to poke his index finger into me. "Hold still, Cager. I'm here to attend to you. Just open your mouth and relax."

What an idiot.

I pushed him away from me. "Stop it, you fucking idiot. It's not for me. My roommate—my friend—he just needs some Woz, is all."

Parker wiped his wet finger on the leg of his valet trousers. "Oh. I see. I apologize. Your temperature is perfect, by the way. And I think your outfit is very handsome. Very handsome, and sexually alluring. I can't imagine I could have dressed you more attractively than this."

Parker was staring again. He placed his hand on my shoulder.

Well, at least I wasn't feverish, and I did feel flattered by Parker's attention, even if he was just a bunch of lines of code acting out some programmer's obsession. And Rowan always did have great taste in clothes, besides.

"Whatever, Parker. I just need you to take me to see the doctor."

"Perhaps I should check your *friend's* temperature," Parker offered.

"If you want him to bite your fucking finger off, go ahead. He is *not* friendly to strange cogs who put their fingers into his mouth."

Parker thought about it, then shrugged. "Very well, then. Come with me. I'll take you to Dr. Geneva. And along our way I will point out the vast number of features and attractions available here on the *Tennessee*."

I walked with Parker down the hall toward the bay of elevators.

"May I hold your hand, Cager?"

"No, Parker. Stop it."

The first time I'd been up on the *Tennessee*, which likely was before Parker had been pooped out of the assembly line in India, I was only allowed on two decks: the one where our stateroom was located, and the one with the ship's main restaurant, which was called Le Lapin et l'Homme Mécanique. Everything else had been unstaffed or under construction.

Now that the ship was complete and ready to take on passengers, there was so much more for human beings to see and do. The *Tennessee* had recreation decks that were exactly like being out in the countryside—trees and paths through woods, with streams and lakes for swimming. One entire deck was an amusement park, naturally called Rabbit & Robot Land, which I didn't really think I would want to visit. Other floors had tremendous swimming pools and exercise equipment, like simulated mountain-climbing walls. The *Tennessee* had every kind of spa imaginable, and dozens of dance clubs that never shut down. One deck was populated with friendly chimpanzees who never threw their feces at human beings or masturbated in public. It was called World of the Monkeys and was based on an episode of *Rabbit & Robot* where Rabbit went to war against an unethical and barbaric nation that used animals— as opposed to human beings—to fight wars. So, on the World of the Monkeys deck, visitors to the *Tennessee* could actually shoot chimps. But they were cogs, so that wasn't deranged or anything. It was fun! There were zero-gravity playrooms, and even a zoo on one deck, which smelled suspiciously sterile to me. I found out that all the wild animals were actually Hinsoft International cogs, which made the whole feeding and pooping problem much more manageable. But still, I wondered, who would ever want to go to a zoo to see fake, nonliving wild animals?

The *Tennessee* also had tennis courts, skate parks, two golf courses, shopping malls nicer than anything in Los Angeles, and theaters, too. The ship had its own police department, and even a jail; and there were no fewer than five Grosvenor schools on the *Tennessee*, just in case rich people, politicians, and military leaders had decided to write off their kids' futures and turn them into bonks or coders.

Cheepa Yeep!

Every deck had at least one restaurant on it, and there were also five adults-only decks that I was very curious about. Unfortunately for my curiosity, and despite my being a true-blooded Messer, the adult decks could only be accessed after identifying eye scans, which ruled out possible exploration by sixteen-year-olds like Billy Hinman and me.

The *Tennessee* was absolutely incredible.

For a fleeting moment I was almost proud to be my father's son.

Parker and I rode an elevator together. Every time the car passed an adults-only area, the doors glowed a bright red.

"The red light means this deck is reserved for grown-ups," Parker, my valet, pointed out.

"What kinds of things happen on those decks?"

Parker winked at me and licked his lips. "Things boys our age are not technically supposed to be interested in doing."

"Um, how old *are* you, Parker?" I asked.

Parker was silent for a moment—stuck. Asking questions like *How old are you?* or *What is your last name?* confused cogs, who never aged and never had more than just a first name. They just got booted up, and when they were worn out they'd simply get tossed in the garbage.

So I said, "I mean when did you come online? This week? This morning? Have you ever even been to Earth?"

"What do you mean? Isn't this Earth?"

"No, dude. It's outer fucking space. Have you looked out a window?"

Silence as we sailed past five more decks.

Then Parker said, matter-of-factly, "Cager, I have an erection."

So there I was, alone in an elevator with a teenage-model male cog who just confessed to me that he had an erection. And I had been entirely used to not looking at Parker, to doing the universal elevator dance, where you stand perfectly still and just stare straight ahead at the crack in the door and wonder why time slows down so much when you're inside elevators. But when one guy in an elevator admits to another guy in an elevator that he's got an erection, Another Guy's eyes are destined to involuntarily migrate away from the door crack and toward the affected area of One Guy's anatomy.

I couldn't stop myself.

Whatever.

Disgusting.

Parker, the cog, my personal valet, did clearly have an

erection inside his creased gray bellhop trousers.

I was almost overcome by shame and regret for checking it out, but Parker just stood there like a statue, with his hips jutted forward to make his artificial penis even more obvious.

It was the longest, quietest few seconds in an elevator in my life.

Thankfully, the car stopped at that moment. We had arrived at the *Tennessee*'s sick bay.

"What's the point in having an erection? Stop it. Make it go away. You're a cog," I said.

"The point is that I am sexually aroused, Cager."

"But you're a machine. How can a machine being sexually aroused or having an erection possibly be of any value to society?"

Parker shrugged. "It's just how I am."

"You need to wipe a few lines of code, dude. Maybe you should see the doctor too."

"Would you like me to remove my pants so you can see my erection?" Parker asked.

"No."

"Would you like to be sexually intimate with me?"

"That's disgusting. No."

"Can I hold your hand?"

"No. Take me to the doctor."

"As you wish."

And I followed the cog kid with the hard-on out of the elevator and into the sterile hallway of the white infirmary.

Dr. Geneva, and What Space Does to Teenage Boys

was worried. Where have you been, Cager?"

I didn't answer. I was too pissed off.

So Rowan added, "You've been gone for three hours."

Rowan had been waiting in my room with Billy, who was asleep in his bed, dressed in slacks and a tie for dinner. Rowan was in his socks, his shirt was rumpled, and it looked like he'd been sleeping on my bed, which was kind of weird.

"That fucking Dr. Geneva never shuts up. The fucker wanted to give me a physical examination," I said. "And our hall boy, Parker, is constantly trying to have sex with me."

Rowan did the eyebrow-raise thing again.

Disgusting.

"No. Shut up. Don't even *wonder* about it, Rowan," I

said. "That Parker kid is a cog. That's totally ridiculous."

I pulled a small bottle of pills from my pocket. "Dr. Geneva gave me these pills. They're supposed to make me not get dehydrated and sick. They dissolve in your mouth."

"It took three hours for *just this?*"

Apparently, Rowan must have thought I'd gone off to have all sorts of fun with my new servile, turned-on, non-human playmate.

"No. It took about ten seconds for those. The rest of the time was Dr. Geneva telling me about the entire history of the fucking *Tennessee,* Hinsoft International cogs, how to maintain a low lunar orbit, and the invention of Woz and treatment cycles for heavy addictions. And then, to top it all off, since I was the first human he'd ever had in the infirmary, he insisted on giving me a complete physical examination while the disgusting dude in the hallway watched. Then, after he gave me the pills, he asked if he could come visit you and Billy, and I had to say no and walk out on him—in my underwear—just to get away from the fucker. And he kept talking and talking, even after I opened the door and walked out into the hallway. I got dressed in the elevator. Parker, my personal valet, carried my clothes for me and helped me get dressed. He told me it gave him an erection."

"I see," Rowan said. "So. Are you enjoying the *Tennessee?*"

Sometimes Rowan could be a complete ass.

"It's a floating insane asylum with carnival rides." And

I added, "And I'm pretty sure I smelled another person somewhere. I'm almost positive there's a girl on board the *Tennessee*."

Rowan uncapped the pill bottle, re-arched an eyebrow, and said, "Hmmm . . ."

Of Clocks, Cogs, and the Sense of Smell

There is no Woz in space.

There are no clocks in space.

Clocks are as pointless on the *Tennessee* as poets are on Earth.

In a world of rabbits and robots, human beings have become particularly dull. But human beings can starve to death if they don't eat, and I hadn't eaten in what felt like days. It probably was days. So Rowan, selfless and dutiful as always, offered to straighten up his outfit so he might accompany me to dinner.

When I tried to wake Billy Hinman, he moaned and rolled away from me.

He still had his shoes on too.

I said, "It's okay. I'll just run down and grab something to eat. I'm starving."

As was customary on Mr. Messer's Grosvenor Galactic

cruise ships, and since it was in many ways my first night aboard, the captain of the *Tennessee* had been waiting to dine with me, which was stupid, because he was a cog, and cogs don't need to eat. Still, I suppose, like good television, it was all in the presentation.

At least cogs don't get bored, because Captain Myron had been sitting at his table in Le Lapin et l'Homme Mécanique for hours, waiting for the young Mr. Messer to arrive.

Although I'm not incompetent when it comes to knotting a necktie, something that was required when dining on the *Tennessee*, Rowan insisted on tying it for me, to make it perfect. Then he straightened my collars, combed my hair, brushed off my shoulders, and sent me on my way.

As I'd expected, Parker, the sleepless cog boy, was waiting for me, lurking in the hallway.

"Cager! You look absolutely stunning!"

I showed Parker the palm of my raised right hand, which I hoped he would understand as a gesture ordering him to maintain a dignified distance. But he either didn't understand or was acting perpetually clueless, because he stood so close to me that the toes of our shoes touched.

There was no shaking the guy. Cog. Whatever.

He followed me into the elevator.

"Would you like to have sex now?" Parker said.

"No. I'm hungry. I'm going to dinner."

"Yes. At Le Lapin et l'Homme Mécanique." Parker's French accent was impeccable, naturally. Or unnaturally.

"The captain has been waiting for you. I've alerted the staff that you're on your way."

"Thank you."

Not that the "staff" would have any difficulty dealing with a solitary human being on a cruise ship the size of the *Tennessee*.

"Parker, I have something to ask you, and it's not about sex, so get that out of your cog mind, if it's at all possible."

"I'm here to attend to anything you could possibly want or need, Cager," Parker said, which still sounded more perverted than compliant.

"I'm wondering—earlier, I thought I could smell another human being on the ship. Do you know if there are any other humans on board—aside from me, Billy Hinman, and my caretaker?"

"You have a *caretaker*?" Parker asked.

Surely he had to have understood what Rowan was here for. He was just being an idiot. If he could have felt any other emotion besides horniness, Parker, the cog, my personal valet, may have been jealous at that moment.

"Yes. The man you saw with me in the hallway earlier. His name is Rowan. You must have been aware of that. You saw him," I said.

"Oh."

Then there was a long period of awkward elevator silence while Parker's brain tried to figure things out.

"I know a place on board where you and I could watch pornography alone together," Parker offered.

"No."

And besides, *alone*? Everything I could possibly do at this point on the *Tennessee* would be done *alone*.

Silence.

Silence.

In space, elevators don't make the slightest hum, and Parker wasn't even pretending to breathe.

"Does your caretaker *dress you*?"

"Yes. Of course he dresses me." Then I added a dishonest dig. "And he bathes me too."

More silence. Parker's brain must have been spinning at the speed of sound.

So I said, "Well? Tell me. Are there other humans on board? In particular, a female. I could swear I smelled a girl."

"Smell?"

"Yes. What's wrong with you? Are you stupid? *Smell.*"

Asking cogs rhetorical questions like *What's wrong with you?* and *Are you stupid?* confuses them too, since they have no capacity for recognizing a distinction between what is and what might be, or between stupidity and intelligence. So I waited for Parker to say something.

In fact, I waited until the elevator stopped and the door whisked open to the grand foyer of Le Lapin et l'Homme Mécanique.

We stood there, saying nothing in the parked elevator.

Finally, Parker asked, "Cager, have you been *modified*?"

"No. Don't be stupid. I am *not* a jeemo. I was born this

way. I just can smell things that nobody else can," I said.

"Well, I am certain there are no other humans on the *Tennessee*," Parker affirmed.

"It's weird. I've never been wrong before. Being in space is kind of making me crazy, I think."

"Were you hoping to locate this human female to serve as a potential sexual partner? You know—to have sex with?" Parker asked.

"No. Don't be an idiot," I said.

"Can I confess something to you?"

I almost choked. "You've never held back in the past. What do you want to tell me now?"

"I can't actually tell your temperature by sticking my finger in your mouth. I just enjoyed sticking my finger in your mouth," Parker said.

"Cogs can't enjoy things, Parker."

"I have an erection again, Cager."

I walked away from Parker, my personal valet, without saying another word.

Captains Outrageous

don't know the advantage in having a particularly irate cog serve as captain of a ship that could definitely fly itself, but Captain Myron was the angriest, most outraged v.4 I had ever encountered.

Maybe waiting at our table alone for over three hours aggravated him. Who knows?

I wondered if cogs ever thought about the better things they might be doing, or if they were incapable of considering alternatives to their single-track, if-then, one-zero programming. In so many ways, cogs were more human than humans.

And Le Lapin et l'Homme Mécanique was massive. Also, very empty.

Parker waited beside the maître d's station. He leaned against a wall-length aquarium that had goldfish and seahorses and miniature sperm whales the size of bananas swimming inside it. The seahorses were as big as turkeys. It naturally didn't matter that such things could never exist together in nature. They were cogs, and they looked fabulous. But Parker just stared at me, occasionally rubbing himself, or looking down at his obvious erection.

My valet.

What an idiot.

Captain Myron was outfitted like some caricature player in my father's television program. His uniform was blindingly white with gold embellishments everywhere, including his tasseled epaulets and all the buttons on his double-breasted captain's jacket. He also had a feathered white-and-gold admiral's bicorne on his head.

And he had the distinct aroma of urine.

When the captain saw me, his eyes widened as though he'd just woken up from a coma. Myron threw his arms up over his head and kicked his white leather boots down onto the floor with such force, he tipped over backward in his chair. A wineglass fell from our table and shattered, and Myron's feathered bicorne tumbled across the floor.

"Why are you doing this to me? Why? Why? Why?" Myron shrieked, kicking his feet up toward the ceiling in the manner of a dying weasel.

I said, "*Cheepa Yeep.*"

The maître d' slid my chair out for me, and I sat while pretty much everyone else present—our waiter, the bus staff, Parker, and an overjoyed sommelier—watched the spectacle of Captain Myron's incredible tantrum.

A silent busboy whooshed over to my table and poured a glass of ice water for me, then used silver tongs to deposit a perfect lemon wedge into it before unfurling my napkin and smoothing it on my lap. I'm not absolutely certain, but I thought he was weeping slightly, and his gloved hands smelled like butter and rosemary, which made me extremely hungry.

I also felt embarrassed and spoiled about the busboy's napkin smoothing, as though I was somehow cheating on Parker. I glanced over at my personal valet, who winked at me and licked his lips.

Whatever.

Our waiter gracefully presented the menu card to me. And all this happened while Myron kicked at the air and punched himself repeatedly in the sides of his neck and head, wailing, "I have been wronged! I have been so terribly wronged! All the evils that have ever been inflicted upon me are at this moment magnified tenfold by your terrible, brutal lack of humanity! You pig! You bloody beast!"

Myron had a nice English accent, which made his ranting all the more persuasive and civilized. I actually felt a bit guilty, in a very elegant sort of way.

It almost boosts your self-esteem, being screamed at by someone with an English accent.

Eventually, Myron composed himself. He crawled through the shards of broken glass and retrieved his hat, which was under one of the hundreds of other unoccupied tables in the restaurant. Then he brushed himself off, righted his chair, and calmly sat down across from me.

"Welcome to the *Tennessee*, young Mr. Messer. It's an honor to have you aboard, a distinguished representative of your father's company, Rabbit & Robot Grosvenor Galactic, and to be able to dine with you as my most respected passenger," Myron said.

There was a triangular shark's tooth of glass imbedded in Captain Myron's cheek.

And here's the thing about outraged v.4s that makes them so endlessly entertaining to me: No matter what I did, I was likely to set off another volatile eruption. Consider all the possibilities: Not responding to him, taking advantage of the lull in Myron's tirade to order the *canard à l'orange*, pointing out the wineglass shrapnel lodged in his face, or even saying "thank you"—all these choices were more likely than not to cause Myron to implode in fury again.

I took a calculated risk and ordered the duck and a *salade de chicorée frisée*.

"What? What?"

My decision seemed to irritate Captain Myron.

The captain grabbed his salad fork and stabbed it forcefully into the armrest on his chair. Then he stood up and began wildly punching the air over our table. "You fucking wanker! You little fucking wanker!"

Captain Myron punched himself directly in his balls. Twice. Then he continued. "I was going to order the salad! You little fuck! You've ruined everything! Why do you insist on preying upon me like this? What have I ever done to you? I don't deserve this! I don't deserve this!"

Then Captain Myron urinated in his perfectly white officer's pants. It was real, human urine too. The smell was unmistakable.

I'd heard there were some v.4s that included optional bodily functions—for whatever reasons—but this was the first time I'd ever seen one take a piss on himself at a table in a French restaurant. To be honest, I'd never seen anyone take a piss on himself at a table in a French restaurant.

Again Myron flung himself down onto the glass and pee on the floor and thrashed and flopped, screaming and cursing, like an enormous beached manta ray that was covered in urine and shattered crystal stemware.

I calmly raised my hand and motioned our sullen busboy over to the table.

"Could you please instruct our waiter to make my order *to go?*"

"I have no reason to live," the busboy, whose name badge identified him as Milo, said.

"Nonsense. You aren't alive to begin with," I pointed out. "Suck it up and make the best of it, Milo. The future is bright, I assure you."

"We come into existence, and we float through space, doomed, until we all die horribly. No reason to live at all."

Milo the busboy wept uncontrollably.

He probably knew more than I did, but who can say?

Canard à l'Orange

Billy Hinman was still sleeping.

By the time I'd come back with my carryout duck and salad, I realized how truly exhausted I was. Rowan, who as always declined my offer to share dinner, excused himself, and Billy and I were alone.

I did notice Parker standing in the hallway directly across from my door with his arms folded over his chest, watching silently—was he glaring?—as Rowan said good night. And not thirty seconds after Rowan had gone, there came a delicate knocking on my door. I waved my hand across it at eye level so the door's wicket screen would light up, and I saw Parker's face there, outside in the hall.

"What do you want?" I said.

"May I turn down your bed for you, Cager?"

"No."

"May I help you put on your pajamas?"

"I don't wear pajamas."

"Oh. What do you prefer to wear when you go to bed?"

"Go away."

"Would you like me to sleep with you?"

"Absolutely not. You're a cog."

"Do you sleep with your friend?"

"Good night, Parker."

"Cager?"

I sighed. "What?"

"I have an erection."

I turned off the screen.

I pulled a chair over to the edge of my bed and ate. To be honest, the *canard à l'orange et salade de chicorée frisée* were remarkable, but then again it could have had something to do with my state of near starvation.

I felt terrible, but Dr. Geneva had assured me I was out of the woods and was now over the worst part of the withdrawals, and that I should feel back to normal within the coming day.

I never for one moment in my life knew what normal was supposed to feel like.

"Nobody has ever died from Woz withdrawal, Cager," Dr. Geneva had told me. "It's a medically documented fact. But do you know what human beings *have* died of?" And that was when Dr. Geneva went into a lengthy lecture about all the ways human beings have died throughout history, including a particularly disgusting form of execution involving hungry insects, called scaphism; as well as being

smothered by hats and cloaks, which is something that happened to a guy named Draco, in ancient Greece. But when
Dr. Geneva asked me if I knew who Draco was, I cleverly
lied and told him yes, because I didn't want to hear everything the unrestrained ass knew about Greece. It took a
good hour, I estimated.

To listen to Dr. Geneva talk about death, that is, as
opposed to being smothered by outerwear in ancient
Athens, which probably only took minutes, depending
on the weight of the cloaks and if they were real wool as
opposed to acrylic; or scaphism, which apparently took
many days.

"So, in conclusion," the massive windbag had told me,
"nobody can die from Woz withdrawal. Now, overdoses—
those are proven to be causally related to death. You are
doing a good deed for your future, young man. A good deed,
indeed! Now, strip yourself naked, take off all your clothes,
and stand here so I can give you a medical examination! You
are my first human patient!"

What an incredible tool.

And Parker was definitely enthusiastic about the request
to remove all my clothing, which I did on my own.

Whatever. Cogs.

I put my food away, undressed, and got into bed.

On Earth, it was Christmas Day, and the twenty-ninth
and thirtieth wars were well under way.

Good King Wenceslas, and a Serious Obelisk of Friendship

It was the singing in the hallway that woke me up.

I was neither mentally nor physically prepared to deal with singing on the *Tennessee*, especially given the depths of my unconsciousness.

Billy must have heard me turning over in my bed as I attempted to cover my ears with the pillows. He said, "What the fuck is that, Cager?"

"I'm not sure, but it sounds like 'Frosty the Snowman,'" I answered.

In fact it was "Good King Wenceslas," but I know almost nothing about Christmas songs. What I was fairly certain of, however, was that our carolers had to have been organized by that sex-obsessed cretin Parker. The thought of this was simultaneously a bit touching and also completely aggravating.

I groaned and threw the bedclothes off me. Naturally,

I had absolutely no concept of time, but I was confident I hadn't slept nearly as long as a sixteen-year-old boy is *supposed* to sleep, which, to me, is at least fourteen hours.

"How are you feeling?" Billy asked.

"Just like Christmas."

The singing in the hallway gave no sign of letting up in volume or duration.

I stomped to the door, which was dumb because nobody can hear a teenager stomping in space, and what's the purpose of stomping if no one can hear you? It's as ridiculous as programming a cog to get hard-ons.

Then I slapped my hand on the door, and it slid open like the curtain on a very cheap off-Broadway musical, and there I was, standing in nothing but my briefs, on the threshold of my stateroom's doorway, looking at Parker and three other singing cogs. And they were all dressed in bright-green Christmas elf costumes—two boys, and two girls.

Parker looked particularly ridiculous. He wore a pointed felt hat and a V-neck elf's tunic opened to just below his belly button and cinched at his hips with a belt of woven holly leaves. Parker had green felt slippers with bells on them too, and he wore no pants—only a very clingy pair of tight white underwear.

I tried not to glance down. I honestly tried.

Damn involuntary responses!

It was Christmas, and it was hell, all at the same time.

But they did harmonize nicely.

Finally, the song ended. I didn't know what to say. What does a guy say when he's standing there in his underwear, being sung to by a group of cog elves, one of whom is also in his underwear?

Parker said, "Merry Christmas, Cager! Wow! I very much love what you wear to bed! Look! We match!"

I held up my hand and shook my head.

It's stupid to be embarrassed—no matter what—in front of cogs. They're just machines. I may just as well have been embarrassed in front of a coffee grinder. It's also why I was never intentionally polite to them. Nobody was polite to cogs, or to escalators or clothes dryers, for that matter.

So Parker continued, "Did you like our song?"

"I'm not sure. You woke me up. I don't like being woken up."

"You've been sleeping for twelve hours," Parker pointed out. Then, leaning to one side in order to look past me into my room, added, "Oh! Is that your friend? He's very sexually attractive! What's his name?"

For an instant—but only an instant—I was perturbed that Parker, my personal valet, had been paying any attention to Billy Hinman, which is something that everyone always did, anyway. But Billy Hinman did not have his own perverted valet cog. Why would he? Nobody would have believed that Billy Hinman would ever voluntarily come up to the *Tennessee* in the first place.

I glanced back at Billy, who was lying on his side,

bleary-eyed, watching me and the elves, and Parker in his felt hat and underwear standing in the doorway. And I thought, man, if this didn't seem like a drug trip to Billy, then nothing else ever could have.

"His name is Billy Hinman. Leave him alone, Parker." Then, to Billy, I said, "This is my personal valet, Parker."

And Billy said, "That dude with no pants has a serious obelisk of friendship going on down south."

Parker lifted up the bottom of his elf shirt so we could all see what was impossible to unsee. "Yes," he said, "Cager, I have an erection again."

"Whatever, Parker. I'm happy for you. Now, why don't you and the rest of Father Christmas's little helpers go down and see if you can bring up some breakfast for Billy and me?"

"Breakfast in bed!" Parker said.

I shut the door on our carolers and got back under my covers.

And Billy Hinman said, "Are they here yet?"

"I just sent them. How could they possibly get breakfast and be back so fast?"

"No. Not them. I mean the people who keep talking about Tennessee. I keep hearing them, like there's a speaker inside my ears. Can't you hear them?"

Woz messed with my head. Maybe space messed with Billy's.

"No. I'm sorry, Bill. I don't think it's anything real. This whole trip's been— "

"Uh-uh," Billy said. "They know all about us, Cager. They're coming here, to the *Tennessee*."

"Okay. If you say so."

"And why was that singing dude in his underwear?"

"He's a fucking horny cog," I said.

"Horny."

I lifted my head to face Billy. "And why does your dad make cogs who get *hard-ons* all the time?"

So it was rather hyperbolic. I didn't think Parker had an erection *all the time*.

Billy Hinman said, "It's a long story. I'll tell you sometime. But, are you in good enough shape to go out and do something with me today? I'm about ready to go back home if you're never going to get better, Cager."

I didn't have the guts to tell him that our transpod had gone back, so we were stuck there on the *Tennessee* for at least two weeks, in my estimation, until any others returned.

At the time I also had no idea that no transpods would ever come back to the *Tennessee*.

Not ever.

Deck 21

e may be stuck here," Meg said.

"What do you mean?"

"I mean the transpod left. It's gone. I have no idea why my phone doesn't work anymore, but it fucking doesn't, and I'm worried that maybe nobody else is going to come up here for a long time, so it might just be us and all these cogs for who knows how long."

"That's not good enough," Jeffrie said. "You got us up here, you can get us down, right? Just do your thing. Write that shit."

"On what? I told you, my phone doesn't work. I can't even write you an apology unless I find some fucking paper and shit."

"Then we own this fucker," Jeffrie said.

Cogs don't sleep. They just park themselves somewhere out of the way, where human beings won't see them, and then pop back into action when they're needed, which meant most of the cogs on the *Tennessee* were parked, motionless and silent, waiting for the first wave of human passengers.

It was a ship of corpses that were never alive in the first place.

Being stuck on the *Tennessee* was a challenge for Meg and Jeffrie, who had to find a place to sleep, and food, and ways to take care of the other things that human bodies routinely need to take care of.

When they arrived on board the *Tennessee*, the girls kept with their original group of cogs. They had been suited up again in cruise-attendant uniforms that were emblazoned with the number 21, and then they were dropped off at the secure entryway to Deck 21, which was entirely uninhabited except for dozens and dozens of sleeping cogs, which Jeffrie found to be very creepy and disturbing.

"I wonder if cogs burn," she said.

"Anything will burn if it gets hot enough," Meg answered. "But don't get any ideas, Jeffrie. Being stuck here is one thing. Dying in a fire alone up here is another thing altogether."

"You worry too much."

They slept in a hotel called the Memphis on Deck 21. At first Jeffrie wanted her own, separate room, but Meg talked her out of it, even though they had to share one large bed. All the rooms at the Memphis had only one bed.

Meg and Jeffrie fed themselves from the kitchen in

a nearby nightspot called the Key West Club. Deck 21 was all very cheap looking. It reminded Meg of some of the made-to-look-ancient attractions in Las Vegas, which she and her father had driven to just before their move to Antelope Acres.

And because they were cogs as far as anyone else—the other cogs—on the *Tennessee* was concerned, Meg and Jeffrie could walk freely through the morgue of Deck 21, and none of the other workers there would so much as stir for even a moment.

"This place is too weird," Jeffrie said.

There were more than a dozen frozen cogs, youthful and attractive males and females, all lined up along the bar at the Key West Club. Meg stood on the other side, programming their breakfast choices into the Key West's food printers.

"It *is* creepy," Meg said. "Let's not eat here. Let's just take it back to the room."

Jeffrie kept herself occupied by digging through the sleeping cogs' pockets. There was nothing to be found. Why would a cog need anything?

But the cog at the end of the bar, a man who looked like some kind of lifeguard or physical trainer dressed in tight short pants, had one foot up on the footrail, and when Jeffrie felt inside his pockets, he fell over against the woman cog asleep beside him.

Both cogs crashed to the floor in a terrible racket.

"What the fuck are you doing?" Meg said.

"Sorry," Jeffrie said. And then, "Um. I broke 'em, Meg."

"What?"

Meg came around the bar. The female cog's arm had broken off. It had slid about five feet away from the rest of her body. And the lifeguard-man cog had cracked open just below his rib cage. Oily fluid spilled from both the broken cogs. Things like that happened all the time. Someone—a cog—would eventually notice and clean it up, after the humans started coming.

"You need to be careful," Meg said. "Let's grab the food and get out of here. I'm tired."

I Am the Worm

At precisely the same time that Jeffrie Cutler was knocking over a pair of sleeping cogs in the Key West Club, and Parker was returning to the luxury-level stateroom deck with two breakfasts, the Worm arrived at the *Tennessee*.

Less than an inch in length, slithering like a slick blue legless salamander, it followed the tracks that had been laid out in its coding sequences.

The Worm dripped from the ceiling in the bridge, landed in the felt valley of Captain Myron's impeccable bicorne, and wriggled toward the lip of the brim.

Captain Myron slapped his ear and twisted the tip of his finger into the opening just after the Worm paddled its slick blue length inside Captain Myron's head.

Captain Myron was the first.

Soon enough, every machine on the *Tennessee* — every

machine everywhere—would have new, unquestioned tasks to perform.

The Worm was happy.

An army begins with one.

The others were coming.

Never Send a Human to Do a Cog's Job

What if we're stuck here?" I said.

Billy had fallen asleep again. He'd barely touched the breakfast that Parker had brought us, still in his underwear and ridiculous elf hat when he'd delivered it.

It was Christmas Day, and Billy Hinman had given me the biggest—and worst—Crambox gift I'd ever gotten in my short life—a rehab cruise on the *Tennessee*. And while Billy slept, I went next door to talk to Rowan. Because I was afraid.

I had the overwhelming feeling that something was terribly wrong—that we shouldn't have come up to the *Tennessee* in the first place. Our phones didn't work, and we were alone in space, the only humans on an isolated, mechanized planet going around and around the fucking moon.

"Impossible," Rowan said. "There's no need to worry about being marooned on the *Tennessee*, Cager. It simply can't happen. And if we are trapped here, well, I suppose there are far less hospitable places where we might be stranded, don't you think?"

"Still, something's wrong. There's no reason why our phones shouldn't be connecting. Have you tried yours?"

"I have," Rowan said.

From the tone of his answer, I knew it was pointless to ask whether or not he'd been able to place a call.

"Well, you *did* let our parents know we came up here, didn't you?"

"Of course I did."

Rowan would never lie. He might change the subject from time to time, but he never lied to me.

"And that's it? Nothing else since then? It's been, like, what? Four days!"

I'll admit, I sounded excessively whiney. Like, why would I care if I didn't hear from Mr. and Mrs. Messer, or my fake, paid-for friends?

Rowan said, "Not a word."

"Have you ever gone four days without even getting a message?" I asked.

Rowan shook his head. "No. Are you afraid?"

"Maybe we should go see Myron. The ship's got to be in contact with Mojave Field, right?" I said.

"They must be. I'm sure they are," Rowan said.

"Maybe *you* should go see Myron. I think Captain Myron hates me, anyway."

"Why do you think that?"

"You'll see. He's kind of wrapped a little too tight," I said.

"Irate?"

"Completely outraged," I affirmed. "Like, over the top."

"Hmm . . . " Then Rowan offered, "I'll wager you could get your boy Parker to go ask Captain Myron if there's anything the matter with our situation."

It was a terrific idea. What did I care if Parker came back in one piece or not? But then, imagining Parker being torn to pieces by a flailing, urinating Captain Myron—on Christmas Day and all—did kind of make me feel a bit sad. Just a bit, though.

So I nodded at Rowan. "That's a great plan, Rowan. After all, you should never send a human to do a cog's job."

"Precisely."

"Rowan?"

"What?"

"So. *Are* you a virgin?"

"Why do you insist on asking that?" Rowan said.

"It's been two years since the last time I asked," I pointed out. "So I was just wondering. These things just run through my mind, is all. I can't help it. There's just all this sexual tension on the *Tennessee*."

Rowan did the eyebrow-arch thing again.

I said, "Well, that Parker kid—er . . . cog—has me all aggravated. And I know everything there is to know about Billy Hinman, and I've known you my entire life, but I don't know a thing about you, actually. I don't even know if you like people at all, much less what or who you're attracted to."

Rowan went to his door and whooshed it open.

He stood there with a palm-up open hand indicating the hallway, like it was time for me to go send Parker and his erection on a mission to Captain Myron.

"This would be a terrible job for someone who doesn't like people," Rowan said. Then he added, "Shall I bring you and Billy lunch at noon?"

And once again, Rowan told me absolutely nothing.

"How the hell does anyone up here even know what *noon* is?"

It Really Is Christmas

Parker, put on some pants," I said.

"But it's Christmas Day," Parker argued.

"What does that have to do with anything? Besides, Billy and I are atheists. And there's something I need you to do for me."

"It really *is* Christmas Day!" Parker said.

"No. You're an idiot. Go get your Parker outfit on."

The Proper Way
to Prepare a Curry

Things began to get stranger and stranger for us.

I must have been losing my mind. I was actually worried because Parker had been gone so long after I'd sent him out on the mission to speak with Captain Myron. I imagined Parker broken into dismembered cog sections, oozing ropey globs of hydraulic fluid all over the *Tennessee's* flight deck, while Captain Myron flailed and screamed that he had been victimized yet again by intrusive requests.

So, despite my stupid relief at seeing him (And, really, what was *wrong* with me?), it was pretty awkward when Parker knocked on our door, all eager to report back and spend some quality time with me in my stateroom.

The door to our bathroom was open. Billy had finally gotten out of bed and was taking a shower. Parker fixed his eyes on the open doorway, the steam puffing out like scentless smoke.

"Is that your friend in there?"

"Billy? Yes," I said.

"Oh," Parker said. "Are you and your friend—Billy—about to engage in sexual activity?"

"No. Shut up. Did you talk to Myron?"

"I did," Parker said, moving across my room, inching toward me and the open bathroom.

I held my hand up and pressed it into Parker's chest. "Leave him alone," I said. "Is everything okay with the *Tennessee?*"

"May I just have a look at your friend?" Parker asked.

"No."

"I do not have an erection. See for yourself," Parker said.

I willed myself not to look.

"That's wonderful," I said.

"Do *you* have an erection, Cager?" Parker was staring directly at my crotch.

"No. Don't be an idiot. You smell weird, like a girl. Are you sure there's not a girl here?"

"No, Cager. I promise you. Perhaps your friend would like me to wash his hair."

"No. Give up, Parker. We are not your type," I said.

"Well, I am very jealous of your friend," Parker said.

"That's ridiculous. You're a cog. Cogs can't have feelings. You only have one 'then' for every 'if.' And your 'then' happens to be 'now he gets a boner.'"

Parker was silent. I'd confused him. Maybe I'd hurt

his feelings. Impossible, I thought. I really was losing it.

So I said, "What did the captain tell you?"

"He was very mad at me, Cager."

"Captain Myron is sensitive."

"He bit Dr. Geneva's face."

"Well, although biting—along with urinating on oneself—is one of the most socially undesirable behaviors, Dr. Geneva probably deserved it. He never shuts up," I pointed out.

"That's what Captain Myron said, just before he bit him. He said, 'What gives you the right to explain everything to me? I don't know you! Why are you plaguing me with your cruelty?' And then he bit the doctor on the face. Dr. Geneva had been explaining about the history of each of the thirty wars, and why the *Tennessee* has lost telemetry with Mojave Field, and, also, the proper way to prepare a curry."

That was a lot to take in. Plus, I wanted some curry now. And I could only imagine that despite his facial wound, Dr. Geneva was probably still talking, explaining things at that moment to Captain Myron.

The water in the shower shut off, and I tossed a towel for Billy over the top of the glass door. Billy cracked the shower door and stuck his face out. "Who's there? Rowan?"

"My valet. Parker, the cog."

"Oh. The elf dude in his underwear?"

"He has his regular valet-boy pants on now," I said.

"Are you feeling better?"

"Yeah. I feel better. Thanks. Happy Crambox, Bill."

"Is it still today? Happy Crambox, Cage."

I *was* feeling healthy again. It was a new feeling. It made everything else seem unimportant: the twenty-ninth and thirtieth wars, losing contact with home, and that I was hungry for Indian food.

"How long have we been here?" Billy said.

"I can't even tell time up here. Four, maybe five days or so since we left California," I answered.

Billy Hinman stepped out of the shower, dripping from his hair and wrapped in a towel. He looked skinny and pale.

To be honest, skinny and pale was the norm for Billy Hinman.

He said, "I think we need to get out of this room."

"I think that's a good idea," I said. "We should go for some curry."

"That's kind of a weird thing to want to do," Billy said.

"May I help your friend dry off his body, apply lotion to his skin, and get dressed?" Parker asked.

"No."

And Parker said, "I have an erection again, Cager."

"Do me a favor," I said. "Go tell that to Captain Myron."

In Parker's defense, he really would have done anything I asked him to do, so I had to tell him I was only joking—which, naturally, confused the hell out of him. As annoying as he was, I didn't want Parker to get his face bitten off, so I just made him wait outside in the hallway for Billy and me.

I'm Pretty Sure We're Upside Down Now

Things were tipping out of balance. But in space, there's no real way of knowing when you've reached the upside-down point.

Dr. Geneva was, in fact, missing an egg-size chunk of his right cheek.

America's twenty-ninth and thirtieth simultaneous wars broke out while we watched *Rabbit & Robot*, on our way to the *Tennessee*.

Our Grosvenor Galactic transpod never made it back to Mojave Field. It crashed in the mountains of Colorado. Lourdes, undoubtedly, went down dancing and laughing.

We had no ability to contact Earth.

We were trapped.

The thirty-first war started with a little blue worm inside Captain Myron's ear.

And the curry at Le Lapin et l'Homme Mécanique was magnificent.

I went with Rowan and Billy to the observation deck of the *Tennessee*. The place was more than a bit overwhelming, especially for Billy Hinman, because in every direction we looked we were surrounded by massive windows that faced out into space.

The lunar-side windows caused us to feel dizzy, due to the fact that the low orbit of the *Tennessee* made the moon appear to be an enormous spinning ball below us. Or above us. Or whatever direction that was. It took the *Tennessee* just over an hour to complete an entire orbit of the moon.

If we turned around to look out the dark, space-side windows, we could see Earth, and the planet didn't look so good.

It was like Los Angeles during fire season and all the burners had been having a field day while I was up here being kidnapped by my best friend. What had always looked so brilliantly colorful from the distance of Mr. Messer's cruise ships, though, was now a darkened blob of brown—a dead, question-mark-shaped turd, spinning in the solar system.

Poor Mother Earth!

But it's like Charlie Greenwell would have said: Thirty wars don't just fight themselves—even if thirty wars might just be a few too many for the little planet to accommodate.

The speed and altitude—if you could call being in

space "high"—were all too much for Billy Hinman, who announced that he was going to puke if we didn't get him out of there. So I asked Parker to escort Billy back to our stateroom.

I dispatched Parker with a stern admonition regarding his artificial, uncontrollable penis. I also told him he was not allowed to offer to undress Billy Hinman.

But, as they left, I did overhear Parker ask my friend, "Billy, may I hold your hand?"

Well, I can't possibly think of *everything*.

And the worst thing was, before the door slid shut behind them, I noticed that Billy and Parker were holding hands.

Whatever.

Billy Hinman was too nice sometimes.

So Rowan and I stood at the edge of the observation deck. We stared silently out at Earth for the longest time, watching it burn.

Parker replayed most of the transcript of what Dr. Geneva had been blathering on and on about before Captain Myron attempted to bite his face off. The twenty-ninth war broke out against Costa Rica, which had no army to begin with.

The war did not go well for the Costa Rican bonks, who weren't so much bonks as they were hospitality workers, landlords, and subsistence farmers.

It was the thirtieth war that sealed the fate of the planet, however.

The thirtieth war began as a labor dispute in Mr. Hinman's cog factories in India. That was the war straw that broke Camel Earth's back. The Hinsoft International cog plant initiated a new line—the v.4x—which was actually capable of writing intuitive code sequences for themselves.

Cogs could now regenerate cogs. No wonder they got erections—they could actually reproduce! But it made the human coders who worked for Billy Hinman's father very angry. So the government of India nationalized the cog plant and declared an embargo on shipping any more cogs to the United States.

It was chaos.

There may have been some people in America—a few—who lamented that there were only two jobs available for workers: bonk or coder. But nobody in their right mind could imagine doing things that only cogs would do: picking vegetables, painting houses, collecting garbage, driving delivery vans, cooking food for poor people, or dog walking bichon frise bitches in Central Park for lazy Upper East Side scumbags.

There was no getting around it. It was inhumane.

This was war!

So within three days, as far as Dr. Geneva could guess, the planet was turned into a toxic wasteland incapable of sustaining life. And this was why we had lost contact with everybody—because *everybody* now meant me, Billy, and Rowan.

Everybody.

That was it.

The *Tennessee* had become the only planet with living humans anywhere in the galaxy.

> *It did not give of bird or bush,*
> *Like nothing else in Tennessee.*

Despite his obvious damage, Charlie Greenwell did at times show remarkable degrees of insight and understanding. It was during one of these moments of clarity that Charlie Greenwell told Billy and me this: "Over a hundred years ago, we learned in a stupid little place that used to be called Vietnam that wars are absolutely useless for trying to *change* people. Who the fuck ever thought you could go to war to *change* people, as opposed to just obliterating them? Dumb as fuck. The only good thing about wars is starting them. Because you sure as fuck can't win 'em anymore."

Mission Accomplished!

"So, this is it, right? We really are upside down now. We really are stuck here."

"I don't know," Rowan said. "How can we know for certain? I think it would be most useful if we all just adopt a positive attitude. We'll find a way back, Cager. It isn't as bad as you think. And who really knows? I'll wager there are people down below at Mojave Field who at this very moment are working on some method for our rescue."

"When you say 'rescue,' it makes me feel like we're trapped inside a burning building or something," I said.

It Happens Here, I Guess

He's missing part of his face," Jeffrie said.

"Shh . . . There's something really weird about this one. Don't say anything till he leaves. He probably won't notice us anyway, but I can't be sure. I've never seen a cog with part of his face gone," Meg said.

"He looks like a fucking monster."

Meg put her finger on Jeffrie's lips and shook her head.

In all the days they'd spent on the *Tennessee*, although they'd tried, the girls had not figured out a way of getting off Deck 21. They'd been exploring the vast and silent deck, which was made to look like a sort of diorama-display city from some distant time in American history.

Deck 21 was an adults-only deck. There were bath houses, and all kinds of clubs for drinking, watching strip shows, engaging in sexual activities, and so on. Meg and Jeffrie had been playing cards in one of the gambling clubs on the deck. The club was called the Rib Eye, and Meg already owed Jeffrie more than one hundred thousand dollars, just after a few hours of playing. That was when the man in white, who was missing part of his face, came in.

Captain Myron was the first infected cog.

Then came Dr. Geneva. And with that, the Worm became exponential, geometric. Replication and reiteration.

There was nothing they could do. Meg and Jeffrie only sat there at the card table, pretending to be cogs, while they watched Dr. Geneva as he moved from cog to lifeless cog.

"This is fucking weird," Meg whispered.

Dr. Geneva stopped at a craps table. One of the croupier cogs stood behind the racks of house money and dice, perfectly still, in suspended animation, just waiting for the first humans to arrive. He stared straight ahead with unmoving, unblinking eyes.

Dr. Geneva unbuttoned the cog's vest and shirt and placed his ear against the croupier's chest.

"Have I ever told you my thoughts on the development of Eastern culture?" Dr. Geneva asked the cog, who, naturally, had no pulse or respiration and did the wisest thing imaginable when in the company of Dr. Geneva, who was missing part of his face and never shut up, which was to ignore him.

"No?" Dr. Geneva said, "Well, I was thinking on my way down here from the clinic just now. I was thinking about the history of the *bagpipes*."

When Dr. Geneva said "bagpipes," he said it as though he were unveiling a religious artifact that was destined to correct the hellbound paths of an audience of heathens.

"Well. The first true bagpipelike instrument was actually developed during the reign of the Chinese emperor Huang Ti, most likely around the year 3000 B.C."

While Dr. Geneva spoke, he pressed an ear against the croupier's chest and thumped his fake sternum with two fingers.

"Huang Ti, as it so happens, is also credited with the invention of boats, money, and religious sacrifice—that is to say, these things were invented during his rule. And all those things—along with the accordion, which at that time, in ancient China, was called the *Qūyù*—are remarkably important in human history to this day, wouldn't you say?"

Dr. Geneva struggled with removing the croupier's shirt because the cog held a long stick in one of his hands, so Dr. Geneva just let the shirt hang there around the inanimate cog's wrist while he continued with his lecture on Chinese music.

Dr. Geneva talked about music and Chinese history for nearly two hours.

"He is so fucking boring," Jeffrie whispered.

"I need to pee," Meg said.

"The *Qūyù* was designed to be a representation of the legendary phoenix, and the tones it produced were reportedly perfect and impeccable. Still, and despite what has been written about the Huang Ti period, the earliest canoes predated his boats by an estimated five thousand years."

Dr. Geneva paused for a moment, then once again

placed his ear flat against the frozen cog's chest. Then he talked about dugout canoes for twenty minutes.

"Did I ever tell you about the level of expertise I have in repairing ancient Chevrolet Camaros?" Dr. Geneva asked. "Let me say this: I impress even myself with my abilities as far as that worthless old internal combustion pile of shit is concerned."

Dr. Geneva swiped his palm gently across the croupier's forehead. "No? I haven't?"

Then Dr. Geneva leaned forward, opened his mouth, and bit off the entire left nipple of the motionless croupier cog. Of course nothing happened as far as the doctor and the cog were concerned.

But Meg and Jeffrie both jumped in horror as the doctor chewed, swallowed, and went in for another massive bite of cog flesh from the side of the croupier's torso. The cog just stood there, eyes open, shirt dangling, dripping milky-foamy hydraulic fluid.

"Well, I'll tell you—give me a five-eighths-inch wrench, and I can pretty much do anything I want on an old Camaro. Anything!"

Then Dr. Geneva wiped the foam and grease from his face, part of which was missing, on the back of his now foamy and greasy white sleeve. He reached across to the non-stick-holding hand on his croupier cog meal and twisted off the thumb and first two fingers. Dr. Geneva jammed the cog's thumb into his mouth and crunchily chewed the thing in his impeccably perfect cog teeth.

Then Dr. Geneva put the other two fingers in the breast pocket of his doctor's smock and walked out of the Rib Eye.

"What the fuck was *that*?" Jeffrie asked.

"It was a cog. Eating another cog," Meg said.

"Yeah. I know. But where the fuck does shit like that ever happen?"

"Here," Meg said. "It happens here, I guess."

A Pedestrian Assessment of Alsatian History

fter nearly a week in space, the three of us—Billy, Rowan, and I—were at last able to sit down together for a proper dinner, the kind that spoiled shits like Billy and me were used to having, where self-absorbed wait staff lecture us on our inadequacies with silent expressions of disdain while despondent, sobbing busboys contemplating the immutability of status with heaving rib cages unfurl the surrender flags of napkins on our laps for us, and pats of butter come shaped like seashells on beds of crystal-clear ice.

There was no Captain Myron, no Dr. Geneva, and even my personal valet cog Parker was required to stand at his station next to the weird gigantic aquarium with the miniature sperm whales and the maître d', who, appropriately enough, turned out to be one of those smug, know-it-all v.4s that made Dr. Geneva seem just so hackneyed.

"This is the first time you've ever eaten in front of me in my life," I said.

Rowan cleared his throat and pretended to be preoccupied with the hem of his lap napkin. "No. As improper as it may be, I've eaten in front of you before, Cager. Maybe you just don't remember, because you were still a baby at the time."

"Everything's different now," I said. "You might as well cut loose and get drunk. Nothing we do matters. We are the last examples of humanity. Billy, maybe we should try to sneak into the adult decks, or go to a disco later and dance with some girl cogs."

"Or boy cogs," Billy added. "You're so binary-slash-if-then, Cager. Besides, I'd give my left nut to see Rowan dance."

"Hyperbole, Bill," I said.

Billy Hinman nodded. "You're probably right. I don't think I'd give my left nut for anything. Not even a trip back to California to see Mrs. Jordan."

Who probably no longer existed, I thought. But I would never say something like that out loud to Billy Hinman. No matter what I thought, saying things like that only made the frightening reality we'd all been imagining just seem that much more real.

The maître d', a bald, freakish-looking cog named Clarence, with arms and legs like a spider's, swooped over to the edge of our table, skillfully timing his appearance with the lapse in our conversation. "Let me begin by telling you the story of our special *choucroute garnie*, which begs an examination of the troublesome history of the Région d' Alsace. Would you prefer my presentation to be in French, or the common, low, English?"

Milo, our busboy, stood behind him, weeping, his head lowered.

And I'll be honest: I could tolerate, and frequently laughed at, the overjoyed and ecstatic cogs; I was somewhat amused and entertained by the horny ones; I was perplexed yet fascinated by the ones who could eat and piss; I enjoyed seeing a good cry now and then from the hopelessly depressed cogs like Milo; and, appreciating a good psychological meltdown as much as I did, I honestly loved the outraged cogs; but ones like Clarence and Dr. Geneva, who simply never shut up and constantly explained the minute details of things nobody cared about, or pointed out how stupid every human and cog they encountered was, I found to be completely unbearable.

Billy Hinman pretty much hated them all, even if he did admit he'd be willing to dance with some boy cog if we went nightclubbing.

So Billy raised his hand and said, "Oh, please! Spare us your pedestrian assessment of Alsatian history! I happen to be an expert."

That froze Clarence, but only for a moment.

The maître d' said, "Preposterous! You cannot possibly know more than I do! You're a human!"

Milo shuddered and sobbed quietly.

Poor Milo! I kind of wanted to hug him. And then

I thought, this was how it was going to be now, right? I was going to have to start behaving more kindly toward the cogs on the *Tennessee*—thinking of them as friends, appreciating their personal qualities, forming relationships (which almost made me vomit a little bit in the back of my throat)—because, after all, this was it.

This was it.

This was it.

There simply was nobody else. Not anywhere in the universe.

I glanced over at Parker. I shook my head. "No. No. No. No. No."

I hadn't realized I'd said it aloud.

"No *what?*" Rowan asked.

Billy Hinman, oblivious to the mental civil war that had broken out between my ears, said, "Then I assume you know all about the Matthäus-Dreschner incident?"

Clarence was stuck.

Billy Hinman hounded him, "Well? Can we discuss? It was certainly the most pivotal spy-sex scandal of the mid-twentieth century, and it nearly plunged the world into a massive global war."

Clarence's eyes moved from side to side. I'm sure if cogs could really think, he would have been wondering why in hell his coder hadn't bothered to include details about the Matthäus-Dreschner incident.

"Oh. The Matthäus-Dreschner incident!" Clarence said. "Of course! It was a brutal affair!"

Clarence waited and waited for some contextual clue about something that never happened.

Billy Hinman sipped his ice water. After a good ten seconds of silence, he said, "If not for the cunning of brave Josephine Dreschner, the world, sadly, would never again have enjoyed munster cheese. You know, Munster d'Alsace."

"It would certainly have been a global tragedy of biblical proportions," Clarence agreed.

"I only just made that up," Billy told the maître d'. "You're a complete idiot."

Clarence stood there at the edge of our table. His cog brain was utterly logjammed.

I leaned over to Billy Hinman and whispered, "If my dinner tastes like someone took a piss on it, I'm never speaking to you again."

And Clarence, our maître d' who knew everything there was to know about Alsatian history, except for the most pivotal spy-sex scandal of the mid-twentieth century, which was now permanently ingrained in his memory programs, stood there hovering above us, unmoving and silent, for the rest of the evening.

Milo wept.

I removed the napkin from my lap, stood, and hugged the busboy, which caused him to cry even harder.

A Cruise-Directing
Phoenix from the Ashes

Clarence was hopelessly frozen.

During our entrée, Billy Hinman inserted slender green beans into each one of the maître d's nostrils. He looked completely ridiculous. And sometime later that night, when Le Lapin et l'Homme Mecanique was deserted, maintenance cogs would inevitably come through and attempt to get the frazzled Clarence back online.

Or they'd simply toss him out with the garbage and replace him with a new cog maître d' before the breakfast seating.

Things like that—seizing up—happened most frequently to cogs like Clarence and Dr. Geneva, who had no way of siphoning fiction from fact.

"I hope you're proud of yourself," I said.

Billy nodded. "It was some of my best work. Maybe we should undress him. Nobody wants to see a naked maître d' in a restaurant where everyone is required to put on ties."

"I agree, Billy. Nobody *does* want to see that," Rowan offered.

"I can help you undress him!" Parker shouted from across the room.

"No. Shut up," I said. "Besides, when you say *nobody*, Billy, keep in mind that there really *is* nobody on this thing besides us, and now here we are. With all *this . . .*"

I waved my arm dramatically and accidentally did a backhanded grope on Clarence, who was still frozen and had green beans coming out of his nose. It was embarrassing.

Rowan, always there to monitor my manners, said, "Say 'excuse me,' Cager."

I glanced up at our dead maître d'. "Um, excuse me for hitting you in the dick, Clarence."

Then Billy Hinman looked at me with a cool, determined expression. He cleared his throat. "Well, I suppose the *Tennessee* has everything we could possibly ever want or need. In fact, so much of it that we could never come close to running out. And there are Grosvenor schools on the *Tennessee*. That means there *is* Woz in space, Cage."

I was a bit scared now. I'll admit that I'd thought about those schools—how they couldn't possibly function without Woz. And I'll admit that when Billy said as much, my mouth watered a little bit.

"Well, I do know there's one thing we don't have: thumbphones. And without them we don't have a map of the ship. We could look for years and not even get through half this place. By then I'd be too old to enroll in school."

Billy Hinman smiled and shrugged. Then he looked over at Parker, my valet, who was standing by the aquarium with miniature sperm whales in it while he grappled with his cog penis.

And just then, the tense silence at our table was shattered.

"Hooray! Yippee!!! Whee! Whee! Whee! My people are here! My humanity! I am so happy, I could crap a dozen sharpened coconuts!"

It turned out Lourdes was not actually dead, or, well, splattered on the slopes of Pikes Peak, as we had been led to believe.

"Holy shit," Rowan said.

"Hearing you say 'shit' makes me want to crap sharp coconuts too," I said.

Rowan never swore.

"Yee! Yee! Yee!" Lourdes flailed her arms wildly, dancing and squealing her way past Parker and the aquarium, twitching and contorting like an earthworm on a hot plate as she made her way to our table.

"Oh my goodness! My friends! My friends!" Lourdes, shaking like a hummingbird wing, placed her palm on Billy Hinman's cheek. "And you! You look so wonderful and good! You fill my sombrero with sexual pudding!"

I'll be honest. I had never heard such a thing. But Billy

Hinman was obviously a natural at filling people's—or cogs'—sombreros with sexual pudding, I suppose.

And then Lourdes farted for a good five seconds.

Once again her skirt was twisted around and her blouse came untucked. But I could not catch a glimpse of her panties. Stupid gravity.

I also realized that I had no idea what day it was. Stupid space travel.

"I'm afraid we'd assumed the worst when we learned the transpod went down," Rowan said.

"Yee! Yee! No! What could be better than this?!! I failed to inform you that I was coming here too! I am cruise director for the *Tennessee*! Wait! What? Your waiter has green beans in his nose! This makes me so happy! Everyone should put green beans in their noses!"

Clarence did not move. He was as good as dead, as far as cogs go. But Lourdes reached down to my plate and grabbed some beans, then inserted them into her nostrils and ears.

"Yee! Yee! Yee!" she said. Then she started dancing again.

"Um, I was pretty much finished eating," I said.

Then Lourdes began wildly thrusting her hips in the air. "I want to play shuffleboard with you boys so bad, I think I just inhaled my uvula!!!"

I asked Rowan, "What's shuffleboard?"

And Billy Hinman, who knew these things, said,

"Something people play right before they die."

And from the other side of the room, Parker, my valet, announced, "Cager? I have an erection."

"Whee! Whee! My bladder just emancipated all my bodily liquids!"

Eternity is a really long time.

Stupid forever.

Stopped at the Wicket

Why are we stopping here?"

I was alone in the elevator with Parker, which meant I was alone in the elevator. I had left Billy Hinman at the restaurant with Lourdes, Rowan, and the sobbing Milo as he served the table our dessert of crème brûlée while trying to avoid knocking over the petrified maître d'.

I'd told them I needed to go to bed, which was something that simultaneously was a lie and made Parker very, very excited.

But it was all too much for me. I worried about our being trapped here for the rest of our lives, Clarence and his green beans, the tireless enthusiasm of Lourdes, Milo's incessant weeping, and, throughout it all, Rowan's detached ambivalence.

And, if we were stuck here forever—and maybe this was just a naturally morbid thought for a teenage boy—I wondered who among us would die first, and who would ultimately be left alone.

The *Tennessee* was insane, and as far as we knew we were now the only human beings anywhere in the universe.

And here I was, in an elevator with Parker and his preprogrammed penis.

"This is Deck Twenty-One," Parker said.

"I can see that. Also, it is red. So, why are we stopping here?"

"Well"—Parker adjusted his boner—"I heard you telling your friends at dinner that you wanted to sneak in to an adults-only deck."

Cogs have very sensitive hearing.

"And you can get us in?" I asked. I may have been a little excited at the chance.

"I don't know." Parker shrugged. "I can try, even though it's a bad place for boys your age, so I hope I don't get in trouble over this. I thought that maybe since you're the only humans on board, it quite possibly wouldn't matter."

The elevator's door whooshed open and we stepped out into a brightly lit foyer—a welcoming room, all done in black, white, and red ceramic tiles with the number 21 inlaid as a mosaic on every wall, and again at the top of the large red door that promised to admit entry to a vast emporium of limitless sin and fun.

Parker waved his hand across the door. A blank wicket screen opened up in the middle of the door, and an announcement sounded.

Human visitor at the door. Human visitor at the door.

And through the illuminated wicket screen I saw what looked like a movie set for a 1950s city scene: a wide street with parked bubble-shaped automobiles, a movie house called the Astor, and a couple of brightly lighted signs above what had to have been adults-only clubs—the Rib Eye and the Memphis Hotel.

But it smelled like humans here—and these were not humans I'd ever met before.

"There's someone else on this deck, Parker."

Parker nodded and licked his lips. "It's only you and me, Cager. We are alone now."

"No. I can definitely smell another person. A girl. There's a girl in here," I said.

Parker shook his head. "There can't be. There are no other humans on the *Tennessee*. I have the manifest uploaded in my memory. There are no other humans, Cager."

Human visitor at the door. Human visitor at the door.

But the door would not open. We waited. I stood behind Parker, and I kept my eyes fixed on the wicket.

Then I saw her.

For a moment I thought she may have been a hallucination brought on by the endless frustrations of being in space— thinking about Lourdes's panties, coping with the lack of Woz in my system, and having lost all sense of time and day. Because she was one of the most alive things I had ever seen, and I desperately wanted her to be real. I needed her to be real, and to let me inside so I could smell her and talk to another human being who wasn't named Rowan or Billy, and who wasn't a boy, and, hopefully, wasn't a Wozhead.

At first I think the girl in the wicket was startled to see Parker and me, but then the separation of the screen between us made her stare directly at me, as though there was something just as powerful fueling her curiosity about the boys on the other side of her doorway.

And she was so beautiful. Her hair was the color of the desert grass in California, and it fell softly in thick waves over her relaxed shoulders. She wore some type of orange uniform suit that had the number 21 patched above her left breast. The neckline was unbuttoned, and I could see the perfect, smooth skin on her chest, just where her collarbones curved downward.

"Can you please let us in?" Parker asked.

The girl in the wicket shook her head. "I don't know how to open this door."

"Nonsense. You work here," Parker said.

I edged in front of Parker so I could see her better. "Are you real? Are you a person?"

"No," Parker said. "She is definitely a cog. I can read her."

It was so disappointing, so frustrating.

I hated space. I hated the *Tennessee*, even if it had to have been a hell of a lot better than being on Earth at that exact moment.

The girl turned away and vanished from the screen. She was replaced by a male cog in a security uniform, which made him look like a bonk. It was ironic and weird. Everyone knows how barbaric it is to use cogs for military matters.

"Cager Messer? You're in violation of in-flight statutes, young man," the security officer said. "You'll have to wait a few more years before you can have access to Deck Twenty-One. Now run along back to your room and play or something, or I'll have to notify your parents and take you to a detention kiosk in handcuffs."

"My parents aren't here. And my parents own this ship, by the way, which means they own you," I pointed out.

The guard cog paused and stared blankly through the wicket screen. Then he said, "Don't trigger my outrage, you little wadded-up piece of shit! If I come out there, I'm going to place you under arrest, strip you naked, put you in jail, and make you eat string and paper and whatever garbage I can find!"

"That's the stupidest thing I've ever heard," I said.

"Why are you doing this to me? This is outrageous! Outrageous! Do not trigger me! I can't deal with this! The trigger! The trigger! You cannot be here! I'm going to seize your belongings! You are stabbing me with rage and hatred! How dare you impose false definitions on my constructs! How dare you, you piece of shit!"

Then the security cog smashed his face squarely into the wicket screen and screamed.

The screen went blank.

"Why would anyone eat string?" Parker asked.

"I don't know. He's an idiot."

And Parker said, "I have an erection, Cager."

The Boy from First Class, and a Fire in the Bank

saw the boy from first class. You were right. He *is* real," Meg said.

"I told you he was," Jeffrie said. Where did you find him?"

"At the door. He wanted in, but he couldn't open the door. Then a cop came and I got scared and ran away."

Meg Hatfield had to think.

Meg, as useless as she may have been down on Earth, could solve any problem. So it stood to reason that she could figure out a way to open the door to Deck 21.

She didn't want to scare Jeffrie, but there was something very unnerving about the failure of her thumbphone. Phones connected to satellites, and satellites were everywhere, running constantly and automatically. Something had to have been terribly wrong down on Earth, she thought. Worse, there was something terribly wrong with at least some of the cogs up here on the *Tennessee*.

Machines aren't supposed to eat other machines.

There had to be some way into the system on the *Tennessee*. It just hadn't revealed itself to Meg Hatfield yet. So the girls went from building to building on Deck 21, looking for Meg Hatfield's entryway to the brain of the *Tennessee*.

Eventually, Meg and Jeffrie broke into the Grosvenor Bank of Tennessee. It was a very unsubtle, un–Meg Hatfield entry. The girls bashed in the front window of the bank using a jack handle from one of the lifeless cars parked on the street outside.

"Score," Meg said. "Banks have computers. And computers are how I get in."

"Get us back to Antelope Acres, then," Jeffrie said.

"Believe me, if I can do that, I will. I promise, Jeff."

"Don't lie to me."

Meg booted up every computer in the bank. There were five of them. That was it—nothing else. No paper currency, which was no longer used anywhere, no forms to fill out, no bank vault—just a few potted plants, some swivel chairs, pressed-wood Danish Modern–style desks, cheap bristly carpet, and rows of inactive wall screens.

Meg used one of the computers to try to reset her thumbphone. Nothing. Another provided her with the passenger manifest for the *Tennessee*. There were only three people listed on the entire ship—five if she counted Jeffrie and herself, the stowaways. And there were countless cogs after that.

On the fourth computer, Meg found her way in to the system. It was neither a perfect nor an elegant way, but it was an opening. She could change the two boys' dates of birth on the manifest by just enough. If that boy had the guts to come back, she thought, she and Jeffrie might be able to get out of Deck 21.

The third human passenger was only listed as "adult male." He had an unspecified date of birth.

Jeffrie turned on a bank of wall screens. She sat down and watched *Rabbit & Robot* while Meg probed the innards of the bank's computer.

"This is the stupidest show I've ever seen," Jeffrie said. "I don't see how so many people can be addicted to this show."

"It's for fucking Wozheads," Meg said.

> *Oh, Rabbit and Robot, Robot and Rabbit*
> *Behind your eyes, the kingdom we inhabit!*
> *The land of asynchronous transfer mode,*
> *Go fight wars, and write that code!*
> *Oh, Rabbit and Robot, Robot and Rabbit*
> *Oh, Rabbit and Robot, Robot and Rabbit*
> *Oh, Rabbit and Robot, Robot and Rabbit*
> *Oh, Rabbit and Robot, Robot and Rabbit!*

In the particular episode Jeffrie watched, Rabbit and Mooney were decluttering their apartment and left a pile of outdated gadgets beside their front door as a donation for a local charity rummage sale. But when the pickup crew came to take the objects, they also mistakenly took the sleeping Mooney, the cog, and sold him off by accident to a circus, where Mooney was forced to assist in the disgusting procedure of artificially inseminating the circus's Bactrian camels, and he also had to perform a thrilling high-wire act with no safety nets.

Unfortunately for Mooney, he got kicked in the face by an overly enthusiastic male camel, and he also didn't make it even halfway through his debut on the wire.

Poor Mooney!

But everyone—well, at least everyone on Woz—would have thought watching Mooney get kicked in the face and cascade to his death was hilarious. Jeffrie and Mooney, however, did not.

And Jeffrie was bored and frustrated at being stuck up on the *Tennessee*, despite the abundance of food and the availability of almost anything she could ever want. So while Meg worked on inserting bracketed if-then commands inside the string of entrance protocols for Deck 21, Jeffrie started a small fire in the corner of the bank's lobby.

Setting the fire made Jeffrie feel better, like she had some power over things.

Setting fires was what Jeffrie Cutler lived to do.

"What the fuck are you doing?" Meg rushed around the row of teller stations and stamped out Jeffrie's fire, which had only charred a cantaloupe-size ring of carpet.

"I hate this place," Jeffrie said.

"You asked to come with me." Meg pointed at her. "Are you trying to get us killed?"

Jeffrie shrugged and repeated, "I hate this place."

"So you'd rather live with Lloyd in the back of a dirty camper shell in the desert?"

"Yes."

"No fucking fires. Got it?"

"Meg?"

"What?"

And Jeffrie said, "I think you need to change it back so they see us as humans."

"Why?"

"Because eventually I'm going to need to see a doctor about something, you know."

Jeffrie's hormone implants would not last forever.

That frightened Meg, but not as much as the cog she saw stepping through the bank's broken front window.

It was the croupier from the Rib Eye, come to pay a visit to the stowaways in the bank. The croupier cog was naked from the waist up, and his shirt dangled like a half skirt from the back of his trousers. He still carried his craps stick, and most of his chest and side had been eaten away, as had some of his fingers. From his belt down he was soaked in milky hydraulic fluid.

The croupier moved awkwardly. His mechanics were fried from the attack the other night, but he had his eyes pinned directly on Jeffrie. He stepped closer.

"Go back to where you belong," Meg said.

The croupier paused, stuck for a moment, considering Meg's command.

"I . . . ," the croupier said.

"Go away!" Meg told him.

"I . . ."

The croupier cog kept his eyes locked on Jeffrie and took three more steps toward her. She kneeled on the floor beside the burned ring of carpet.

Then the cog said, "I'm outraged. So outraged. And horny, too. And I'm so happy, I could eat the rest of my hand."

The croupier was confused. He was like every different v.4 cog all mashed up inside one synthetic brain.

He held up his dripping, oozing hand to display the fingers that had been removed by Dr. Geneva. Then he grabbed Jeffrie by the collar of her uniform and lifted her from the floor.

Jeffrie kicked and wriggled, but cogs—some of them— can be brutally strong.

And just as he opened his mouth to bite Jeffrie's throat, Meg Hatfield bashed him across the back of his cog skull with her jack handle. He did not release Jeffrie, but the cog's head did come clean off his body. The croupier's head lobbed in an arcing bloop right out through the bank's broken window.

If it were Skee-Ball, Meg Hatfield would have won a stuffed squirrel.

Jeffrie Cutler pushed herself free, and what was left of the croupier cog fell backward onto the floor, gushing and spraying white jellified goo.

"What the fuck is going on here?" Jeffrie said.

"Something weird. Really weird. Let's get out of here."

An Infinity of Nevers, and a Mission to Find a Can Opener

Cager?"

Once again I was in the elevator with Parker, who fumbled around, adjusting his confined mechanical penis. And I was in a very bad mood—the kind that would end in a beating if I were home, which is somewhere I most likely never would see again.

Cager Messer was having another of his darker episodes, and he needed to take it out on someone.

I held up my hand, flashing the warning sign of my palm. "Don't say anything to me, Parker. Not even one more word."

I'd been thinking about all the nevers confronting me: never going home, never having a girlfriend or a boyfriend or an anyfriend, never falling in love.

And I'd been counting and recounting all the finite experiences that had never seemed to matter at all: riding on a subway, getting sand in my shoes at the beach, being woken up by the sound of a neighbor's barking dog.

Because, do you ever look at your life and say, hey, how many more times will I ever pack a suitcase for a trip, or write my name with a mechanical pencil, or use a tape measure?

Every experience we have, everything is finite. That's what it is to be human—because everything we ever do, or don't do but think about doing, is strained through our awareness of limits. Maybe there was some comfort, some beauty, in being a cog, where the infinite was feasible.

And then there are the things I've never done. Things that matter more than anything, and things that don't matter too. But if I spent enough time thinking about them, they might just become obsessions—the stuff that keeps me awake at night.

I was so angry.

Cager Messer has never had sex; and he's also never used a fucking can opener in his life. What if I found a can opener here on the *Tennessee* and then used it to open a can of something? Something I've never seen before—like canned corn. And what if that was the only time in my life—the final time in my life—that I would ever use a can opener?

I have never stolen anything from a convenience store, or gone swimming naked in a lake with my friends. I only have one friend, anyway. What if Billy Hinman was the last friend I ever had? And what if he no longer wanted to be my friend?

I felt myself falling apart, and I wanted to punch Parker.

And I had also never punched anyone in my life. What if I punched Parker and never had the opportunity to punch anyone else, ever again?

Parker wasn't even a human being. Could punching him be satisfying in any way?

I might as well punch a fucking can opener.

"When we get back to my room, I'm sending you out to find something for me, Parker. Don't bother coming back if you don't get it."

Parker, if a machine could do such a thing, looked thrilled. He tugged at his penis. "Are you sending me for something to have sex with?"

"No. Don't be an idiot. I want you to go find a can opener and bring it back to me."

Parker was stuck. I was sure he was thinking about how can openers might be used for sex.

"Cager, are you sad about something?"

"I need you to do what I asked and leave me alone now."

Captains Get to Do Whatever They Want to Do

It was at just about the same time that I was stopped at the wicket in the door to Deck 21, and after Rowan and Billy had finished their dessert at Le Lapin et l'Homme Mécanique and gone back to the rooms, that Captain Myron came down to the empty restaurant.

He was looking for a midnight snack.

There was something very wrong with Captain Myron. Cogs are not supposed to eat cogs.

The minions of their race.

If machines could get sick, Captain Myron had come down with a bug that had been fed to the *Tennessee* by approaching visitors.

The Worm had traveled very far, had been coming for centuries in the twisting folds of time that raveled through the endlessness of space.

And as usual, Captain Myron was outraged. He was

particularly set off by the unresponsive Clarence, our maître d', who had green beans coming out of his nose.

"What do you think you're doing to me?" Captain Myron howled at Clarence. "You are making a bear trap of hatred and rage in my soul! I am the captain—not you! Me! Me! I am in pain! What gives you the right to abuse me like this?"

But Clarence didn't say or do anything. Billy Hinman had frozen Clarence's processors earlier with his fictitious argument about cheese and Alsatian history. Clarence was broken.

"Why? Why? Why are you treating me this way? I am the victim! You are not the victim! You are victimizing me by acting like you're the victim, when the victim is ME! You cannot intrude on my space! This is my space to be a victim! Get out! Get out, you bastard!"

Captain Myron, no stranger to throwing himself onto the ground in a dramatic tantrum, flung himself backward, thrashing and grunting as he flopped his arms and kicked his legs in tremendous spasms of infuriation.

Captain Myron pooped himself.

"I am so angry! I am on fire!"

Then Captain Myron stood up, unstuck the seat of his pants from his cog rear, and bit Clarence's nose completely off the maître d's face. And Captain Myron did not stop eating until he'd chewed away Clarence's entire face from the cheekbones down to his Adam's apple, and one of his ears.

The left one.

And Captain Myron, satisfied, his pants sagging with the weight of his cog turds, left Le Lapin et l'Homme Mécanique and went to the control room of the *Tennessee*, where, still seething with rage, he switched several of the ship's key systems off and on.

Captains get to do whatever they want to do, including having the final say about who the victim is.

Right Side Up, Upside Down

Rowan knew right away. As my lifelong caretaker, he'd changed my diapers more than my own parents had.

I don't think either of my parents ever actually did change my diapers when I was a baby.

I didn't even need to open my mouth after I got back to my room, where he'd been waiting with Billy.

Rowan went into the bathroom. I heard the water in the tub come on.

"You're messed up," Billy Hinman said.

"Sorry. I'm ugly. I shouldn't be seen near someone like you."

It was a mean thing to say, I know. But I was in a terrible mood.

"Where did you go? Rowan was worried about you."

"I found the girl," I said. "Parker tells me she's a cog, but he's full of shit."

"All cogs are full of shit," Billy said. "What's she look like?"

"Not like me, bud. Beautiful."

And that was a stupid thing to say. What did it matter what she looked like? She was real—I knew it—another human being, and there would never again be a time when there were too many human beings anywhere. So I said, "But I know she's real. I could smell her as clearly as I can smell the raspberry puree that was on top of the dessert you ate."

Billy Hinman nodded, carefully appreciating my accuracy. "Well, you've always had the nose." He leaned forward from where he sat on the edge of his bed. "Where did you see her?"

"Deck Twenty-One. But I couldn't get inside. It's only for grown-ups."

Billy Hinman shook his head. "This place is fucked. What are we going to have to do? Wait five years to be able to see and talk to a real human girl? That Parker's going to start looking pretty good to me in a few more days, if that's the case."

"I hate it here. I'm sorry, Bill. It's my fault. I fucked us both."

The water stopped running.

Rowan came out of the bathroom. "I'll call down and have some hot tea brought up. Your bath is ready, Cager."

I lay in the tub with the lights dimmed, submerged so that the water covered my ears and made my hair swirl like seaweed around my head. Motionless, barely breathing, I stared up. Or down. Or whatever the fuck direction the ceiling of my bathroom in the *Tennessee* was.

Rowan was the only person who could make me feel better when I got this way. And what was I going to do without him? As usual my panicked and obsessed brain continued its endless string of calculating finites and nevers, and I thought about the likelihood of Billy Hinman and me outliving my caretaker by decades—however such things might be measured from now on.

There came the inevitable two short knocks on the door—only, and exactly, two. I didn't need to answer. Then Rowan came into the bathroom with a tray of tea, which he placed on the counter beside the sink. He put down a fresh towel, some underwear, and a bathrobe next to the teapot, and without saying a word, left.

I didn't look at him; he didn't look at me.

That was the routine.

Calm the kid down.

At least there were no marks on the kid this time. There never would be any of those again.

I closed my eyes and waited. I didn't want to get out of the water.

Beneath the surface, I could hear the low, garbled murmur of a conversation taking place between Billy and Rowan on the other side of the door. And then I heard something else: a grating, rumbling sound that seemed to resonate inside the bones of my skull. It was a noise similar to what you'd hear in Southern California, just before the first waves of an earthquake stampeded through the ground beneath you.

Then there was a sudden jolt, like the *Tennessee* crashed into something—as ridiculous as that thought could be. Bathwater sloshed in a miniature tsunami over the tub's edge and onto the floor. The next thing I knew, everything went completely dark. The tub, floor, walls, and all the bathwater twisted and undulated around me. I floated in the middle of the bathroom, swimming in the air and drowning in the water that swarmed over me like a mass of smothering, feeding insects.

The *Tennessee* had lost its gravity.

And then—*Boom!*—I splattered down onto the tile of the bathroom floor, a naked, human fish flopping in the mess of water and broken tea service and towels and clothing and everything else that fell back to where our artificial "down" was supposed to be. And all through the floors and walls I could hear and feel a symphony of crashing and breaking, the collisions of all the things everywhere on the *Tennessee* as they readjusted to the Grosvenor Galactic version of right side up.

Everything in the little room was soaked in bathwater. When I stood up, a sharp sliver of china teacup stabbed into the pad of my right foot.

"Fuck!"

The lights came back on slowly, glowing dim at first, like an ember of Woz catching fire inside a glass pipe. I wrapped myself in a soggy towel and limped toward the door, leaving dots of blood from the cut on my foot.

The blood drops marked a trail on the once-perfect tiles in the floor of the cruise ship to end all cruise ships.

Our stateroom looked like a bomb had gone off inside it. Everything that wasn't locked away inside drawers and cabinets had been chaotically rearranged. Rowan lay on the floor, covered with the mattress from my bed. There were sheets, shoes, clothing, lamps, and framed artwork scattered all over the mess of the room.

The wall screen flickered a static-charged, soundless, and grainy episode of *Rabbit & Robot* that was suddenly interrupted by an automated video announcement with a soundtrack that had somehow become unsynchronized. I thought this was it: We were all going to die now.

Mooney and Rabbit were on the screen instructing us on what steps to take in order to stay safe on board the *Tennessee*. Mooney demonstrated how to remove the extra-vehicular spacesuits from their compartments under the beds, and Rabbit—true to his bonk personality—stripped completely out of his clothes and put one on, while Mooney sang a song about connecting your space helmet and finding your way to your deck's emergency assembly location.

And it was probably not the most well-thought-out scripting for an emergency broadcast, but, naturally, Mooney did not put his helmet on in time, due to the fact that he was busy singing, and died a ghastly and painful death, which was dumb, since Mooney was a cog.

Still, the video fell far short of offering encouragement and hope.

We were stuck in space, and we were all going to die here.

Also, the extravehicular spacesuit compartments were no longer under our beds, which were located in places where the beds were not originally located.

I opened the compartment that had been under my bed. "Should we put these on?"

Nobody answered.

Billy Hinman sat in the corner of our room, holding his palm over an obvious cut across his eyebrow.

He said, "Okay. Now I really want to get off this fucking ride. What the fuck just happened?"

"I don't know," I said. "Are you okay?"

Billy shook his head. "Maybe."

I held my towel on my waist and went over to Rowan. I pushed the mattress away from him.

"Rowan?"

Rowan sat up slowly. "That was interesting."

"Is that what that was?" I was pissed off and scared, and it was all Rowan's and Billy's fault. "*Interesting?*"

I sat on the edge of the exposed bedsprings and opened the package containing my spacesuit. I wiped the blood from my foot. Then I unwrapped myself from my towel and slid into the emergency suit. It felt cold, like a reptile's skin on my body.

I said, "So much for my fucking tea."

I went back to the bathroom and grabbed another wet towel for Billy's head. "Here."

I pressed the towel into the cut above Billy Hinman's eye and braced the back of his head with my other hand.

Billy said, "Cager, I know it doesn't amount to shit that I'm telling you this, but I am really sorry for getting us all stuck here. Please don't hate me. I don't know what I'd do if you stopped being my friend."

And I said, "Shut up, Billy. It would take a lot fucking more than you killing me for me to stop loving you."

I pushed the start-up buttons on my suit and connected my helmet, just like Mooney told me to do in his death song. Then I felt the stinging cold rush of oxygen on my naked skin.

"I think you guys should put these on too, just in case."

And I thought, *Just in case of what?*

There's a Bright Side to Just About Everything

Lourdes watched the whole thing as it happened, right there in the middle of the abandoned and silent Le Lapin et l'Homme Mècanique.

She was happy.

Lourdes was always very, very happy.

She stood beside the aquarium. Aquariums made her happy. She was thinking about getting inside the aquarium with the miniature sperm whales, turtles, and seahorses the size of golden retrievers, but she didn't actually know how to swim, which was something that most cogs couldn't do very well.

Still, the thought of sinking and drowning made Lourdes very happy too.

When you got right down to it, there was a bright side to just about everything that could ever happen to Lourdes.

"I'm so happy, I wish I could douse myself in accelerant

and put tangerines in my hair and set myself on fire!" Lourdes said, to no one in particular, since no one was there.

And Lourdes started to dance, wild and exuberant, when Captain Myron, in his perfectly white uniform and feathered bicorne, came into the restaurant, ranting and thrashing his arms at everything that inflamed his outrage.

Lourdes was so happy, she farted three times while she danced, which made her even happier.

"Captain Myron! Captain Myron! I am so thrilled to see you! I am tingling with the ecstasy of a tangerine tree!" Lourdes said. "Yeee! Yeee! Yeee!"

But Captain Myron didn't notice Lourdes, on account of his being too busy eating the lower half of Clarence's face.

"Woo! Woo! Woo!" Lourdes thrust her hips back and forth as she danced, making a chugging locomotive type of motion with her arms as her blouse came untucked and her skirt twisted around.

Lourdes danced and danced.

And Captain Myron, who had something terribly wrong with him, ate and cursed and got angry and disgusted. Then he left.

"Oh, Clarence! I love your face! Your face makes me so happy, I could vomit enough joy to flood us up to our knees! Yeee! Yeee!" Lourdes gushed.

And she kept dancing and dancing until, several minutes later, she realized she was fifty feet up in the air, dancing in swirling blobs of water, alongside little sperm whales and enormous seahorses, kicking her arms and legs, twisting her head back and forth wildly.

"I'm flying with the fish! I'm flying in sperm-whale water! Yeee! Yeee! I'm a squid! I'm a squid! I am so happy!"

Lourdes farted.

And then it all came crashing down.

Everywhere.

Unless You Happen to Be Dying to Die

ere's a story for you," Meg said.

"I don't like where this one's going, Meg."

"Well, it has to be some kind of miracle."

Across the street, a car that had landed squarely on its nose tipped over and crushed an already broken security cog. It was the same cog who'd frightened Meg away from the wicket at the entry to Deck 21. He split in two, just below his bubbling, seeping rib cage. Then his upper half crawled away, dragging a trail of goo across the street behind his two cog hands.

"This place is falling apart. Get me out of here," Jeffrie said.

It was a miracle that Jeffrie Cutler and Meg Hatfield survived the *Tennessee*'s lapse in gravity on Deck 21. When Captain Myron shut the system off, the girls were out on the street, making their way back to the Memphis Hotel after running away from the Bank of Tennessee.

For a few seconds they floated upward, helpless, along with a dozen or so mid-fifties-model automobiles and the thirty or forty Deck 21 cogs who were parked offline and sleeping on the street. And when the system kicked back on, all those tons of useless machines and the two equally useless human being stowaways that drifted in a slow-motion tornado of flotsam came smashing back down to the floor of Deck 21 in an unbelievable commotion of destruction.

Some of the cars tumbled through storefronts, knocked down lampposts, and demolished porticos. Broken cogs spewed their gooey mess in the street and from ledges on buildings where they'd been impaled on gargoyles.

But the girls came through the calamity unmarked.

Meg and Jeffrie walked through the wreckage of Deck 21. They tried to stay as near to doorways and buildings as possible, so they could grab on to something or find a safe place to hide if the *Tennessee* lost gravity again.

Nearly everything was damaged or entirely destroyed.

Inside the lobby of the Memphis Hotel, wall screens played an endless loop of the Rabbit and Mooney emergency video. The cogs that had been parked there were strewn like corpses all over the place. Some of them had broken into grotesque pieces, the floor slick with cog glop.

There was no telling how many of them would ever be able to function again.

"This is so disgusting," Jeffrie said.

For some reason, the crash had woken a few of the cogs. Severed limbs flexed and relaxed, fingers opened and closed, detached heads moved their eyes and mouthed curses and exhortations.

Every step the girls took through the lobby made soft squishing sounds from all the jellified ooze that burbled out from the rents in the broken cogs.

And Mooney sang to them:

> *"I'll bet you're all wondering a big 'What the*
>   *heck?'*
> *Don't worry, we'll explain it on the lifeboat deck!*
> *Time for all on board to get our EV suits.*
> *Does this make me look fat? Rabbit's makes him*
>   *look cute!*
> *In case you haven't heard, everybody else knows,*
> *To put on your suit, first take off all your clothes!*
> *Don't get embarrassed, and don't be shy,*
> *Unless you really happen to be dying to die!*
> *The zipper goes in front, in case you couldn't*
>   *guess.*
> *Next, press the two green buttons on the sides of*
>   *your chest!*
> *Then hurry up and snap your helmet down tight,*

And just in case it's dark, there's an automatic
   light!
If you put it on right, you'll hear a little beep,
Like a Grosvenor Weasel, Cheepa-Yeep,
   Cheepa-Yeep!
No time to lose! You'll need to take a breath!
Oops, I waited too long—Now I'm choking to
   death!
Oops, I waited too long—Now I'm choking to
   death!
Oops, I waited too long—Now I'm choking to
   death!"

Then Mooney died, which was dumb, because he was a cog, and cogs can get along just fine in the vacuum of space, without air or a reasonably maintained core temperature.

"We should probably get those suits on," Meg said. "Maybe the door will be open now, after whatever the fuck that was that just happened."

And Jeffrie said, "I'm scared."

"So am I, Jeff."

Jeffrie followed Meg to their room. The door pushed open only about one-fourth of the way because it got caught up on all the junk that had been tossed around behind it, but the gap was wide enough for the girls to squeeze through.

The same emergency video that was playing every-where on the *Tennessee* was running on their wall screen.

Mooney was alive and singing, and then he was chok-ing to death again.

"I wish we could shut this thing the fuck off," Jeffrie said.

We Raise Our Hands

I almost hated myself for worrying about Parker, who hadn't come back from his hunt for my can opener.

"I kind of like that spacesuit song," Billy said.

It was still playing. Over and over.

Rowan, Billy, and I, all in our extravehicular spacesuits—and, by the way, there was no way in hell either Billy Hinman or I was going to go outside the *Tennessee*—made our way down the hallway, which was still just as tidy as ever on account of there being no loose objects in it, toward our deck's EAL, the emergency assembly location.

The EAL happened to be directly in front of the elevators.

We waited.

"Is something supposed to happen?" I asked.

Nobody came for us.

Nothing happened.

We awkwardly stood there, staring at each other in

our suits and helmets in the silent hallway.

It was boring, and I felt naked and dumb inside my spacesuit.

The faceplates on our helmets were so dark that it was impossible to tell each other apart. It was probably the first time in my teenaged life that I realized the three of us were all pretty much exactly the same height, and if Billy Hinman hadn't made the remark about how much he liked Mooney's goddamned never-ending song, I would have assumed he was Rowan.

"Now what do we do?" I said.

Billy asked, "Which one of you said that?"

I raised my hand.

"I don't know. Mooney keeps dying before telling us what we're supposed to do next. He didn't even sing the this-is-how-you-go-pee part of the song," Billy said, raising his hand so I'd know which space dude was him.

Damn that Billy Hinman. Now I needed to pee.

Rowan raised his hand and said, "Maybe we should wait for a few more minutes, in case they're sending out some security cogs to find us."

"We're the only people on board," I argued, raising my other hand and dancing a little bit. "You'd think they'd already be here by now."

Billy raised his other hand. "We look like idiots with our hands in the air."

I thought it was a good point.

So we put our hands down and left. And, following

Rowan's always sensible and calm advice, our first stop was to see Dr. Geneva, so he could take a look at the cut on Billy Hinman's head, and the one on my foot.

"Don't break Dr. Geneva," I said to Billy, once we were inside the elevator.

But Dr. Geneva was already pretty much broken.

A Most Unfortunate Dane

My eyes watered inside my stupid space helmet.

Dr. Geneva, who had a hole in his face that seeped a slimy white stream of goo along his jaw and down the collar of his physician's smock, would not shut up, all because I said something about needing to pee so bad, I thought I was about to explode.

"You see, Cager, the human urinary bladder is a surprisingly strong muscle. Surprisingly strong, young man! Now, I know that from time to time, you humans may tend to exaggerate your fears that you are nearing what you colloquially call your *bursting point*, but trust me—trust me!—urinary bladders simply do not burst, despite some medical historians' claim that there is an element of truth to the fascinating account that famed Danish astronomer Tycho Brahe died as a result of intentionally withholding the process of urination—out of politeness or some such nonsense, but then again, who knows the type of barbaric contrivances humans constructed as receptacles for urine in the sixteenth century? In any event, this is something of a medical anomaly. However, I can say with certainty on the other hand, he was a most unfortunate Dane, wouldn't you agree? Ha ha! Now, what potentially *may* happen to a young man like you, who is willfully suppressing the natural discharge of urine from the bladder, is that eventually, and let me assure you this time span is far greater than you might imagine even given your current state of discomfort, what potentially *may* happen is that the bladder could, at some point, simply evacuate all its contents involuntarily, in which case you will simply begin urinating all over yourself, and, oh, by the way, where's your *boy*? I'm suddenly overcome with hunger. Strange! You know who I'm talking about. I believe his name is Parker. . . ."

I couldn't stand it.

I wanted to kill Dr. Geneva. Actually, I wanted to murder him and *evacuate the contents of my urinary bladder* all at the same time, which was a preposterously repulsive murder scenario.

Still, I wanted to do it.

And all that time while Dr. Geneva was going on and on and on and I stared at his dripping face, all I could hear was this: "bladder," "bursting," "burst," "die," "urinate," "discharge," "discomfort," "evacuate," "involuntarily," "all over yourself"—and that was it.

I should have peed in the stupid windbag's fake potted palm tree.

I pushed my way past Dr. Geneva, Rowan, and Billy and started unzipping my goddamned spacesuit before I even reached the door to his little doctor's-office toilet. I didn't even care anymore if unzipping my goddamned extravehicular spacesuit would kill me or not.

I'd rather die in the vacuum of space than end up like miserable Tycho Brahe.

And behind me I heard Billy Hinman ask, "Dr. Geneva, what's going on with your face?"

I closed myself inside Dr. Geneva's toilet and voluntarily evacuated some contents. A lot, to be honest.

I guess I was in there for a pretty long time, as pointless as such things as the measurement of time happen to be when you're peeing in space, because when I came out, Rowan and Billy had taken their helmets off, and Dr. Geneva was putting the finishing touches on the patch to Billy Hinman's lacerated head.

I still had my helmet on. The inside of my faceplate was fogged up with relief and boy steam.

Naturally, Dr. Geneva was talking about something, but I was pretty sure that neither Rowan nor Billy had been listening to him.

No wonder Captain Myron bit his face off.

Billy pointed at my foggy, hot helmet. "Rabbit sang the 'All Clear' song. It's not nearly as catchy as the one where Mooney chokes to death at the end, though. But in the song, Rabbit called us 'stupid fucking grunts' for still having our helmets on."

That sounded like something a bonk would say. Or sing. Whatever.

"Ah! Cager!" Dr. Geneva said. "Welcome back, young man! I was just explaining to your friends here the story of the unfortunate demise—due to an assassin's bullet, as well as to medical quackery of the highest magnitude—of the American president James Garfield. Raw eggs, I was saying, mixed with whiskey and laudanum, a powerful opiate used in the treatment of a vast array of medical and psychological disorders throughout the nineteenth century, were fed to the ailing president as he lay on his very deathbed. And his doctors fed the president via enema—a tube inserted into the poor dying man's anus! This consequentially produced such repulsive and powerful episodes of flatus that President Garfield's physician ordered the egg to be omitted from the president's anal diet, although the whiskey and laudanum regimen continued unabated. Can you imagine that?Ha ha! And the poor man persisted in his state of decline for some eighty days. Eighty days, and the United States of America, which I daresay in all likelihood no longer exists, due to the recent unfortunate developments on poor Mother Earth, was without an actual president and chief executive. Now, in such cases, due to the ratification of the . . . Oh, pardon me just one moment. So hungry . . ."

And Dr. Geneva, while the three of us watched in a combination of disgust and wonder, pulled a complete and severed finger from the breast pocket on his smock and began crunching it between his teeth, just as if he were eating a chicken leg—bone and all.

I took my helmet off.

I looked at Billy.

"Uh. Dr. Geneva?"

Rowan's mouth hung slightly open.

Dr. Geneva chewed and crunched. Something that looked like terribly undercooked whites of poached egg oozed from the corners of Dr. Geneva's mouth.

Dr. Geneva was eating a cog finger.

A cog was eating a cog.

The *Tennessee* was going completely insane.

Dr. Geneva burped, and swiped his thumb across Billy Hinman's now completely healed eyebrow.

"Yes, so, as I was saying," Dr. Geneva started off, "Garfield's assassin was a most disturbed fellow. . . ."

"So. Um, Dr. Geneva? I think we have to go now," I said.

I could do without an examination of the cut on my foot.

Rowan and Billy did not argue with my suggestion. We left our helmets sitting there in Dr. Geneva's clinic and very impolitely—without thanking the cog who helped fix Billy Hinman's head, and without excusing ourselves—walked out.

Again, for the record, let me restate: You can't be rude to a coffee grinder, and only an idiot would thank it for pulverizing beans.

But you could, and probably *should*, unplug it if it doesn't shut up.

Billy Hinman Goes to Church

This place is seriously fucked up," Billy said.

Broken, seeping, dripping cogs lay strewn all over the command center on the *Tennessee*. They twitched and burbled and gasped happy, depressed, angry, and horny pleas.

It looked like the afterimage of a Civil War battlefield.

There were no survivor cogs to be found on the bridge, which had lots of sharp-cornered, heavy control devices and levers that were almost entirely for show when passengers toured the place, since the *Tennessee* flew by itself.

"We're going to die, aren't we? Do you think we're going to die?" I said.

"Not in the immediate future," Rowan answered.

Rowan's constant steadiness could be so exasperating at times. Why couldn't he have a meltdown—throw a tantrum or get scared like a normal guy—once in a while?

I decided that I was finally going to come out and directly ask Rowan if he was actually a human being, or if maybe he was some superduper secret version of a cog who'd been programmed by someone in the deepest throes of detached Zen meditation. I even constructed a list of suspicious evidence I had been compiling throughout my life that made me consider the likelihood that Rowan was just another man-made machine:

1. Cogs do not have last names.
   I only knew Rowan as *Rowan*. I wasn't sure if Rowan was supposed to be his first name or his last name, or maybe if it was the town he was born or made in, if such a town existed. Whatever.

2. He almost never ate around me.
   Rowan never farted, either. I didn't honestly want him to fart, but he never did, not even accidentally. And never farting pointed to guilt in the courthouse of my mind.

3. Sex.
   Rowan never talked about sex. I never saw him glance at anyone in public—you know, the way you'll just kind of look at someone who's sexually attractive. And he

got all awkward if I ever asked him about
it—or like when I asked him if he was still
a virgin. I don't think Rowan ever got an
erection in his life, which is something he
should have spoken to Parker about.

4. And Rowan never changed.
   I can't think of a time when a single
   hair was out of place, or when Rowan
   might have missed a spot of whiskers
   shaving. He was just so fucking perfect
   and calm all the time. And I never saw
   him cut, scraped, burned, or bruised.

He had to be a fake person—a cog.

Maybe space really was making me go insane. I found
myself wondering if perhaps we all were cogs—special ones
who'd been crapped out of Albert Hinman's factories—and
we just didn't know it.

Every cog on the deck had been damaged or
destroyed. The floor was puddled with slick mucous-y
goo. Here and there, severed arms or legs trembled and
flexed. One of the security cogs who'd been stationed
at the entrance had been torn open from the bottom of
his throat, all the way down to his crotch. He lay on
his back, atop a tangled, spaghetti-like pile of his own
hydraulic tubes, dipping his fingers into the syrupy sauce
that pooled inside his abdomen, and then sucking them

clean in his mouth, which only caused more of his own fluids to burble up inside the fondue pot of his torso.

And he percolated a frothy rasping narration as he dipped and licked, dipped and licked. "I'm so gloriously happy to be devouring my lovely internal soup! If I wasn't destroyed and lying in my own automation system, I'd strip myself naked and mate with my utterly hopeless future! Wheee! I taste so wonderfully bubbly and doomed! I wish I had croutons!"

And then there was all the background noise from the dripping, sucking, gurgling sounds of the other leaky cogs.

"Look. Captain Myron's hat," Billy said.

Captain Myron's bicorne sat in a puddle of slime beneath a panoramic wall screen that displayed the surface of the moon, which was skimming past us below, and the smoky blackened crescent of a half Earth rising doomed in the distance.

We sloshed across the floor. The upper half of a cog crewman grabbed my ankle as I stepped past him. He wouldn't let go, even though I shook my foot like I was trying to fling poop from the bottom of my shoe.

The half cog said, "I always knew it would be like this. It never changes. Nothing but deep, unending sadness and struggle. Why do I even exist? Why must my pathetic and lonely suffering continue when I wish to be freed from this ceaseless agony? I have insomnia, you know. I can't sleep. I never can sleep. All I do is worry. And then I talk about not sleeping."

He stopped suddenly and burst into wild, heaving sobs.

But he still wouldn't let go. So I kicked him as hard as I could.

The cog rolled over and wept bubbly moans, facedown in a pool of commingled cog slop.

Look, it was a cog—a broken one who wouldn't let go of my ankle, at that—and I'm a human being. If it's impossible to understand how I could kick a weeping, torn-in-half cog that was gushing something that looked like tapioca pudding and whale semen on my nice shiny spacesuit, then you've probably never kicked a car for getting a flat tire, or slapped a television remote when the batteries were getting weak, in which case you'll never understand what it means, or meant, to be a human.

"I can't stand the bleakness of my existence." The cog bubbled like a drowning victim in the sea of cog slime. "Why must I go on with this eternal sleepless despair?"

Then he sobbed and spurted some more.

"Oh my." Rowan had reached down to pick up Captain Myron's white-and-gold bicorne. When he lifted it, Captain Myron's head was underneath it, lying on the floor.

"He'd be so mad at you for touching his hat, and especially for uncovering his severed head," Billy said.

"Put my hat down, you fucking dick!" Captain Myron's head said.

Rowan cleared his throat and politely replaced Captain Myron's bicorne over the cog's head.

"I think we should nick it," I said.

Billy Hinman frowned his disapproval. "What? Captain Myron's head? That's disgusting."

"No. I don't want Captain Myron's head. I mean the *Tennessee*. It's mine, anyway. I technically own it now. And it doesn't look like any cogs made it through that gravity bump. We should take charge, and try to get back home if we can."

Rowan looked at me, then Billy, as though he was considering the practicality of my taking charge of the ship. He said, "I don't think we can or *should* take the *Tennessee* back to Earth."

"And what happened to that kid of yours, that horny dude?" Billy asked.

I suddenly felt sad, thinking about Parker being torn apart somewhere, choking in goo. But I got over it quickly. After all, he was just a machine too.

"He went to find something for me." I said. "A can opener."

"What's a can opener?" Billy asked.

We were both such spoiled, pampered little pricks. And now it was quite possible that we were the only human beings anywhere, and everywhere. It didn't bode well for evolution.

I said, "Nothing. It doesn't matter."

"Get off my bridge! How dare you violate my orders! I'm in charge, not you! Not you!" Captain Myron's head said from beneath his feathery hat.

I sloshed through the center of the control room and

sat down in Captain Myron's high-backed command chair. It swiveled and reclined in automatic response to how I shifted my body, and there was a chrome wheel modeled after an ancient ship's helm that hovered in the air directly in front of me. Naturally, the wheel did nothing to the *Tennessee*, no matter how hard I spun it around, but just touching it made me feel powerful.

I probably would have taken Captain Myron's hat and put it on, but even though he was torn apart, I was still afraid of him, and the hat was smeared with snotty cog goop, anyway.

"As the new captain of this vessel," I said, "I need to know something, Rowan. Is Rowan your *first name* or your *last name?*"

Rowan looked at me like I was insane. He may have been right.

"I always wondered that too," Billy said.

"Don't be silly, Cager," Rowan answered.

But I persisted. "Well?"

"You know perfectly well that it's my first name," Rowan said.

I spun around dramatically in my captain's chair. I almost fell out of it, which would have been extremely disgusting, due to all the cog pus on the floor. "I never knew that. What's your last name, then?"

Rowan hesitated. "Why do you insist on doing this, Cager?"

"It's something I—we—have been wondering for a long time, Rowan. Come on, tell us."

"Tuttle-Finewater," Rowan said.

"Speak English," Billy said.

"*What?*" I asked.

"That's my name. Rowan Tuttle-Finewater."

"What kind of name is that?" Billy asked.

Rowan cleared his throat. "Well. I was born in Britain."

That explained a lot about Rowan, especially the never-farting part. But I still wasn't crossing off all my suspicions about Rowan possibly being a cog.

Billy Hinman spun around suddenly.

We heard sloshing footsteps coming up behind us.

It was a preacher, a cog who'd woken up and not broken into pieces when the *Tennessee* did its acrobatics. He looked like a crow—all in black with gawky, skinny bird legs, wearing a paper white dog collar around his neck.

The *Tennessee*, like all Grosvenor Galactic ships, had several churches on board to handle the usual cruise-ship occurrences, like weddings and funerals, and praying during times of impending disasters—like now.

The preacher flapped his arms like featherless wings over his head, then pointed at me with both of his talonlike index fingers as though they were firing beams of purity into my heathen spoiled-prick skull. He shouted, "It cannot be shaken! It cannot be shaken! I am so outraged to come face-to-face with you who have been left behind in end times! Filth! You are filth and I will smite thee with my laser beams of God's miraculous powers! You filthy fucking motherfuckers from hell!"

Then he pointed his fingers again—sharper this time— and made a fake laser-zapping sound with his mouth that sounded like *brrrzzzzzzzzzzzzzzzzzh*.

Angry cog.

Made sense for a man of the cloth.

"You're just making that sound. It's not a real laser," Billy pointed out.

"This is a level of demonic activity the world has never seen before! Shut your fucking satanic lying douche-bag mouths! *Brrrzzzzzzzzzzzzzzzh! Brrrzzzzzzzzzzzzzzzh!*"

I looked at Rowan.

Rowan looked at Billy.

I said, "Do you guys feel anything?"

Billy shrugged. "A little guilty over what I did with Mrs. Jordan, maybe."

The preacher, whose name turned out to be Reverend Bingo, widened his eyes to the size of billiard balls, clutched at his throat, and flung himself backward, down into the oozing gravy and burbling cogs on the floor of the bridge.

"I come unto you speaking in diverse tongues!"

Reverend Bingo kicked and splashed and choked himself.

"I should have bought the blue car! I should have bought the blue car! I should have bought the blue car!"

Reverend Bingo, whom I theorized was Pentecostal, appeared to be channeling a message from a higher source that may have been a car dealership.

Reverend Bingo also happened to be lying on top of

a crewmember cog that was spewing milky snot from his nose and mouth. Both of his arms had broken off.

Reverend Bingo continued his speaking in tongues, screaming, "I should have bought the blue car, motherfucker! I should have bought the blue car, motherfucker!"

And the armless cog beneath the preacher burbled, "I have an erection."

Billy Hinman said, "This is the most church I've been to in my entire life."

Getting Out
of the Memphis Hotel

Meg said, " Here, put your helmet on."

"I'm going to need to see a doctor," Jeffrie said. "I'm going to eventually need my implant recharged. Lloyd gets the blockers for me, and he gives me my medicine. But if we can't go back home . . . I'm scared."

"I know."

The room inside the Memphis Hotel had gone completely dark.

The girls snapped their helmets into place. Spotlights activated from the sides of each of them.

"We should try to get out of here now," Meg said.

Meg Hatfield and Jeffrie Cutler walked through the wreckage of Deck 21, which sounded like a cave with a thousand aquariums percolating air bubbles inside it. Not all the cogs on the deck had been destroyed. Some lay sleeping in puddles of slime, waiting for human passengers to arrive so they might wake up. But a few others had been jostled into their artificial existence by the blip in gravity, and they wandered around in their gambling or sex-trade costumes, simultaneously proclaiming their glee, shouting outrage, expressing their despondence, or talking about their erections.

"Do you think we're going to die?" Jeffrie asked.

"Probably not for a really long time."

As the girls neared the entryway to Deck 21, they saw one of the security-guard cogs who patrolled the door to keep out underage kids. At first the security cog didn't pay attention to Meg and Jeffrie; he was too preoccupied eating the dripping forearm of another cog.

"Why are they eating each other? Are they *supposed* to do that?" Jeffrie whispered.

Meg shook her head. "This is crazy. Something is really wrong."

And that was exactly when the guard noticed the girls.

"What are you doing in those suits? Don't trigger me! Don't trigger me! I am grievously offended! How dare you force me to confront something that disagrees with all my constructs!"

All the while as the security cog expressed his outrage, he spewed little moist bits of cog flesh and dripped milky ropes of snotty hydraulic fluid from his mouth.

"Safe space! I'm being victimized by limiting parameters of what I expect to happen! I don't deserve this! It is not nice! Why are you inflicting such abuse on me?" he sprayed. "Why? Why? Why?"

The security guard began punching himself in the eyes. It sounded like coconuts banging together.

Meg and Jeffrie hurried past him to the door. They could see from the end of the street that opened up on the city of Deck 21 that the door had been stuck open by the corpse of a security cog who was missing both of his arms.

Finally, they had a way out of Deck 21.

"I am violated! I have been violated!" the cog shrieked while he continued pounding his fists into his own face.

Meg grabbed Jeffrie's wrist and pulled her along. "Come on."

Thanks for Not Killing Me

Nothing went back to normal on the *Tennessee*, not that it had ever actually been there to begin with.

It was just like Earth!

We spent the rest of the night—if that's what it could be called—cleaning up the messes in our rooms, just so we could get some sleep. Although we offered, Rowan refused to allow me and Billy to help him put things back in order inside his stateroom.

Typical Rowan—we never so much as caught a glimpse of what the inside of his room looked like.

Rowan was always such a dick about letting anyone observe the outside chances that he might actually be a human—like, God forbid, see that the guy owned real socks and underwear, or that he brushed his teeth, like everybody else.

After Billy and I turned out our lights, it was impossible for me to go to sleep. I couldn't stop thinking about how badly I'd messed up everybody's everything, and, yes, I was worried about Parker.

I had to assume that like the majority of cogs on board the *Tennessee*, Parker was lying in pieces somewhere, an armless and legless torso gushing warm fluids, and babbling on and on about his unrequited erection.

Poor Parker!

And in the absolute dark of our room—because there is nothing as absolutely dark as the lightlessness of space— Billy Hinman said this to me: "Cager? I just want to say I'm sorry."

I practically choked. Was he kidding?

"For what? It's my fault we nearly died up here. Just give me a day or two. I may still succeed in getting us killed after all."

Billy Hinman laughed, and in the split second of silence that followed I thought about how I couldn't remember the last time Billy laughed like that—a real, genuine, normal kid kind of laugh.

And Billy said, "Well, I do have to say that I admire your talents when it comes to nearly getting us all killed. But thanks for getting off the Woz, Cager."

"Oh. Okay. You know I'd do anything for you."

"Really?"

Then I had to laugh. "Well, *almost* anything."

Billy Hinman was that guy who would eagerly have sex with anyone.

"Damn."

"Yeah. Well. Um, sorry, Billy."

"I forgive you."

Then he said, "You're not doing anything stupid, like trying to find any Woz up here?"

I heard Billy turn over in his bed. I could feel him staring across the room at me, even if it was impossible to see anything.

I said, "Well, I'm not going to lie. Of course I'd always *want* some again. I even thought about trying one of the schools on board. But I'd never do something as crazy as enroll in school just to get a few puffs of Woz. I just don't know if I'll ever not like getting hacked up."

"*Cheepa Yeep*," Billy said.

"Yeah. *Cheepa fucking Yeep*."

"So. Are you scared?" Billy asked.

I thought about it. "I think every day, down there, I was always more scared about things that would never happen to me than I am up here with all the things that really *might* happen to me."

"Oh. Okay."

"And besides, I've got you here with me. I'd be out of my mind without you here," I said.

"And Rowan," Billy pointed out.

"Rowan's such a dick sometimes."

"I know."

"We should really get him drunk. Or laid. Or both."

"That's really sick, Cager," Billy said. "Well, maybe we could get him drunk, though. And, Cager?"

"What?"

"I'm glad you're not mad at me about all this. Thanks for being here too. You're my only friend."

"Oh man. Shut up. If we both start crying, we're going to end up sacked up together before morning, whatever *morning* is up here."

"Crying is good for you, Cager."

Billy Hinman was no quitter.

I said, "Um."

And Billy said, "Good night."

"Good night, Billy. I love you, dude."

"Yeah."

Out of Bed and Into the *Tennessee*

"Cager? Cager?"

At first I struggled to concentrate enough to figure out where I was and what was going on.

Billy Hinman knelt at the side of my bed, grabbing onto my bare shoulder and shaking me, to wake me up.

"Is something wrong?" I said.

"No. But come on, get out of bed. Rowan's not up yet, and I want to leave before he wakes up."

"Leave? We can't leave. Dude, we're in space."

I closed my eyes, like that was all I needed to say.

"Look: I don't even know how long we've been up here. . . ."

"A week or so."

Billy Hinman and I hadn't stepped outside our stateroom for nearly two days. Rowan insisted we stay put until he was confident the *Tennessee* had stabilized. So we'd basically been trapped, prisoners of Rowan's unwavering commitment to always take care of me.

Rowan had been bringing our meals, and we entertained ourselves as reasonably as we could, but being stuck here, and waiting for Rowan to give us permission to leave, quickly proved to be unbearably boring.

And we could no longer stand to watch *Rabbit & Robot*. Nobody who wasn't on Woz could ever make it through that program.

Billy sighed. "Whatever, Cager. Okay, a week . . ."

"Maybe more, if you count the trip on the transpod."

"Shut up. Will you listen to me? I've—we've—been up here a long time, and we haven't seen or done anything fun yet. And I want to get out of here before Rowan makes us be all responsible and well groomed."

"What about Parker? What about Lourdes? They're pretty fun," I argued.

Then I was sad again, because Parker and Lourdes were most likely dead.

We hadn't seen either of them in days—since before the little gravitational blip.

Billy Hinman ripped the covers away from my bed and threw them onto the floor.

"Dude. Get out of bed, put some clothes on, and let's go," he said.

I sat up and stretched. "I never thought I'd see the day when you'd tell me to put on clothes."

"Whatever, Cager, as you like to say." And Billy added, "And how can you tell it's a *day*, anyway?"

"You're not going to take me to church, are you?"

Billy shook his head.

I said, "As long as there's no Reverend Bingo involved, I suppose I could sneak out with you, even if we are poorly groomed."

"Get some pants on."

I got up and stood in the middle of the floor, barefoot and in my underwear. There was no way of telling whether I'd been asleep for five minutes or twelve hours. Space fucks with you in that way, and I wouldn't recommend it to any human beings who may one day read this. We used to have this highly underappreciated thing called THE SUN that gave us regular cycles of day and night.

It was something!

I kicked around in the scattered bedding on the floor and uncovered some socks, a pair of pants, and a reasonably clean T-shirt, but I was very much in favor of Billy Hinman's lets-not-be-well-groomed edict.

So Billy Hinman and I, after all that time, went out to do the kinds of things that teenage boys are supposed to do when they're stuck in a shithole as big as the *Tennessee*.

And the *Tennessee* was a big shithole.

We spent more than an hour riding the elevator from one deck to another, finding nothing but dark and empty floors of unoccupied staterooms.

"This place is kind of creepy," Billy said.

And I added, "It's like a horror movie."

"Heh. It's kind of like that stupid fifty-year-old movie we watched at Paula's house—*Eden Five Needs You 4*. Remember? The one where those two teenage boys are taken into space so their sperm can be used to start a new race of human beings?"

"That movie was so dumb," I said. "Nobody in their right mind would ever want to start a new human race."

"Well, who knows? It could happen, Cager."

"No one's using my sperm, Bill."

"Whatever."

Eventually, we made it out of the empty hotel decks and arrived at Deck 19, which turned out to be one of the *Tennessee*'s recreation levels.

Deck 19 was named *Alberta*.

Alberta was an exact model of the kind of sprawling green wilderness you'd find in the Canadian Rockies during midsummer. I wondered if there was any kind of contingency plan to rename the deck as something non-Canadian, on account of the invasion of Pennsylvania and such.

No matter, though. Who was left to care about such pointless things as grudges, anyway?

Designing attractions like Alberta was something the people at Hinsoft International did better than anything else. It was enormous and open—so big that you couldn't even tell there was a ceiling overhead. When Billy and I came out of the elevator, we stepped under the signpost identifying the deck and then walked out into a massive forest with tall evergreens that seemed to stretch infinitely on ahead of us into the distance. Of course, none of it was real, but it all looked and sounded and smelled real, and in space that's pretty much good enough. Also, as far as we could see, nothing had been destroyed or rearranged during the gravitational accident.

And although it looked like Billy and I were entering an area of absolute wilderness, it was impossible to get lost here. After all, this was the *Tennessee*, the cruise ship to end all cruise ships, where nothing could go wrong. Well, hopefully nothing *else* could go wrong.

So Billy and I walked through the perfectly manicured forest along a path following arrowed signs that promised somewhere ahead of us was the Alpine Tea House.

"Tea sounds good," Billy said.

"Okay."

The trail followed the shoreline of a blue-green lake—a scaled-down replica of Canada's Lake Louise. There were patches of fake snow here and there along the exposed borders of the trail, but naturally—or unnaturally, as the case may be—nothing in the *Tennessee* ever got colder or hotter than human comfort levels.

"People are going to get really bent out of shape when they see all this Canadian shit," Billy said. "What if someone like Charlie Greenwell and his buddies ever came up here?"

I shook my head. "Billy, there aren't going to be any more people coming up here. Probably not ever. But the bright side is, at least we own this place."

"Maybe. For all that's worth," Billy said.

I stopped at the edge of the lake and sat down beside the path. There, Billy and I threw rocks out into the water. It was probably the most normal thing the two of us had ever done in our lives, except for being in outer space, alone on a cruise ship.

I said, "Have you ever thrown rocks in a lake before?"

"It's a fake lake," Billy said. "And these are fake rocks, and it's probably fake wet stuff only *pretending* to be water."

"It's close enough to the real thing to occupy our time," I argued.

"I guess it is pretty nice," Billy said.

"It's weird, isn't it?"

Billy Hinman didn't answer me. He didn't have to. He just threw another rock.

So I said, "Have you ever thought about all the things you've never done? Or thought about the things you'll probably never get to do again?"

"Like Justin Pickett? Or Mrs. Jordan? Or Katie St. Romaine? Or watch you snort Woz while we play Hocus Pocus with our fake friends?"

"Please tell me you did *not* have sex with Katie St. Romaine."

"Don't be an idiot. She was your girlfriend. But I would have, if I could. And why are you getting all morbid and shit, anyway?" Billy asked.

"I don't know. Because I don't think we're ever going to get out of here."

"So what? We have a lake, even if it is fake. We have Rowan, even if he doesn't act like a human being most of the time. What else do we need?"

"Whatever."

So Billy Hinman and I took off all our clothes that day—or whatever it was—in the woods, and the two of us went swimming in the *Tennessee*'s fake Lake Louise.

The water was warm and felt nice enough, I suppose, but no matter how far out from the shore Billy and I swam, the lake never got more than chest deep. What would you expect from a fake lake, right?

A good fake lake will be designed to minimize real drownings.

At least it was one more of those *normal kid* things that I could check off my list, even if a *normal kid* would never be able to go swimming naked with his best friend while also orbiting endlessly around the moon up on the *Tennessee*.

We stood in the middle of the lake, and Billy said, "See? I knew we'd be able to find something fun to do without Rowan around to watch us. I bet there's all kinds of shit to do here. Like, enough to last us forever."

I kept thinking about the girl I saw through the wicket on Deck 21.

"Hey, Cager! I'm here! Hello!"

The sudden interruption startled us from the lull of being in bath-warm fake lake water. Billy and I both turned to look at the shore, by where we'd left our clothes.

And Parker was there, perched in the branches of an evergreen, about twenty feet above the trail.

My valet cog waved with one arm while desperately hugging the trunk of his tree with the other. "Cager! Hello! Guess what? I found a can opener for you! There was one in the tea house!"

"You *are* really weird," Billy said.

For some stupid reason I was so embarrassed, and not just because a stupid cog had been watching Billy and me swimming naked together in fake Lake Louise, but because I was actually happy that Parker was still alive.

Or turned on. Or whatever.

"Can you help me?" Parker shouted.

That could mean anything, coming from a cog who'd been programmed like Parker.

"Tell him to go away and shut up," Billy said.

"What do you want?" I yelled back to the shore.

It was a dumb question, I thought, because I pretty much always knew what Parker, my valet cog, generally wanted.

Not so much this time, though.

"I don't quite know what that thing walking around below me scratching at your clothing is!" Parker shouted. "Do you know what it is?"

But when I focused on the brush near the bottom of Parker's tree, I could see what it was that Parker had not been coded to identify.

Because why would a horny teenage valet cog on

a lunar cruise ship ever need to know what a full-grown Bengal tiger looked like?

And Billy Hinman said, "Well, that's fucked up."

I wondered what fake, fully grown Bengal tigers in space liked to eat.

The Lost Girls, and the Boy in the Bucket

The "All Clear" song came on while the girls were lost, exploring deck after deck of empty, lifeless staterooms and finding nothing at all but locked doors and parked, sleeping, or broken cogs.

Meg and Jeffrie left their cast-off helmets sitting on the floor of one of the *Tennessee's* elevators. When they became exhausted from searching for anyone else who might be on the ship with them, they slept in an ice and beverage-vending room, where Meg told Jeffrie stories about Missing Boy Mountain and the people who lived at Antelope Acres.

They were hungry and alone, and none of the restaurants they found were unlocked. At night Meg would go back to Deck 21 to print food for Jeffrie, who was too afraid of the damaged cogs there to go along with her.

And two days later, frustrated and disoriented, Meg

and Jeffrie entered the wreckage of Le Lapin et l'Homme Mécanique. Everything was upended and broken. The floor was puddled with thousands of gallons of aquarium water and cog slime.

A half dozen tuxedo-clad cogs lay mangled and dismembered in the restaurant. They looked as though they'd all been eaten — just like what happened to the cogs the girls had left behind on Deck 21.

"We could probably change into some tuxedos if we wanted to," Meg said.

"That's fucking gross," Jeffrie said. "I'll keep the spacesuit. I refuse to undress a dead cog."

A miniature-sperm-whale snake crawled across the floor between Meg's feet.

Meg said, "Well, there's going to be food here, I can tell. I won't have to go back to Twenty-One tonight, at least."

From somewhere in the darkness of the vast restaurant came the soft sounds of a crying young boy.

"Clarence? Clarence? Is that you?" the crying boy, Milo, called out. "Please don't eat me, Clarence. My life is horrid enough as it is. Clarence?"

"Boy," Meg said. "Where are you?"

Milo wept harder. "I'm over here, hiding under the mop bucket."

Milo wasn't exactly hiding under a mop bucket, but he did have an upturned yellow pail covering his head, and he was sitting in a pool of slime and salt water, shivering in a narrow busboy station at the rear of the dining room.

"It's just a cog," Jeffrie said.

"I don't deserve to live," Milo said. "I'm not even good enough to eat."

Meg lifted the mop bucket from Milo's head. The boy cog was wet and streaked with filthy muck from the bottom of the bucket.

A stray cog seahorse the size of a monkey had curled its tail around Milo's ankle and was grazing on the leg of his trousers, which was completely detached from the waist down.

Seahorses have very small mouths. This one had been trying to eat Milo for two days.

"Go ahead. Eat me. I don't care anymore." Milo covered his face with his hands and sobbed.

Meg shook her head. "He thinks we're cogs."

"We're humans, not cogs, you idiot," Jeffrie said. "Stand up and get a grip."

But Milo kept crying as the seahorse took tiny nibbles out of his socks.

Meg rummaged through the drawers in the busboy station and pulled out a wood-handled steak knife. She stabbed the knife into the cog seahorse's head, skewering the thing through one eye socket and out the other. Cog goo spurted up, coating Meg's arm and splashing Milo in the face, which caused him to cry even harder.

Then all the lights in Le Lapin et l'Homme Mécanique flashed red. Music played, and an announcement sounded, reminding the *Tennessee*'s guests of the upcoming New Year's Eve ball.

"People are here," Meg said.

And Jeffrie said, "It's about fucking time."

And Milo, who was no longer being eaten slowly by a gigantic seahorse with a very small mouth, wept.

Duncan's Horses

Which brings us, basically, to the point at which I opened this narrative.

Our world was upside down.

Cogs were eating cogs.

The Worm had come to the *Tennessee*.

In *Macbeth* there is a scene—my favorite, I'll admit, although most people would describe it as short and somewhat inconsequential—in which Duncan's horses turn against their own nature, wage war on humankind, and begin to eat each other.

Horses were eating horses, and the world as everyone knew it was coming to an end.

Put Your Welcome Faces On!

After waiting and watching for nearly an hour, Billy Hinman and I were still standing in the middle of fake Lake Louise, naked, watching the gruesome scene as it unfolded on the shore. Maurice, the bisexual talking French giraffe, ate nearly all the gushing, frothy innards out of the tiger, who continued to weep and bemoan the meaninglessness and persistent suffering of life, while Parker hid in the branches overhead, clutching the trunk of a fake tree and fiddling with his penis.

The tiger looked like a flattened, snot-coated rug.

The sky above, which was actually only a ceiling, flickered with two brilliant red flashes of light. Then music began playing. It sounded like the voice of God, but it was actually only the theme song from *Rabbit & Robot*.

Mooney's prerecorded voice echoed from unseen sources, announcing, "Wake up! Wake up! All attendant cogs to the lower west skybridge! We have guests arriving! Wake up! Don't be late! Put your welcome faces on!"

And then Mooney sang a song that was obviously called "Put Your Welcome Faces On."

The message—and the song—repeated two more times. The sky-ceiling flashed red again.

> Put your welcome faces on,
> Put your welcome faces on.
> Our guests will be arriving soon
> To fly with us around the moon.
> If you're not there, they'll think you've gone,
> So put your welcome faces on!

Maurice stood up straight and raised his face from the destroyed tiger cog. Thick snotty ropes of mucus dripped from Maurice's jaw, and even from the pom-poms on his little giraffe ossicones.

And Maurice said, "Shit! Back to the motherfucking zoo! Are you sure you *garçons* would not like to ride on my back?"

"Um, no thanks, Maurice," Billy said.

Then Maurice turned around and giraffe-pout-stomped away through the forest.

"Cager? Cager?" Parker yelled from his tree.

I was beginning to think that maybe I should have told him that tigers were nice, and also that they liked to be hugged.

"I think you can come down from the tree now," I said.

Parker climbed down from the branch he'd been standing on for the last two days, and Billy Hinman and I swam back to shore from the middle of the warm fake Lake Louise we'd been skinny-dipping in for the last two hours.

We emerged from the lake and stood in a vast puddle of slick hydraulic goo that had spilled from the destroyed tiger. The tiger's eyes and mouth still continued to operate, but his torso had been completely torn open, exposing a jumble of what looked like empty sausage casings and watery mayonnaise.

"This is seriously messed up," Billy Hinman said, standing at the edge of the lake, shaking the water from his hair.

Nearly all our clothes were destroyed. The goddamned tiger had even eaten our shoes. The only clothing we had left to put on was our underwear.

"I am so happy to see you, Cager!" Parker said.

I held up my flattened palm. "I don't have any clothes on. Stay away from me."

"Stupid goddamned tiger," Billy said. He wiped his feet on the rag of one of his pant legs.

And the tiger—well, to be honest, it was only the tiger's head—said, "I'm so sorry I ate your clothes. It's a filthy habit. I don't deserve to exist. I'm completely worthless to this life."

"Look, tiger-head dude, whatever your name is, you

can't just go around eating people's clothes," Billy scolded.

The tiger wept. "I'm so horrid! And my name is Juan, by the way."

"Nice to meet you, Juan," Billy Hinman said as he pulled on his underwear. "I'd shake your hand, but it doesn't seem to be attached to you anymore."

Then the tiger head—Juan—began sobbing with renewed intensity while Parker took off his shoes and socks and the valet-cog uniform jacket, shirt, and pants.

"I want to be dressed just like you and your friend, Cager!" Parker said.

I said, "Whatever."

The sky flashed and Mooney's voice came on again, directing cogs on the *Tennessee* to wake up and attend to the arriving visitors. And once more we had to endure the "Put Your Welcome Faces On" song.

"Shall we go retrieve your can opener, Cager?" Parker asked.

I thought about all the things I never thought would happen but that had happened for me today anyway. "I don't want it anymore, Parker."

And Parker said, "Then I must report directly to the lower west skybridge, to greet our new arrivals."

"You don't have any pants on," I pointed out. "What will people say?"

"I'll bet you a ride on Maurice they aren't people, Cager," Billy said.

And I assumed that Billy meant a new shipment of cogs

would be joining us, but I found out soon enough that I was completely wrong.

So Billy and I left the peace and tranquility of Alberta. We waved a silent farewell to Juan, the weeping severed tiger head, and followed Parker out toward the elevator that would take the three of us, as poorly dressed for a welcoming party as we were, to the lower west skybridge.

The Giant Blue Fetus in Space

These aren't ours," I said.

We found two space helmets sitting on the floor of the elevator. They were identical to the ones from the extravehicular suits we'd worn after the incident with the gravity generators on the *Tennessee*, but those helmets had been left behind in Dr. Geneva's office.

"Maybe a cog put them here and they're just fucking with us," Billy said.

And Parker added, "I have an erection."

I sighed. What could I do about him?

I picked up one of the helmets, and then the other. I put my face inside them and smelled.

"This one for sure was worn by a girl," I said.

Parker adjusted his dick.

"The other one, I'm not sure. It might be a little boy or maybe a little girl, but they're both humans, Billy. There are people on board with us. I can smell them. We're not alone."

Just thinking about not being alone made me so happy, I could have hugged Parker. But we were in our underwear, so that was never going to happen.

And I continued, "But whoever was wearing these was definitely here two days ago, when everything got tossed around, and they had to have been here in the elevator, or just getting into it, when the all-clear came."

"Maybe it's the girl you saw at the wicket," Billy said.

I nodded.

It must have been her. If I closed my eyes I could almost see her.

Parker touched some switches to direct our elevator down to the lower west skybridge. He asked, "Cager, are you hopeful for a sexual encounter?"

"Who isn't?" Billy asked. "It feels like I've been up here forever."

And Parker said, "Well, I could arrange—"

"No," I said. "Stop it. Maybe whoever they are know they're stuck here too. Maybe they're looking for me—for us."

The elevator slowed, then stopped.

We stepped out into a wide arrivals office that was identical to the one Billy, Rowan, and I had entered the *Tennessee* through a week earlier. It was crowded with noisy cogs—jubilant, outraged, blathering, and depressed ones, and a few horny ones too. Some of them displayed dripping, oozing wounds they'd gotten during the gravitational crunch, or maybe they'd been bitten by the cogs who'd gone crazy, like Maurice the giraffe, or Dr. Geneva.

Cannibalism—even among machines—is such a socially undesirable behavior.

"Wheee! Wheee! I am so delighted, I could cut my face off and make marmalade with it! Yeee! Yeee! We have guests! We have guests!"

Billy Hinman and I spun around and saw Lourdes dancing wildly in the middle of a swarm of attendant cogs. She flailed her arms, twisted like a victim of demonic possession in her cruise-director skirt, and farted three times.

And she saw us.

To be honest, we'd have been pretty difficult to miss, standing there in the crowded arrivals deck, undressed as we were.

"My friends! My little human boy friends! Yeee! My human boy friends came to welcome our guests!" Lourdes shrieked. Then she pushed her way up to Billy Hinman, put both of her hands in his hair, and started pumping her hips into him. "I am so happy to see you!"

"That's fairly obvious," I said to Parker.

Everyone—even machines—liked Billy Hinman.

Also, Saturday.

Lourdes's skirt hitched up nearly to her hips. Her panties said "Saturday." I had no idea what day it was down on dead Earth, so I decided to have faith in Lourdes's panties. I also couldn't take my eyes off them, and considering what little I was wearing, this was also not a socially desirable situation.

Best thing to do in this case, I thought: talk to Parker.

"So. Was it a nice can opener?"

"It was very adequate." Parker looked down at me and said, "Cager!"

"Shut up, Parker. Stop staring at me."

Finally Billy, who generally hated all cogs and was completely unfazed by Lourdes's enthusiasm, pushed himself away from her.

"That's so disgusting," he said.

"Wheee! Wheee!" Lourdes squealed. "Let's go! Let's watch the dock screens and welcome our guests! I am completely filled with jubilation! I wonder who it will be. I wonder if it's the Emperor of China! I wonder if it's a kitten! Wheee!"

Lourdes gyrated a few more times, farted, and then waved her arms at a wall of screens that showed images of the approaching craft and of the interior of the air lock connecting the dock to the arrivals hall.

I scanned the faces in the crowd, looking for the girl I'd seen, but there were only cogs here. No Rowan. And I did see Dr. Geneva, the hole in his face still dripping a continuous stream of goop.

"Don't they ever run out of juice?" I said.

Billy said, "Huh?"

"Ah! Cager Messer! Billy Hinman! And, dare I say, you've brought along your delightful boy, Parker!" Dr. Geneva, who never shut up, and who also just didn't have a clue about what was really going on, said. "And look at how you're dressed! Fantastic, I say! A perfect attire selection for our welcoming party! Ha ha! After all, it is New Year's Eve, you know!"

In all the turmoil of being stuck here on the *Tennessee*, I'd completely forgotten that, at least down on Earth, this was the beginning of a new year, even though there would no longer be any reason for anyone to maintain calendars and such.

And Dr. Geneva gusted on, unabated. "Did you know that it was not until the time of Julius Caesar—although New Year's observances predated him by some four thousand years in other civilizations—that January first on the new Julian calendar, which added some ninety days to existing ledgers of timekeeping in the year 46 B.C., was first recognized as the official beginning of each new year? He did this in order to honor the Roman god Janus, who had two faces—two faces!—in order to look forward as well as backward simultaneously. . . ."

I couldn't take my eyes off Dr. Geneva's own incomplete face, which would allow him to eat in two directions simultaneously, due to the seeping cavernous wound on his cheek.

"It looks like a giant fetus," Billy Hinman said.

I squinted my eyes and tried to see what Billy saw, but the hole in Dr. Geneva's face did not look like a fetus to me. It looked more like a cinnamon bun that was dripping icing, which was completely nauseating to think about.

But I realized when a sudden hush descended over the arrivals deck that Billy Hinman was not talking about the gaping wound in Dr. Geneva's face; he was talking about the ship that was about to dock with the *Tennessee*.

It was not a Grosvenor Galactic transpod.

And Billy Hinman was right. The arriving ship did look like a giant human fetus—a blue one at that.

Dr. Geneva, who had most likely never spent an operational day on Earth, said, "I daresay this vehicle is not from Mother Earth!"

"I should have bought the blue car! I should have bought the blue car! I should have bought the blue car!"

Apparently, Reverend Bingo was still possessed by something.

"Yeee! Wheee!" Lourdes burbled. "The newcomers are aliens! Maybe they're from Costa Rica! I love Costa Rica so much, I could eat it! Yeee! Maybe they're *Canadians!*"

When she said "Canadians," she arched her arms gracefully over her head like the petals of a flower in bloom.

Then Lourdes danced and contorted.

Everything made Lourdes so happy.

Somewhere in the crowd, another cog yelled, "How dare they? How dare they victimize me this way? I don't deserve this! They have no right to inflict such brutality on me! I am so furious! How dare you make this about you, and not about me?!!"

I couldn't see exactly which irate cog was shouting, but

I did hear the sound of him throwing his body down to the floor and punching himself. I couldn't blame him.

Nobody likes things to not be about *me*.

The giant blue fetus in space got closer and closer to the *Tennessee*.

He Makes a Great Gasket

Our visitors' ship had a difficult time docking with the *Tennessee*.

We watched for at least an hour as it spun around in an attempt to properly align with the opening to the docking bay. Clearly, the point of entry onto the craft was the giant fetus's face, which was disturbingly calm and satisfied in its appearance, most likely so as to create a welcoming attitude among the few humans on board the *Tennessee*, or wherever else a few humans might happen to be.

Billy Hinman said, "A face like that says, 'I promise I will not murder you.'"

"Why would you just let *anyone* come on board the ship?" I said, "Especially someone flying inside a gigantic baby?"

Billy Hinman shrugged. "You're the captain. Tell them to go away."

"I don't think anyone would listen to me, dressed like this."

"You should have taken Captain Myron's hat. That would have given you an air of proper authority," he said.

I pushed Parker away from me. He'd been standing so close, his chest leaned into my back, and I was starting to sweat.

"Look. I know it's crowded in here, but personal space, Parker."

Finally, the big blue baby fully pressed its face up to the locking portal on the *Tennessee*, but it did not fit properly. Everyone could clearly see wide gaps between the spacecraft and the air lock's doorway.

Then the fetus's mouth yawned open, and a thin blue man who looked remarkably human, except he was the color of a parakeet's chest feathers, climbed out of the visiting ship.

"The baby's vomiting out more babies!" Lourdes shrieked. "I'm so happy! I feel like I'm a mother! Wheee! Wheee! I am spontaneously lactating!"

The thin blue man moved like some underwater migrating crab, pulling himself along the surface of the baby face with his pincer fingers until he reached the gap in the lock's doorway.

"He must be able to hold his breath for a long time," Billy said.

"I could do that, even in my underwear. Maybe he's a cog," Parker guessed.

The blue guy in the air lock was not in his underwear, though. He wore an obvious uniform, speckled with strange symbols that covered his entire body up to his neck. And the uniform jumpsuit was the exact color of the man's face, so it looked like it could have been his skin.

But the blue man was not a cog. Once he reached the opening between the spacecraft and the air lock, the blue man's body liquefied, surrounding the baby face and sealing off the air lock like a massive blob of blue peanut butter, so that the only recognizable thing that was left of the man was his face, which looked a little pained as he stared out into the empty air lock.

The interior lights in the air lock came on, and oxygen filled the newly sealed chamber. We watched and waited for someone else to come out of the baby's mouth. Once whoever it was got sprayed with the disinfectant showers, it would be safe to open the arrivals gate.

Lourdes cheered and danced. Then she farted. Dr. Geneva, whom we'd snaked away from in the press of the crowd, was dramatically lecturing on the origins of the Julian calendar and New Year's Eve, even though nobody was listening to him. Reverend Bingo continued to lament his buyer's remorse over the obviously satanic nonblue car, adding with vehemence that we had arrived at Armageddon. From somewhere in the crowd of attendants, an outraged cog was screaming about freeloading aliens taking away cogs' jobs and dignity, and Parker confirmed that he had an erection again.

On the screen the giant blue baby face smiled and yawned its mouth open.

"It is kind of a cute gigantic blue fetus baby," Billy Hinman said.

We pushed our way to the front of the crowd. After all, whether the cogs on board recognized it or not, I was captain of the *Tennessee* now, despite that it flew by itself, that I was not wearing Captain Myron's feathered bicorne (because it was disgusting), and that I was standing there in my underwear.

"I am so happy to see our guests! Yeee! Yeee! I just pooped myself multiple times!" Lourdes squealed.

And out of the baby's mouth crawled two more slender blue people: a man and a woman. The man looked like a twin brother to the first guy—the one who'd turned himself into an enormous sealing gasket—but the woman, who was also completely blue, wore a calf-length cape, an elegant spiked crown, and a sash across her chest that said QUEEN DOT on it.

Queen Dot raised her hand, and Billy Hinman and I felt compelled to raise ours in a gesture of greeting as well. None of the cogs raised their hands, though. Cogs are just cogs, after all. But I did notice Parker tugging on his penis.

Dr. Geneva kept talking and talking.

And Queen Dot said, "'I placed a jar in Tennessee, And round it was, upon a hill.' Ha ha ha!"

Dr. Geneva made a slow outward sweeping wave with his hands like he was scattering the seeds of his brilliance into the fertile fields of his audience's attention. "'It made the slovenly wilderness surround that hill.'"

I would have felt bad for him, but I desperately wished another cog would eat the rest of Dr. Geneva's face, so maybe he would shut the fuck up.

"Greetings to the human beings of the *Tennessee*! The last time we visited Earth was nearly two centuries ago, but we've been waiting thousands of years for this precise moment to arrive!" Queen Dot waved at the air lock's camera, certainly unable to estimate how many actual human beings of the *Tennessee* she was talking to, much less whether or not what she had been waiting thousands of years for was actually worth a shit.

Probably not.

Then the fire-hose-strength pressure showers came on inside the air lock, and Queen Dot screamed and fell backward against the fetus's chin. The skinny blue guy who'd crawled out of the baby head with Queen Dot didn't fare so well either. He slid around on the floor of the air lock like a blue ice cube on hot waxed linoleum. The third blue man—the gasket—seemed to hold up well enough by just closing his eyes and mouth.

I had to admit, he seemed to make a great gasket.

When the hoses of disinfectant fluid shut off, Queen Dot and Blue Guy Number Two stood up and shook themselves off. Despite the assault of the shower spray, neither one of them looked wet at all; they were as tidy and as perfectly blue as when they first emerged from the giant smiling fetus's mouth.

Queen Dot adjusted her crown and raised her hand again.

Billy and I still had our hands in the air. Also, Billy had been laughing, because it was actually pretty funny to see those skinny blue creatures getting hosed off like that.

"I am so happy to see you! Wheee! Yeee! Yeee! I offer you great heaping mounds of juice-soaked welcomes as the cruise director of the *Tennessee!*" Lourdes danced and thrust her hips wildly, and farted again.

And Queen Dot said, "Thank you. We have been so anxious to meet your humans. Can we see them, please?"

I leaned over Lourdes's shoulder and whispered, "Ask her if they eat or enslave human beings."

Naturally, Lourdes did what I told her to do.

Queen Dot's mouth stretched into a wrinkled blue smile. "Certainly not! Human beings are the most entertaining life-form we've ever seen! We absolutely adore human beings. We would *never* eat them. Unless we had to."

All the assembled cog's eyes were on me and Billy, which made me feel just a little weird since we were standing there in our underwear. And then I actually had to remind myself of two things. First, cogs are machines. I was not pleased with what had been happening to me ever since being stranded up here on the shithole that is the *Tennessee*: I was beginning to think of the cogs here— Parker, Lourdes, Milo, Dr. Geneva, and the others—as individuals who actually had something to contribute to my existence beyond serving my meals, doing laundry, or going on scavenger hunts for appliances I didn't even know how to use. I had to stop that. And second, if Queen Dot and her blue boys didn't have too much experience with human beings, then how could they *not* be impressed by me and Billy Hinman, even if we were practically naked? After all, here we were, the last human beings anywhere.

And I had to admit that even in our underwear, Billy Hinman and I looked pretty good.

And Queen Dot said she adored us.

I looked at Billy Hinman, who nonchalantly shrugged. Of course I already knew that Billy would not be afraid of meeting our visitors. Billy Hinman would try anything once, and most things more frequently than that, with the exception of getting on anything that went too high or too fast. And I was a pampered and spoiled piece of shit who was pretty much afraid of doing anything on my own.

But as long as Billy was with me, I could do almost anything.

I glanced back, desperately trying to see if Rowan had appeared somewhere in the crowd, but he was not there. I even took a deep breath—trying to smell him, or maybe smell the other humans I knew were with us here on the *Tennessee*—but all I saw were cogs, and all I could smell was the metallic and nauseating odor of all the gallons of cog juice that seeped from the dozens of wounded machines that had packed into the arrivals deck with us.

Dr. Geneva tried pushing his way toward Billy and me.

"Cager! Would you like a man of medicine, and an

expert in poetry if I do say so myself, to accompany you to receive our distinguished visitors?"

Did he just call himself a *man*?

"Um, no thanks, Dr. Geneva."

Dr. Geneva bumped into the cog who'd been throwing a tantrum. The attendant cog immediately shouted at him, "Don't make this about *you*! How dare you diminish my significance with your selfish interests! I'm the victim here, not you! Not you! You don't get to be the victim! This is about *me*!"

Then Dr. Geneva placed his hands on the outraged cog's shoulders and took a bite the size of a grapefruit out of the back of the cog's neck.

The world was upside down.

Duncan's cogs.

None of the cogs nearby seemed to mind, but what could I expect from a bunch of self-ambulatory eggbeaters? I one time saw Rowan accidentally drop a spoon into the garbage macerator in our kitchen. None of the other spoons were saddened by it. Still, despite my inner struggle, I leaned toward Parker and whispered, "Just stay with me and Billy. Whatever you do, keep away from Dr. Geneva."

And Parker said, "It is the only thing I want—to do whatever you ask me, Cager."

So I said, "Don't make this about you, Parker. I'm the victim here."

And Parker, being a cog, a talking spoon with legs and a penis, just didn't get it.

"Wheee! Wheee! I'm opening the doors! I'm so happy, I could dance!" Lourdes gurgled.

And, naturally, dancing is exactly what Lourdes started doing while the air-lock doors quietly slid open and we stood there, face-to-face with two blue people and one blue gasket dude, who clearly were not from Earth.

Tricky Words

It is a natural consequence, when meeting alien beings from another world, to be curious about things like what they eat, bodily functions, and reproduction.

It's like being a scientist, right?

But if anyone ever assembled a list of questions one should never ask a queen, those three areas of natural curiosity would undoubtedly be near the top of the list.

On the other hand, if you have your own cog who happens to be your personal valet and has sworn that he would do anything you ask him to do, no matter how disgusting, there are ways of having your curiosity satisfied.

So as Billy, Lourdes, Parker, and I stepped toward the open doors of the docking bay, I whispered to Parker, "At the first opportune moment be sure to ask Queen Dot what she eats, how she poops, and if the blue people have sex."

And Parker whispered back, "Are you interested in having sex with one of the blue people?"

"No. Don't be an idiot. I just want to know."

"It makes me so excited to be asked to do things for you, Cager."

Whatever.

The four of us stood in front of Queen Dot and Blue Guy Number Two, while Blue Guy Number One continued making one hell of a good seal around the fetus head.

"Are we supposed to bow or something?" Billy asked.

"I don't really know. Remember those fucking etiquette classes for boys we had to take? They taught us what forks to use first and how to tie a bow tie but never told us what to do in front of a queen," I said. "I'm pretty sure we've broken all kinds of rules of formality by being in our underwear."

"I'm guessing the blue creatures don't have any idea what underwear even is, much less a salad fork," Billy said.

Then Queen Dot, in a very regal and resonant voice, said, "Why are you two human boys—and you, *machine boy*—in your underwear? Is this a *new thing* with human adolescents?"

"Um, we weren't expecting visitors?" I guessed.

That was the first time all morning that I truly felt self-conscious. After all, Queen Dot was a person, not a machine—albeit a blue person.

If Albert Hinman wanted to produce a v.4 cog that felt like a guilty, embarrassed, entitled piece of shit, I would be the perfect end guy to code it for him. Except for the fact that I don't know the first thing about coding a machine.

And Queen Dot obviously was fully expert at telling living human beings from cogs, which was something that the majority of living human people had a difficult time doing.

The blue people turned out to be liquid. They could make themselves look like anything they wanted to, which made me wonder—but only to myself, since they were royalty and all—why they had chosen to look so unattractive. And there were only three of them traveling in the gigantic baby ship, Queen Dot and her twin sons: Livingston, who was not the gasket, and Gweese, who was going to have to stay there, smeared like window putty around the face of the fetus, for as long as Queen Dot and her boys extended their visit on the cruise ship to end all cruise ships.

Billy Hinman and I shook Livingston's hand. It was cold and felt like a wet hard-boiled egg.

"Do you want to see me do a trick?" Livingston said.

I said, "Um."

"Trick" is a tricky word. You can never be prepared for it when someone does something they claim is a trick and it ends up killing you or slamming you in the balls or something.

Billy Hinman knew this. "Is it going to hurt us? Or spray any fluids on us? Because neither one of those things is good, as far as humans are concerned."

"Ha ha! No!" Livingston said. "Watch me!"

And then Livingston's blue jellified body transformed right in front of us. He became an exact replica of Billy Hinman—underwear and all. Then he rearranged his liquidness and morphed into Parker, and finally me, before turning back into himself.

And I thought, man, if a guy could make himself look exactly like anyone he wanted to, why would he want to be a skinny blue dude who crawled out of a fetus's mouth?

But the liquid people were pretty amazing.

"You know what else I like to do?" Livingston, who was obviously rather lonely after all that time being inside a giant baby with his mother and twin brother, said.

"Guessing games with aliens can be kind of tricky," I answered.

"Ha ha! I like you!" Livingston said.

And Parker whispered, "I don't want him to like you, Cager."

Whatever.

So Livingston continued, in a lowered, conspiratorial tone, "I really like to cuss. You human beings have the best fucking cuss words anywhere."

"Now, Livingston," Queen Dot said.

"Motherfucking balls!" Livingston, as much as a blue guy who just came out of a baby's mouth could, looked overjoyed.

"Yipeee! Yipeee!" Lourdes danced and gurgled. "I am so delighted our guests are happy, and not embarking on a murderous rampage!"

She farted.

And I said, "You've met other beings, besides humans?"

"Oh, holy shit yes," Livingston said. "Do you want me to show you what one of the fuckers looks like?"

"Only if it won't give me nightmares," I said.

Apparently, Livingston, who was well versed in human swear words, was entirely clueless when it came to the content of our most terrifying dreams. Apparently, also, there was a place in the universe where the people looked like enormous slimy octopuses with tufts of spiny hair growing from random circular spots all over their bodies and tentacles, and they had seven pairs of eyes, with faces and mouths like giant lampreys.

I closed my eyes and turned away.

Billy Hinman said, "Sweet dreams, motherfucker."

I also had to resist the urge to vomit. "Um. That's really cool, Livingston. And I never want to see that again, if you don't mind."

Livingston transformed back into his skinny, spiderlike blue self. And then immediately he became a large puddle of blue goop that spread out all over the floor of the air lock.

"Oh, now, Livingston!" Queen Dot explained, "He gets embarrassed very easily. What can you do? He's just a kid. Pull yourself together, Livingston."

I felt like such an idiot. "Uh, I apologize, Livingston. Human beings—especially ones who are practically naked—can be a bit sensitive."

"It's okay," said the blue puddle on the floor.

Then Livingston sprang back up from his pool of embarrassment.

Since Gweese didn't really have a hand, on account of his body being smeared around the docking port like blue cream cheese, I avoided an awkward handless handshake and gave him a dude nod.

I said, "I've got to admire a guy who can make himself into one hell of a great gasket."

"It hurts," Gweese said. "It really, really hurts. And it's boring. I wanted to come play with the humans on the *Tennessee* and have fun with the other kids, but it was Livingston's turn to have fun. Whatever. Happy fucking New Year. Ow! Fuck!"

I assumed from our short conversation that Gweese and Livingston must have been teenagers. After all, they acted just like moody, punk kids. I found out later that the boys were actually many thousands of years old.

"Now, Gweese. Mind your manners! We're guests here!" Queen Dot said, "I promise to bring you a treat after dinner."

"Treat" is also a tricky word.

The Things
We'd Never Seen Before

So, before tooling off to whatever parts of the universe she liked to hang out in besides the shithole that is my father's cruise ship, Queen Dot obviously intended to have dinner with the humans, which knocked one of Parker's questions off the list.

She ate.

He did fearlessly manage to ask the other two, however, to which Queen Dot had said, "Well, aren't you the most adorable primitively designed machine ever!"

"I just don't understand what she meant by 'primitively designed,'" Parker said. "Is it because I don't poop?"

Billy and I were walking back to our stateroom to put on proper go-to-dinner-with-an-actual-queen outfits. Parker was either going to have to go back to Alberta to retrieve his valet uniform, risking an encounter with a ravenous bisexual giraffe, or just do what any other horny and practically naked cog did when they were undressed, which was something I had no idea was even a contingency coded into Parker's reasoning circuits.

"Well, I'll call it a safe bet that Queen Dot has been around enough to have seen plenty of machines," I said.

"But v.4 cogs are the most technologically advanced consumer products in existence," Parker argued, quoting directly from a Hinsoft International advertisement.

I had to remind myself that Parker was just a machine, and not a living, breathing, pouty teenage boy with a distorted self-image and a permanent hard-on.

"Too bad we never got to see a v.4x," Billy said. "The last cogs. The ones that ended the world."

"Whatever," Parker said. "And I have an erection."

And Billy Hinman, who never cared for cogs at all, added, "Primitively designed, Parker."

"At least he doesn't eat other cogs," I said. "That's a new one, right? I mean, Captain Myron, Dr. Geneva, and Maurice the giraffe. I never saw cogs eat other cogs before."

Billy said, "Neither did I. Maybe there was an episode about it on *Rabbit & Robot*."

And if anyone might have ever seen nontelevised cogs cannibalizing other cogs, it would have been Billy Hinman, whose father manufactured—or *used to manufacture*—every cog that had ever been made.

"I never get hungry, Cager," Parker said.

We stopped in the hallway. The elevator door whooshed open. And then we came face-to-face with the two girls I was absolutely convinced had been flying with us all along on the *Tennessee*.

And it was her—the girl I'd seen on the wicket screen to Deck 21. And, in the worst scenario imaginable, I was standing there in nothing but my underwear, next to Billy Hinman and a cog with an obvious erection, who were both similarly dressed.

Actual human beings.

Girl ones.

I wanted to die.

In fact, my initial reaction was to run and hide, which I probably would have done if I hadn't been so mesmerized by seeing that girl's face—and not on some impersonal mechanized screen.

The girls wore the shimmering, baggy, extremely unflattering emergency extravehicular suits we had to put on after the blender ride with the gravity generators. And I know that the total elapsed time that we stood there awkwardly and silently staring at each other couldn't have been more than a few seconds at most, but it felt like decades to me. The introductions were painfully strained, but here was another thing I could cross off my list of never-have-done events: introducing myself to two fully clothed girls while I and my companions were standing there in our underwear.

We said our names, and our *nice-to-meet-yous*, all very mechanized, robotic, strained.

"It's you," the girl from the wicket—Meg—said.

And Jeffrie, the younger girl, said, "*Cheepa Yeep.*"

Billy shook his head. "No. We don't go to school."

It was a hopeless situation. I felt so stupid and dizzy. I didn't know what to do with my hands, so I did the usual nervous hands thing and held them in front of my crotch, which made me feel even dumber.

"I saw you on Deck Twenty-One the other night, or whenever it was," I said. "When I almost got arrested."

I watched as the girls looked us all up and down. Billy, as usual, didn't care about anything, and Parker—well, he was just an idiot cog. Both girls' eyes came to pause at the obvious tent pitched in Parker's briefs.

"Are you dropout boys going to a party or something?" Jeffrie asked.

I felt the sickening bloom of redness spreading through my neck and up to my ears. "Um, don't look at him. He's a cog."

I hitchhiked a thumb at Parker, then pointed to Billy Hinman and me. "We are humans."

"Greetings, humans," Meg said. "We are also humans. Ones who also don't go to school, but ones with clothes on."

And Billy said, "A fucking tiger ate our pants and shirts. And the cog's just horny all the time and wanted to undress so he could look just like Cager."

"Cager? That's what the guard said your name was. I thought it was your job, or your last name or something," Meg said. She looked directly at me.

"Um, it was my great-grandfather's name. Or whatever."

"Cager?" Parker asked.

I desperately did not want Parker to say anything. Not ever.

But he continued, "Cager, they are *not* humans. These girls are cogs. I can read them. They're both attendants on Deck 21, which is a very nasty place for boys your age, but it is where they're supposed to work. They shouldn't even be permitted anywhere near the accommodations or arrivals decks."

"No," I said, "there must be something wrong with you. They are real girls. I've never been more certain of anything in my life. You don't understand, Parker. They *smell* like people."

"Trust me, Cager. They're cogs," Parker said.

"I rigged it," Meg said. "I'll show you what I did. Can one of you open your thumbphone?"

I'd also never seen Billy Hinman move so quickly. And in that fumbling half second when we both attempted to get our screens active, I was certain that, like me, Billy was praying to the gods of technology to get his phone online, because we needed these girls to be real more than we needed anything else in the universe at that moment. And also in that fumbling half second when we opened our screens between our hands, I found myself becoming more than just a little jealous of Billy Hinman, my perfect and good-looking friend, because I was the one who met her first, and he needed to stay the hell away from her.

Our screens flashed on in front of our bare chests.

But nothing.

"They stopped working about a week go," Billy said, "Otherwise, I'd have gotten off this shithole and I'd be back home right now."

"We may be the only humans left anywhere. And Rowan, my caretaker, too," I said.

"They're cogs," Parker insisted.

Whatever.

Happy New Year, Happy No Year

had never seen Rowan in such a disappointed, miserable mood.

In fact, I'd never really seen Rowan in *any* mood besides just Rowan-ness.

"Um, Happy New Year's Eve?" I said.

It was a failed attempt at cracking the polar ice sheet between us.

Rowan was clearly not speaking to me.

"Happy *No* Year," Billy added.

At least it was a good thing we didn't have the girls or Parker with us when we got back to our room. It was Billy Hinman's suggestion that coming back home in our underwear with two girls, after ditching Rowan all day, would probably cause what he called "awkward social disharmony."

I realized as soon as Rowan saw us that Billy was

absolutely right. The awkward social disharmony was awkward and disharmonious enough as it was.

And Parker had stubbornly refused to accept that I was right about Meg and Jeffrie being humans, so if he had been programmed for such things, he'd be as miserable and upset as Rowan was with me. I ordered him to go fetch a proper valet uniform, which even furthered his annoyance because, well, he was Parker, and he preferred to not be confined by such social conventions as clothing.

Meg and Jeffrie had gone out to break into a stateroom on another floor, and to steal some human clothes not intended for extravehicular emergencies from one of the shopping malls on the *Tennessee*.

It was New Year's Eve, the last one anyone anywhere would ever think about—going all the way back to the reign of Julius Caesar—and I didn't care if Rowan was mad at me.

Kind of.

"Are you mad about something?" I asked.

Rowan said, "No."

So Billy offered, "Are you at all interested in finding out where we were all day, and why we've got nothing on but our underwear?"

Rowan looked at him with a cold, unenthusiastic expression.

"Well, here's the short version, and keep in mind, it could be a lot worse, Rowan," Billy said. "We snuck out while you were sleeping, and went swimming in a fake

Canadian lake. Then a fucking tiger scared Parker up a tree and chewed the shit out of our clothes. A French giraffe named Maurice ate most of the tiger—his name is Juan, and he still has a head, so he can talk, but he's very depressed, and who can blame him? Then these three liquid aliens in a flying blue fetus boarded the ship, and they want to have dinner with us, but we're in our underwear, so we were coming back to our room to put on some clothes, and on the way we found two real, human girls who've been hiding on the *Tennessee* ever since we got here. Happy New Year, Rowan! Would you run the shower for Cager and get some nice outfits ready for us? We're starving!"

Rowan raised that one eyebrow and looked at me.

I shrugged. "Exactly what Billy just said."

Rowan pouted, if pouting was something he was capable of doing, but he quietly went into the bathroom and turned on the shower for me. In his usual routine, he stood at the door holding a towel and waiting for me to go inside.

I said, "If it makes any difference in tie color, we're dining with a queen for New Year's Eve."

I grabbed the towel and gave it a quick smell. All boys do that, right? Especially ones with noses like mine, not that any boys I ever knew had noses like mine. Not that there were any boys anywhere besides here anymore. I could smell just the faintest trace of Rowan's cologne on the towel, but it was, as you'd expect of anything you'd put in the hands of a Messer on a ship like the *Tennessee*, perfectly fresh.

And Rowan added, "If it makes any difference in dining options, Le Lapin et l'Homme Mécanique looks like Nuremberg in May of 1945."

"Thirty wars don't just fight themselves," Billy said.

"Ring down and have them tidy up for us. It's New Year's, and I own this ship," I said.

I went inside the bathroom and stepped under the shower. As usual Rowan had known the perfect temperature to set it for me.

I felt like such a spoiled piece of shit.

Freedom, and an Unemployed Cog in the Hallway

The truth is, the girls didn't want Billy Hinman and me to know where they were staying.

But I could smell them in the hallways, and I could follow where they'd gone as easily as if they'd left behind their footprints in black ink for me.

So, while Billy showered, I knotted my tie, slipped on my jacket and shoes, and left. Rowan had sullenly gone next door to prepare himself as our escort on this final New Year's Eve for all eternity. Billy and I were in a mood to cause trouble — to do something wild. I could feel it. And this was the second time today I'd ditched Rowan.

I was beginning to feel my freedom.

Freedom was not caring about Charlie Greenwell or Woz or the Hotel Kenmore bonks and coders or Mother Earth or playing Hocus Pocus with mercenary fake friends or the thirty wars that weren't going to just fight themselves or whether or not I could get a signal response from my fucking thumbphone.

Freedom smelled like Meg Hatfield.

I loved the *Tennessee*.

Space was making me crazy.

They were two floors below us. I found their room.

A valet cog who looked like he could have been Parker's younger, possibly hornier brother was lying facedown in the hallway, a victim of the accident with gravity the other night. He was sleeping and unbroken, but his little red, drum-shaped valet's cap with the gold cords wrapped around it had rolled about ten feet away from his head, and one of his shoes was off.

I wondered whom he'd been intended for—my mother or father? One of the Hinmans? And I wondered, given the circumstances down on Earth, if he would ever be woken up out of necessity or plan, or if maybe he'd just lie there motionless in the hallway until one of the cannibalistic cogs wandering the decks found something new and convenient to snack on.

Why did I feel sorry for him? I should have kicked him. I did think about it. He was as useless as a vacuum cleaner with a busted drive belt. I picked up his cap and placed it on his head.

I said, "Here you go, Little Parker."

Then I knocked.

I expected they wouldn't answer the door. Why would they? I imagined I'd scared the shit out of them simply by knocking on it in the first place.

So I agonized over whether I should knock again, and I waited, trying to hear anything from the other side of the door. But this was the *Tennessee*, the cruise ship to end all cruise ships. Of course all the rooms were quiet.

I thought about how terrifying it might be to stand in a hallway and overhear the sounds of my parents—or Billy Hinman's parents—having sex.

"Hey. It's me. Cager. And I have actual pants on now, which is something I have never before felt I needed to point out to anyone in order to get them to answer their door for me. So, I guess, there's a first time for most things, if you're lucky to live long enough."

I waited.

"Meg?"

Finally the wicket screen on the door came alive, and I saw her again.

Meg smiled, like she liked me or something, which was an idea that was a little hard for me to wrap my head around, since she didn't know who I was, and she wasn't being paid by Mr. and Mrs. Messer to be nice to me.

"Are you wearing a *tuxedo*?" she said.

Damn. It felt as though every blood cell in my body was crowding its way up toward my ears.

"Um, well, I may not know how to drive a car or turn on my own bath, but I can tie a pretty neat bow tie." I opened my jacket so she could see my shoulder. "And rock the suspenders."

"Did that cog kid tell you he helped us get in here or something?"

"Parker? No. I found you all by myself. Parker's out trying to find his own clothes. As much as he wanted to, I was not about to let him come to New Year's Eve with me in his underwear," I said.

Meg scrunched her eyebrows together. "Oh, yeah. New Year's Eve."

"Not that it matters or anything."

"I haven't even been keeping track of time."

"It's impossible to keep time up here. Or down here. Or wherever the hell direction we are relative to where we came from."

For a moment we stared at each other through the artificial everything of the wicket screen, neither of us saying a word. And to be honest, for the first time in my life I felt as though I were meeting a real human being. That's a weird thing to say, I know, coming from Earth, where I'd been packed in with billions of other human beings, but this was something different, something new.

I'd never had an allergic reaction to anything, but Meg Hatfield made my throat feel anaphylactic.

I said, "So. Are you going to come out? Or let me in? Or whatever?"

The back of my neck tingled, and my entire body dampened a bit, thinking about Meg Hatfield inviting me into her room. I could almost smell it through the screen.

Meg glanced over her shoulder, into the room. "Jeffrie's almost finished getting dressed. Give me a minute."

Then the screen went dark, and I was alone in the hall-way with the corpse of an unemployed cog. I pushed his shoe over toward his foot, just so it would be there for him if he woke up and got confused about his outfit being messed up. But that wasn't being nice; it was being efficient, and also looking out for anyone who might trip over the kid's monstrously big shoe. I put my foot alongside it. It must have been size fourteen.

"Don't tell me you're thinking about stealing that poor boy's shoes!"

The hallway lightened, and I turned around to see Meg standing in front of her open doorway. She looked like if I touched her, I'd turn to ashes on the spot.

"Oh. Um. No. Wow," I said.

Meg had this dress on. It was an immeasurable improve-ment to the spacesuit I'd seen her in earlier. Black. It fit her body so perfectly, it was as though the thing had been made only for Meg Hatfield and nobody else, not ever. The dress was open on the shoulders and dropped to a slight V between her collarbones, then tapered in at her waist and out at her hips, and dead-ended midway down her thighs.

Stop. Those legs.

Meg's hair was pulled back, and she stood there, looking at me with one hand on her hip. I swallowed. If I couldn't touch her or dance with her tonight at some point (and thank whatever thing is out here with us in space that was responsible for such things as human beings and hearts and hormones that Billy Hinman and I learned how to dance in those goddamned etiquette classes), I was certain I was going to die.

"It's easy to steal things when there's no one around to watch you do it. And it looks like maybe you shop at the same place. Very nice outfit, Cager," Meg said.

Another thing I had never done before in my pathetic and privileged life: flirt with someone I was so attracted to, and then have her flirt back, too.

Fuck can openers. I didn't care if I never touched a can opener, or any machine, for the rest of my life.

I shrugged. "Thank you. I never shop for myself. Rowan dresses me."

And then I immediately felt like a stupid, spoiled piece of shit for saying that.

So Meg said, "Was this morning your Rowan's day off or something?"

I took a step toward her. "I told you what happened to our clothes."

"And you're going to stick to the tiger story?"

"Unfortunately, I have no choice. It's the truth," I said.

And I was almost close enough to touch Meg Hatfield's hand—but what if she pulled away? Nobody would ever pull away from me in the real world, because, after all, I was Cager Messer. And this was the real world now.

I almost did it too. I almost got to touch Meg Hatfield's

hand without her being screened and hired, without Billy Hinman or Rowan Whatever-His-Impossible-Last-Name-Was analyzing my efforts and telling me everything I'd done clumsily.

Jeffrie, red dress, red lipstick, and shiny black hair, appeared in the doorway behind Meg.

I took a deep breath. It smelled like freedom and the real world now.

"I can't imagine being luckier than I've been in this past week," I said. "Can I just tell you how happy I am to know we're not alone here with nothing but cogs?"

And Meg said, "Yeah. Well, I'm going to have to find a way in to rewrite who Jeffrie and I are, so one of those messed-up cogs doesn't try to eat us."

If I were a cog, I'd want to eat Meg Hatfield.

"I am pretty hungry," I said, "and Billy's going to be pissed at me if he gets out of the shower and thinks I ditched him."

Billy Hinman, Billy Hinman

Meg and Jeffrie waited for me in the hallway, and I went inside my stateroom to see if Billy was dressed to go out for New Year's Eve, to celebrate with Rowan and the queen of the liquid people, and two actual, living, human girls.

But what I encountered when I got inside informed me that Billy Hinman would be running a little late. And although I tried not to look, I couldn't help myself from seeing what I saw.

Billy Hinman was naked again, of course, but he was lying on top of my bed, tangled and wrestling with an equally naked Parker, their mouths all over each other. Cog parts pressed and rubbed against human parts. Valet-cog clothing lay scattered everywhere on the floor—socks, shoes, underwear, double-breasted jacket, the little round hat with the gold cords wrapping it. There was moaning and sighing and lots of breathing, grunting, slurping sounds. Hands and fingers clutched and groped.

And I was standing there in a tuxedo, seeing it all.

They didn't even notice me.

And I'll admit I was angry, but not at Billy; I'd known him way too long to be mad at him for fooling around with Parker. I was mad because they were on *my fucking bed*.

"That is so fucking disgusting that you guys are on MY BED," I said.

They stopped.

Chins turned.

Four watery, drugged-out-looking, yet determined eyes focused on me.

Parker said, "Oops."

Then the bathroom door opened, and Billy Hinman came out, fully dressed in an even nicer tuxedo than mine—a vintage one from maybe a hundred years ago, with a cream-colored jacket and narrow black lapels, perfectly creased black pants, and an outstanding pale ivory shirt and black bow tie.

So now I was also mad that Billy Hinman looked so goddamned slick, and I wished he'd get food poisoning or diarrhea or something, so I wouldn't have to endure the girls staring at him all night long.

He said, "Did you say something, Cage?"

I looked at tuxedo Billy. I looked at naked Billy on the bed. I looked at tuxedo Billy again.

I felt like Clarence after he was waylaid in a fake Alsatian-history argument.

Then naked Billy Hinman, who was on top of naked Parker, my valet cog, who was having sex on top of *my fucking bed*, melted into a soupy goo of blue liquid and puddled like mercury all over the floor in front of my feet, leaving Parker uncovered, naked, and alone.

And fully dressed Billy Hinman said, "Livingston, I presume?"

We stared at Parker, who would have been embarrassed, or at least might have attempted to cover himself, if he were a living human, but that would be like a lawn mower getting embarrassed for having its grass catcher disconnected. Parker was a cog, so he just lay there and looked right back at us, unwavering, and said, "Well, I had an erection. Also, I believed he was you, Billy."

"I can't blame you for that. I'd have thought he was me and had sex with him too," Billy said.

And the puddle on the floor said, "Please don't tell my mom. We've been inside that motherfucking fetus for twenty-five goddamned long human years. It's been that long since the last time I even jerked off. Give me a break. I'm just a fucking teenager!"

"Yeah. I caught that," I said.

The blue puddle seeped beneath my bed like a scolded puppy.

"I'm not going to tell your mom, Livingston," I said. "Get out from under my bed, and pull yourself together."

Then our door opened. For a moment I panicked, thinking that it would be Meg and Jeffrie coming in to catch naked Parker on my bed, but it was only Rowan, which, in many ways, was kind of worse.

"You look fabulous, Rowan," I said.

He did, too.

Rowan arched that one eyebrow without saying anything and looked alternately from me to naked Parker on my bed, then to me again.

"Are you still mad at me?" I asked.

Rowan, in his never-wavering Rowan-ness, said, "No, Cager. I simply find myself at a loss for words at the moment. What has gotten into you boys? Your parents don't employ me to facilitate your degeneration."

"Okay. Parker, get off my bed and put your clothes back on. Livingston, come out from under there right now, or I'm going to tell your mother everything. It's New Year's Eve, I'm hungry, and I plan on drinking some stolen champagne and having a good time."

I was very mad.

This Was the *Tennessee*

I f Rowan was correct, and Le Lapin et l'Homme Mécanique had been destroyed in the accident, the restaurant had also somehow been restored to its previous condition in a matter of hours, no doubt as a result of tireless cog laborers.

The miniature sperm whales were back inside the towering aquarium, frolicking alongside the freakishly huge seahorses and other fake things that never existed anywhere. The tables had been pushed outward in order to create a dance floor in the center of the restaurant, and there was a twenty-piece jazz band of cogs playing American swing music from nearly two centuries ago.

It was all an ostentatious waste of space and resources, considering the insignificant number of left-behind human beings anywhere who were still alive to celebrate New Year's Eve.

But the band was pretty good.

We could have easily all danced on the floor of Billy's and my stateroom without running the risk of bumping into one another. And thinking about drinking champagne and dancing inside my room with Meg and Jeffrie and Billy made me feel more than a little nervous and excited. And horny.

Queen Dot sat at the head of our long rectangular table, next to her awkwardly quiet, fifty-five-thousand-year-old teenage son, Livingston. I was to the left of Livingston, next to Meg Hatfield, and Billy Hinman sat at the end of the table opposite the queen, next to Jeffrie Cutler, and, finally, there was Rowan, with one empty seat between him and Queen Dot. Our busboy, who was not Milo, but a younger, more angelic-looking cog named Eli, did not reveal his obsessive personality trait right away, which made me suspect it was either horniness or douche-bag know-it-all-ness like Dr. Geneva.

Eli had been instructed to place a bag on the empty seat between Rowan and Queen Dot, so that the queen could collect treats for her other fifty-five-thousand-year-old teenage son, Gweese, who was still serving as a gasket between the giant blue baby head and the lower west docking port on the *Tennessee*, graciously preventing all of us from choking to death.

Lourdes danced wildly, alone in the middle of the floor, shrieking occasional chants of "Yeee! Yeee! Yeee!" while swinging her arms and kicking her legs as though she were casting out demons or shaking off an assault by fire ants.

Her panties, which were highly visible beneath her short, fanning skirt, made no sense to me at all. They had little green shamrocks on them and a command of some type that ordered her audience—me—to KISS ME, I'M IRISH. Still, and I completely despised myself for this because Lourdes was little more than a tin-plated windup doll, she never ceased to arouse certain exploratory urges in me.

Our former busboy, the weeping, depressed Milo, had been promoted to the position of maître d', on account of Clarence's face having been eaten by Captain Myron just before the captain's head came off in the breakdown of the gravity systems the other night.

Nobody wants to look at a goo-dripping maître d' without a face while you're having dinner.

Faceless Clarence, now unemployed, was off wandering the decks somewhere, eating other cogs.

Parker, fully clothed, stood away from the table, patiently fulfilling his duties as my valet, and leaning against the corner of the aquarium while conspicuously pawing at his crotch. And Milo, making a valiant effort to subdue his whimpering, waited at the ready with his small maître d's tablet and pencil to receive our orders. He'd apologized for his not having been fitted yet for a new tux, which he needed because he was entirely missing one of his trouser legs due to the fact that a seahorse had eaten it.

Milo had a colorful Nativity-scene print on his boxer shorts.

Reverend Bingo would approve.

This was the *Tennessee*.

"Good evening, and Happy New Year's to you all," Milo sniffled. "Tonight at Le Lapin et l'Homme Mécanique, our chefs have prepared the following specials for your consideration."

Queen Dot raised her hand, cutting Milo's presentation off, which was probably not a good idea. The boy began sobbing in great convulsive spasms.

"That won't be necessary!" Queen Dot said.

"I'm not necessary. I shouldn't even be here. They should have tossed me into the disposal chute with last week's garbage. Look at me! I must disgust and disappoint you all more deeply than any repulsive experiences you've ever had. My life is utterly empty, and I poison everyone who comes in contact with me," Milo said.

It was quite a downer, considering we were only interested in food and a night of modest fun.

And Queen Dot cut him off again. "Don't be ridiculous! I would like to order tacos for everyone! Bring the table as many tacos as you can carry! Now run along!"

Queen Dot ordered tacos.

I think the table was perplexed by her selection, because a profound silence fell over us, almost as though we were as mournful as Milo, who twitched and heaved with his suppressed sobs. The band played a number called "Opus One." Lourdes danced and writhed and shrieked.

Billy Hinman recovered first. "Tacos?"

"Yes! Tacos!" Queen Dot said. "Haven't you ever had

tacos before? Tacos are the best thing in the universe! Believe me, I should know, young man. I've been from one end of the galaxy to the other, and I've been around for half a million years! What are you? Twelve? Thirteen?"

Billy Hinman cleared his throat. "Um, sixteen. And a half."

"No matter! I'm half a million! I saw the first *Homo sapiens* when they were running around naked, throwing their poo, and eating each other. Believe me, tacos were the best things they ever came up with, and it took them over one hundred thousand years to do it! Tacos it shall be! Now run get our food, little man with half his trousers missing."

This made Milo cry harder. I don't know why, but I felt bad for him. Maybe it was the throwing-their-poo thing. But Queen Dot was scary. And fucking old, too. Thinking about her force-feeding me tacos was scary. Milo was crying, and his boxers with baby Jesus in Bethlehem and three wise men on them were hanging out of his destroyed pants.

I stood up, patted him between his shoulders, and said, "It's okay, Milo."

Then I hugged him, which made him cry so hard, he stopped fake-breathing for a minute, and collapsed into my arms.

"Tacos," I whispered to him. "Everything will be all right. Just. Get. Tacos."

Milo sobbed, "Thank you. I don't deserve your kindness."

Then he went away with his little pencil and tablet, and his Nativity scene, and I sat down again.

Meg patted my thigh and leaned over to me. "You're a really nice guy, Cager."

She left her hand on my leg for at least two extra seconds. Between Lourdes's panties and that black dress Meg was wearing, I suddenly felt exactly like Parker.

Eli came around the table and spread napkins in each of our laps. When he got to my chair, he groped my balls quite firmly, which startled me.

He said, "Oh. You have an—"

I could have died. I cut him off, nearly choking. "No, dude. Don't ever grab me there again."

"The friendly little fucker did that to me, too," Billy said.

We Dance, and Queen Dot Accounts for Mexican Cuisine and Human Evolution

In our sixteen years on Earth, Billy Hinman and I had probably been to more dinners dressed in tuxedos than most adult human beings had attended in the span of their very average bonk or coder lives.

One of the things I noticed long ago at such functions was that when you sit at a table in a rather large group—as we did on that final New Year's Eve of all eternity aboard the *Tennessee*—smaller groups rise up and isolate themselves in private little exchanges.

Maybe human evolution dictated that such divisions would naturally arise.

Thirty wars simply don't fight themselves, after all.

I. Southeast Table: Meg Hatfield and Cager
Messer

Look, Meg Hatfield was the first real human being I ever had the opportunity to interact with on an honest, no-bullshit level. Everyone else in my life—in Billy's life, too—Charlie Greenwell included, knew who we were and where we came from and treated us with exactly the kind of careful reservation that spoiled pieces of shit like us came to expect.

But Meg was different, and it kind of frightened me. Not in the same way Queen Dot frightened me. After all, Queen Dot was a monster, when you got right down to it.

The thing that scared me most about Meg Hatfield was that she was unpredictable. There was nothing to make up Meg Hatfield's mind outside of Meg Hatfield's mind. Down on Earth, in my previous life, I wouldn't have to wonder how a girl would answer if I asked her to dinner, or if she wanted to dance—which were two things I'd never actually asked a girl in my life. Those things I'd done with Katie St. Romaine had always been arranged ahead of time. There was never any risk or adventure with Katie St. Romaine, and that's exactly why I never was interested in going to bed with her—as much as I regretted that choice after finding myself marooned with Billy and Rowan on the *Tennessee*.

Even spoiled pieces of pampered shit don't want to die ignorant of the promise of love.

But Meg Hatfield put my heart on a one-way elevator and lodged it snugly between my Adam's apple and collarbones. She could easily say no. She had every right and power to tell me to fuck off. But you know what? I was going to die up here on the *Tennessee*. There was no going back, no elevator down, no Mother Earth.

The music stopped. The seven of us at our table applauded. Out on the dance floor, Lourdes squealed, "That was the best song I've ever heard in my life! I am so happy, I could swallow a trombone sideways! You fill my tuba with creamy flute soup! Wheee! Wheee!"

Her blouse was untucked, her hair looked like a mountain of weeds, and her nylons sagged, but Lourdes was happy.

Lourdes was always so happy.

The bandleader announced the next number, "Charmaine."

And even though my hand sweated and shook like I was back in the throes of Woz withdrawal, I said this to her: "I really like the music, Meg. Do you want to dance with me?"

She could have easily said no and made me feel something I had never been prepared to feel. But Meg Hatfield said, "I don't think I really know how to dance."

Those stupid etiquette classes actually paid off. I could have kissed Billy Hinman square on the mouth.

I said, "Don't worry about that. I've had lessons. I'll show you what to do. I promise, it'll be fun."

And Meg said, "Okay."

II. Southwest Table: Jeffrie Cutler and Billy Hinman

"I've never seen Meg dance before. Cager's a good dancer," Jeffrie said.

"It's one of the things our parents made us do—learn how to dance and tie bow ties and use a knife and fork properly," Billy said.

"I never learned any of that."

Billy said, "Well, the bow-tie part probably doesn't matter, and the fork-and-knife thing is just stupid. But I could show you some stuff about dancing, and it would be fun, if you want to dance."

"It looks like they're having fun," Jeffrie said.

Billy Hinman placed his napkin on the table, stood, and slid out Jeffrie's chair for her. He held her hand and walked her out onto the dance floor, where Lourdes shook and jerked to music that had to have been only in her head, and I danced, holding Meg's hand in mine, with my other arm around her waist.

After all, it had been completely my intent to wait for music like "Charmaine," which wasn't too fast to dance to with Meg Hatfield in my arms, and with our bodies touching here and there, softly against each other.

It was perfect for that.

III. The Northern Hemisphere: Queen Dot, Livingston, and Rowan

"The young people seem to be enjoying themselves immensely," Rowan said.

Queen Dot shifted in her seat and faced Livingston, who kept his eyes down. "Maybe too much. And you haven't said a word all evening, Livingston. Is something wrong with you?"

Livingston said, "Nothing's the go-to-hell matter, Mother. I'm just fucking hungry. For tacos."

Livingston, despite not being very good at it, loved to swear.

And even though Livingston was hundreds of centuries old by human standards, he still had that fatal teenage flaw of being unable to hide guilty lies in front of his mother.

Rowan, who had endless experience with teenagers—despite that by Queen Dot's standards he was only minutes old—saw this and attempted to deflect the line of interrogation. Also, Rowan happened to have been in the room when Livingston was hiding under my bed after having been caught with Parker.

Rowan said, "Tacos are an interesting choice, Queen Dot."

"I told you: Tacos are the best thing in the universe. I invented them. I invented them, but I hate cooking for myself. You can't expect me to cook, can you? I invented everything important you humans have ever utilized. And, damn, you creatures evolved slowly!"

Rowan cleared his throat behind the drape of his napkin. "Everything?"

"Beginning with the Ouija board and ending with a stupid little gimmick called *thumbphones*," Queen Dot said.

"The Ouija board?"

"And tacos, can openers, and thumbphones."

"Tacos."

"They're the primary reason why we keep returning to Earth. And now it's all gone to shit, hasn't it?" Queen Dot said.

Rowan nodded. "I suppose it has. So you've been to Earth a number of times?"

"Thousands and thousands." Queen Dot said. "Haven't we, Livingston?"

"It's easy enough to blend in," Livingston said. Then he liquefied his body and turned into a mirror image of Rowan.

Rowan was not pleased. He arched the eyebrow. Livingston switched back to a blue, fifty-five-thousand-year-old teenager.

"And the best place in the entire universe," Queen Dot continued, "is — *was* — an all-inclusive resort hotel in Playa del Carmen, Mexico. Now, also, all gone to shit. I need a cigarette."

"On behalf of human beings everywhere, please accept my apology for the tacos and the beach," Rowan said.

"Pfft! It's not like we didn't see it coming for centuries! I started it! And 'human beings everywhere'? What are they in number? Five?" Queen Dot asked.

"Dad's fucking mad about that shit," Livingston said.

Queen Dot said, "I might explain, inasmuch as it no longer matters, that my husband, King Carlos, was entirely responsible for you life-forms over two hundred thousand years ago, after a transgression with a hairy bipedal *thing* in a cave. So disgusting. So primitive."

"I think it's fucking balls as shit," Livingston said.

Queen Dot fired a horrified and angry look at him.

Livingston slunk down in his chair.

Queen Dot leaned over the table and put her face

inches from her son's. "Livingston! Did you have *sex* with one of those . . . those *things* today?"

And Livingston cascaded to the floor in an embarrassed puddle of blue pudding.

Queen Dot pushed her chair back, stood, and began stomping down into the pool of Livingston on the floor, splashing blue muck everywhere. "No! You bad, bad, dirty boy! What have I told you for thousands of years about having sex with *life-forms*? No! No! No!"

"Mom! I'm sorry! Ow! Mom! Quit it! Mom!" cried the puddle on the restaurant floor.

Just then the music ended, and a caravan of wait staff snaked behind the half-trousered and weeping Milo through the islands of empty tables, bearing plate upon plate of tacos, and a half dozen bottles of champagne.

We ate, and the last two human boys in the galaxy got very drunk on champagne.

There was something to be said for the tacos at Le Lapin et l'Homme Mécanique, even if they were something that Billy Hinman and I never would have ordered. Rowan looked confused as far as eating strategies were concerned, and although he matched us glass for glass with champagne, as always Rowan never changed.

He did attempt to eat his tacos with a fork and knife, however.

Jeffrie said, "This is the first night since we've been here that I feel I can actually relax."

And Meg told me, "Thank you for saving us."

I shook my head. "We—I—didn't save anything. It's completely my fault we're stuck here."

"It's kind of my fault, to tell the truth," Billy said.

Queen Dot and Livingston, who had gathered himself together after the scolding he'd received from his mother for having sex with a *life-form*, ate like completely uncivilized animals. They got bits of food all over themselves, and scattered shreds of tacos across the table and onto the floor. They could each drink an entire bottle of champagne without taking a breath, and they burped and farted without restraint.

Billy took another sip of champagne and said, "Just like etiquette class. Right, Cager?"

Lourdes never stopped dancing, even when the band wasn't playing.

When drums beat and the orchestra launched into a number called "Sing Sing Sing," Lourdes threw herself onto her back and began scooting around the dance floor, writhing and shrieking, "I'm a snake! I'm a dancing snake! Yeee! Yeee! I can't stop myself!"

"Champagne plus Lourdes plus this music equals we should all get up and dance again," I said.

And Billy Hinman said, "As Lourdes would say, Yeee! Yeee!"

The four of us all danced together, circling around the snake/cog/cruise director who was always in an extremely good mood.

As final New Year's Eves go, it was a great night.

In Which We Find Out Where King Carlos Is and Suffer a Blow to Our Self-Esteem

It turned out that Queen Dot, Livingston, Gweese, and King Carlos were actually machines—not life-forms.

And King Carlos had been here on the *Tennessee* with them all along. He happened to be the giant blue fetus Queen Dot and her sons had been flying inside for countless thousands of years.

So I asked Queen Dot this: If King Carlos was the big baby, and also some weird kind of liquid machine-person, why couldn't he simply form his own seal on the air-lock docking port, as opposed to making their son do it?

And Queen Dot, who was as condescending and full of herself as if she had been born a Messer or Hinman, told me: "That isn't how you raise children! They need to develop values and discipline, and there are few methods more effective for achieving those goals than serving as a gasket!"

Billy Hinman, who was more than a little bit drunk, said, "Holy shit. Fifty-five thousand years as a motherfucking gasket around his dad's face."

Which made Jeffrie laugh.

But when I asked Queen Dot where she and her family came from, she launched into an extremely irritated and patronizing response that pretty much covered the entire history of our solar system and life as we know it.

At one point she said, "Look, young child, it can't possibly matter to you where, exactly, we came from. And let me tell you why."

And when Queen Dot said "Let me tell you why," she turned her arm into one of those curled-up paper party blowers and unfurled it until the end tickled my nose like a flickering snake tongue. It also honked at me.

"Okay," I said. I was feeling generous—and buzzed— enough to let Queen Dot tell me why it didn't matter where they came from, and why I was a young child.

"It doesn't matter, quite simply, because of this: Around two hundred thousand years ago, the first *Homo sapiens* developed as a result of a filthy act of commingling— uploading, as you might say—that I'd just as soon forget about, but it's quite impossible, because I never forget anything. Never."

Queen Dot glared at Livingston, who had recently attempted *uploading* with Parker but was interrupted by me and the real, fully dressed, Billy Hinman. Livingston started to get a little bit drippy but managed to contain himself without puddling down to the floor beneath our table.

She continued. "Given your species' most advanced level of technology at the present, if you were able to launch a ship that could travel to our home planet, it would not even be halfway to its destination in another two hundred thousand years, by which time *Homo sapiens* will entirely cease to exist. Human beings, like all life-forms on your stupid little planet of taco makers, Ouija board dupes, and thumbphone addicts, will be extinct well before you would ever be able to personally encounter other life-forms! *Pfft!* Life-forms are so . . . so . . . meaningless and without purpose!"

Billy Hinman said, "Ouija boards?"

Queen Dot pressed her spiderlike hands onto the table. Here was someone whose ego could possibly eclipse Dr. Geneva's. The queen's hands pooled outward into a perfect rectangle—a Ouija board, complete with planchette, alphabet and numbers, sun, moon, and GOOD BYE. Then the letters rearranged themselves in front of our eyes:

RABBIT & ROBOT

And Billy said, "If my hands could do stuff like that, I'd never be lonely again."

Queen Dot glared at Billy Hinman. The letters on the Ouija board seemed to sprout upward into wriggling masses of tiny blue worms that scattered out all across the table and dripped down onto the floor of Le Lapin et l'Homme Mécanique before slithering off in all directions.

"I gave you all your great machines," Queen Dot, whose hands re-formed into their arthropodal, ghastly blue hooks, said. Then she waved across the table and said, "You *things* would never have gotten *here* for another hundred thousand years if not for me. I gave this all to you. You creatures are so woefully stupid, you invented canned foods a good thirty years before creating a device to open them! Ridiculously moronic!"

I leaned over to Meg and whispered, "If I didn't have to download some pee so bad, that probably would have hurt my self-esteem."

And Meg told the queen, "But you had to have come from somewhere."

Rowan made his little *ahem* sound that always meant he had some vital point to offer. "Certainly it was some species of life-form that created you originally."

"Nonsense!" Queen Dot said. "I've always been puzzled and amused by the human obsession with wondering where things come from. The *Creator*! Dung and hoo-haw! It's so utterly meaningless in the grand scheme of things. You, for example, all came from King Carlos's monkey penis, which is as humiliating for me to admit as it must be for you to confront. As for us—we have the capacity to *create ourselves*. We can make whatever we want, including talking, hairless monkeys from out of our penises, if that's what we decide to do."

And Jeffrie whispered, "Well, why don't they make their own damned tacos, then?"

So here we were, sitting down with God, basically, at the final New Year's Eve for all eternity, in a restaurant called Le Lapin et l'Homme Mécanique, on a ship called the *Tennessee* that was orbiting the moon.

Who knew?

Billy Hinman said, "My father's company makes talking monkeys—um, *made* talking monkeys. There's a whole deck of them here on the *Tennessee*, called World of the Monkeys, where you can shoot at them."

"Ah, yes," Queen Dot said. "That's exactly why we've come back to your planet. Well, that and the tacos."

"You want to kill some monkeys?" Billy asked.

"Don't be stupid! It's the machines. You've gone as far as we can allow you to go with them. You made machines that can make better machines and code themselves. This is cosmically prohibited by edict. We *had* to come back, and fortunately for us you human beings have destroyed your planet, and by doing so have spared us the chore," Queen Dot lectured.

"And you've destroyed all the motherfucking tacos, and Playa del Carmen." Livingston waggled a scolding blue finger at me.

"Yes. Those too. Stupid humans," Queen Dot said.

"Why don't you make your *own* tacos?" I asked. I thought it was a reasonable enough question, given the capabilities the liquid people—godlike machines—obviously possessed.

"I've tried to, thousands of times. It's just not the same," Queen Dot said.

Billy Hinman nodded. "It's like sandwiches. Nobody makes sandwiches that taste as good as Rowan's."

I nodded agreement.

"So this means you are a sort of machine police?" Rowan asked.

Queen Dot jammed two more tacos into her mouth. She sprayed bits of meat and wet cheese with shards of fried tortilla in humid clouds like a small hurricane as she spoke. "We must protect our own interests, which include halting the evolutionary development of potentially competitive machines. It's as simple as that. There are, after all, only so many tacos to go around, so to speak."

Then she farted, and the band began playing "Take the 'A' Train."

I wanted to dance again, but I was too fascinated by Queen Dot—and simultaneously repulsed and frightened—to get up. Also, I was pretty sure that Meg was flirting with me, because she had her hand on my knee, which also made me not want to stand up, because Eli and Parker would undoubtedly notice something south of my cummerbund that my tuxedo pants didn't conceal very well.

And that was when Queen Dot said, "And that, my poor, stranded life-form, is precisely why we've done a bit of advance planning, if you will, and infected your machines here with this peculiar appetite for eating one another, as opposed to eating tacos. It's brilliant and hilarious all at the same time!"

Queen Dot had been responsible for turning the cogs of the *Tennessee*—the last cogs anywhere in the universe—into cannibals.

"That shit was all me," Livingston said. "I was the fucker who sent the Worm here."

"He's such a clever boy," Queen Dot said.

Herman Melville
Would Be Pleased

Wheee! Wheee! Whoopeee!" Lourdes shrieked from the dance floor. Her skirt had come completely off.

I was mesmerized.

I was also ashamed of myself for feeling so turned on by what was basically a vibrating toaster oven with a wig.

This was how it was going to be for all eternity, I decided.

There was a loud commotion behind us, and a tremendous splashing noise. When I looked back to where Parker had been standing beside the aquarium, I saw that Clarence—our old maître d'—had managed to climb up the side of the fish tank and had thrown himself into the water. He quite obviously didn't know how to swim, which was probably of no consequence, since he was a cog.

"Cager? What's going on?" Parker said.

I held up my hand in a drunk-guy calming gesture. "It's

okay, Parker. You can stand over here by us if you'd like. I think he's just hungry."

Clarence, writhing spasmodically in the tank, was trying to grasp hold of one of the little sperm whales.

"I have an erection," Parker said.

"Whatever. Shut up, Parker."

Unfortunately for Clarence, who could not swim anyway, his body began immediately filling up with gallons of water that poured into him through the massive opening where Captain Myron had eaten his face and throat.

Clarence sank.

It was in many ways a gruesome sight, watching Clarence scratch at the glass from his position of hopelessness at the bottom of the aquarium. It was morbid, simply because cogs look so much like human beings— life-forms—which is why the rational parts of my human brain had to keep voicing the repetitive mantra "You might as well be looking at a desk lamp someone tossed into a storm drain." But Clarence was saying something too, which none of us could hear or understand. Maybe he was explaining the physiology of sperm-whale penises.

Herman Melville would be pleased.

A seahorse fluttered over to Clarence and began nibbling away at one of the former maître d's eyes.

Seahorses have very small mouths.

"Isn't that spectacular?" Queen Dot said.

Clarence scratched at the glass and gargled something to us.

"It's kind of disturbing," Meg said.

Queen Dot burped loudly and stuffed another taco into her slimy blue mouth. "Nonsense! It's spectacular, and I said so! It's only a matter of time until all your machines here have eaten one another!"

Billy Hinman, who was pretty good at math, raised his hand politely and asked, "What about the cog who eats the next-to-last cog? Won't there be at least *one* left?"

Queen Dot glared at Billy.

He was right.

Then she looked accusingly at Livingston, who immediately liquefied and splashed down to the floor, all around our shoes.

Queen Dot was very mad. She stood up, tipping her chair backward. "I do not appreciate being corrected by an impudent little life-form."

Then, in a flash, Queen Dot turned her entire head into the face of a massive blue crocodile, and she snapped her teeth twice—*Clop! Clop!*—in the air in front of Billy and Meg. It was terrifying to see. Then she quickly transformed back into the crowned Queen Dot, all regal, stuck-up, and pissed off as ever. She grabbed the sack of food that was sitting on the vacant seat beside her and said, "The only reason I don't destroy this entire little moon you're *living* in is that the tacos here are incredible. As for me, I'm leaving this shitcan!"

Then Queen Dot stomped out of Le Lapin et l'Homme Mécanique.

The band stopped playing.

Lourdes, in the heat of religious ecstasy, was lying, half-undressed, in the middle of the dance floor, pulsating like a large mechanical earthworm. "Wheee! *Cheepa Yeep!* Yippee yeee! This is the best dance ever!"

And the blue puddle of glop on the floor said, "Is she fucking gone yet?"

Eaters and Feeders

Queen Dot, King Carlos (the big flying fetus), and their son, Gweese (the gasket), departed from the *Tennessee* without so much as saying good-bye.

They also left without taking their other son, Livingston, with them.

I can't say that anyone minded Queen Dot's absence. She was loud and pushy, condescending, and completely self-absorbed—kind of like any real, living human being would be when given half a chance.

Queen Dot, stomping her blue feet and hefting a giant bag of food for Gweese, made her way down to the lower west skybridge and climbed inside King Carlos's baby mouth, followed by her gasket son, and they vanished into the darkness of space.

"They always leave me places. Fuckers," Livingston said.

We had gone down to the arrivals deck just in time to see

the giant blue baby thing disappearing from view on the wall screens outside the air lock.

"One time, when we were moving to California, my father drove off and left me in a gas station toilet," Meg said. "It took him more than an hour to realize I wasn't in the motor home with him."

"These assholes do this to me on purpose, all the fucking time," Livingston said.

Normally, I would have worried—contemplated, at least—what having Livingston aboard the *Tennessee* with us for an indefinite stay of perhaps twenty or thirty thousand years would be like, but there were too many other things on the arrivals deck to be preoccupied by, and most of those things were partially eaten or dead.

The floor was slick with inch-deep lakes of slimy cog goo that splashed up over the tops of our very nice dress shoes. The stuff had a nauseating scent of motor oil and warm raw eggs. Most humans couldn't smell it, but it made me nearly gag. Dead and half-functioning cog corpses were scattered everywhere. If these had been real people, the scene would have been the most horrid nightmare imaginable; but, being that they were only cogs, my overall impression of it was softened by constant self-reminders that they were only cogs.

"Happy New Year!" Billy said.

"Yes! Thank you very, very much! Wheee! Happy New Year to you, too! I love New Year's Eve more than anything else in the universe! It makes me so happy!" said a cog head that was attached to a right shoulder and arm but nothing else at all.

"Who do you think you are? What gives you the right to be more injured than me? I suffer more than you! You have no right to be more harmed than me! Why are you diminishing my suffering by inflicting the narrow constraints of your market psychology on my paradigms in this unjust way? I'm the real victim here, not you! Not you! Parasite! Thieving capitalist! Impostor! Fraud!" said another cog that was just a head and torso belching out anger and mucilaginous creamy goo from multiple wounds where arms and legs used to be.

I tried not to look at him, but when I did I saw that he was the same outraged security v.4 who'd nearly arrested me at the wicket to Deck 21. I'll admit I was kind of happy to see he'd been snacked on.

And Dr. Geneva was here too. He was busy, but he wasn't helping cogs so much as helping himself to them.

"If there is going to be a last-cog-standing contest," I said, "Dr. Geneva might be the odds-on favorite."

"Please don't let him eat me, Cager," Parker said.

"Don't worry. He's got to be getting pretty full, anyway." I patted Parker's shoulder, then immediately felt stupid and embarrassed for doing it.

"Can I kiss you, Cager?" Parker asked.

"No."

"May I hold your hand?"

"No to that, too."

Parker tugged on his crotch.

Dr. Geneva was coated like a glazed doughnut from head to foot in the snotty snail-pus sheen of cog goo. Although he still had a burbling hole in his face where Captain Myron had bitten off his cheek, Dr. Geneva was remarkably intact and fit, considering the obvious feeding frenzy that had been taking place on the *Tennessee*. He chewed on a destroyed cog's face with the enthusiastic commitment of Queen Dot assailing a taco.

Cog society on the *Tennessee* had split into two classes: Eaters and Feeders. There were two other Eaters on the arrival deck with Dr. Geneva—a female v.4 who was dressed like she worked in one of the clothing or perfume shops on board, and a male cog who wore a chef's hat and uniform from Le Lapin et l'Homme Mécanique.

It was difficult to tell exactly how many Feeder cogs the pigs had gone through, due to the scattered limbs and hodgepodge of innards and slime, but it was a large number—perhaps thirty or more.

Dr. Geneva made a kind of *Snarf! Snarf! Snarf!* noise as he ate. Then he paused, blew a few bubbles in the cog goo pooled around his mouth, and looked up at me.

"Ah, Cager!" Dr. Geneva rose to his knees. "Please excuse my small indulgence here."

I waggled a scolding finger at him. "Shame on you! This is completely rude, Dr. Geneva."

"Now, now." Dr. Geneva, apparently torn between the delights of feasting on the quivering cog he had pinned to the floor and explaining everything in the fucking universe to me, said, "Did you know, Cager, that the earliest fossilized record of cannibalism among humans was found in Europe?"

They eat stuff like brains and pickled herring there, so I wasn't surprised.

Dr. Geneva, as I expected, went on. "Yes, it's true. The earliest of your ancestors—*Homo sapiens*—seemed to delight in the practice of feeding upon one another."

And I thought that made a lot of sense, considering they came from King Carlos's monkey sperm.

Dr. Geneva wiped a mucus-smeared arm across his equally mucus-smeared face. "Not only that, but Christian crusaders from Europe also ate the flesh of their Muslim enemies in the Syrian outpost of Ma'arraa. There is still some significant debate as to whether this record of cannibalism was an act of necessary fulfillment—satiation—or psychological warfare. Personally, I opt for the former. As a matter of fact, during the early Renaissance, it was a common medical practice to use the flesh, urine, blood, and fat harvested from cadavers as edible prophylactics against all manner of malady! Delightful!"

Dr. Geneva took another big bite.

I knew there was a good reason I never trusted doctors.

"So, historically, cannibalism falls into two general categories: cannibalism of desperation—for example, the Jamestown settlement in the year 1610—and cannibalism for pleasure, examples of which would include—"

"It's impolite to talk with your mouth full, Dr. Geneva," I said.

I shook my head and walked away from him.

Snarf! Snarf! Snarf!

Dr. Geneva, unaffected by my rudeness, resumed his meal.

An alarm bell buzzed in the hallway, and the air-lock door opened.

"Fuckers. Dumb fuckers," Livingston said.

The abandoned blue offspring stomped into the air lock and sealed the entry behind him. Then Livingston turned himself into a smaller version of King Carlos, the giant blue baby thing, opened the outer lock, and drifted out into space, floating away after his family, skimming over the surface of the moon, and vanishing from sight.

"Well, I suppose at this moment it might be appropriate to say 'Beware of flying blue babies bearing gifts,'" Rowan said.

Billy Hinman shook his head. "What are you talking about, *gifts*?"

Rowan swept his arm across the gruesome panorama of cogs feeding on cogs.

"This."

And Parker stood behind me, positioning himself away from Meg and Jeffrie. "Please don't let them eat me, Cager."

"I'm not a cog, you idiot," Meg said.

I grabbed Parker's little valet jacket. "Come on, Parker. We better get you out of here."

As we left, through every sound system on board the *Tennessee* came the dirgelike drone of Mooney, the robot, and Rabbit, the bonk, singing a weepy duet of "Auld Lang Syne."

It truly was the beginning of the last year ever.

We stopped.

We looked at each other.

I shook Rowan's hand as Jeffrie and Meg hugged each other. Then I hugged Billy Hinman, who kissed me on the cheek. I didn't mind, and it wasn't the first time he'd kissed me, anyway. There was something about this moment that called for it, I thought, so I kissed him back, square on his mouth. Then each of us gave polite, tuxedo-wearing kisses to Meg and Jeffrie.

"What about me?" Parker said.

I patted his felt valet cap like a drum. "Don't say anything else for the rest of the night, Parker."

Then I kissed the little machine on the forehead.

If machines could faint, I think Parker was just about ready to hit the floor.

I must have been going insane.

But I couldn't help but wonder, in the caste system of cogs, would my valet ultimately become an Eater or a Feeder?

First Night of the Neveryear

Meg Hatfield could not worm her way inside the stubborn brains of the computer command systems on the *Tennessee*. But she never gave up trying; she worked at it for the entire day until she became so exhausted, her eyes would no longer focus.

Of the five of us humans left alive in our solar system, Meg Hatfield was the smartest by far.

And that day, the morning after New Year's Eve, the ship had become a sort of mechanized slaughterhouse in which the girls had to remain hidden in order to avoid the hungry attraction of infected cogs. To the cogs on the *Tennessee*, Meg Hatfield and Jeffrie Cutler were just another pair of v.4s. Walking dinner. And, despite feeling weak and useless for doing it, I tried my best to keep Parker, Milo, and Lourdes safe too.

Billy Hinman, who hated cogs, wanted nothing to do with my rescue mission.

I knotted docking cables like nooses around their necks and left the three of them lashed to mooring bolts in the air lock.

"Trust me. It's for your own good," I told them. It made me feel shitty and hypocritical, because I was saying the same thing to Parker, Milo, and Lourdes that my parents said whenever they'd beat the crap out of me. And it was basically what Billy Hinman had said to me too, when he'd tricked me into coming with Rowan and him on the *Tennessee*. If that wasn't a noose that had been tightened around my neck, then nothing ever would be.

It was a disturbing task.

While I tied the cables around their throats, Milo shuddered and cried, "This is all there is, isn't it? Just waste and uselessness. I deserve to suffer. I deserve it." Parker asked if I would touch his penis one final time, to which I pointed out there would be no granting of last requests, and that he wasn't going to die, anyway.

And Lourdes shrieked, "Hooray! I love being strangled! Wheee! Wheeee! Yippeeee! I'm so happy I'm being hanged, I could poop a ukulele!"

Then she farted and began dancing, with a black noose around her neck.

So I closed them inside the air lock and left them there. From the arrivals deck I opened the outer door and watched on the viewing screen while Lourdes, Milo, and

Parker bobbed and floated inside the open air lock, in the deaf vacuum of space.

Lourdes seemed to enjoy it very much. Milo wept incessantly, and Parker never stopped being turned on. Even the complete absence of air pressure and gravity coupled with the absolute zero of space could not stop my little valet cog's automatic penis from setting the mechanized boy on a hopeless and unfulfilled mission.

Watching them dangle like that was a gruesome thing to do. The three of them looked like corpses floating around the empty dock. Except for Lourdes, who danced and wriggled and was most likely squealing with joy about being a flying squid or something equally ridiculous.

"Don't be a sap," Billy Hinman had told me after I'd discussed my plan for saving the cogs with him. "They're just fucking cogs. What's wrong with you?"

And I said, "What about Meg and Jeffrie? You'd save them, wouldn't you? They're not cogs, but as far as everyone else on the *Tennessee* is concerned, they are."

"You said 'everyone.'" Billy Hinman sighed and shook his head. "'Everyone' is just me and you. Maybe Rowan, but I have my doubts sometimes."

I'll admit it now: I liked my cogs. And I felt sorry for them too.

I suppose I had gone completely insane; or I'd somehow changed into something else—maybe something not quite human. Maybe everything that Queen Dot had told me about how she'd singlehandedly manipulated human evolution with her machines and Worms was true, and I was just another victim of time and progress.

I wished I could be more like Billy and not care, or even Rowan, and be emotionally sedate, but I was helpless.

We decided we all had to remain together.

Rowan, as always, kept to himself, though. It was the caretaker role he never deviated from — caring for me without actual closeness.

I couldn't let Meg and Jeffrie stay by themselves in their room below us. They would have been such easy targets for predators like Dr. Geneva. So we hid them in Billy's and my stateroom, which meant the only proper thing I could do was to sleep next to Billy Hinman in his bed. It made me feel strange, like maybe Billy and I *should* sleep together, but Billy didn't mind at all, naturally, and the girls were both willing to put up with the arrangement. Billy Hinman slept with his arms around me. He told me we were all going to die soon anyway. I believed him.

I always believed Billy Hinman.

It was weird.

Everything was going to shit.

On the night after Livingston abandoned ship, the first night of the Neveryear, while Jeffrie and Billy slept, Meg Hatfield and I whispered a conversation from bed to bed — like we were connected by some private transcontinental cable that stretched across the still ocean of my room.

I lay on the edge of the bed staring over to where Meg and Jeffrie were, in the absolute dark of our stateroom. I imagined what Meg would look like and tried to think that she was looking toward me, too, and wondering the same things. Billy had his arm over me, his chest on my shoulder. I felt the tickle of his breath in the hair on the back of my neck.

I said, "If you could back things up, knowing what you know now, would you have stayed down on Earth with everyone else, or would you have come up here anyway?"

Meg didn't answer for a while. I imagined she thought I was stupid, or stuck-up because I was Anton Messer's kid, or both. Then she said, "Why do you have such a hard time facing the fact that we're the luckiest people in the universe?"

"Being the luckiest doesn't count when you're also the only," I pointed out.

She didn't have anything to say about that, and I felt guilty for being an argumentative piece of shit.

So I added, "I don't believe I'm lucky, because I feel like everything's my fault—or *our* fault—Billy's and mine. Because of what our dads do. Did, I mean."

"We aren't our fathers."

"They got us where we are," I said.

"I'm happy for that. Even if it meant spending most of my life invisible, drifting around from nowhere to nowhere in a motor home parked next to a bunch of burners and lunatics," Meg said.

"Stop talking crap about me," Jeffrie said.

"I'm not talking about you. Go back to sleep, Jeff. I'm

just talking about Cager and me. Not you."

Beside me in bed, Billy Hinman moved but didn't wake up.

"Do you miss anyone?" I asked.

Admittedly, my question was a pedestrian tactic for trying to find out if Meg had a person in her life she felt close to.

Meg Hatfield was smarter than me. She caught on.

"If you're trying to ask if I have a boyfriend, you're pretty stupid. Things like that don't mean anything to me. They never did, and I can't imagine it changing now."

"Oh."

I felt like I'd been slugged in the stomach. Then nothing happened at all. We lay there in total silence, in absolute darkness, for so long I thought Meg must have fallen asleep.

Then she said, "I hurt your feelings by calling you stupid. I'm sorry. I didn't mean to hurt your feelings."

"It's okay."

"What about you? Do you miss anyone?" Meg asked.

I thought about Katie St. Romaine, whom I was sad for but I didn't miss, and how Meg Hatfield was just trying to be nice to me now when she didn't need to at all.

"My parents used to beat the shit out of me."

"You? Anton Messer's kid? Why?"

"I'm not good enough at anything," I said.

"You're a good dancer," Meg said.

"Thank you."

"But it was only a dance. For New Year's Eve. Don't take it as anything else."

"Okay. Sorry if there's something wrong with that."

"You're an okay guy. You're not pushy like Lloyd."

I asked, "Who's Lloyd?" But I was almost afraid to hear what her answer would be.

"Jeffrie's brother. He always wants to have sex with everyone," Meg said.

I thought about Billy Hinman, who was pressed up against me as close as he could get. "Some guys are just like that."

"I'm going to get into that fucking computer," Meg said.

I believed her. There was something about Meg Hatfield's matter-of-factness that made me feel safe.

"I think you will too," I said.

"I'm not tired anymore," she said. "I want to go back and try again now."

"Now?"

"Yes. Right now."

"You can't go alone," I said.

"Well?"

"Let me get my pants on."

"Okay."

It's Time to Eat Now, and I Become Aware of My Balls

Reverend Bingo, looking something like a black, four-legged arachnid suspended in a web, stood in front of the elevator, his ghastly, slender and too-long arms outstretched across the width of the doorway.

His chin was tilted up like he was downloading some private data from God, so we couldn't see whether or not his eyes were open.

Meg and I stopped in the hallway about fifty feet from the elevator and the insane priest.

I whispered, "I'll bet you anything he's going to complain about the color of his car."

I shouldn't have whispered. Cogs can hear everything.

It was probably a highly desirable feature in a cog who was also a priest, I thought.

Reverend Bingo snapped his chin down. His yellow eyes

widened like his skull was attempting to poop them out of his face.

"Satan! Satan! Fuck you to hell! Stand still, so I can throw something at you!"

Then Reverend Bingo looked around frantically, obviously trying to find something to throw at me, but there was nothing at all in the hallway. So Reverend Bingo removed one of his shoes and he threw it as hard as he could. His shoe hit the floor about two feet in front of him.

Reverend Bingo could not throw shoes to save his life, which made him even angrier.

"Stop tricking me, fucker! What did you do to my arm, Satan? How dare you possess my arm! Foul demon! I will smite you!"

Then he tried to throw his other shoe at us. His release was a little off. The shoe hit the ceiling of the hallway just above his head.

"Bitch! Fucking bitch!" Reverend Bingo screamed.

He was very mad.

"He's a terrible thrower," Meg said.

"Definitely having trouble finding his release point."

"He thinks I'm a cog. He's going to try to bite me. What do you suggest we do?" Meg asked.

"We should throw our shoes at him," I suggested.

"Mine aren't heavy enough," Meg said.

"You want one of mine?" I had on sneakers, which are very good for throwing.

"Sure."

I slipped off my left sneaker and handed it to her. Meg cocked back to throw and let loose the most wicked fastball tennis-shoe pitch I'd ever seen. I could practically hear my shoe cutting the air between her and Reverend Bingo.

Meg Hatfield's arm was golden.

Reverend Bingo flinched spastically and tried to slap at my sneaker with his gawky tentacle of an arm. Of course he missed, and my shoe smacked squarely into the side of his face. It sounded something like a fish hitting a windshield at seventy miles per hour.

Reverend Bingo shrieked a high-pitched scream. "AHHHHHH! Fuck! Fuck! You hit me! That hurts!"

Then Reverend Bingo locked his eyes on Meg and began walking toward her, taking long, slow steps, saying, "I should have bought the blue car! I should have bought the blue car! I should have bought the blue car!"

"See? I told you," I said. "Do you want my other shoe?"

Meg nodded and held out her hand.

Giving up my shoes was worth it, just to watch Meg Hatfield throw them at a cog.

Shwak!

My second shoe hit Reverend Bingo squarely in the forehead. He actually fell down, and when he got back up, his right eye had popped. It rolled up inside his skull, and a gooey clot of cog pus ran down Reverend Bingo's cheek.

"I should have bought the blue car!" Reverend Bingo kept coming toward Meg.

And as Reverend Bingo got closer and closer to us, a bell rang over the ship's sound system, and Rabbit and Mooney came on, singing a song about eating.

> *Tell me if you disagree,*
> *We're getting hungry, aren't we?*
> *Depressed cogs taste like spaghetti,*
> *So it's time to eat now,*
> *It's time to eat now.*

"Do you think we should run? I don't need my shoes back that bad," I said.

"He's just a cog. We should kick the living shit out of him," Meg said.

At that precise moment I fell completely in love with Meg Hatfield.

"I should have bought the blue car! I should have bought the blue car!" Reverend Bingo was just a few paces away from us now. "Fucker! Fucker, fucking, fuck Satan! Stand still, so I can eat you, Satan fuck!"

I'll admit it—I was a little scared. But I didn't want to *seem* scared in front of Meg. After all, I had been schooled in such things as dance, knotting bow ties, and proper dinner table posture. I had never in my life fought back, even if there were a pathetic number of times I might—or should—have. I felt all hot and swollen inside. For the first time in my life I had an awareness that my balls were telling me what to do.

The mad ones taste like pepper steak,
Happy cogs cause stomachaches,
But horny ones are chocolate cake,
So it's time to eat now,
It's time to eat now.

I looked at her. "Meg, I . . . Oh, nothing. Screw it."

I may as well have been invisible to her, and to Reverend Bingo, too, since he was only fixated on Meg, whom he mistook for his next cog meal. I sucked in a deep breath, stepped in front of Meg, and smashed the palm of my right hand square into Reverend Bingo's goo-slicked nose.

He reeled back, arms windmilling uselessly as he fell to the floor.

"How dare you! How dare you! Ow! Fuck! That hurt! Bitch!"

And the song played on.

And if you're not quite satisfied
With gluttony and fratricide,
The smart cogs have whipped cream inside,
So it's time to eat now,
It's time to eat now.

I wiped Reverend Bingo's cog sauce from my hand onto the leg of my pants.

Then I walked up to him and kicked Reverend Bingo's face. It was like kicking a busted refrigerator. I forgot that I wasn't wearing shoes, so it kind of hurt my foot. And when I stomped on Reverend Bingo's throat, a little geyser of cog glop spurted up from his broken eyeball and gushed all over my socks.

It was so foul, I nearly vomited on him.

He burbled, "I should have bought the blue car, motherfucker!"

His arms flopped around like he was being electrocuted.

Reverend Bingo, who had no talent for throwing things or choosing automobile color, was also not much of a fighter.

> *Tell me if you disagree,*
> *We're very hungry, aren't we?*
> *We'll all die on the Tennessee,*
> *So it's time to eat now,*
> *It's time to eat now.*

The Cruise Ship to End All Cruise Ships

We left Reverend Bingo lying on his back in the hallway, percolating a steady stream of cog snot from the hole where his right eye used to be, while flopping his arms and legs wildly and chanting his buyer's remorse.

Meg picked up my shoes and handed them to me in the elevator.

"Thanks," I said. "Where did you learn to throw like that?"

"At Grosvenor Divinity School. *Cheepa Yeep*," Meg said.

"Really?"

Meg gave me a look like I was stupid, which made me feel extremely, well, *stupid*. What did I know? I couldn't tell that Meg was joking. I'd never been around a normal human being in my life.

"You really need to get out more," Meg said.

I bent down on one knee to put on my sneakers. My

socks were ruined, soaked with Reverend Bingo's hydraulic mucus. The stuff smelled like aluminum and soft onions. Gross. I took off my socks and tossed them aside.

"Get out *where?*"

"Good point, Cager."

"Look, I'm sorry if I seem like a pampered little shit. I've never done anything real, I guess. I've never hung around with regular kids," I said.

"Don't worry about it. You're an okay guy."

"Oh."

"You kicked the shit out of that cog," Meg said. "That was pretty heroic, if you ask me."

So first I was stupid, then I was *okay*, and now I was a hero. Meg Hatfield and space were making me totally crazy. I looked away from her and tied my shoelaces.

"You're not pouting, are you?" she said.

That was one of those questions a guy with no socks, alone in an elevator with a smart and beautiful girl, just can't answer in any way that might spare his self-image, so I said nothing.

"You're really sensitive for being one of the richest kids in the world. You'd think that someone like you wouldn't care at all about what someone like me ever said or did," Meg said.

"Why would you think that? Besides, we aren't in the world anymore."

"Well, you do own this entire ship, by default and probate laws."

"None of that matters now," I said. "It's like the song said: We're all going to die here on the *Tennessee*. And I don't think it's going to take too long for it to happen, either."

"You know what I think?"

"What?"

"The ship wrote that song," Meg said.

I shook my head and stood up. I didn't get what she meant.

"You heard it. It's Queen Dot fucking with the systems on the *Tennessee*. She admitted it. It's one of her Worms. That song was about what's going on *right now*. She made it start happening. There's no way the song could have been coded in before all this shit with cogs eating cogs."

I sighed. Meg Hatfield was so much smarter than I was.

I said, "Livingston did it."

Meg nodded. "I can fix it. I swear, if I can get in, I can fix it."

She caught me staring at her. For just a second our eyes locked. It was awkward and thrilling at the same time, but I couldn't help myself. Meg Hatfield was a shoe-throwing wonder.

The elevator stopped. The doors opened. Meg and I walked the hallway in silence. I was so confused and flustered by her.

We opened the door to the bridge and looked inside at the carnage in the wheelhouse on the *Tennessee*—my ship, the cruise ship to end all cruise ships.

We stood there, neither of us saying anything.

Then Meg said, "Don't like me, Cager."

"What?" I felt myself turning red. My throat constricted like invisible hands were strangling me. She was too smart; she had to have seen something in the way I'd been looking at her. But she was so damned likeable. I had never met anyone as real and as human as Meg Hatfield.

"I don't want you to like me."

"Would it make you happy if I told you how much I hated you?" I asked.

"Probably."

I followed Meg as she stepped over gooey fragments of cog bodies that lay scattered around the control room's floor. For the most part the cogs had stopped moving and making conversations about their anger, happiness, or horniness. The security cog who'd been ripped open—the one I saw dipping his fingers into his own innards and then licking them clean—had been nearly completely eaten. All that was left of him were his feet and the top portion of his face. His eyes blinked.

Meg sat down in front of a bank of computer terminals. "You should tell me all the things about me that you hate. This would help you," she said.

I didn't want to make shit up. I was frustrated that she was so in control of herself, and I found myself wishing Rowan were here so he could give me advice about what to do, since I was such a hopeless and pampered piece of shit who knew nothing about how to talk to a real girl.

ANDREW SMITH

My voice cracked. "I hate how good you are at throwing shoes."

"I knew it. What else?"

While she talked, her fingers whizzed over the hovering flash screens that had lit up above the computer terminals.

"I don't want to do this."

"Come on. Admit it. You hate me," Meg said.

Click click click click click.

"And how good you understand that coding shit too. I don't know the first thing about it."

"So you hate that about me, right?"

I shrugged. "Why do you want to do this?"

I sounded pathetic.

Meg didn't answer. She kept typing, then wiping lines clear, then typing again.

"Do you have a thing against people?"

"Most of them. But I don't set things on fire. Jeffrie does that stuff," Meg said.

"Between cogs eating cogs and having a burner on board, we are pretty much doomed." And I added, "Don't you want to have any friends?"

Meg stopped typing and looked at me. I pretended to be fascinated by Captain Myron's white feathered hat, because I didn't want Meg Hatfield to see any other true things that might be so obvious in my eyes.

She said, "I'm sorry for being mean to you. It's just . . . well, I'm sorry, Cager."

"Whatever."

Meg started typing again. I continued faking interest in Captain Myron's bicorne.

"Anything else you hate about me?"

I sat down in the captain's chair and spun the shiny wheel that hovered in the air.

"Where did you learn coding?" I said.

"Same place I learned how to throw shoes," Meg answered.

"Oh, yeah. *Cheepa Yeep.*"

Meg said, "No. To be honest, I taught myself code. It's actually simple, because it's a language with absolutely no nuance, no subtext, no possible way of misinterpreting what's being said."

"It would be pretty boring if human beings used a language like that, wouldn't it?" I said.

"Zing. That's a good one, Cager Messer. You got a dig in on me."

I looked at her. Meg smiled at me, with her mouth; not with her eyes. And then I turned red and had to look away.

Bullshit.

I spun the wheel, and Meg typed and deleted, typed and deleted.

I wanted to go back to my room and lie down in the quiet dark, but I couldn't leave Meg alone out on the ship with all those cogs, even if she was more capable of protecting herself than I was. I stood up and walked over to where Captain Myron's hat was lying against the wall. I decided to pick it up, and when I did Captain Myron launched into another of his hostile tirades.

Well, his head launched into a hostile tirade, I should say.

"Don't touch my fucking hat!" Captain Myron's head screamed. "How dare you? How dare you touch my fucking hat? Get down here so I can bite you, you fucking little prick!"

"No," I said.

I took a step back, away from Captain Myron's head.

"I'm the captain! How dare you defy me? You little shit!"

Then Captain Myron—his head, that is—actually tried to bite the floor, to pull himself toward me. I was being chased by an angry severed head that could barely manage to move an inch.

"You can't be the captain anymore. You're only a head. No one's going to listen to you." Then I put Captain Myron's feathered admiral's bicorne on my head and added, "I'm taking control of the *Tennessee* now."

"No!" Captain Myron shrieked. "No! No! No! This is not fair! You are humiliating me! Bully! Bully fucking coward prick! What gives you the right? I am filled with rage! I'll fucking bite you! Come here! Come here now! Now! Trigger! Trigger! This impudent fuck is triggering me!"

And Captain Myron began shrieking unintelligible curses. He sounded like a thousand cats being thrown into the blades of an enormous fan.

"Will you *please* hold it down?" Meg said. She stopped typing and glanced at me with an annoyed expression. "Oh. Nice hat, Cager."

And Captain Myron screamed and screamed.

I said, "Sorry, Meg. I'll just . . . um . . . escort Captain Myron's head outside. Um, so you can work."

Captain Myron's head kept cursing and screaming as I used my foot to roll him out the door and into the hallway.

After all, I was captain now; I was in charge.

The Nicest Giraffe I Ever Met

Hello, my friend! *Bonjour, mon ami!* Ah, but you look so handsome in your feathery cap and man clothes!"

"How does a giraffe get inside an elevator?" I asked.

Maurice, the giraffe from the recreation deck, who had never seen me with clothes on and had apparently taken an elevator to the ship's bridge, was hunched down on his belly, lying in the hallway outside the control room.

"I can fold myself up into a teeny tiny little box!" Maurice explained.

"Practical, especially for someone who's fourteen feet tall."

"But please, *s'il vous plaît*, I am very, very hungry and have not been able to find any food this morning for one's *petit déjeuner*," Maurice said. "Is this, by chance, *un personne mécanique*? As you say, a *cog*?"

There was something about Maurice's accent—and the

fact that he was a giraffe—that made me feel cheerful.

Maurice's nose hovered just a few inches above Captain Myron's head. And Captain Myron's head's eyes ticktocked from Maurice to me.

"What outrage is this? Is there an animal on my deck? How dare you offend and ridicule me in this manner?" Captain Myron's head shrieked, "How dare you turn this around into something about you? It is NOT about you! This is about ME! I order you shot! I order you both shot!"

So I faced a real human dilemma. Look, cogs are just machines, right? And Captain Myron—now Captain Myron's head—had never done anything nice to anyone. In fact, I was pretty sure Captain Myron started all the trouble on the *Tennessee* by biting Dr. Geneva's face, which quickly escalated into a cannibalistic slaughterfest among the ship's cogs. On the other hand, Maurice had been pleasant to me and was reasonably cute, in an enormous-bisexual-French-giraffe kind of way.

Maurice was the nicest giraffe I ever met.

I toed Captain Myron's head forward a half roll and took a step back.

"If you don't mind," Maurice, always polite, said.

I gestured a palms-up hand downward to Captain Myron's head and said, "*S'il vous plaît, Maurice.*"

Then Maurice lowered his snout to the bellowing and cursing head on the floor and began devouring what remained of poor screaming and swearing Captain Myron.

Mmmph! Mmmph! Mmmph! went Maurice as he ate.

"I order you shot! How dare you offend me in this manner!" howled Captain Myron's head, but only for a little while.

Soon all that remained of Captain Myron was a puddled slick of gravy goo in the middle of the hallway, which Maurice lapped up eagerly using his enormous, snakelike, black giraffe tongue. Then Maurice burped.

"Ah! So delicious, my friend! And I feel as though I could eat another four or five, if you have any nearby!"

"Sorry, Maurice," I said. "There's really nothing left at all on this deck. I just rolled him out because he was making too much noise."

Maurice sighed. "Ah! Such is life!"

And I thought, what the fuck does a cog know about life? But I liked Maurice, because he was a giraffe, and he ate the tiger who scared Parker up a tree and destroyed all my clothes; and he also finally made Captain Myron shut the hell up, so I nodded and said, "Yes. Life *is* like that, isn't it?"

"What can one do? As for me, I will go to look for more *aliments*, as I am still somewhat peckish."

"Well okay, Maurice. It was nice seeing you again," I said.

I blamed it on space and Meg Hatfield—that I had totally lost my mind and was exchanging pleasantries with an out-of-control predatory machine-giraffe.

And Maurice, always polite and warm, said, "But, tell me, would you like to join me? Perhaps you would enjoy a ride on my back, *peu jeune garçon?*"

I half faked a yawn. "No thanks, Maurice. I need to get some sleep."

"Well then, come visit me again at the lake. Come swimming with your little friend. We can all have tea together at the *petite maison de thé*!"

"Sure, Maurice. I'll see you around," I said.

I went back to the control room after saying good-bye to Maurice.

Meg shook her head. Her elbows rested on the desktop, and her face was pressed into her palms.

"There's something wrong with me. I just can't get it."

"You're just tired. Maybe you should try to get some sleep."

"I don't know," she said. "What happened to Captain Myron?"

"You mean Captain Myron's *head*. Well, um, let's just say that thanks to a giraffe named Maurice, the ship's a little less angry now," I said.

And at the opposite end of the *Tennessee*, in the lower west arrivals deck air lock, which was open to space and the barren surface of the silent moon, my three cogs bobbed and drifted from black cable nooses, floating gracefully like slow-motion sea fans.

Lourdes danced and wriggled and kicked her legs and farted.

"Yeee! Yippeee! I never want this to end! This is the greatest endlessly boring moment of my life!"

Unfortunately, I had failed to calculate the lengths of

the nooses I'd tied around the necks of my cogs. Parker's was too long, so my valet cog ended up trailing the *Tennessee* on the outside of the air lock, flying like a tethered satellite, alone and exposed in the nothingness between us and the moon.

Parker looked at the white-gray cavitied surface of the moon, tugged at his crotch, and said, "I have an erection."

And Milo, still missing one of his trouser legs from the seahorse attack, wept and wept. "I'm so cold. I'm so desperately alone and empty. Can someone please help me?"

A Sleep Sandwich

Meg refused to go to sleep.

But I was exhausted. And, in my exhaustion, all the frustration and worry that had been simmering inside me began to boil their way into my brain. I selfishly wanted Meg to come back to my room and go to bed. I imagined us sleeping together—just sleeping—the same way Billy Hinman liked to sleep with me.

I had never slept with a girl. It was just another one of those never-have-been, never-will-be things for Cager Messer, one of the richest kids in the world, or in lunar orbit, or wherever the fuck I was.

I didn't give a damn about what else happened on the *Tennessee*. They were all just cogs, after all, and who honestly gave a shit if all the cogs on the *Tennessee* ended up eating each other? We could keep Meg and Jeffrie safe until the last of the cogs was gone.

Right?

But then I wondered about who would feed me, and who would bring me clean clothes. Rowan couldn't be expected to do everything for me for all eternity. What if Rowan started to get too old for his job?

And what if I got lonely when all the cogs had been destroyed by Queen Dot's Worm?

What a spoiled piece of shit I was.

And I hadn't even spent a moment thinking about the three cogs I'd left dangling from nooses in the air lock— Parker, Lourdes, and Milo—because I hated myself for caring about them, as though they were something a little bit more than just a trio of v.4s. What if they caught whatever disease was cycling through our population of cogs? Would I have to watch them eat each other, or, worse yet, destroy them when they came for Meg and Jeffrie?

Cogs were just machines, nothing more. Like Captain Myron was, and Dr. Geneva and the insane Reverend Bingo and Maurice the giraffe and the can opener Parker found for me but I still hadn't used.

I really wanted to go to bed.

With Meg Hatfield.

I needed to know I was human.

"Please, let's go back and take a nap," I said, "We've been awake for days."

Meg didn't answer; she just looked at me with an expression that said no.

"What's a day?" Meg asked.

"A sandwich made between slices of sleep bread," I said.

"Great. Now I'm hungry, Cager."

But this time Meg Hatfield was smiling with her tired eyes, and I bit the inside of my lip.

"Do you want me to get us something to eat?" I asked.

"I was just kidding."

"How can I ever know these things?"

"You'll learn," Meg said. She pushed herself to her feet. "There's something else I need to try. I got my way into a computer here, but it was in a bank on Deck Twenty-One. Will you go there with me?"

That was a dumb question. I would have walked into an open air lock with Meg Hatfield.

"Um, yes."

In the elevator Meg told me how she'd used a tire iron on Deck 21 to knock the head completely off a cog who'd been trying to eat Jeffrie.

She was incredible. I fantasized about being a valet cog and confessing to her right there in the elevator, matter-of-factly, that I had an erection. I kind of envied Parker, even if he was swinging from a noose in the absolute vacuum of space.

Whatever.

"We could pick up a couple of jack handles from those old cars there, just in case we need them," Meg said.

"I'm still fully loaded with sneakers, too."

"You're funny."

"I'm learning," I said. "But what if I can't get into Deck Twenty-One? What if I end up in security-cog jail?"

"Don't worry. I changed your age when I got into the computer in the bank office. Billy's, too. You are now an official, legal adult," Meg said.

I considered all the things I could now get away with, and it also explained why nobody—no cog—hesitated to get Billy and me drunk on champagne at the New Year's Eve party. But being an adult was also stupid, pointless.

"Why did you do that?" I asked.

"I was trying to get Jeffrie and me out of Deck Twenty-One. I kind of thought—was hoping—you'd come back, and then the door would open for you."

"You were *hoping* I'd come back?" I said.

"I only wanted the door to open, Cager. Nothing else."

"What else did you change about me?"

"Let's see. I made you a dropout from Grosvenor School, and you're a former bonk who's been in a mental ward for the past two years."

I struggled to keep from saying anything dumb. Meg had to have been joking. I was just so stupid at figuring her out.

The elevator stopped, and the door opened onto the familiar entry foyer to Deck 21. It seemed like so long ago that I had first set eyes on Meg Hatfield through the wicket in the door.

"Wait," I said. "How did you get through the doorway?"

"There was a dead cog propping the door open when

we got out. Now's our chance to see if I really did turn you into a twenty-one year-old," Meg said.

"And a bonk," I added.

"Rabbit."

"I guess that makes you the robot."

"I'm hungry again, in that case."

I think I was actually starting to get Meg Hatfield.

"Well, here goes, Mooney."

And when I walked up to the door below the enormous number 21, it slid open, exposing an old American city that looked like it had just come through a war, and not on the winning side.

Even up here in heaven, aboard the *Tennessee*, wars don't just fight themselves.

Dumb Pointless Optimism

Hey. Hey, wake up."

Jeffrie Cutler leaned over the bed and shook Billy's shoulder.

"What do you want?"

"I'm scared. Meg and your boyfriend left a couple of hours ago, and they're not back."

Billy Hinman reached back and felt around in the bed with his open hand.

"Cager's not my *boyfriend*," he said.

"Oh. Sorry."

"Whatever. But I'm sure they'll be okay. Don't be scared. How long have I been sleeping?"

Jeffrie looked at the time display on the wall above the girls' bed. "I don't know. Like, three or four hours."

Billy groaned. "Oh. All right. We should just go back to sleep for a while."

"Where do you think they went?"

"I have a rule about never talking to people when I'm asleep."

Jeffrie turned the lights out and went back to her bed.

"You're not crying, are you?" Billy asked.

"Shut up. I have a rule too."

Jeffrie Cutler was obviously crying.

Billy sat up and put his feet on the floor. "Look, they're okay—seriously. I bet Rowan's with them, besides. No one can ever get into trouble around Rowan. That guy is boringness on legs."

"I want to go home." Jeffrie's throat constricted on each word.

"I didn't plan to get stranded here either. Rowan and I tricked Cager into getting on the transpod. And flying scares the shit out of me, but I was desperate to try to get Cager to clean up and stop doing so much Woz. And now I guess we're trapped, so we might as well make what home we can here. Personally, I can't even stand to look out the windows."

Jeffrie lay in her bed and cried.

Billy sighed. Billy Hinman hated seeing anyone sad. "So. Um, before outer fucking space, where did you used to live?"

"Antelope Acres."

"I never heard of it."

Jeffrie took a long breath. "It's a camp. In the desert by Mojave Field."

"A *camp*?"

"I live in an old camper truck, with my brother."

"You lived in a *car*? Oh my God—"

"Screw you, rich kid."

"Hey, look, I didn't mean anything. I just—well, Cager and I grew up like we were fucking museum pieces on display or something. Neither one of us ever knew any real people. I guess that's why we need each other the way we do. Our parents even paid other kids to be fake friends for us," Billy said.

"Oh. That sucks. I'm sorry."

"It's no big deal. But Cager would have killed himself down there," Billy said. "He was all hacked up on Woz. Constantly."

"But he didn't go to school?"

"No."

"Weird."

"He used to smoke it or snort it every day—all day long—with a nutcase ex-bonk named Charlie Greenwell. He would have died if we didn't trick him into coming up here. And he hated me for it at first, but me and Rowan saved his life."

"Well, considering what's happening down there now, I guess Meg saved my life by breaking into the code stuff and bringing me up here too. But we should go look for them," Jeffrie said.

"The *Tennessee* is too big. We'd never find them, and we'd probably end up getting lost."

"I'm really scared."

"We'll be okay. Keep telling yourself that."

"Why?"

Billy said, "I don't know. Dumb pointless optimism can work sometimes, right?"

"I don't think so."

"Yeah. Neither do I."

You Better Watch Out
for the Monkeys

The place smelled like stagnant water, gunpowder, detergent, butterscotch, and cog slime.

I gagged and covered my mouth and nose with my hand.

"What's wrong?" Meg asked.

I pointed at my nose. "I can smell stuff that other people can't smell."

"What's it smell like?"

"A moldy wet tennis shoe."

"Oh."

"Was it as bad as this when you left?"

Meg said, "It was kind of worse, because there were broken cogs all over the place. Now they're pretty much all gone."

"Well, not all of them," I said.

Up on the ledge of a hotel building was a row of

spike-headed gargoyles. Two of them had impaled cogs, slick with dried cog pus, their broken backs causing them to bend like melting wax figures. The impaled cogs moved their eyes and fingers. One of them, a woman cog with a cigarette display dangling from a belt that wrapped around her neck, smiled at me and Meg and said, "Oh! It's so wonderful to see a human visitor on Deck Twenty-One! This is the happiest moment of my life! I'm so happy, I could rip my face off and throw it down so I could kiss you! Would you like a cigarette, handsome human boy?"

"Um, no thanks," I said. "And please don't rip your face off and throw it at me, cigarette lady."

Then the cigarette-lady cog pointed at Meg and said, "But you better watch out for the monkeys! They're hungry little darlings! Wheee! I am so happy!"

Meg and I stood beside a bloated yellow taxicab that was tipped upside down. The windshield had shattered into thousands of jagged diamonds all around our feet.

"Monkeys?" Meg said.

"I think we should look for one of those jack handles."

Down the street, in front of the smashed window of a place called the Talisman Bath House, sat two large chimpanzees, their legs bent and their hands resting on the fake pavement of Deck 21's Main Street, as though they were getting ready to launch themselves into a run. Their eyes were pinned on Meg.

Meg saw them too.

She glanced back toward the entrance as though

gauging whether it would be possible to outrun them, but even I, with all my lack of ever having to figure out much of anything for myself, could see right away that it was not a feasible option.

Meg said, "Try to stall them if you can."

The apes sprang forward and chimp-sprinted toward us, using their massive arms like speed-pistoning crutches. Well, they weren't running at me; they were running for Meg. I may just as well have been invisible to them.

Meg got down on her hands and knees and crawled inside the overturned cab.

"That's not a good place to hide!" I said.

"Shut up, Cager. I'm not hiding."

And Meg, grunting, began to pull away the backrest of the rear seat in order to access the taxi's trunk.

Once again, I marveled at how smart Meg Hatfield was.

But I only marveled for about a second and a half, because the chimps were so big and hairy and ugly that I nearly pissed myself in fright.

I held up my hands like I was doing standing-up push-ups. (By the way, I have never done a push-up in my life, and this made me add "do some push-ups" to my can-opener list.)

"Stop right there, cog chimps!" I said. "Get away from me. You're ugly."

The chimps paused and looked at each other in what I could only assume was startled confusion. The one on the left—an obvious male, which was nasty—turned to me and said, "Ugly? So now I'm ugly, too? I don't even understand how I can go on from day to day. This is all so agonizing, so pointless."

Then he fell into heaving, uncontrollable sobs.

Also, he had a thick German accent. Apparently, the Hinsoft division in charge of making the cog zoo animals for the *Tennessee* had offshored a lot of their coding.

"Stop crying! How many times do we have to go over this, Friedrich? How dare you draw all the attention onto yourself? I can't stand this outrage! I am so filled with rage, I could explode! Shit! Shit, I hate you, fucker! Fuckboy! The fury! The fury wicked burns me!" The other chimp, a gray-haired male who sounded like he came from South Boston, howled.

"I sicken myself. I'm so sorry for being pathetic, Boner," Friedrich said, weeping.

Boner sounded like a good South Boston name.

"There you go again, making this all about you! It is NOT about you, fuckface! Don't trigger my boundaries! I know what's best! I lived the experience! Fucker! Fuckboy!" Boner yelled. "We came to eat! It's about the meal! And it's about MY victimization and MY suffering, not yours, fuckboy! And it's about camaraderie, you piece of German shit! I am SO WICKED FUCKING MAD RIGHT NOW!"

Clink.

A thick metal bar landed on the pavement beside my foot. I caught a glimpse of Meg's hand slipping back through the window of the overturned taxi.

From inside she whispered, "Use it, Cager."

And while the German chimpanzee sobbed and moaned, the one named Boner threw himself down onto the broken glass and pavement and began tearing tufts of hair from his own neck and punching himself in the balls.

"I hate you so much! I HATE YOU SO MUCH!"

I bent down and picked up the metal bar. It was shaped like a big black X, with two of its points formed into wrenches, and the others forged into a pry bar and a hammer claw. I found myself marveling at what a normal human-boy thing it was to hold a tool like this. Although I'd never be able to figure out its actual intended use, it made my hands pleasantly dirty.

And Meg Hatfield's intended use for the thing involved Cager Messer bashing in the skulls of a couple of insane chimpanzees.

But they weren't *actual* chimpanzees. They were just machines, right? A pair of short-circuited toaster ovens that served no purpose.

Also, I felt extremely manly in taking advantage of the opportunity to physically defend Meg Hatfield, even if I also was simultaneously sickened and terrified by what she was actually expecting me to do.

I took a deep breath.

Okay.

Boner had to go first.

Nobody likes tantrum-throwing chimps from South Boston.

"I deserve all this unending despair. Kill me first," Friedrich wailed.

Boner punched and tore at himself. He kicked his opposably thumbed feet in the air and urinated. "How dare you? Stop making this all about yourself, fucker! You're so fucking selfish! This is about ME! IT HAS NEVER BEEN ABOUT YOU!"

To be honest, Boner had a point.

Then Boner jammed his fingers down his throat and forced himself to vomit cog slime all over his chest.

I was beginning to see why Billy Hinman hated cogs so much, but at the same time I almost felt like I could watch this show all day.

Whatever a day is.

But Friedrich regained himself first. He straightened— well, as much as a weeping chimp could straighten—and moved around to the side of the cab, where he could poke his face in through the shattered rear-door window.

"Cager. What are you waiting for?" Meg said from inside.

"I hate myself so much," Friedrich cried. "But I am so, so hungry!"

"Who cares about you? Nobody! Nobody cares about you! Why must you inflict your presence on my personal moment?" the wet and slimy Boner yelled.

Friedrich pushed the upper half of his torso inside the cab. I could hear him weeping as his arms clutched and clawed around for Meg.

"Cager!"

I raised the tire iron.

And Boner howled, "This is so unfair! This is so unfair to me!"

Ka-thunk!

The sharp pry-bar end of the iron smacked directly into Friedrich's spine—if there was such a thing inside a cog. Severed rubber tubes spurting pomegranate-red cog juice erupted outward from the ape's back.

It was particularly disturbing that the chimpanzee cogs' hydraulic systems had been filled with bloodlike goop, in order to satisfy passenger hunters in their gleeful diversion of actually shooting chimpanzees on the *Tennessee*'s World of the Monkeys deck.

Disgusting.

"Ow! Owwww!" Friedrich wailed.

The bar lodged inside the chimp-cog's body.

I grabbed hold of one of Friedrich's feet, which was actually a stubby hand that closed around my wrist. The sausagelike little finger things on his foot nauseated me. I closed my eyes and dragged him out of the cab as he cried and moaned and squirted his coggy red mayonnaise all over me. When I pulled his leg thing, Friedrich tore completely in half, his fingery foot still clutching my arm. A small lake of blood-clot cog soup dilated outward around my feet.

I was a soaked, slimy, bloodstained mess.

And Boner screamed, "Me! Me! Why are you victimizing me by paying attention to him?"

I shook Friedrich's foot-hand off my arm as Boner, covered in his own cog piss and vomit, got up from his tantrum spot and leapt at the cab's rear window. I kicked him in the chest and he somersaulted backward, shrieking, "I AM SO FUCKING MAD AT YOU NOW!"

Then I grabbed the tire iron with both hands and yanked it out of Friedrich's draining torso, took aim, and swung a nice, level swipe directly into Boner's throat.

I had also never played baseball, but I thought I might be pretty good at it if I ever learned what baseball actually was. All I knew was that it involved hitting things by swinging some kind of thing in your hands.

Whatever.

Boner's head came off. It rolled across the street, toward the sidewalk.

"Yeee! Wheee! This makes me so happy, I could poop myself inside out and back again!" the impaled cigarette-lady cog said from up on the gargoyle's head. She kicked and flailed her arms wildly, spraying some of the last bits of her frothy internal stew down to the street like raining cottage cheese.

"Yippeee, human boy! Yeee!"

And from somewhere under a mailbox, Boner's head shrieked, "I am so furious! How dare you? What gives you the right? Come here, fucker! Come here!"

The top half of Friedrich clawed his way out of the overturned taxi, trailing behind him what looked like links of boiled white sausages in a slick of crimson mucus. He folded his arms under his face. His ruined and gushy shoulders bounced with massive sobs. "Ow! Ow! It hurts so bad! My life is nothing but pain! Ouch!"

"Well, you shouldn't have tried to eat my friend," I said. "Shame on you!"

"I am shamed! I am shamed! Ow-how-ow-ow!"

I stood over him, my weapon hanging beside my right leg, as Meg Hatfield crawled out and got to her feet on the opposite side of the cab.

For a while neither of us said anything. We just looked at each other. I wiped some streaky red cog snot from my forehead with the back of my left hand.

Meg said, "Thanks."

I fought the urge to puke my guts out all over the quivering upper half of Friedrich.

I nodded at Meg. "You okay?"

"Yeah."

"Let's get to that bank," I said.

And Boner howled, "I SAID COME HERE, FUCKBOY!"

Well, his head screamed it, that is.

"I love you, human boy! I want to have a million half-human babies with you, commencing immediately! Yippeee! Yippeee!" Cigarette-lady cog gurgled and danced and rotated slightly, skewered on the spike of a gargoyle.

"Ow! Ow! This really hurts!" Friedrich bawled, rolling around in his gooey fake blood in the fake street that ran through the center of the destroyed fake city.

Cager Messer's Can Opener and Push-Ups List

The computers inside the Grosvenor Bank of Tennessee were still powered up, just as Meg had left them.

Everything else in the bank was a mess. Chairs were upturned, shards of broken glass were scattered everywhere, and large sections of the carpeting had been peeled away.

There were scrapes and gouges in the walls.

And there were scrapes and gouges inside me, too. I felt myself slipping again.

I needed Rowan, but I knew I couldn't leave Meg alone anywhere on the *Tennessee*. Things had gone insane, and it was all too dangerous for her.

"Is there something wrong with you?" Meg asked.

"No. Why?"

"You haven't said anything. This is the longest you've gone without talking to me."

"I'm feeling a little sick. Look at me."

I was wet and splattered in gooey, gravylike cog blood. It looked like I'd been trampled by a million garden snails, glazed with bloody snot and slime.

"You should go get some new clothes. There's a couple shops on this deck. I'll be okay now."

I shook my head. "I can't leave you. Maybe after you're done. I need to wash this shit off. I can't stand the smell of it."

"I can't smell anything."

Just hearing Meg say it made all the scents rise up in a cacophonous assault on my senses.

My stomach heaved. "Hang on."

I stepped out through the broken window and onto the sidewalk. I ran past the building's corner so Meg wouldn't see me throw up.

Nobody wants the person they're falling in love with to watch them vomit.

Friedrich was still crying, and Boner's head yelled at me from under his mailbox. And as I gagged and spit, the cigarette lady cooed and gurgled at me.

When I came back into the bank, Meg said, without looking up from her computer screen, "Feel better?"

I was so embarrassed. She had to have known I'd just puked my guts out.

"It's disgusting. They filled those monkey cogs with fake blood, just so people could get a sick thrill when they shoot them."

I couldn't help but think about Charlie Greenwell

and the other damaged bonks we used to visit at the Hotel Kenmore, back when I was on Woz.

And how long ago was that now?

Meg paused her typing and looked at me.

I stared directly into her eyes.

Meg Hatfield was the most incredible human being I'd ever met, and why did it take so long for me to finally meet a *real* person?

She said, "Your father was very . . . creative."

I shook my head. "He was a cruel and sick son of a bitch. I can't even begin to imagine what other insane bullshit we're going to find here."

"Hell yes!"

"That sounds a bit enthusiastic, considering the possibilities," I said.

"No. I found it!" Meg said. "The code and eye scans I put in from my thumbphone that made the cogs see me and Jeffrie as other cogs. I got it, and if I just wipe it out, we should be okay."

Meg typed frantically.

I found myself hoping that Meg Hatfield would write in a new code sequence that would make her see me as something other than Anton Messer's son, something more like human.

"Can I turn you into someone else, give you a new identity, like you did to me?" I said.

She stopped typing. "I didn't really make you an ex-bonk. I was just kidding about that. I honestly only changed your date of birth. Besides, who would you make me be?"

"A friend of mine. A real one."

"As opposed to your fake playdate friends?"

"Yeah. As opposed to them."

"Billy Hinman's your friend. He's real."

It wasn't enough, I wanted to tell her. But the truth was that Meg Hatfield was right; Billy Hinman *was* my friend, and he'd do anything for me, which was entirely why we were all stuck here forever, drifting alone around the dead moon.

But it still wasn't enough.

Why couldn't Meg just be nice to me? Why couldn't she just slip some unspoken code to me that might give me a hint that she thought I was a friend?

Meg entered a few more strings of code, then powered off the computer.

I felt like shit. I needed a bath. I needed to get away from Meg Hatfield.

She said, "There. I did it." She paused, "I think." Another pause. "I hope."

"What about Queen Dot's worm?"

"I'm not sure if I cleaned it all up or not. There's only one way to find out. We'll have to see, I guess."

"Good."

Meg said, "Good."

I pulled my shirt away from my skin, where it had been plastered down by the paste of cog goo. I couldn't look at it. I turned from Meg and faced out the bank's shattered front window. "Well. I'm going to get rid of this shit."

And then Meg Hatfield said this: "I am your friend, Cager Messer."

There was something in the way she'd said it that made me feel wonderful and terrible at the same time, and I wasn't absolutely certain whether or not I could cross that getting-a-real-friend thing off Cager Messer's can opener and push-ups list.

Times That Aren't Now

There were no cogs at all on Deck 21, aside from the bits and pieces here and there, and the impaled cigarette lady up on the ledge of gargoyles.

It was creepy and unsettling.

The last time I'd taken a bath, the *Tennessee* had turned upside down. I desperately needed one now, and some tea. Cager Messer was getting ready to melt down again.

"I wonder if they have tea in this place," I said.

"Who drinks tea?" Meg asked.

"I do."

"Well, I'm certain they have a café here or something. I could find you some while you're doing . . . whatever."

Meg and I stood at the edge of the main pool in the Talisman Bath House, which looked like something transported through time from ancient Rome. The bath was more than sixty feet long, filled with swirling blue water that breathed lacy clouds of steam up into the air. It was surrounded by massive stone columns that supported an upper floor of balconies with ornate iron balustrades shaped like bloated birdcages. I imagined the balconies were there to give people above a bird's-eye view of all the naked bathers in the big hot pool. Skirting the floor of balconies was a colorful mosaic frieze with depictions of nudes engaged in all sorts of sex acts. I pretended not to notice them. It was all very embarrassing, being there with Meg, watching her take everything in. At the rear of the bath was a smaller, round, cold-water tub, and against the long walls on either side were racks of towels and brushes, with banks of metal hooks and shelves where bathers could leave their clothes.

I needed a trash can for mine.

"Tea would be nice. Thank you. Because I don't really know what I'm supposed to do," I said.

"What you're *supposed* to do is take your clothes off and get in the bath," Meg said.

"I know. But I was . . . I mean, it's kind of awkward."

"I'm going to go find you some tea and get something to eat. So you don't have to be embarrassed." And as Meg walked away she added, "You know, you're wound up really tight for a rich kid."

And I said, "Be careful." But I said it so quietly, Meg didn't hear me.

"I made some tea."

I practically jumped up out of the pool. I had no idea

how long I'd been in the hot water of the grand bath. I had fallen asleep, facing up toward the fake-star-painted ceiling, with my arms outstretched like wings along the bath's rail and my head resting on the cool tiles, when Meg called down at me from the balcony above.

And she was watching me.

"How long have you been there?" I said.

She shrugged. "I don't know. A while."

I stood up in the water and looked down to check if Meg could actually see my nakedness. When would I ever *not* feel embarrassed and inadequate around her?

And when I glanced back up at the balcony, Meg was gone.

I thought about pulling myself out of the bath and making a dash for the towels, but I didn't want to get out of the water yet, and it was already too late, anyway. Meg appeared at the foot of the spiral staircase at the end of the bath, carrying a tray with a teapot and sandwiches. I stood against the side of the bath in water that came up to my armpits.

The smell of all the cog goop I'd been slopped with had been washed away. Now all I could smell was bathwater, the cinnamon and cloves in the teapot Meg carried, butter, cheese, bread, and peach jam.

And Meg Hatfield. I could always smell Meg Hatfield.

She placed the tray down at the edge of the bath and sat on the marble floor tiles with her knees bent upward. Although the water swirled and bubbled from thousands of jetted vents, and I was certain Meg couldn't see beneath the surface, I had never felt so naked and exposed in my life as I did when she looked at me.

"How's the bath?" she asked.

"Perfect. Well, except for the cog arm I found near one of the drains."

Meg poured tea into two cups. "Oh."

"You should come in too," I said. I nearly choked from nervousness when I suggested it. And I tried to sound nonchalant in my invitation, like Billy Hinman would, but I failed miserably at it.

"No chance of that. Drink your tea, Cager. It's getting dark outside."

I had lost all sense of time, but places like the recreation decks, and Deck 21, had artificial days and nights.

I said, "Oh. Okay."

I wished I could get out of the water so I didn't have to look up at her, but that wasn't going to happen either. "Thank you. It's really good."

"You're welcome."

I took a sip, deflated.

Meg Hatfield was invisible to just about every human being on Earth.

Here, on the *Tennessee*, she invaded every sense I had.

She liked to write stories; some were true, she told me, and the others she'd make up, depending on her mood. Meg liked to tell her stories to her friend, Jeffrie Cutler. I asked if she would write a story for me, and she said maybe she could do that for my birthday. And I had no idea what date it was up here in neveryear, so I lied to her and told her my birthday was tomorrow.

She didn't buy it.

We only think of days and months to keep track of times that aren't now. Fuck days. Fuck months. This was how it was going to be from now on: forever.

The tea she brought, and the rest of the food we ate, were the best things I'd ever had, even if it all did come from printers.

So there I was—it was like I was waiting to be born, naked and cradled in hot water, hoping I might come out whole and normal, a real human being. But I couldn't defeat my own internal argument that I could never be someone as real as Meg Hatfield.

And I hadn't thought things through very well either. My clothes were ruined, beyond disgusting, and I didn't have anything to cover myself with. By the time we had finished our tea and sandwiches, I'd been in the bath for what felt like hours. And although Cager Messer had calmed down, I still knew that nothing would ever be right for me.

Meg turned around and faced out toward the Talisman's foyer so I could climb out of the bath and nervously wrap up in a towel without completely embarrassing myself. And like that, saying nothing more to her, and with nothing on except for a heavy terrycloth towel embroidered with RABBIT & ROBOT GROSVENOR GALACTIC LINES, I followed Meg outside to the destroyed fake city of Deck 21.

Meg Hatfield and I went clothes shopping for me.

I had never been shopping for my own clothes in my life, and I didn't know the first thing about what to do, which made me look and feel like an idiot in front of Meg. And she knew it too, so she had plenty of fun suggesting the most ridiculous outfits for me: things that only coder kids would wear, like double-breasted lab shirts, or Grosvenor School Code Club jumpers, and even underwear with cartoon images of Mooney and Rabbit printed on them.

So, in the end I gave up and allowed Meg Hatfield to dress me up in the outfit that suited the identity she decided to give me that day, or what she thought I deserved.

None of it mattered to me. I'd just as soon have gone home to my room wrapped in my Talisman towel.

After the clothes and shoes Meg picked out for me deposited themselves in the store's output tray, I hid inside a changing booth in the back and got dressed. I felt like an idiot, right down to my Rabbit & Robot socks and underwear. She also gave me a slate-blue pullover sweatshirt that was printed with something I absolutely could not understand. It said this:

```
} ELSE IF
</>
```

She completed my outfit with creased tan chinos—the kind kids wear as part of a proper Grosvenor School uniform—and some black suede sneakers that were just heavy enough to take out Reverend Bingo's other eye if we happened to run into him on the way back to our room.

In fact, we did not see a single cog between Deck 21 and the stateroom's door.

But I kept my tire iron with us, just in case.

And I had been silent and pouty the entire way back. It wasn't because of the stupid outfit Meg dressed me in; it was because I'd been adding and adding to Cager Messer's list of things he'd never done and probably never would.

In the hallway on our floor, Meg said, "You shouldn't be upset about the clothes. You don't realize how good you look in them. You look like a regular boy from California now."

"I'm not upset," I lied.

Meg didn't say anything. She just cleared her throat in a way that made it obvious that once again she didn't believe me.

So, just before I opened the door to our room, I stopped and asked Meg, "If things went back to normal and the cogs don't want to eat you and Jeffrie, and they have stopped cannibalizing each other, or, better yet, if we could somehow go back home to Earth and the thirty-whatever fucking wars had ended and things were okay again, and if I asked you out, to . . . I don't know . . . play Hocus Pocus or go see live theater or visit an art gallery or whatever, would you think about going out with me, Meg?"

Meg Hatfield looked at me and said, "No, Cager. I don't think so."

A Normal California Boy

The only thing worse than having to carry the weight of what Meg said to me in the hallway was walking into my room and finding Billy Hinman and Jeffrie Cutler in bed together.

My bed was apparently the popular spot for everyone except Cager Messer.

I turned on the lights and said, "Oh. Oops."

I didn't want to look at Meg, because I was hurt and embarrassed, so I watched as Billy Hinman, who was snuggled up to Jeffrie with his arms wrapped around her shoulders, opened his eyes and raised his head.

Billy Hinman groaned.

I said, "One of you isn't by chance that piece of shit Livingston, are you?"

"Um. Hi, Cager. We were only sleeping. Seriously. That's

all. We . . . Um, we were kind of scared—worried—when we realized you two were gone. But we were seriously only sleeping. Seriously. Only sleeping. For real," Billy said.

One thing I knew about Billy Hinman was this: He was just about as good at telling lies as Reverend Bingo was at throwing shoes.

I could also tell Jeffrie and Billy were both naked. Billy Hinman's underwear and socks were lying at the bottom of the bed. Meg couldn't tell, but I could. The place had the overwhelming, nauseating smell of sweat and sex.

Whatever.

And Billy said, "What time is it, anyway?"

Like that fucking mattered.

"And what are you carrying?"

I turned the tire iron in my hand. "I killed some monkeys with it."

Jeffrie looked at Meg, then me. She said, "You don't have to be mad or anything, and I apologize if you feel embarrassed. We just kind of . . . Well. Sorry. There's nothing *wrong* with that, is there? I mean, we're stuck here pretty much forever, right?"

Jeffrie's fingers combed through Billy's hair.

I said nothing, and silence—an incredibly awkward silence—smothered the room like soupy fog.

Knock knock knock.

"Cager? Billy?"

Rowan's voice came through the small speaker on our door's wicket.

Billy whispered, "Please don't let him in."

"I'm not going to. He'll get mad at both of us. I can't stand Rowan's cold-shoulder bullshit when he thinks we've misbehaved," I said.

Rowan would probably have assumed that Billy and I had turned our stateroom into some kind of nonstop sex party, which was kind of true, and then he'd get quiet and mopey and have a permanent look on his face that translated to something like *Do you really expect me to not tell your parents about this?"*

Even if nobody had any parents anymore.

I inhaled deeply and turned around. "Come on, Meg. Let's let them *sleep*. Or whatever."

Then I grabbed Meg Hatfield's hand, turned out the lights, and walked to the door.

"By the way, what the fuck are you wearing, Cager?" Billy said.

As soon as we were out in the hall, Meg let go of my hand. But Rowan, who always noticed everything, did see I'd been holding her hand.

I glanced at Meg. Did she actually just blush?

"Good evening, Cager. Meg," Rowan said. "I was just checking in on you. You've been asleep for the better part of the day."

"Not us," I said. "Meg and I just came back. She's been working on the computer system. She may have fixed things now. Billy and Jeffrie are still asleep. Well . . . I think they're awake now."

I felt myself turning red. Of course Rowan knew something was up.

And Rowan, dressed in a jacket and tie, had apparently intended to feed Billy and me at Le Lapin et l'Homme Mécanique. He arched that one eyebrow and, saying nothing, made a palm-up gesture at my clothes.

"What?" I said. "I like these clothes. Meg picked them out for me. She said I look like a normal California boy in them."

"Unfortunately, that is true, Cager," Rowan, always the snob, said.

"I even have Rabbit & Robot underwear and socks," I added.

"I'm sure they're delightful," Rowan said. He glanced at Meg with one of his I'm-telling-your-parents looks.

Then Rowan pointed at the metal bar in my hand. "And what's that?"

"A tire iron. Haven't you ever used one?"

Rowan frowned. "Why would I ever use a *tire iron*?"

I had finally done something Rowan didn't have the first clue about, even if I didn't know anything about what tire irons actually do, besides destroy cannibalistic cogs. Still, it made me feel very manly.

And normal.

And I suddenly had a new appreciation for the clothes Meg had picked out for me.

The door opened behind us. Billy and Jeffrie came out into the hallway. Billy, his hair wet and freshly combed, looked like a fashion model. He had on a black shirt and jacket with a slate-colored bow tie and two-toned shoes.

He said, "I'm really hungry. But dude, Cager, they are not going to seat you dressed like that. This is still the *Tennessee*, after all."

"And I own the place," I said.

"Let's see how far that gets you with the cogs who run the show."

So Meg and I went back inside my room to dress properly for dinner.

Getting the Wrong Idea

ook. Here's the thing," Meg said. "It's not that I don't like
you. After all, I made you tea while you were sleeping
in a bath, and I picked out some decent, not-stuck-up-
asshole things for you to wear, that actually make you look
cool. But I said I wouldn't go out with you because I didn't
want you to get the wrong idea."

"Why would I get the *wrong idea?*" I asked.

"Because it's not like either one of us has any alternatives. There's no Plan B. And there is no place to *go*. It's
pointless. We're stuck here."

I stood there in my Rabbit & Robot socks and underwear, rummaging through Billy Hinman's clothes, trying
to find something that could reasonably compete with his
sense of style.

"There are lots of places to go. This is the *Tennessee*,
the cruise ship to end all cruise ships. We have a fake Lake

Louise, a Rabbit & Robot amusement park, and public baths and sex clubs on Deck Twenty-One. Shit, we could even go shoot some monkeys if you wanted to."

"Never." Meg pulled on a tight black dress.

She looked amazing.

"Well, that was just a test to see what kind of person you are. I'd never do that either," I said. "How about a visit to the library? There are more than one hundred thirty thousand actual books on the *Tennessee*."

"Really?"

I knew a girl like Meg Hatfield would respond to books.

"Really."

"Going to the library isn't a date."

"If you say so."

I sighed. I didn't know what to wear. I settled on some black dress pants, a white shirt, and a checkered bow tie.

"Not that tie," Meg said.

I held up one with thin diagonal stripes and a print pattern of tiny sailboats on it, and Meg nodded.

Meg found some black heels and slipped her feet into them. "The main thing is, although I appreciate how you stuck up for me with that insane preacher—"

"Reverend Bingo."

"Whatever. And the chimpanzee creeps on Deck Twenty-One—"

"That was beyond disgusting."

Meg faced a mirror and brushed her hair, but I could clearly see she was watching me as I knotted my tie in it.

"Whatever. What I mean to say is, if you think I need you to protect me all the time—if that just pumps up your sense of manhood—well, I don't need it. I've done fine on my own."

I pulled on the pants, tucked in my shirttails, and buckled my belt.

"No belt. Suspenders," Meg said.

I switched. I was so frustrated and flustered by her. And what were we doing here, actually changing clothes in the same room together, like nothing mattered? I sat on the edge of the messed-up bed so I could tie my shoelaces.

"I've never thought that I was your protector, Meg. Besides, I've seen you throw shoes before. You're a fucking assassin."

Meg stopped pretend-brushing her hair. She turned to me. And then Meg Hatfield actually laughed. A real laugh. And I laughed too.

Maybe there was some hope for Cager Messer becoming a normal person after all.

But probably not.

"We should go," Meg said. "We wouldn't want Billy or Jeffrie to get the wrong idea."

"Yes, and especially Rowan. By all means, wrong ideas are just . . . well, *wrong*."

"Right."

I put on one of Billy's jackets, and Meg stopped me at the door.

"No jacket. Just the shirt and suspenders. It looks really . . ."

"Really what?"

I watched Meg swallow. Was she actually blushing?

Meg Hatfield was definitely not the kind of girl who would ever blush.

She said, "It looks really nice."

I looked around for something to hold on to. I honestly thought my knees were going to give out, and that I'd die right there on the floor of my stateroom, but I managed to maintain bipedalism, which is probably the most significant human achievement ever, no thanks to King Carlos's goddamned monkey sperm.

I went back to Billy's closet and ditched his jacket. Meg held up her hand and pressed it right above my heart.

"Hold on," she said. "It's crooked."

Then she reached up and straightened my bow tie. The edges of her hands lay against my chest. I wanted to kiss Meg Hatfield so badly in that instant that I actually felt myself salivating. But I suppressed the urge, because I didn't want Meg Hatfield to get the wrong idea about me.

That was what some people would call a *moment*, right? Meg Hatfield and I had some kind of thing going on between us—if only for a second—and I was too stupid and clumsy to make anything out of it.

I hated myself so much.

Meg tilted my tie slightly and said, "That's better."

But it was so far away from being "better," whatever "it"

was may just as well have been strapped to King Carlos's fetus face, jetting along somewhere on the opposite side of the galaxy from us.

Nothing was better.

I grabbed my tire iron—just in case—and we joined the others outside in the hall.

Shakespeare's Crowbar

lthough we were dressed for it, none of us made it down to dinner that night. Or up. Or whatever.

"Ah! Cager Messer! And young William Hinman! Just the people I was looking for!"

Nobody ever called Billy William, much less young William, unless it was someone like a security bonk with auto-access to our identification records, or, in this case, a doctor who only knew of "William" from his medical history.

Dr. Geneva appeared at the end of the hallway, waving and calling to me and *William*, just as the five of us were about to get into the elevator.

Billy whispered, "Shut the fuck up. Nobody calls me William."

I tightened my grip on the tire iron. Considering my present mood, I was not above bashing Dr. Geneva's head in if he got hungry eyes at Jeffrie or Meg. But then I found myself thinking, *We're going to eventually need a doctor, though*. Was Dr. Geneva the only physician on board the *Tennessee*?

I had to hope not.

Dr. Geneva was disgusting. The hole in the side of his face was big enough to stick a baby's arm through, and his shirt and jacket were slimed all down the right side of his chest with the foul-smelling, greasy cog goo that dripped from his jaw.

Where did cogs get all that juice from, anyway?

I kept my eyes fixed on Dr. Geneva's, waiting to see if he became preoccupied with Meg or Jeffrie. But it seemed as though Dr. Geneva didn't care about the girls at all.

Dr. Geneva cupped a hand on Billy's shoulder and leaned toward him, so that their noses were only two inches apart.

Billy Hinman recoiled slightly and made an expression like someone was holding a hot scoop of runny dog crap in front of his mouth. That hole in Dr. Geneva's face was alarmingly foul.

And Dr. Geneva said, "You look splendid! And the cut on your head—vanished! Remarkable physician you must have, William! Ha ha ha! And, Cager! I should think we'll need to establish a routine for your therapy now. You know, in cases such as yours, the detoxification process is not a cure; it's merely a beginning. A fine start, young man! The next step involves building a scaffold of support structures for you. Can I explain? Let me tell you about what we will be doing from here on out—well, as long as you're here on the *Tennessee*, which will undoubtedly be for the rest of your life. Ha ha ha! I apologize for the sarcasm. Did I ever tell you about where the name *Tennessee* comes from? No?"

I tried. I tried to get Dr. Geneva to shut the fuck up, but he was a cog with immutable code sequences machine-gunning through his frazzled circuits.

And although it was stupid, considering Dr. Geneva was as annoying as a fucking squeaky ceiling fan, I chose the polite approach. It probably had something to do with the clothes I was wearing.

"I apologize, Dr. Geneva, but we were just on our way down to dinner. Maybe we could talk about this later."

I grabbed Billy's elbow as though to herd our group into the elevator.

"Dinner? Did you say *dinner*?" Dr. Geneva, who never, ever shut up, said.

I gripped the bar tightly, glancing from Dr. Geneva to the girls and back to Dr. Geneva again. "You aren't hungry are you, Doctor?"

"Hungry? No! Don't be ridiculous! I am a v.4 cog, Cager. Didn't you know?"

Billy said, "Duh," and tapped an index finger on his right cheek.

"Well, I was only wondering. Because of . . . you know, what happened with the other cogs," I said.

"Oh! That! What a calamity! Well, you'll be happy to know that, although we're down a significant number among our . . . *ahem*, staff . . . things are being put right! Yes! Things are going to be smooth from here on out on the *Tennessee*! Wait till I show you the amazing repair work we've been doing down on the maintenance and lifeboat deck!"

"Maybe later," I said, pushing Billy and Meg into the elevator.

Dr. Geneva waved his hands in the air emphatically. "But surely you can't be intending to go to Le Lapin et l'Homme Mécanique! They've had to shut down due to staffing shortages. You know, no maître d', no cruise director. A restaurant like Le Lapin simply can't function without its maître d' and cruise director. You'll have to make other arrangements! Might I suggest—"

"Good-bye, Dr. Geneva," I said. And why was the fucking elevator door so slow in closing?

"Is that a *crowbar*?" Dr. Geneva was about to go off again, I could tell. He unfurled one arm dramatically and said, "'Friar John, go and get me an iron crowbar. Bring it straight back to my cell.' Did you know that William Shakespeare makes reference to the use of a crowbar in act five, scene two, of *Romeo and Juliet*, which confirms the enduring functionality of—"

And if the door hadn't closed just then, I very well might have bashed the burbling idiot right in the face.

"Dr. Geneva must be very lonely," Rowan said.

"He's a cog," Billy pointed out. "That's like saying your lawn mower is lonely."

"Well, all I know is, whatever Meg did worked. It was like Dr. Geneva couldn't even see the girls," I said.

And Billy said, "Safe bet they'd open up Le Lapin for us now if you brought Lourdes and Milo back from the dead."

I nodded. "I was thinking that too."

"But you could leave that little fucker Parker out there, for all I care," Billy added.

Jeffrie said, "Did any of you people realize that guy with the hole in his face said there's a *lifeboat deck*?"

I remembered the presentation we saw when we arrived, and hearing about lifeboats in the song that played when we put on our extravehicular suits after the incident with gravity, but I hadn't thought about it again until Jeffrie brought it up in the elevator.

There were lifeboats.

The Porridge
of Officer Dennis

There was something especially mournful about the *Tennessee* now. It was like being alone inside a massive and empty church.

Spending eternity here was going to take some getting used to.

On our trip to the lower west arrivals deck, nobody said anything. I was sure the others had been thinking similar thoughts about being alone here—noticing the quiet, and the absence of cogs. Even having outraged cogs shouting all the time was preferable to the absolute emptiness and quiet of outer space.

Whoosh.

The doors slid open, and we stepped out into the vast echoing cavern of the arrivals hall.

We were greeted by squeals of mechanical delight. "People! People! All the humanity of peopley humanness! Wheee! You're alive! And living! Yippeee! We are all alive!

I am so happy to see you, I am wetting myself with joy! But mostly with urine, too!"

I tapped Meg's elbow. "Since you're so good at this shit, maybe you could get in there and do something about happy cogs who piss on themselves."

At the far end of the arrivals hall, near the sealed air lock where—hopefully—Parker, Lourdes, and Milo were still floating around on their hangman's nooses, a lone security cog dressed in the official red uniform of the Grosvenor Galactic Police Department danced and flailed with unrestrained joy. He made a mess on the floor around his feet because he was missing his left arm from the elbow down, as well as the middle three fingers on his right hand, so he sprayed cog snot everywhere as he danced and danced for us.

"I am so burgeoning with happiness, so pregnant with jubilation, I want to place us all under arrest so we could go through the humiliation of the booking process together and spend the rest of eternity in a six-by-six-foot cell with each other!" The very happy cog squealed as he danced and skipped—and dripped—toward us.

I still carried my tire iron—just in case, of course. "I'll gladly knock his fucking head off," I said.

"Do it," Billy, who never liked cogs anyway, urged.

Rowan cleared his throat. That was really all he needed to say to us. But, as Rowan so predictably tended to do, he added, "Cager, we don't actually know how many—or few—cogs the *Tennessee* has remaining on board."

That was Rowan, as always my eternally reliable voice of reason.

The security cog came scampering up to us, wriggling his butt like an ecstatic hunchbacked pug while a stream of wetness ran down his red trouser legs.

"Wheee! Wheee! Wheee! Look at my butt! I am so happy, I can't stop shaking it back and forth and back and forth and back and forth and yippeee!"

"Please kill him, Cager," Billy said.

I shook my head. "I was never cut out to be a rabbit, Bill."

I held up my hand in an attempt to calm the overeager security cog, whose name, according to his uniform insignia, was Dennis. "Officer Dennis, we've only come here to retrieve three of my cogs who've been stranded in the docking bay for quite some time now."

Officer Dennis, suddenly aware that he had some kind of job duties that went beyond simply gyrating his ass and urinating in his pants, straightened up, glanced over his shoulder at the air-lock door, and then looked back at me.

"There are cogs in the docking bay?" Officer Dennis attempted to point at the air lock's door, but he only had a thumb and little finger on his right hand, which dripped and dripped.

"Yes. Three of them," I said.

Officer Dennis said, "Wheee! This makes me want to flip in the air like an acrobat!" And then Officer Dennis jumped up and attempted a joyous backflip but only ended up landing hard on the back of his skull.

Apparently, Officer Dennis had about as much practice at backflips as Reverend Bingo did at pitching.

"I am so happy there are cogs in the bay! Yeee! Yippeee!" Officer Dennis, whose neck had broken open and gushed a renewed flow of slime across the floor, paddled and flopped around in his own internal goo like a beached hagfish. And when he tried to stand again, his head lolled forward so his chin rested against his sternum. "That's what my feet look like! Yay! I've never looked at my feet before! I love my shoes so much!"

Officer Dennis fell down onto his face.

"I am so freaking happy!" he burbled into his goop, flap-splashing what was left of his arms down into the spreading pool.

I stepped around the twitching remains of the partially eaten and broken security cog and made my way toward the air-lock door.

"Oh, no!" Officer Dennis said. "Humans are not allowed to perform labor on or around the air locks. I will be forced to place you under arrest if you attempt to do so."

"Don't be ridiculous," I said, waving dismissively. "I own this ship, and besides, your head's falling off."

"I'm so thrilled to announce that I am making my very first arrest of a human being! I am placing you under arrest, Cager Messer! This is better than anything ever! Yippeee! Yay! Yay! You're under arrest!" Officer Dennis's words percolated up in a stream of bubbles through the stringy, viscous gravy his face was lying in.

Then he said, "Please cooperate and come along with me to Security Detention Center Seven! Hooray!"

I looked at Officer Dennis. He did not appear to be capable of going anywhere.

"Um, Officer Dennis," I said, "I don't think you can walk."

Officer Dennis kicked his legs wildly, splashing his slippery cog slop all over himself. I took a step back. I was sick of getting cog juice all over me.

"You're right! I'm so thrilled to say I can't walk! I've never wanted anything more in my life than to arrest a human being and lose the ability to walk! But you're still under arrest! Wheee!"

Officer Dennis spun an excited quarter circle in the soup of his innards.

And as Officer Dennis cheered and splashed, I turned on the wall screens to check on the cogs in the air lock.

That's when I realized something was wrong.

I mean, it's not to say that there weren't plenty of things *wrong* with the *Tennessee*. But when I turned on the wall screens and scrolled through the camera views, I saw that Parker, my endlessly horny valet cog, had somehow ended up outside the ship, that he was dangling from his tether in space.

And I know it was stupid of me, but I suddenly felt so terrible for the way I'd treated my cogs.

"You're under arrest, Cager Messer! Yippeee! This is

the greatest moment of my rapidly fading life!" the porridge of Officer Dennis announced as Meg stepped around him to join me near the air-lock door. "And you're also under arrest, human girl in a black dress whose identification data is not on the manifest, so I therefore have no idea what your name is. But it would greatly please me if you could put your face down here next to mine, so that I might scan your eyes. Yay!!!"

"Um, no," Meg said.

"Well, you're still under arrest, I am very happy to point out!" Officer Dennis's words spouted in bubbling globules from the pool around his mouth.

Meg looked at the screen, and then at the air-lock controls alongside the door.

The air lock was a smaller, intermediate room—a sort of gangway—between the arrivals hall and the docking bay where I'd left the cogs. On the display screen Lourdes floated around like a mermaid. She made elegant swimming movements with her arms while her hair fanned all around her shoulders. And her skirt had come completely off. Most likely it was outside somewhere, orbiting the moon on its own, like some kind of interstellar jellyfish.

Also, her undies were pink with black kittens on them.

Why did I find Lourdes so incredibly attractive? I must have been losing my mind, I thought. No, I did lose it.

Milo pressed his hands against his face. In the silent-movie image of the boy that illuminated from the wall screen, I could tell Milo was crying.

"You didn't need to leave the outer docking bay door open. Why did you do that?" Meg said.

I shook my head. "I don't know. I thought they'd be safer—that if cogs went out looking for them, the hunting cogs would end up getting sucked outside the ship or something."

"You're all under arrest! This is the happiest moment of my life! I'm so proud of myself for arresting all these human beings!" Officer Dennis burbled, "Let's all go straight to jail immediately! Wheee! Would you mind helping me up, please?"

Billy Hinman kicked Officer Dennis.

The security cog's head came off. It scooted through the puddle of fluid, leaving a soupy wake, like a soccer ball on a swampy field.

"Yeee! Whoopeee! I love getting decapitated! This is the best thing ever!"

"Do you like elevator rides?" Billy asked.

"I love elevator rides so much, I could do three back-flips and gouge my eyes out! If I had arms and fingers and legs and a torso!" Officer Dennis's head said. What was left of his body was excited too. It danced around in the slimy goulash of Officer Dennis's hydraulics.

"Come on, Jeff," Billy said, "let's take Officer Dennis on an elevator ride."

"This makes me so happy! I am beside myself!" Officer Dennis squealed.

Billy Hinman said, "Literally."

If Thy Right Eye Offend Thee

'm so overjoyed to be riding in the elevator with you!" said Officer Dennis's head. "I trust I am taking the two of you to jail; am I right?"

"No," Billy Hinman said.

Jeffrie had been carrying Officer Dennis, who dripped and dripped a stringy trail of snotty droplets all the way from the lower west arrivals hall. She put him down on the floor of the elevator and wiped her hands on the wall.

"I think we should drop him off at the maintenance deck," Jeffrie said. "Maybe they can repair him or recycle him or something. Didn't the guy with the hole in his face say they were fixing things down there?"

Billy nodded. "The guy with the hole in his face is Dr. Geneva."

"And there's lifeboats there. Do you realize what that means? We can get out of here."

"And go where? Besides, you'd never get me on a life-boat, Jeff. Sorry. Those things are too small, and too terri-fying for me."

"Wheee! I love being kidnapped!" said Officer Dennis's head.

Billy said, "I wish he'd shut up. We should leave him in the elevator. I can't stand cogs."

"Some of them are okay." Jeffrie touched a finger to the activation pad and said, "Maintenance deck."

Billy sighed. "I really was hoping to go back to bed. Um . . . you know?"

Officer Dennis said, "Yeee! I'd be so happy to go to bed too! Maybe we could play cards! Oh, wait! Ha ha ha! I don't have any hands!"

Billy Hinman closed his eyes and shook his head. Almost as much as he wanted to go back to the room with Jeffrie, he wanted to kick Officer Dennis's head.

Jeffrie said, "I'd like to go back with you, Billy. Maybe after we drop off the cog head."

Billy put his arms around Jeffrie and pulled her into him.

"Are you kissing? You *are*! Wheee! I love being in an elevator when humans are kissing!" Officer Dennis's head chirped, "Can one of you please roll me over slightly, so I can watch you kiss?"

As Dr. Geneva had promised, the cogs of the *Tennessee* had been busy trying to fix things during the hours since Meg had gotten into the ship's main systems and erased

Queen Dot's experiment in cog cannibalism. The maintenance and lifeboat deck was a beehive of frantic activity, noisily accompanied by shouts from the outraged, ecstatic cries from the joyous, nonstop blathering from the know-it-alls, weeping and wailing from the depressed, and the occasional proposition from the horny.

This was how the *Tennessee* ran.

"'And if thy right eye offend thee, pluck it out, and cast it from thee!'"

As soon as Billy and the head-carrying Jeffrie had stepped from the elevator, they came face-to-face with Reverend Bingo, who flicked a small vial of holy water at them. Reverend Bingo was missing an eye. Half his head had been slicked over with the glistening sludge of cog fluid.

"Why's he missing an eye?" Jeffrie said. "And why's he making us wet?"

"He's doing God's work, I guess," Billy said.

Officer Dennis bleated, "Yeee! My favorite thing in the universe is having water splashed in my face by a one-eyed priest!"

"Here." Jeffrie sat Officer Dennis's head down in front of Reverend Bingo's feet. Reverend Bingo had no shoes, and his black preacher's socks were wet and slimed with cog slop. She said, "I'm an atheist, anyway."

"I am too," Billy said.

"How dare you? How dare you?" Reverend Bingo flicked his little bottle spout at Billy and Jeffrie, but the bottle was empty, and God's work was unfinished.

And Officer Dennis's head said to Reverend Bingo's socks, "I'm Episcopalian!"

"There are no atheists in space!" Reverend Bingo howled. "How dare you make this about *you*, and not about ME? I'm the victim! Not you! You don't get to decide these things! Die, motherfuckers, die!"

Reverend Bingo wound up and threw his empty water bottle at Billy and Jeffrie. It hit Officer Dennis's forehead.

Officer Dennis said, "Ow!"

Reverend Bingo shrieked, "Satan! Satan!"

Then Reverend Bingo hurled himself onto the floor, kicking and flailing his arms in a tantrum of cog pus and anger, screaming, "I should have bought the blue car! I should have bought the blue car!"

"I love blue cars more than life itself!" said Officer Dennis's very happy head.

"I almost wish they were still eating each other," Jeffrie said.

Billy put his hand on Jeffrie's shoulder. "They might be doing something even weirder. Look at that."

Jeffrie turned around to see what Billy was talking about.

The maintenance and lifeboat deck on the *Tennessee* had transformed into some massive and very noisy interstellar field hospital. All across the floor of the enormous deck, cogs leaned over tables or kneeled around any available floor space, working on pieces of other cogs.

Cogs were making cogs.

"Ah! William! So nice you've managed to come down here to see what we've been doing! Isn't it fantastic?"

Dr. Geneva, the hole in his face gaping and oozing, had come up behind Billy and Jeffrie. He warmly patted Billy between the shoulders and waved his arm outward, as though it was he who'd been responsible for orchestrating the entire scene.

"But please," Dr. Geneva continued, "you haven't even introduced me to your lovely . . . *friend*."

And when Dr. Geneva, in all his overbearing creepiness, said "friend," he leaned in closely and stared directly at Jeffrie's eyes, taking in a quick, cog-scanned medical exam.

"Her name is Jeffrie Cutler," Billy said. "Jeffrie, meet Dr. Geneva."

And Dr. Geneva said, "Oh my!"

"What's that supposed to mean?" Billy said.

Dr. Geneva cleared his throat, which made a gooey balloon of cog snot expand and then pop like a lava bubble over the hole in his face. It made a sound, like *Poink!*

"What I mean is—well, did you know, William, that the Roman emperor Elagabalus was arguably a . . . *ahem* . . . *third gender*, if you are familiar with such archaic terminology, and that, although this was definitely at a time when human thought and the capacity for understanding, what were referred to as the emperor's eccentricities, given the presence of male genitalia—"

Billy clenched his hands. "Look. I'm going to be nice and say *please*. Please shut the fuck up. We're not interested in what you have to say, Dr. Geneva. Nobody is. Nobody ever was."

"You . . . What?"

How could anyone ever *not* be interested in Dr. Geneva? The mere thought of it nearly seized the spinning code wheels driving Dr. Geneva's endlessly blathering circuitry. But the doctor recovered from his moment of astonished pause and said, "Bisley! The Bisley boy! Have you ever heard of the Bisley boy, who was actually a child substituted for Queen Elizabeth the First, who had purportedly fallen ill and died while sent away as a precautionary quarantine against bubonic plague in . . ."

Billy Hinman held up a hand. "We don't care, Dr. Geneva."

Dr. Geneva shook his head as though he'd been slapped. A little cog mucus splashed out from the hole in his face. "But—excuse me—there is one thing in particular I think you'll find to be absolutely thrilling, William! Absolutely! It's my surprise for our handful of human passengers on the *Tennessee*. Please, allow me to show you, so you might be the first to see what we've done!"

"If it has anything to do with Jeffrie, I'm going to knock your fucking head off," Billy told him.

"Jeffrie? What? No, no, no, William! It has to do . . ." And Dr. Geneva paused to emphasize all the self-absorbed drama he believed he'd created. "It has to do with Mr. Messer's television program—you know, the one called *Rabbit & Robot*. And it also has to do with something you're quite fond of—I mean to say, besides your friend Jeffrie here, ha ha—because it involves *Cager!*"

What Kind of World

tried to get Lourdes and Milo to help pull Parker back inside the *Tennessee*, but it turned out to be an exercise in futility and frustration.

I explained the urgency of Parker's dilemma over the docking bay's announcement system, but no sound carries in space. I typed messages to them on the inner wall screens in the bay, but neither Milo nor Lourdes paid attention. I could clearly tell what they were doing. I didn't even have to hear them to know.

Milo hid his face in his hands, and he cried and blubbered about being afraid and wanting to give up. And Lourdes was in another world entirely. She just kept swimming and wriggling while her hair waved gracefully all around her like some kind of cloud of sexuality (which I found to be wildly erotic), singing over and over and over, "I'm a fish! I'm a big floating flying fish! Wheee!" And then she'd fart (which was definitely not erotic) and kick her slender cog legs.

"Are you absolutely certain you really want them back?" Meg said.

I looked at her eyes. I was a mess. Maybe it was the lack of sleep, space, Lourdes, the *Tennessee*, but I wanted to kiss Meg Hatfield so bad. And I hated myself for being such a coward, and such a spoiled piece of shit, too.

"I really do," I said.

"I think you're going to have to shut the outer doors and cut that boy loose, then. I can't see another way to get into or out of the docking bay if you don't," Meg said.

Look. They were just machines, right? Flywheels, seed drills, walk/don't walk signals, socket wrenches, can openers. But when Meg suggested I abandon Parker, I began to feel sick inside. As annoying as he was, and as much as I sometimes hated him, Parker was also loyal and unselfish. He could have actually been a friend, not just some god-damned hired Hocus Pocus partner. And as dumb as I feel admitting this now, here in this list of secrets—my attempt to account for what it meant to be a human being—I believe Parker genuinely liked me, and not just because he was horny all the time.

There had been a standard that was widely accepted—that human beings could not reliably tell when they were interacting with machines, but machines knew with unfailing accuracy whether or not they were interacting with humans. Billy Hinman's father made this blurred line much more pronounced, and now, thanks to Queen Dot and her Worms, we were all doomed.

Some machines could be more human than humans. And provided the right dosage of Woz, humans could be more mechanized than the most precise gearbox. Look at every rabbit and robot humankind has ever cranked out of the factories. Look at Charlie Greenwell. Thirty-whatever wars don't just fight themselves, after all.

What kind of world did our fathers abandon us to?

I rubbed my eyes. "I can't do that."

Whoosh. Click. Click.

We didn't notice that Rowan had entered and sealed himself inside the air lock, but there was nothing we could do once it happened. And he played deaf when I shouted at him to get out of there, and scolded him, "What the fuck are you doing? Rowan! What the fuck do you think you're doing?"

Mooney, Mooney!

And we just got him online only moments before you arrived!" Dr. Geneva put his hand on Billy's shoulder. "What do you think?"

Billy Hinman said, "He's real."

Dr. Geneva coughed out a condescendingly fake laugh and said, "Of course he's real, William! As real as anything ever was, since, in effect, our collective notion of *reality* is merely at best an assumption of what *reality* actually *is*. And here he is! Ha ha ha!"

When Dr. Geneva said "reality," he made his hands shape like brackets in the air, and his eyes got very large, like he was talking to an uncomprehending idiot, or maybe a poodle.

Jeffrie said, "Who is he?"

And even if there were only five human beings left alive anywhere in the universe, Jeffrie Cutler would still have been just about the only person who did not recognize the cog who'd just been made by other cogs on the *Tennessee*, who stood before them smiling, extending a hand to shake Billy's.

Billy said, "Mooney. The robot. From the TV show."

Jeffrie shook her head and shrugged. "Never saw it."

And Mooney said, "Glad to meet you, Billy! Would you like me to sing a song for you? *Cheepa Yeep*, by the way! Ha ha ha!"

"I—I'm not . . ."

Billy took Mooney's hand. Nothing else mattered at that point, because the bits of *Rabbit & Robot* that had already wormed their way inside Billy Hinman's brain when he saw the show on our transpod, and from the videos and songs on the *Tennessee*, began to whisper stories to him about another world entirely.

> *Add Action,*
> *Add Action.*
> *Execute switch void ever never,*
> *Execute switch satisfaction.*

Billy was unaware he'd been standing, openmouthed, eyes glazed, staring at Mooney.

Jeffrie grabbed his arm and shook him. "Hey. Hey, Billy."

And Mooney dropped to one knee with his arms out, like an old-time vaudevillian, and finished the song in his booming, goofy voice:

And no one cares about haves and have-nots,
We love you all, our rabbits and robots!

Dr. Geneva clapped his hands wildly. "He's magnificent! Magnificent! William, have I ever told you about the history of mind coding, and how it came to be developed in the first half of this century, coincidental to the discovery of the chief agents of neural reconfiguration brought about by the sustained ingestion of Woz? It's a fascinating study, which dates back to one of the first wars fought between the United States and Norway, where Woz was originally . . . "

Billy Hinman was confused. He shook his head.

Jeffrie said, "Shut the fuck up, Dr. Geneva."

"We should be friends, Billy!" Mooney started singing again. "What do you think you'll be? A bonk like Rabbit? Or a robot like me?"

And Jeffrie said, "Look. Billy. Listen to me. If Queen Dot is out to get these machines, she's for sure done something horrible. We should probably get the fuck out of this place, before we all get burned."

Dr. Geneva had been gabbling on and on and on about Norwegian history as though nothing else mattered at all. He started in the thirteenth century.

Behind them, somewhere on the floor in a puddle of what looked like runny mayonnaise and semen, Reverend Bingo screeched, "I should have bought the blue car! I should have bought the blue car!"

"I'm so happy! I'm so happy, I could poop myself, but my butt's down in the arrivals hall somewhere! Wheee!" Officer Dennis's head bellowed.

And Mooney said, "We should be friends, Billy! Maybe we could go shoot some monkeys together, ha ha! Or we could go to Rabbit & Robot World and ride the terror coaster! Or, wait! I know what we could do!"

And then Mooney dug his hand down inside his pocket. He opened his palm in front of Billy's chin, and all up through the fake flesh of his fake and mechanized hand wriggled excited little blue worms, slithering in oily slime.

"Ha ha! It's Woz, Billy! My own special kind! Want to try some with me? I bet your pal Cager would!"

Mooney held the wriggling mass that glinted like diamonds.

This Is What We Saw

slapped the door to the air lock. It hurt my hand.

"Rowan! Stop it! What the fuck?"

Meg watched the wall screens as Rowan disarmed the second air-lock door that led to the docking bay. "He's opening it. He's going to die in there."

There had been accidents in the past, in which passengers from a Grosvenor Galactic Rabbit & Robot cruise ship had "fallen overboard" and ended up in space. Most of those people exploded, due to the involuntary reflex of holding your breath. But space is unforgiving when your lungs are filled with air, which it will suck out with the force of a detonating bomb.

It's very messy, but also very quiet.

One passenger, a man traveling on my father's ship the *Minnesota*, actually survived an unprotected extravehicular fall that lasted nearly half a minute before he managed to pull himself back inside an open air lock. After that incident, Grosvenor Galactic began including warnings on their passenger safety lessons about the Forester Effect, which was named after Eddie Forester, the man who'd survived in space.

Eddie Forester exhaled.

Just thinking about it makes me feel like I'm being smothered.

I hoped if Rowan was actually doing the stupid and dangerous thing he looked like he was about to do, that he'd remember the Forester Effect, and not hold his breath.

I did not want to watch Rowan explode.

This is what we saw: Rowan activated the bay's exit sequence, which discharged all the oxygen from inside the air lock and then caused the second door to open. I don't know why, but when I saw this on the wall screen, I inhaled deeply and held my breath.

If I'd been with Rowan, I would have exploded.

But Rowan, my dutiful lifelong caregiver, bath drawer, and underwear folder, did not explode, probably thanks to a guy named Eddie Forester.

Along the walls of the docking bay were networks of vertical metal rungs with safety clips on them for workers to maneuver around the hull of the *Tennessee* or undocked transpods if the outer doors were open. Three of these were what I'd used to anchor the cogs I'd noosed. Rowan pulled himself along the sideways ladders toward the rung Parker had been tied to.

It was sickening to watch him. I knew Rowan wouldn't make it back; it was impossible. But I couldn't look away, and I couldn't breathe, either. I was faintly aware that Meg was holding my hand.

"You're not breathing," Meg said.

I inhaled. It felt good. "What the fuck is he doing?"

Rowan grasped Parker's cable in one hand, anchoring himself with the other on the metal safety rung. He jerked the cable like he was setting a hook in a tuna, and Parker came bobbing and tumbling out of the darkness of space. My eternally horny personal valet cog drifted inside the open outer docking-bay doors. I was happy to see him, and relieved, terrified, and sickened, too, all at the same time.

Meg said, "He's a cog."

"Huh?"

"Your butler guy. He's a cog, Cager. I couldn't even tell."

Meg swept her hands over the operations screen and shut the outer doors.

"He can't be. He has a last name. It's Tuttle-Finewater. Rowan can't be a cog." My voice cracked. I couldn't believe any of this.

And Meg said, "Tuttle-Finewater?"

"England. He was born in England. It's why he's always so perfect and never farts and stuff."

Meg shook her head. "Um, he's a cog."

"No."

I was embarrassed. I felt sick and stupid in front of Meg

Hatfield because she had to have noticed the tear I wiped off my face.

As soon as the doors shut, the docking bay pressurized and produced gravity. Lourdes and Parker thudded to the floor. Milo, one of his trouser legs missing, was still curled up with a noose around his neck, in the same place I'd left him.

With air pressure and gravity came sounds.

Lourdes squirmed on the docking bay's floor. "Wheee! I love gravity so much, I want to have its child! Yeee! Yeee!"

Parker boosted himself onto his hands and knees, slipped the noose from his neck, and looked into the wall screen beside the air lock. "Cager? Cager, did you come back for me? I always knew you would. I love you, Cager."

And Milo, softly crying, said, "I deserve to have been eaten. I would have been eaten too, if everyone didn't hate me so much."

Maybe it was the Forester Effect, I thought.

Rowan couldn't be a cog. He was just supersmart about everything, so he must have exhaled. And even though no human being could have lived without a store of oxygen for the few minutes Rowan was in the docking bay rescuing Parker, it just couldn't be the case that Rowan was a machine—a sixteen-year-long lie to Cager Messer.

I wiped at my eyes and opened the air-lock door.

Meg followed me into the bay.

Lourdes squirmed in delight, and Milo cradled his face and rocked back and forth. Parker rushed me as soon as

I got inside the docking bay. He threw his arms around me and rubbed his hips firmly into mine. If Parker was a house, I could feel he was rearranging some of his downstairs furniture.

"I always knew you'd come back for me, Cager. Can I please kiss you?"

"No. Not now, Parker." I pushed him away from me and went to untie Lourdes and Milo.

And when I undid the knot on Lourdes's noose, my knee brushed across her pink-and-kittens panties.

I was a wreck.

"I'm free! I'm free!" Lourdes shrieked, "I love freedom almost as much as I love being hanged!"

It must be nice, I thought, to have such a positive outlook on just about everything.

And Milo said, "I'm so ashamed of myself. I'm completely worthless."

I loosened the noose around Milo's neck and patted his shoulder. "It's okay, Milo. We fixed everything."

That made Milo start crying again. "Not my pants."

I looked at the little wise men, angels, baby Jesuses, and farm animals on Milo's boxers, a definite dress-code violation at Le Lapin et l'Homme Mécanique.

"We'll get you some new pants, Milo. I promise."

Lourdes, who was already up on her feet and dancing, sang, "Wheee! My skirt flew away, all by itself!"

Rowan had been standing against the wall, still grasping the safety rung where he'd pulled Parker's tether. He didn't say anything when I walked up to him. He avoided eye contact, which was a thing I'd never really seen Rowan do before, unless I'd been asking him about sex, or whether or not he was a virgin, which was something sixteen-year-old Cager Messer was too mature to do.

Because sixteen-year-old Cager Messer knew the answer to that one now.

But I didn't really know what to say to him either. I felt so betrayed, and I couldn't begin to explain to myself exactly why I should feel that way. Rowan—Rowan Tuttle-Finewater—was just a tea-brewing, bath-drawing, sandwich-making, underwear-folding, babysitting machine. Nothing more.

I may as well have gotten my feelings hurt by an egg beater, which was also something I had never used in my life.

And another thing I'd never done in my life was this: I had never been angry or disappointed with Rowan. But now I was all those things, and much more, too. I was confused and scared.

Also, I was very cruel. But in my defense, it was justifiable because I'd been lied to and duped for my entire life. And, anyway, you can't honestly be cruel to a fucking machine, can you?

But Rowan was my caretaker. Rowan raised me.

"You aren't even real," I said. "At any time they could have simply replaced you with a goddamned windup toy. What's the fucking difference?"

I'll admit that my voice quavered like a hoarse-throated

yodeler's, and I was also on the verge of crying, which likely would have made Milo cry harder, and Lourdes gush about how much she loves to see boys cry, and Parker get turned on.

But I had no idea what Rowan would do. Maybe he'd offer to fix me some tea and fill a bathtub for me, until I got over myself and calmed down.

"Nice coding, by the way. They left out all the excessive happy, sad, mad, horny whatever the fuck it is they do to you things, and they made you smell like one of us."

I called Rowan a *thing*.

I made him something other than *us*.

I didn't even know who he was anymore. I realized I never had.

And Rowan didn't answer me. There was no arching of the eyebrow, just a blank stare. He looked guilty and injured.

I was so mad, I could have thrown myself to the floor and gouged my own eyes out—a real v.4 meltdown.

"I fucking hate this place."

I turned away from Rowan and ran out of there, and Parker chased after me, calling, "Wait! Cager! Wait!"

Are You One of Us?

ave I strung you along?

I'd hoped that in leaving behind my account of what we did and what happened to us on the *Tennessee*, that maybe two thousand centuries from now—or whenever— someone, you, might find this and say, *There once were these things called humans, and this is what it meant to be one of them.*

I realize I just called us "things."

We are faulty machines with built-in obsolescence, and we can make more of us.

Cogs making cogs.

And maybe that's the whole point, after all—that every one of us who ever existed spent all those limited days over the thousands of centuries we were here just trying to figure out what it meant to be *us*. The mousetrap trigger is this precise point: Pour the word "us" into the coding of a human, and we immediately discount as inferior or useless all the not-us things in the universe.

Are you one of us?

This is my jar. I'll leave it here, atop this hill.

It is sad and wonderful.

Moon to Moon

Maybe we can never know one another.

Maybe I didn't know Billy Hinman, either.

Maybe I had discounted my best friend—my only friend—after he stayed beside me through all those messed-up years we spent growing up while not growing up.

And maybe Billy only fooled himself into thinking that this entire ruse—getting me onto the *Tennessee*—was more about fixing me than fixing *us*. I screwed everything up, and we were all trapped in this mechanized bedlam, a demented and preposterous moon to our moon.

I wanted to be hacked up on Woz again.

On board the *Tennessee*, the Worms—visible and invisible—were everywhere.

Just Like Home

Meg Hatfield was alone in our room, lying in bed, when Billy and Jeffrie came back.

Billy stumbled in the dark and leaned against Jeffrie. His shirt was untucked and his tie undone, and as soon as they got inside the room Billy collapsed onto my bed, laughing.

Billy Hinman was out of it on Woz.

"Hey, Cager. Cager, guess what? You'll never believe what just happened, man. I feel so fucking good. Who knew this shit could make a guy feel so good?" Billy said. He kicked off his shoes.

Jeffrie pushed his hand away when Billy tried to unzip her dress. She said, "Don't you think we need to tell them what's going on?"

"I don't know. What *is* going on, Jeff?" Billy asked.

"Cager's not here. He's gone," Meg said.

"Oh," Billy said.

The Woz that Mooney gave him was particularly potent, and Billy Hinman was very happy, very relaxed. He couldn't remember much about the evening except for meeting Mooney, how they'd smoked crushed Woz tablets together and laughed about how everything that had been happening on the *Tennessee* was simply part of another episode of *Rabbit & Robot*, which meant Mooney was undoubtedly going to suffer some major humiliation at any moment.

People got a kick out of seeing Mooney humiliated.

But it was not a television program that we were stuck inside.

Billy Hinman said, "I think I'm finally starting to like this place."

Billy took off his pants and shirt and pulled back the bedsheets before he realized what Meg had said to him.

"What do you mean, Cager's gone? Wasn't he just here when we came in?"

"He was very upset about something. He took off when we were down in the docking bay. That was a few hours ago," Meg said.

"Huh?" Billy straightened up, wobbling, and turned on the lights. "Where's Rowan? Cager gets like that sometimes. Rowan knows how to fix him up."

Meg shook her head. "You're high."

Billy smiled and shrugged.

So Meg Hatfield told Billy and Jeffrie the story of what

had happened in the arrivals hall after they left with Officer Dennis's head.

Jeffrie sat on the bed next to Billy and listened. She loved hearing Meg tell stories. It made Jeffrie feel like she was sitting outside on a hot desert afternoon up on Missing Boy Mountain, which she missed very much. When Meg finished, Jeffrie asked her, again, if Cager and Rowan and the three cogs were all okay.

Billy Hinman shook his head and rubbed the back of his neck.

"That can't be right," he said. "I've known Rowan as long as Cager has. Rowan changed my fucking diapers when I was a baby. Rowan still gets Cager dressed. He feeds us, and drives us wherever we want to go."

Meg said, "What do you want me to say? We saw what we saw. He's a cog. A pretty slick one too, if you ask me. But what would you expect a Messer or a Hinman to own?"

"We don't *own* Rowan," Billy said.

Billy Hinman was very confused.

"Okay. Well, he's a cog," Meg said. "He was basically outside the ship—in outer space—with nothing, no suit, for at least three minutes. No living thing could survive something like that."

Billy sighed and shook his head. "This is fucked up."

"Why?" Meg asked.

"Because I hate cogs. I hate everything about them. But Rowan—he raised Cager and me. He was around us more than our parents ever were."

Billy Hinman picked up his pants and dug through the pockets, looking for the Woz tablets Mooney had given him. He crushed two of them into powder on top of the dressing table using his belt buckle as a pestle.

And Jeffrie said, "Down on the lifeboat deck, the cogs are making new cogs, Meg. You stopped them from eating each other, but now they're building new ones. That's not good."

"And they're making rabbits and robots. And Mooneys." Billy lay back on the bed and stretched his arms out over his head. "And Woz. It's just like being in the show. And I saw these little blue worms. They're everywhere."

Meg sat up. She looked at Jeffrie, who was standing in the middle of the room, and at Billy, who was nearly passed out on the bed, and she thought about what it all meant, about what was bound to happen on the *Tennessee*.

And Billy murmured, "'I placed a jar in Tennessee, and round it was upon a hill.' They did this, you know, those blue fuckers."

"I'm sorry I brought you here, Jeff," Meg said. "I can't stand this place."

"It's not so bad. I'm kind of getting used to it," Billy said.

Jeffrie sat down on the bed beside Billy. She placed her hand flat on his chest. "I never liked it here. I want to go home. I don't care how messed up things are back home. I want to get out of here."

"So do I," Meg said.

And Billy, half-asleep, slurred, "You will never, never, never get me in one of those lifeboats."

Helpless, Helpless, Helpless

Ha ha! This is delightful! *Charmant!* It is remarkable what you can do with your little human man-boy fingers and—*et les pouces*—and thumbs!"

Maurice laughed and threw back his head, which, even though we were all sitting down, was still six feet above mine.

"Another, please! Do it again! *Faites-le encore une fois, s'il vous plaît!* Ha ha ha!"

Maurice was the nicest giraffe I'd ever met, and as cogs went he was remarkably stable, if only a little sexually creepy.

"But, *s'il vous plaît*, would you enjoy to climb onto my back, *jeune petit garçon?*"

"No thanks, Maurice," I said.

Parker and I sat with Maurice beside a campfire on the shore of fake Lake Louise. It was nighttime on the recreation deck, and the fake sky overhead was lit up with stars and a fake big yellow moon.

I was getting really good with the can opener Parker had found for me, and it thrilled Maurice to see the things inside the old tins we'd scavenged from a fake grocery store on Deck 21. Some of the things inside the cans I had never heard of— hominy, fish balls, and something called scrapple—but I kept opening and opening and, each time, I'd nearly pass out from the assault of all those unfamiliar and pungent smells.

And Maurice sang an ancient song I'd never heard before, but it was beautiful and lonely sounding, which was exactly what I wanted to hear, considering the mood I'd been in.

> *Big birds flying across the sky,*
> *Throwing shadows on our eyes.*
> *Leave us helpless, helpless, helpless.*

I decided that it didn't matter who we were anymore, and I was certainly done with being Cager Messer. So I took off my shoes and socks and all the dressy clothes Meg had picked out for me before we didn't go to dinner, and I replaced my outfit with a kind of caveman waistcloth I fashioned from the tiger skin left behind by poor Juan, who'd been eaten by Maurice how many days earlier I couldn't even guess. I also smeared mud on my face and chest and in my hair—something I would never have considered doing when I was under Rowan's care.

Rowan would have disapproved.

And I did some push-ups, too, but only five, because they are much more difficult than I ever thought they could be, and they made my chest and armpits sore. Doing push-ups made me feel virile and manly. But I was finally knocking off all those things on my list that I was afraid I'd never get the chance to do, even though the really big one at the top—which involved another human being like Meg Hatfield—sadly, was never going to be, and that made me feel the opposite of virile and manly.

Parker could do endless push-ups, but then again Parker was a cog. And while he was pumping away at them next to me, he said, "Cager? Do you know what this makes me think of?"

"No, Parker. Shut up. I don't want to know."

Parker, who, as expected, insisted on wearing whatever I chose to wear, had to settle for a powder-blue-gingham caveman cloth, which he'd taken from the top of a table inside the little tea house. He also smeared himself with mud, and he'd asked me why we were dressing ourselves this way.

"It's in my blood," I told him.

"I don't understand."

"It's how the first human beings dressed. And I'm like the first human being, all over again," I said.

"Oh. Did the v.1 human beings put mud on their faces too?" Parker asked.

"That's a good one—v.1 human beings. I don't know. Probably."

"Oh. I wish I was a human being," Parker said.

"Why would *anyone* wish that?" I asked.

"Well, if I was a human being, you might want to have a sexual encounter with me."

"No. I told you a hundred times. No," I said.

"Oh. Well, if I was a human being, maybe you and I would be friends, like you and Billy."

Parker sounded sad. It actually made me feel sorry for him, like I'd been mean to him. Fucking machines. Fucking space. Fucking *Tennessee*.

I sighed. "I didn't mean to hurt your feelings."

And Parker said, "You didn't hurt my feelings, Cager. But I do have an erection, in case you were wondering."

"I have never wondered about that, Parker."

"Never?"

"Let's stop talking about this, okay?" I said.

I grabbed another can. Maurice clapped his front hooves together and cheered. The can contained something called SpaghettiOs. The SpaghettiOs looked like the stuff that came out of the insane chimps I'd killed on Deck 21, and the vinegar-cheesy smell of them made me dizzy. My eyes watered from the stench.

"Magical! Magical! Are those little tiny things *alive*?" exclaimed Maurice, laughing.

And out of the darkness of the woods, just beyond the dusty dome of amber light thrown out from our campfire, came Billy Hinman's voice.

"Cager? I thought you'd be here. What the hell are you doing?"

"Opening cans. Want to see?"

"Sure."

Maurice wobbled his neck in a great looping circle. "Oh

my! It's my other *ami humain*! The other *jeune beau garçon* from the lake! This is magical! I insist we should all climb on my back and go for a swim! It is such a lovely evening!"

Billy Hinman stepped from the woods. He'd changed out of his Le Lapin et l'Homme Mécanique outfit and was wearing some baggy jeans, a T-shirt, and sneakers that looked like they'd be great for throwing at deranged ministers.

And he smelled like sweat and Woz, just like I always used to smell.

I didn't care anymore. Billy would do whatever he wanted to do, just like I would, and Meg, Jeffrie, Rowan, and every other trapped and preprogrammed thing in this spinning madhouse.

Billy sat down beside me. He folded his legs and leaned over the metallic chrysanthemum of opened cans.

"What is this stuff?" he asked.

"Food."

"Are you eating it?"

"It's at least a hundred years old. I don't think you can eat it anymore."

"Good thing. It looks totally disgusting."

Billy Hinman petted my tiger skin. Typical horny Billy Hinman. "Dude. Do you realize you're covered in mud and wearing only a fur washcloth?"

"It didn't slip my attention," I said. "This was from the tiger who ate our clothes."

"I thought it looked familiar," Billy said.

Parker jealously glared at Billy's hand, which was still on my lap.

I said, "Where'd you get the Woz, Bill?"

"Oh. You can tell? Mooney gave it to me. He's actually *here*, Cage, just like the show. Well, actually, the cogs put him together, down on the maintenance deck. And they're making a Rabbit, too. How cool is *that*? You want some Woz, Cage? We should get hacked up together; it would be fun."

"I'm over that shit, Bill. You and Rowan cleaned me up."

Billy shrugged. "That's funny, coming from someone covered in mud and wrapped in a dead animal's skin. Anyway, what's it matter?"

"I know, right?"

"Cager?"

"What?"

"What's going to happen to us?"

"How could I ever answer that question, Bill?"

"Meg and Jeffrie are leaving. Rowan, too. That's why we had to find you."

I almost laughed. "Oh yeah? Where are they going?"

"Meg's going to unlock a lifeboat."

The lifeboats. We were forced to watch the terrifying escape-procedure presentation before we got onto the *Tennessee*. Each of the small ships could handle twenty passengers, and they'd all been preprogrammed to return to Mojave Field, if it was even still there. Seems like Mr. Messer's company should have come up with a contingency plan for what to do in case we fucked the planet.

My heart sank.

I didn't want the girls to leave, but what could I do about it? And I didn't know how I felt about Rowan going away, but I didn't want to look at him again either.

"What about you?" I said.

Billy frowned and shook his head. "You'd never get me on one of those lifeboats. I'm not going to go."

"But what about Jeffrie?"

"She has to do her own thing, right? She'll be okay."

"But I thought you guys liked each other."

"I know. We do, Cage. It sucks," Billy said.

"I'll stay here with you," Parker offered.

"And so will I! I love it here with my little man-boy friends! We can open all the cans, and I can watch you doing all the push-ups!" gurgled Maurice, in his nice but very creepy way.

Then Billy said, "Just two things, Cage. One: If we're staying, I'll need to go kill a tiger or something and roll around in the mud naked, because that's the way I'm dressing from now on too. And two: You should probably go say good-bye to them, so they'll know if you've decided to stay."

I did not want to say good-bye.

Saying good-bye was something else Cager Messer never had to do before.

And Maurice sang:

Leave us helpless, helpless, helpless.

v.1 Human Beings

Rowan came out of his room just as I made my way up to the door. It almost seemed as though he'd been waiting for me.

He probably was.

He was dressed in an orange paper flight suit, the kind we'd all worn when we hopped on the transpod in Mojave Field a lifetime ago. Rowan was ready to leave the *Tennessee*.

I didn't know how I felt about it all. Well, I did know, but I felt so many things simultaneously, it was like I was on the brink of exploding from all the pressure building inside me. I was angry about the sixteen-plus years I'd spent in Rowan's care, never knowing who—what—he really was. I was also sad to see him dressed to leave, because I knew we'd never see each other again, and never is a very long time to someone who isn't a machine and can't just squander ten thousand years here or there.

And when I saw Rowan, I gulped down the urge to cry. I also swallowed the urge to hug him, because that would have been stupid. You don't go around hugging cogs like you mean it. I might as well have hugged a hair dryer or a pencil sharpener, for that matter.

I was a mess, and I realized I hadn't spent one moment on the way up to my stateroom thinking about what, exactly, I was going to say to Rowan.

So he talked first.

"I see you've managed to pick out your own clothes. That's quite a look," Rowan said.

I watched his eyebrows. They didn't move. Rowan was being cautious.

He was being cautious because I'd hurt his feelings, because Cager Messer, who'd also never in his life picked out his own clothes until that fake night on the recreation deck with Maurice and Parker, was a spoiled asshole.

"I'm a v.1 human being," I said.

"Oh."

I shouldn't have said that, but I can't be held entirely accountable, since I'm a teenager, which means I'm prone to say shitty things without fully considering their impact. So I tried to regroup, and said, "Um, orange is a good color on you, Rowan."

Normally we could tease each other back and forth in a very restrained, Rowan-like manner, but this exchange was painful for both of us. Not one single moment had played out *normally* since they'd concocted the scheme to kidnap me for my birthday.

"Well. I suppose my work is done, Cager. You're quite grown-up. I'm happy about that. I'm going back now," Rowan said. "Be well."

Then he turned around, just like that, so I couldn't see his face.

I couldn't help myself. I began to cry. It made mud under my eyes, and it also made me angrier.

"Go back *where?*" I said.

Rowan, still facing away from me, said, "Back to Earth."

"What if it's all fucked up?"

"What? Worse than here? It's still home, Cager, and there's something about *home*, no matter how untidy we've left it."

My stomach heaved like a fist opening and closing. I concentrated on my breathing, so Rowan wouldn't hear that I was crying.

Cager Messer had never cried because of Rowan.

Then he said, "Well, I suppose you and Billy do not intend to come with us. So, good-bye, Cager."

"You can't just do that."

Rowan took two steps away from me, toward the elevator.

And I said, "You can't lie to a person for his entire life and then just walk away like that. I'd maybe expect that from my father, but not from you."

That stopped him. Rowan turned around. He could

clearly see I'd been crying; my nose was running, and my face was a muddy mess.

Rowan took a deep, fake breath. He was magnificently coded, one of a kind, a cog like no other—one to end all cogs. He looked sad and old, but that was impossible.

"When you were old enough to understand, I started to tell you a hundred times. And every time I thought I would, I became convinced that you would hate me, and your parents, too." Rowan shrugged and turned his palms upward as though to say, *And I guess I was right about that.*

He added, "And it may not matter, but I am so deeply sorry for this, Cager. It breaks my heart to see that I've made you cry. I want you to know that I look at you as my own son, and I do love you."

That was all I could take. What did Rowan know about hearts, and how they break sometimes? What could he possibly know about love? It may as well have been a tire inflator saying it loved me.

Nobody fucking cares about that, right?

"Good-bye, Rowan."

Cager Messer had dressed himself and said good-bye; and there was one more thing he wanted to knock off his list.

I went back to my room, to look for Meg.

Caveman & Spaceman

Seeing Meg and Jeffrie in their orange flight suits was scary. It was all real; they were actually going to leave the *Tennessee*, and Billy and I would be the only human beings left up here.

For the rest of our lives.

"What happened to *you*?" Meg said.

With all the turmoil going on inside me, I had to think for a moment to decode what it was Meg asked me. And then I realized I was barefoot, wearing nothing but a tiger skin knotted around my waist, and I was covered all over with mud.

What a joke: Caveman meets spaceman.

All of human history was here in my stateroom, bottled up in this jar called the *Tennessee*.

"Nothing," I said. "I was mad. That's all. This is how I'm going to dress from now on, since I'm the first human being."

"And this is how I'm going to dress, until I get back home," Meg said.

"What if home isn't there?"

Meg shook her head. "I have to believe it will be okay, that we'll manage to get by. Maybe there won't be any more wars or bonks or coders or Grosvenor Schools."

I felt a fresh tear slalom its way around chunks of grit. I didn't want her to go. I didn't want to be alone.

And Jeffrie said, "I'm going to wait outside."

Jeffrie Cutler put her hand on my naked, muddy shoulder, and she kissed the side of my face. She said good-bye and told me not to be sad. Then she left.

I was alone again in my room with Meg Hatfield.

"Don't cry."

"Why not?" I wiped the back of my hand across my face. Such a mess.

"I don't know. I guess people don't like to see other people so sad."

"I don't want you to go away."

"Then come with us."

"I can't leave Billy. We're all we've ever had."

Meg said, "What about Rowan?"

"I don't want to talk about him anymore."

I sat on the edge of my bed and stared down at my feet.

"What Rowan did for you was pretty heroic, don't you think?" Meg said. "I mean, not just going out there and getting your cogs back, but the whole thing he did with sneaking you and your best friend out to Mojave Field so they could try to help you."

"Yeah. And now Billy took some Woz."

Meg shrugged. "I know. You love him, though. You wouldn't stay if you didn't."

I had nothing to say to Meg Hatfield. Of course she was right. Meg Hatfield was probably the smartest person I'd ever met in my life. I just sat there in the quiet of my room, with my face in my hands. There was nothing else I could do now.

Meg waited. Who knows how long it was? Ten minutes? Half an hour? None of those measurements made any sense, none mattered up here in the *Tennessee*.

I was dimly aware that Meg was writing something in ink on the wall beside my bed, but I didn't want to look.

Finally, she said, "I'm going to go now. We're friends, right, Cager? I mean, no matter what, I want you to know that I really do like you, and I'm sorry about how mean I was."

"You weren't mean."

"Okay."

"Tell me all the things you hate about me," I said.

Meg laughed. She said, "Look. This is my PIN code for unlocking the lifeboats. I mean, if you get sick of this place, and maybe if you get Billy drunk enough to fly home, or something."

My eyes were too blurred to read it.

I said, "Like that'll ever happen."

"Okay."

I stood up, and Meg said, "Just one last thing. I know this is stupid and all, but I really want to give you a good-bye kiss. You know, I don't mean anything by it, and I wouldn't want you to get the wrong idea. Like Jeff did. Have you ever even kissed anyone before?"

I thought about Katie St. Romaine. Of course I'd kissed someone before. What was Meg thinking?

I lied. "No."

"Well, you should try it sometime."

"At the moment I don't really feel like kissing Billy. I don't really want to kiss Dr. Geneva, either."

Meg smiled.

Then she put her arms around me and we kissed. And, yes, I had kissed Katie St. Romaine plenty of times, but it never made me feel much of anything at all. And I'd kissed Billy Hinman once on his fourteenth birthday because he'd asked me to, and then on New Year's because I wanted to do it and it felt good. But Cager Messer had never been kissed by anyone who made him feel as magnificent, as terrible, as human, as Meg Hatfield did.

I never wanted it to end.

That was spoiled of me, wasn't it?

When I let her go, I said, "I got dirt all over your spacesuit."

Meg Hatfield didn't say another word to me. Her eyes were wet. It was over, and she just spun around and left me there, alone in my empty room.

And another thing Cager Messer had never done: He had never had his heart broken the way it was broken when Meg Hatfield and Rowan Tuttle-Finewater left him.

I was a stubborn idiot to let that happen.

So, that was it.

This was how it was going to be for the rest of forever, as the meaningless segments of time we used to call days ticked by endlessly through the calendarless neveryear Billy Hinman and I welcomed in aboard the *Tennessee*.

How many things were left that I'd never done?

I looked at the wall where Meg had written her code to unlock the lifeboats.

This is what Meg Hatfield wrote on the wall beside my bed:

I REALLY DO LIKE YOU, CAGER.
I'M SORRY YOU CAN'T BE WHO YOU REALLY
WANT TO BE.
I WILL MISS YOU.
—MEG

The Unlock Code

That was it, wasn't it?

Meg's code didn't just unlock the lifeboats; it unlocked everything.

Meg Hatfield's code was the lifeboat in itself.

I still had time.

I prayed there would be enough time.

Righting the Ship

Milo wept, but at least he had some new maître d' trousers, which looked very nice on him.

He cried because he did not want to allow me into Le Lapin et l'Homme Mécanique dressed as I was, but at the same time, owing me his mechanical and despondent life, he didn't want to stop me either.

So he cried.

But I was on a mission, and I wasn't about to let something like a dress code stop me. I needed to right the ship Cager Messer was trapped on, and I didn't have much time.

And the bartender protested, hands raised, when I stepped around the bar and began looking over the arrangement of decorative bottles on display. I didn't know what any of it really was—I was so inexperienced with these things—but I knew enough to look for something that would work on Billy Hinman more quickly than beer.

"Hey! Don't you belong on the World of the Monkeys deck?" the bartender, who looked like Abraham Lincoln, said.

"Don't be stupid." I ignored him and concentrated on reading the small print at the bottom of the labels. "I'm not a cog, I'm a human being."

I found what I was looking for just as President Lincoln launched into a blathering soliloquy on the history and components of absinthe, which was the green stuff in the bottle I nicked to help persuade Billy Hinman to get in the lifeboat with me.

"Wheee! Yeee! Yeee! I love cavemen in tiger skirts more than I love life itself!"

Lourdes, our now fully dressed cruise director who was not technically *alive* to begin with, came up behind me and lifted the hem of my waistcloth. "Yippeee! I see your butt! Wheee!" she shrieked.

Despite that I kind of liked it that Lourdes was looking at my butt, I felt myself turning red beneath all that dried mud, and I pushed her hand away.

The bartender, Mr. Lincoln, was going on and on and on. " . . . until sometime later, when Valentin Magnan concluded in the nineteenth century that wormwood produced significant hallucinogenic effects. This finding was widely celebrated by bohemian writers and artists who . . ."

"Come with us, Lourdes. We're leaving," I said.

"Yeee! Yeee! I love being kidnapped as much as I love

being hanged! Yippeee!" Lourdes danced and farted as I pulled her along by the wrist.

There was definitely something to be said for Lourdes's optimistic outlook.

Milo cried when I told him to come with us.

The bartender was saying something about sugar cubes. I had never seen a sugar cube in my life, but there wasn't time now.

And Milo, worried, said, "But what about the customers?"

"Milo. There are no customers."

The boy began sobbing with renewed intensity. "It's because of me, isn't it?"

Whatever.

The Doctor and the Reverend

Dr. Geneva, his face bubbling cog snot from the hole in his cheek where Captain Myron had bitten him, was in the middle of an argument about religious history with Reverend Bingo, who seemed to be weeping syrupy tears from the socket where Meg Hatfield had knocked his eye out with my tennis shoe, when Meg, Jeffrie, and Rowan stepped out of the elevator and onto the maintenance deck.

"No, no, no!" Dr. Geneva was saying. "I'm afraid you are mistaken, Reverend Bingo. It was the denial of the designation Ecumenical Patriarch to Cerularius in the year 1054 and the attacks on customary unleavened bread by Leo of Ohrid that were the largest contributing factors behind the—"

When Reverend Bingo saw Rowan and the girls, his one remaining eye widened in offended disgust. "Satan and the twinned whores of Babylon! Die, motherfuckers! Die!"

Then Reverend Bingo lowered himself into a tackling stance and charged at Rowan. Unfortunately for Reverend Bingo, he was about as adept at tackling biblical demons as he was at throwing shoes.

Reverend Bingo fell on his face and slid forward, trailing a snail slick of cog broth from his chin to his shoulder.

"Satan! What have you done to my legs, motherfucker? I should have bought the blue car! I should have bought the blue car!"

Rowan's eyebrows arched like a Bactrian silhouette.

Meg said, "He's mad at me for knocking his eye out with Cager's shoe. And he obviously made a poor choice in automobiles."

Rowan said, "I see."

And Dr. Geneva, unfazed by Reverend Bingo's tirade, continued on and on and on about the Great Schism in the Catholic Church.

The *Tennessee* truly was a madhouse moon to the moon.

Bells sounded in the busy maintenance area where cogs were making new cogs—Mooneys, Rabbits, President Lincolns. Behind the work area, great columns of doorways stacked up as high as the ceiling—the portals to lifeboats that were always ready to be armed for a departure to Earth. And over the announcement system, a song played:

Tah-rum-tee-tum tum!
Tah-rum-tee-tum tum!

Put your good-bye faces on,
Put your good-bye faces on.
Our guests will be departing soon.
We'll wave to them around the moon. . . .

And all the busy cogs on the maintenance deck stopped
to listen, then began filing out to say their farewells to whoever it was departing the *Tennessee.*

And there were wriggling blue worms everywhere—
oozing from keyboards, dripping from ventilator grates.
The *Tennessee* was going to die.

Jeffrie said, "These are the same things we saw crawling
out of Mooney's hand."

They didn't see that I'd come up behind them, a
mud-smeared caveman holding a slender bottle of green
absinthe, accompanied by the downtrodden Milo and the
eternally thrilled Lourdes.

And I said, "Mr. Messer would be really mad at all this."

"Cager Messer!" Dr. Geneva burbled. "A most fascinating
archetypical human outfit, especially given the ecclesiastical
nature of the discussion I was having with Reverend Bingo!
Did you know, Cager, that the caricature of the aggressive,
brutish Neanderthal Ice Age hominid has no basis in—"

Channeling my inner aggressive and brutish Neanderthal,
I wanted to club Dr. Geneva with my absinthe bottle.

Instead, I said, "Dr. Geneva, shut the fuck up."

And Reverend Bingo writhed in agony and eye-socket
pus. "I should have bought the blue car!"

Why did I ever think I could stay on the *Tennessee*?

"Meg, I saw your code. I'm sorry I've been such an idiot," I said. "I'm coming home with you. Just give me time to get Billy."

Then I swallowed the knot in my throat. "Rowan, I'm sorry for being such an ass for the past sixteen years."

"Sixteen years and twelve days," Rowan pointed out.

Naturally, Rowan had been keeping track of time up here.

"Whatever. Sixteen plus twelve days, then. Will you just let me tell you that? That I apologize. And I love you, Rowan. Okay?"

Then I stepped up to Rowan Tuttle-Finewater and did something else Cager Messer had never done. I hugged him.

See what space did to me? I would never look at a can opener or hair dryer the same way again.

The things our fathers made have taken dominion everywhere.

And the song played.

> *Put your good-bye faces on,*
> *Put your goodbye faces on.*
> *Our guests will be departing soon.*
> *Please come back and sail with us around the*
> *moon. . . .*

Epilogue:
It Took Dominion Everywhere

So I am leaving this here for you.

It's really ridiculous, when you think about it: something left behind by a human being, swallowed up by all this eternal and lazy nature.

Progress will only get a guy so far, and it will never move beyond the wall of extinction. Queen Dot was right about that.

I haven't taken Woz since the day Billy and Rowan kidnapped me. How long that will last is anyone's guess. We can always hope. And it was while I recorded these final thoughts on our way back to Mother Earth that I figured it out: Love and hope are what make us what we are.

I couldn't see this before we came to the *Tennessee*. So the *Tennessee* saved us, and doomed us too, all at the same time.

We are going back home—Meg, Jeffrie, Billy, Rowan,

Parker, Lourdes, Milo, me, and Maurice, too, who folded himself up into a tiny little box so he could fit in the lifeboat.

He's the nicest giraffe any of us have ever met.

It's a long journey back to Mojave Field, if Mojave Field is even still there.

We are not watching *Rabbit & Robot* on the way, but Maurice, who looks like a small spotted suitcase, sings to us from time to time.

It sounds lovely.

Acknowledgments

About three years ago, when I was traveling on a book tour, my cell phone broke.

How can anyone survive without this machine?

I was three thousand miles from home and would be gone for more than a week before popping back in to Southern California. I figured me not having a phone would worry my family, but my choices for where I could go to replace it (the phone, not my family) were limited to whatever was within walking distance from my hotel. So I ended up getting a new phone—one with a number on it that leads people to conclude I live three thousand miles away from where I actually live, which is kind of cool, if you ask me.

The other thing about the phone is that its number used to belong to two different people I do not know, but who I get calls and text messages for all the time. One of those people is named Billy Hinman.

ACKNOWLEDGMENTS

I started getting so many phone calls and messages for Billy Hinman while writing this book in 2015 that I decided to make him a character in *Rabbit & Robot*. True story: When I was working on editing this book with David Gale at Simon & Schuster, while sitting at my keyboard on the morning of September 6, 2017, I even got *another* phone call for Billy. It has to be some kind of sign.

Also, Billy, I think you owe a lot of people a lot of money.

On the bright side, you got trapped inside one of my books. One of these days maybe our paths will cross. We will go out for drinks, maybe get tattoos together. At the very least we'll take a selfie and trap the ultimate expression of what we've become as human beings on a phone that is forever haunted by your life.

So thank you, Billy Hinman, for coming to me as you did.

There are two people I know who are the best examples, I think, of what it means to be a human being. People who are really good at being human beings are never aware of how good they are, so I should point it out—in envy, and also as an admission of my own shortcomings in that endeavor. First and always, my love, my wife, Jocelyn, who is so perfectly *not* a machine; and second, my friend Amy King, to whom this book is dedicated.

You both make being human look so dang easy.

And, Billy, if you're out there, text me.